Praise for the novels of ~~Patricia~~

GIRLFRIENDS

"Grab your girlfriend and read *Girlfriends*. Who knows what will happen!"
Rita Mae Brown, *New York Times* bestselling author

THE WAY IT IS

"A witty tale about single women searching for friendship, unconditional love and the perfect dessert."
Booklist

"Lots of drama and truly hilarious moments make this a fast, enjoyable read that readers will devour!"
RT Book Reviews

TIGHT

"A frank comedy of manners that exposes both the highs and lows of the modern quest for youth and beauty."
Kirkus Reviews

ONCE UPON A NERVOUS BREAKDOWN

"The writing is brisk, and the emotional undertones treat nicely the ups and downs of life, love, children and aging parents."
Publishers Weekly

Books by Patrick Sanchez

GIRLFRIENDS

THE WAY IT IS

TIGHT

ONCE UPON A NERVOUS BREAKDOWN

And don't miss

MURDER WITH FRIED CHICKEN AND WAFFLES
the first book in the Mahalia Watkins Soul Food Mystery
series coming soon!

Published by Kensington Publishing Corporation

Girlfriends

Patrick Sanchez

KENSINGTON BOOKS
Kensington Publishing Corp.
http://www.kensingtonbooks.com

KENSINGTON BOOKS are published by

Kensington Publishing Corp.
119 West 40th Street
New York, NY 10018

All Kensington Titles, Imprints, and Distributed Lines are available at special quantity discounts for bulk purchases for sales promotions, premiums, fund-raising, and educational or institutional use. Special book excerpts or customized printings can also be created to fit specific needs. For details, write or phone the office of the Kensington special sales manager: Kensington Publishing Corp., 119 West 40th Street, New York, NY 10018, attn: Special Sales Department, Phone: 1-800-221-2647.

Kensington and the K logo Reg. U.S. Pat. & TM Off.

ISBN-13: 978-1-57566-924-3
ISBN-10: 1-57566-924-2
First Kensington Trade Paperback Edition: August 2001
First Kensington Mass Market Edition: September 2002

10 9 8 7 6 5

Printed in the United States of America

ACKNOWLEDGMENTS

Much thanks and gratitude to:

My parents, Patricia and Guillermo Sanchez. My three sisters, Donna, Maria, and Laurie. My extended family, Cal, Paul, Allison, Helen, Caroline, and CJ. My grandmother, Bertha Herbert and my Uncle Murry.

My editor, John Scognamiglio: For appreciating my sharp (some might say caustic) sense of humor, being a genuinely nice guy, and helping me take my manuscript to a higher level.

Yvette Chisholm: For always coming through for me, being knowledgeable about virtually everything, and all your wonderful ideas for this book.

Steve Stark: For all your tips, advice, and guidance, but mostly, for being the first person to tell me that I might actually have something here.

Karla Mahoney: For helping out a complete stranger and doing more than just proofreading my manuscript.

Tony Smith: For creating my Web site.

William Sloan: For crafting such a fantastic cover.

Wendy Corsi Staub: For doing a great job with the cover copy.

Johanna Tani: For doing a super job copyediting my manuscript.

All my current and former colleagues at ValueOptions.

The following individuals for helping out in one way or another through friendship, support, encouragement, inspiration . . . or proofreading: Jennifer Amato, Dorothy Barry, Jennifer Carroll, Whitney Clark, Tony Curtis, Lucia Ferguson, Teresa Glaze, Mike and Kerri Gray, James and Mindy Harrington, Barry Hirsch, Lyn Laparan, Mary McDonald, Andrea Newsome, Cindy Ostrowski, Jim Palumbo, Angela

Perri, Joe Russell, Tasha Tillman, Holly Tracy, Alev Volkan, and Sandy Wells.

And, most important, to everyone who takes a chance on me and buys this book. I'd love to hear from you at *author patrick@yahoo.com* and please check out my Web site at www.patrick-sanchez.com.

Always the Bridesmaid

Gina Perry was uncomfortable in the hard church pew. Damn Catholics, she thought. Their weddings are just too fucking long. She'd take a quickie Protestant or Jewish ceremony over this foolishness any day. And what was the deal with all that kneeling and standing and kneeling again? If she'd known there was going to be a whole Mass along with the wedding ceremony, that would've done it—she definitely wouldn't have come. And to top it all off, Linda didn't show. At least as far as Gina could tell, Linda wasn't there. The church was so damn packed, Linda may have been somewhere in the crowd, but Gina wasn't able to find her.

Gina's mind wandered a little while a friend of the groom's read the Bible story about God taking Adam's rib to create Eve, blah, blah, blah. She'd heard it too many times over the last few years as, one by one, virtually all her friends took the plunge and became MOHs (married old hags). It was like all her friends had joined a club that she couldn't. She didn't even see most of them anymore. She hated going out with couples and feeling like a third wheel. It had been nearly ten years since high school, a fact she was recently reminded of when she received the invitation to her reunion a few weeks earlier. She couldn't believe ten years had gone by already, nor could she believe that virtually all her friends had gotten married, and some had even started families.

The classic church was decked out in white and pink roses—white and pink roses on the altar, white and pink roses in the sanctuary, white and pink roses on every windowsill in the God bless-ed church. Earlier, when Gina spotted the bridesmaids getting out of the limo, she was quite taken aback. They were all wearing pink dresses (the same shade of pink as the roses) with white bows on the sleeves and a big white bow on the bustle. Penelope had asked Gina to be a bridesmaid, but Gina couldn't bear being the bridesmaid one more time. She had enough pastel puffed-sleeve dresses in her closet to clothe a cross-dressing army, and she wasn't eager to add to the depressing collection. Besides, she was tired of being paraded down church aisles looking like Glenda, the Good Witch. She just lied to Penelope and made up a lame excuse about how she was out of vacation time and wasn't sure if she would be able to get off from work the day of the wedding.

The whole idea of Penelope having a church wedding was so ridiculous. Penelope barely knew Jesus Christ from Jesus Jones. But, like many of Gina's wedded friends, who hadn't stepped foot in a church in years, Penelope suddenly returned to her Catholic roots when she needed a place to have her wedding ceremony.

The entire scene should have been unbelievably tacky, but to Gina's surprise, the pink-and-white display was stunning. It was a pleasant summer morning, and the pastel colors gave the church a soft, warm feel, which just added to Gina's disgust with the whole thing. Penelope had been a good friend to her, and Gina really did care for her, but Gina couldn't help wishing some disaster would happen. Maybe Penelope would get overly nervous and vomit all over her wedding gown. Or, better yet, Donny would have second thoughts right in the middle of the ceremony and walk off. That way, at least Gina wouldn't be the only straight girl she knew without a relationship.

Gina looked around and saw couples everywhere. She seemed to be the only single person in the church.

God! There is nothing more pathetic than a dateless girl at a wedding, Gina thought to herself as a middle-aged woman slid into the pew next to her. The woman was wearing a tight navy blue skirt and a cropped sleeveless top. She looked old beyond her forty-six years. With her thin, dry hair, raspy voice, and fine lines all over her face, she could have easily been the poster child for an antismoking campaign. Fresh from the salon, her hair was an even brassier shade of auburn than usual.

"Shirley," Gina whispered. "Why are you so late? You probably should have stayed in the back until the ceremony is over."

"I had a hair appointment. It took forever. Did I miss anything?"

"Just the whole wedding."

"Good. Weddings are a drag. Just show me the way to the open bar."

"Mother!" Gina droned. The only time Gina called Shirley "Mother" was when she was aggravated with her.

As the service came to a close, Gina contemplated going home and skipping the reception. She was considering potential excuses as she watched Penelope and Donny glide arm in arm down the center aisle while joyous music blared from the church organ.

Gina followed the crowd outside. The wedding party had already scampered around to the rear of the church and back inside to begin taking pictures. With Shirley in tow, Gina walked toward her car after giving one final sweep for Linda. She sat in the car, trying to decide what to do. She wasn't thrilled about going to the reception with just Shirley, looking like the only escort she could get was her mother. Not that Shirley was Gina's escort at all. Shirley was chums with almost all of Gina's friends, at least the ones Gina would let her get near, and was an invited guest as well. Shirley certainly lacked maternal inclinations, but she was always good for a few laughs at a high school slumber party or college barbecue.

Gina's neighbor and former boyfriend, Peter, had agreed to be her date for the wedding but called the day before to say he was a little under the weather and wouldn't be able to make it. After he canceled on her, Gina figured she would just hang out with Linda and drink wine and make fun of the bridesmaids all afternoon. She eventually decided she would get through the introductions and the entrée, then sneak out after congratulating the happy couple.

When Gina and Shirley arrived at the Marriott on 14th Street, they proceeded to the ballroom and stopped at the gift table. As Gina added her gift to the table, a place setting that Penelope had registered for at Hecht's, Shirley whipped a card out of her purse.

"Gina, sweetie, you got a pen?"

Gina rummaged through her purse and handed a pen to Shirley, who signed the card. Shirley then gave the table a good once-over and snatched the card off one of the larger gift-wrapped packages, crumpled it up, and replaced it with her card.

"Oh, no, Mother! You are not doing that again."

"Oh, please, I do it all the time. Saves some major cash."

"Look, just sign my card, and my gift can be from both of us. Okay?"

"What did you get her?"

"A place setting. It's the one she registered for."

"Hell no. You think a place setting is as good as what's in that big ole box?"

"Whatever, Shirley," Gina said, raising her hands at Shirley and walking away.

Gina entered the ballroom and walked up to the bar. She ordered a glass of wine and took a sip. Gina didn't recognize anyone at the reception. Other than Linda, Gina and Penelope didn't really have many friends in common. After college, Gina and Penelope grew apart, especially when Penelope started dating Donny about three years earlier.

Gina stood close to the bar and slowly drank her wine. While the crowd waited for the bride and groom to make their grand entrance, a mature woman approached Gina and tried to make small talk.

"Lovely ceremony, wasn't it? The church was just beautiful."

"Yes, it was," Gina paused. "Looked a little like the Easter bunny threw up, but it was quite beautiful."

The woman laughed at Gina's little joke. "Yeah, all that pink was a little overwhelming. Penelope always did like to go overboard. Are you a friend of hers?"

"Yes, we went to college together. I'm Gina."

"Nice to meet you. I'm Sally, Penelope's aunt. I just got in from New Jersey this morning."

"Oh . . . how long does it take to get to D.C. from New Jersey?" Gina asked, already bored with the woman but appreciating her company. It beat standing there alone.

"Just a little over three hours. It's not too bad, but doing it alone can be a little tiresome."

"Alone? Are you married?"

"Oh, no, dear. I never married."

Before Gina could inquire any further, the room quieted, and the deejay asked the crowd to welcome the newly married Mr. and Mrs. Donald Weils.

Gina watched Penelope and Donny stride into the ballroom while everyone stood up and boisterously clapped their hands. Penelope was certainly not what one would consider a pretty girl, but, like most brides, she did look radiant on her special day. As Gina eyed the couple walking toward the head table, she wondered what was running through Penelope's head. She looked so happy and confident, but most of all, Gina figured she must be relieved—relieved that she had gotten married and didn't have to worry about growing old alone.

Gina hated the way she felt as she stood next to Sally, clapping for the couple, a forced smile on her face. A big part of her really was happy for Penelope. But, God, Gina would have been so much happier for Penelope if she were in a relationship herself. Here Gina was, on the verge of thirty, and she hadn't had a serious relationship since her long stint with Peter about five years earlier.

"Is there one of those dumb seating plans, or can we sit wherever we want?" Shirley asked Gina, approaching her from behind.

"We're seated over there at Table Eleven," Gina said, part of her glad Shirley was there, so she at least knew someone at the wedding. Her other half worried that Shirley might do something to embarrass her.

"Do you know who else is seated with us? Anyone good?"

"No, Shirley. I don't. Why don't we just go over there and take our seats."

After Gina excused herself to Sally, she and Shirley made their way over to the table and introduced themselves to the four other people who were sitting there as well. They were distant relatives of the groom, who drove up from North Carolina and were a total bore.

Over lunch the group discussed some benign topics, learning each other's connection to the newlyweds, what they did for a living, how lovely the weather was for the ceremony. . . . As Gina began to wonder if it really was possible to die of boredom, the photographer approached their table and requested a group shot.

"Sure, hon," Shirley said, trying to fluff her hair.

"Smile," the stocky, middle-aged man said as he clicked the shutter on the camera.

"Thank you," he said to the group and turned toward the neighboring table.

"Is that it?" Shirley asked. "You know, I just got back from the salon. You could take a few more."

"Sure, miss," the man said politely.

"Hold on just one sec," Shirley said, reaching for her purse and pulling out a tube of lipstick and a compact. She applied

some lipstick and dabbed some powder on her nose and forehead.

"Okay, I'm ready," she said, and put one hand behind her
head and gave the camera a seductive smile.

"Nice!" the photographer said, clicking the shutter as
Shirley put both hands behind her head and puckered her
lips for the camera.

"Shirley! How much have you had to drink?" Gina asked
her mother. She knew it was too early for Shirley to be
drunk, but Gina was hoping the rest of the table might think
too much alcohol was to blame for Shirley's behavior.

"Oh, I'm just having fun, sweetie," Shirley said as she
continued to pose. Realizing that the photographer was
shooting only Shirley, the rest of the guests at the table
leaned back in their chairs and got out of the way—except
for Gina, that is. She got up from the table altogether and
walked back to the bar just to get away from the whole
scene.

After Gina ordered another glass of chardonnay, she
searched the crowd for a familiar face but wasn't able to locate anyone she recognized from college or even Penelope's
family. Lunch was finishing up, and the guests were starting
to disperse around the room. When she got back to the table,
it was empty. Everyone was on their feet and mingling.

Gina sat down, thankful Shirley was done with her im-
promptu photo session. She decided she would finish her
wine and then make her way over to Penelope and Donny.
She would wish them well and get the hell out of there.

As Gina sat at the table, sipping her wine, she saw
Penelope and Donny walking toward her.

"Hi, Gina!" Penelope said with more glee than Gina
could stand. "I'm so glad you're here."

"Me too," Gina said with as much enthusiasm as she
could muster and gave Penelope a quick hug. "You look
beautiful."

"Thank you."

"Congratulations," Gina said, turning to Donny and giving him a hug as well.

"Thanks, Gina," he replied before turning to Penelope. "He must be around here somewhere."

"Who?" Gina asked.

"The photographer. We're going to start the dancing soon, and he seems to have disappeared. We've cased the whole room for him."

"He was over here just a few minutes ago," Gina said.

"Well, we had better go hunt him down. Thanks again for coming, Gina. I'm glad you were able to get the day off."

"Sure," Gina said as the couple departed.

Gina set her wineglass down on the table and started off for the bathroom. She would run to the ladies' room, then fetch Shirley and be on her way. As she strode toward the restroom, she heard some voices coming from behind the coat-check counter, which was unattended during the summer. She poked her head over the edge and saw two pairs of legs sticking out on the other side.

"Shirley!" she shrieked, recognizing her mother's shoes.

Shirley hurriedly hopped up from behind the counter and began rebuttoning her blouse.

"What are you doing? Who's back there with you?"

"Just me," the photographer said, stumbling on his feet and fiddling with his loosened tie.

"I'd better run," he said to Shirley, gathering his camera and awkwardly touching her on the arm. He nodded to Gina and hurried back toward the ballroom.

"Shirley! What the hell were you doing?"

"He was taking a little break from photographing the reception."

"A little break? On the floor behind the coat-check counter?"

"Oh, loosen up, sweetie. We were just having a little fun."

"We're leaving, Shirley," Gina said curtly. "You've embarrassed me enough for one day."

"Oh, please! No one saw us."

"I saw you! We're leaving, Shirley," Gina said again. "Now!"

"All right, all right. Let me get my purse."

"I've got to run to the ladies' room. I'll meet you back here in a minute if you can manage to behave yourself for that long," Gina told Shirley, not bothering to lecture her mother any further. Gina was annoyed and embarrassed by her mother's inappropriate conduct at the reception, but, truth be known, it wasn't that big of a deal. Shirley had behaved far worse in her time, and Gina had come to expect such behavior from her mother. She was just thankful no one knew about this particular incident.

"Let's go," she said to Shirley in a cool voice as they met in the hallway.

Gina was silent as they walked out of the hotel toward the car.

"Is that it?" Shirley asked as they got inside the car.

"Is what it?"

"No lecture? No reprimand?" Shirley asked.

"Why? It obviously doesn't do any good."

"Yeah, but it's so fun to see you get all riled up."

"Shut up," Gina said, cracking a smile. One thing about life with Shirley—it was erratic, unpredictable, and often embarrassing—but never boring.

"Hand me the phone, would you?" Gina asked Shirley, who was lighting a cigarette. "And put that thing out the window, would you? You know I don't like you smoking in here."

Shirley retrieved the phone from the glove compartment and passed it over.

"So where were you?" Gina said into the phone as soon as Linda answered.

"I had one of my killer migraines, Gina. I'm sorry. Was the wedding bearable?"

"I guess, until Shirley ended up on the floor with the photographer," Gina added, looking over at Shirley and grinning.

"What?"

"I'll tell you about it later," Gina said. Linda was probably the only person Gina didn't mind knowing about Shirley's antics. That was the kind of relationship she had with Linda. Gina knew she could always count on Linda and confide in her.

"Are you feeling better?" Gina asked. "Maybe we can go out tonight and have a few drinks. I'll tell you all about the wedding."

"Yeah. I'll probably be up to it by the evening. Why don't I meet you around nine or so. I'll come by your place."

"Sure," Gina said, and hung up the phone and handed it back to Shirley.

Shirley lowered the antenna and put it back in the glove box.

"I'm sorry if I embarrassed you, sweetie. I'll try to behave myself from now on."

Gina turned to her mother "You do that, Shirley," she said, both of them knowing full well it wasn't going to happen.

Princess Charming in
a World of Toads

Gina and Linda were at one of their regular haunts, a dance club called Rumors, one of many in a cluster of bars and nightclubs in downtown Washington, D.C., that were known as "meat markets" for young professionals. In fact, the entire neighborhood was jokingly referred to as the "herpes triangle." On weekends these clubs were filled with D.C.'s singles—mostly young men and women who were employed by the federal government or had jobs with government contractors. Aside from the young crowd, there were always a few middle-aged businessmen searching for a little love while their frumpy wives thought they were working late. Gina spent more time than she cared to admit at these bars, hoping to find Mr. Right or at least Mr. I'll-Do-for-a-While. But even in her worst moments of desperation, she never dreamed of getting involved with one of the old farts with the tight starched dress shirts—shirts so tight you could almost hear the buttons screaming *Help me! I can't hold on!* She would *never* talk to one of those guys. Not until she met Griffin anyway.

Gina was standing against the bar, waiting for Linda to come back from the restroom. The bartender had just handed her a rum and Coke, and as she reached in her purse to grab some cash, a short, balding man intervened and paid for her drink. He must have come straight from work, because he was wearing the remnants of a business suit—no blazer or tie but those formal creased pants that look really awkward when worn without the rest of the suit. Of course, the shirt was too tight, especially around the belly. And the icing on the cake—he was wearing some ridiculous baseball cap that had "The Big G" printed on the front of it. Gina smiled, not knowing quite how to react. The kind of smile that said thanks for the drink. I'm flattered. Now get lost. She sipped the drink and smiled again, wondering how long she had to stand there. Hoping he wouldn't make her talk to him, she scanned the bar for Linda, wishing she'd come back soon.

"I think you're absolutely beautiful," the pudgy little man said with a hopeful smile.

Of course you do. Fat, ugly guys always think that, Gina thought, returning his smile, and again hoped that if she just stood there without saying anything, he'd go away.

The bald, potbellied man persisted. "And your name is?"

"Hi, I'm Gi—Mary," Gina replied, feeling obligated to say something to him. As much as she wanted to just ignore him and walk away, she couldn't do it. He was truly pathetic; she just couldn't be rude to him. Besides, there was no harm in chatting with him for a minute or two and then saying she had to go find her friend or run to the restroom or whatever it took to get away from him.

"Mary, what a pretty name. I'm Griffin," he said, pulling a pack of cigarettes from his pocket, lighting up, and offering one to Gina.

Gina shook her head. Short, fat, bald, *and* you smoke. How *do* you keep the women away? "Yeah, my mother's name was Mary, and her mother . . ."

She almost said "And her mother too" but caught herself before the lie seemed too ridiculous. It wasn't so much that she was afraid to give out her real name. She just got a kick out of making one up, especially around guys like Griffin, whom she knew she would never really be interested in. Just as she was thinking of a good occupation to tell the loser (maybe a nurse or, what the hell, how about a personal assistant to Laura Bush), Linda emerged from the crowd. Gina gave her *the look,* and Linda immediately went into action. She frowned and put her hand to her forehead before telling Gina that she had a headache and wanted to leave.

Gina turned to Griffin, not remembering his name. "Oh, ah . . . ?"

"Griffin," he replied.

"Griffin, my friend really isn't feeling well. I think we have to leave."

"I'd be happy to take you home if you'd like to stay for a while."

"Oh, I need to go anyway. I have an early day at the White House tomorrow."

"The White House?"

"Yeah, it was nice to meet you."

"Can I call you?"

"Sure," Gina said as she walked away, hoping he wouldn't have the guts to ask for her phone number.

"Mary," Griffin called. "Your phone number?"

Gina kept walking pretending not to hear, and fortunately Griffin didn't persist.

Gina and Linda hit the street.

"Where should we go now?"

"I don't know, Linda. There are so many trolls out tonight. Here a troll, there a troll, everywhere a troll troll." Gina was getting frustrated. It had been months since she'd met anyone who even remotely interested her.

"Why don't we go over to the Phase?" Linda suggested, referring to Phase One, a bar near Capitol Hill.

"The Phase? That's clear across town. Besides, what are the chances of me finding a man there?" Gina said, exasperated.

"Would you forget about finding a man for once in your life and just try to have some fun? Come on, we'll have a few drinks, and dance, and maybe *I'll* get lucky."

"All right, Linda, let's go." Gina was feeling a little re-signed anyway. Maybe just relaxing and getting stone drunk was what she needed.

Booty Call

"You know, you're a royal pain in the ass."

"Yes, but you love me anyway. Come on, Peter, if you had a dog, I'd do the same for you," Gina said, calling from her cell phone outside Rumors.

"I don't know, Gina. I think I'm coming down with something. I don't feel like going outside."

"Please, Peter, it will just take a minute."

"Yeah whatever," Peter said, and hung up the phone.

He was in the middle of taking his daily vitamin regimen when Gina called. He recently switched all of his vitamins into a handy pillbox with seven compartments. It was so much easier than finding seven different containers in his gym bag and then opening each bottle individually. He got up from the chair, muttering to himself, "Gina, out having a good time and wants me to make sure her dog doesn't pee all over the place." He got the key from the hook and went down the hall to Gina's apartment.

Peter and Gina met when she was still an undergraduate at American University and he was in his first year of law school there. They dated for just over a year, and it was actually after they had broken up, and after Peter dropped out of law school, that he moved into Gina's building. Gina's grandmother owned her unit and leased it to Gina for a nominal rent. When a unit a few doors down from her opened up, she mentioned it to Peter, and he moved in a few weeks later.

"Hi, Gomez. Hey, boy. How ya doing? Yeah, your owner's out drinking and trying to find a man," Peter said to Gomez in what Gina had come to call his Gomez voice. He sounded like he had just sucked down helium and some angry woman was pulling on his balls. Gomez always got so excited when Peter came over—or when anyone came over for that matter. Peter picked up Gomez and stroked him on the head.

"How are you, Gomez?" he said to the little dog, putting him up to his ear.

Silence.

"Oh, you are?" Peter said back to the dog.

Silence.

"Oh, you did? Wow, that's cool, Gomez."

Peter wasn't sure what kind of dog Gomez was. He thought Gina mentioned something about him being a miniature dachshund, but Peter had never seen a dachshund like Gomez. He had the elongated body and short legs, but he also had a long, fluffy fur coat like Peter had never seen on a dachshund. Peter sat down on the floor with Gomez and rubbed the dog's belly and scratched his neck before getting up and grabbing a leash from the table by the door.

"Hold still, boy. I can't get the leash on you if you don't hold still. I'm going to leave you here if you don't calm down. God damn it, you stupid mutt . . ."

When Gomez and Peter finally got outside, they traipsed straight to the grassy area in front of the apartment building. Gina and Peter lived in one of the few buildings in the neighborhood that actually had a small grassy patch between the building and the sidewalk. Gomez knew it was stupid to do his business right away, because then Peter would just take him back inside. Playing the moment for all it was worth, he searched for a lightning bug or moth to chase. No such luck, so he just kept walking and sniffing the ground. Once again Peter and Gomez caught the attention of some fellow apartment dwellers. This time an Asian couple just getting out of their car. They had the typical reaction most people had when they saw Peter walking Gomez—a six-foot-tall, burly Italian walking a miniature dachshund. It didn't help matters that the dachshund constantly tugged on the leash while prancing around with his tongue hanging out. Gomez insisted on pulling too hard on the leash, causing him to make harsh choking noises every few minutes as he meandered around the neighborhood. The couple gawked a little and laughed under their breath as they walked toward the lobby.

"All right, Gomez, shit or get off the pot. We're going inside," Peter called to the dog, who continued to trot ahead of Peter, ignoring his walker's frustration.

When Gomez finally watered the lawn, Peter dropped him off at Gina's and went down the hall to his apartment. After he finished thoroughly washing his hands with antibacterial soap and super-hot water, a ritual he performed whenever he came back into the apartment, he saw that the message light on the answering machine was blinking.

BEEP. "Hi, Peter, it's Cheryl. I just got in. It's about eleven-thirty. Call me if you get in soon. I rented a couple of movies if you want to watch them with me."

Peter grinned when Cheryl mentioned the movies. She was probably calling for a little midnight action, and rented movies were an easy segue. Although Cheryl did have other excuses and sometimes got quite creative. The time she actually took the drapes off the window so he could come over and help her put up some "new" curtains was probably one of her best. The whole facade was silly, but then, leaving a message on Peter's machine saying "Hey, I'm horny as hell. Want to come over and fuck me?" might have seemed a tad blunt.

"Hi, I was just out walking Gina's dog," Peter said, playing with the phone cord.

"You let that tramp walk all over you. Isn't that mutt of hers dead yet?"

Peter couldn't help thinking how ironic it was that in the midst of making a booty call at midnight, Cheryl managed to call Gina a tramp. "Careful, Cheryl, your claws are show-ing. What are you doing just getting in at eleven-thirty?"

"I went for a drive. I have a lot going on right now. Do you mind if I come over for a while? I really could use some-one to talk to."

"No, not at all. I'm kind of tired though. I had a long day myself."

"Okay, I'll be over in a bit."

"Bye."

Perky Cheerleaders

Gina and Linda were on the dance floor at the Phase, moving to the music played by the heavy set (all right—fat) deejay up in the booth overlooking the room. She must have been a guest deejay. Linda and Gina had never seen her before. Apparently, her name was Tanya and she never took song requests. Actually, she accepted them, saying, "I'll try to get it on for you," and then played whatever her fat ass felt like playing. But Gina figured it worked. The place was packed every weekend.

Gina was buzzed to the core. Her vision blurred just a little as she left the dance floor and headed for the bar. She felt really good, or at least numb, and one more beer would only intensify this state.

"Another draft, Pearl," Gina asked the bartender. She was probably the only straight girl in D.C. on a first-name basis with the bartenders at the Phase.

"Okay, darlin'. Are you sure you haven't had enough?"

"I most certainly have not had enough. In fact, I haven't gotten any in months."

Pearl grinned, twisted the cap off a bottle of Miller Lite and handed it to Gina. "On the house, darlin'."

Gina barely had a chance to taste her beer, when someone approached her from behind.

"Gina? Is that you?"

Gina hesitated for a moment before recognizing the woman. "Annie! My God! How are you?" Gina replied with a look of surprise on her face.

"I'm great. Never thought I'd see you here."

Gina never thought she'd see Annie there either. "Yeah, well, I'm here with a friend. She's on the dance floor."

"Why would she leave you all alone over here?"

"I just don't feel much like dancing right now," Gina replied.

"Not even with me?"

"I suppose I could be convinced to go out there for a little while."

Annie took Gina's hand and led her to the dance floor. They joined the lesbians under the lights and started swaying to the music. Gina was feeling the beers, and, a few minutes into the dancing, she started seductively straddling her partner and dancing like she was in the movie *Dirty Dancing*. She wasn't interested in women, but in her drunken state she enjoyed teasing Annie, who Gina assumed was a lesbian. After all, the Phase was one of the few lesbian bars in the city. Gina had gotten used to lesbians, and lesbian bars, and lesbian book clubs, and lesbian this and lesbian that. Linda always asked her to come along to various events, and Gina figured a night with a bunch of lesbians was better than a night with Gomez and the television set.

"I didn't know you stayed in the area, Gina. So many people have moved away," Annie said after they stepped off the dance floor.

"Well, after college I got a job here in the District, so I decided to stay."

"Do you live downtown?"

"Yeah, near Dupont Circle," Gina said. "Just a few blocks from here." If the lesbian bar scene was anything like the straight scene, Gina figured Annie was trying to decide if it was better to suggest going back to her place or to Gina's.

"How about you, Annie? Where are you living these days?"

"I'm just over in Adams Morgan."

"Are your parents still in the District?"

"No, they moved out to Maryland a few years ago," Annie said. "The city just got to be too much for them. You know, the crime and stuff."

Fact was, there wasn't a huge amount of crime in the Cleveland Park neighborhood of D.C., where Gina and Annie grew up and went to high school. It was one of a handful of neighborhoods left in the District that wasn't declining. In fact, it was one of the most prestigious areas of the city. In high school Annie was a cheerleader, and perky, and, in Gina's eyes, a bitch. Gina was too tall, too thin, and too lanky—at least she thought so. Not to mention shy and somewhat awkward. Gina hadn't cared for Annie ever since they tried out for the cheerleading squad during her freshman year.

Gina was eager to be popular and make new friends when she started high school. What better way than to be a cheerleader. The first day of tryouts, Annie went around and introduced herself to everyone as the obvious choice for captain of the junior varsity squad. She explained that she had extensive training and had already won various awards during middle school. Gina didn't even know awards existed for cheerleading but was eager to be liked and decided to approach Annie and offer her support. She was shy about approaching a stranger, especially one who seemed to be as self-assured as Annie. Nonetheless, Gina finally gathered her confidence and tapped Annie on the shoulder.

"Hi, Annie. I'm Gina Perry, and I just wanted to say I think you'd make a great captain."

Annie looked Gina up and down and crinkled her nose. "Really? Are you trying out for the squad?"

"Yes," Gina said humbly, seeking Annie's approval.

"Honestly, Jennie," Annie said, already forgetting Gina's name. "I just don't think you'd be a good fit. You're quite a bit taller than the rest of the girls, and we're really looking for girls with flair. Have you thought about the volleyball team? Or what about basketball?"

Gina was dumbfounded and just wanted to cry. Holding

back the tears, she said, "Yeah, maybe volleyball is a good idea." With that, she slumped back to the locker room and cried like a helpless baby. That was a defining moment for her personality and self-esteem for years to follow. For the next four years she and Annie barely exchanged words and ran with different crowds. Annie would eventually be captain of the squad and maintained a tightly knit circle of friends, which consisted of other cheerleaders and girls with "flair." Gina hung with a small circle of friends that would eventually include Linda, and spent most of high school fading into the woodwork. It wasn't until college that Gina outgrew her somewhat gawky demeanor and made some repairs to her self-esteem.

She hadn't seen Annie since graduation about ten years earlier. Now, about twenty curve-enhancing pounds later, one-hundred-dollar-a-month hair-foiling sessions with Dennis, and a nose job that she was still paying for, Gina was certainly the more attractive of the two and was well aware of it. Despite this, Gina had days when she looked at the people around her and wished she resembled this person or that person. But she also had days, particularly when Shirley dragged her to the Shoppers Food Warehouse to save a buck on groceries, that she looked at the people around her and felt like a beauty queen. Annie had gained weight in all the wrong places and must've gone to one of those "fast food" hair salons for her latest do.

"Would you like to see my place?"

"Sure," Gina said, hiding the smirk that was trying to come out on her face. "Let me run to the little girls' room, and I'll meet you outside." Gina staggered to the bathroom and pulled a notepad from her purse. It was handy to have in case anyone wanted her phone number at the bars. She quickly scrawled on the pad and returned to meet Annie.

Sorry-Assed Chick

From across the bar, Linda saw Gina leaving with Annie. Now, that was a new one. She'd seen Gina take off with a guy once or twice but never with a girl. Linda had a short but feminine haircut and her hazel eyes were a nice match to her light brown hair. She was about five feet four and maybe ten or fifteen pounds overweight. You certainly wouldn't call her fat, but she was by no means thin either. She was standing just off the dance floor, pondering the situation, when a petite, middle-aged woman came up to her.

"Hi. This is kind of weird, but I was wondering if I could ask you something?" the woman inquired.

"Sure," Linda replied.

"Well, you see, I'm not gay, but I lost a bet with my husband. See him over there?" the woman said, pointing to a man, who then smiled and waved at Linda. The woman continued. "Like I said, I lost a stupid bet and agreed to let him watch me . . . well . . . you know . . . 'do it' with another woman."

"I see," Linda said, bewildered. This was one sorry-assed chick!

"I guess I was wondering if you'd be interested in helping a girl out?"

"Oh, this is a joke. Did Gina put you up to this?" Linda asked.

"No, no, I'm quite serious. I'm cute. Don't you think? You could do much worse. It'd be for only a couple of hours."

"What would be for only a couple of hours?"

"Just a little lesbo action to please my husband."

"What are you? Some kind of freak! What on earth makes you think I'd go anywhere with you and your buffoon husband? Is this what you two do for fun? Go to lesbian bars and pick up chicks?"

"I didn't mean to offend you. I just thought . . ."

"Honey, you need some serious help. You know there are people who can help you and your so-called husband," Linda said, annoyed but starting to feel sorry for the woman.

"Yes, I know. But some hookers can be really nasty, not to mention expensive."

"No. God! Not hookers. I mean a therapist or a counselor or something." Only Linda would start giving sound advice to a woman who just asked her to have sex in front of her husband. Linda was constantly trying to help the down-trodden. She surmised that this woman certainly had issues, and that her husband, who must have had major issues of his own, was taking advantage of her.

"We can't afford a hooker. How we gonna afford a therapist? Look, you're a sweet kid, but I don't have time for chitchat. I gotta find me a woman." With that, the woman stepped away from Linda to continue her search.

"Ma'am," Linda called, feeling a genuine concern for the woman. "Here is the number for the Whitman Walker Clinic." Linda handed her a card from the clinic where she volunteered once a week. "They have all kinds of counseling programs at little or no cost. Think about it."

The woman took the card and said nothing before walking away.

Linda watched her go. She pitied the woman, and the whole incident made her feel a little sorry for herself as well. She was so *over* the singles scene. She was tired of smoky bars and lesbians with attitude. Linda would sometimes give

Gina a hard time for always harping on the fact that she was alone. Linda always told Gina that she didn't need to be in a relationship to be fulfilled, and Gina needed to learn to make herself happy. Linda only wished she believed that herself. She didn't think of herself as desperately trying to find a partner, and she certainly was more content with her life than Gina was with hers, but Linda still longed for someone to really share her life with—someone to lie on the sofa with and watch *Xena* or kiss good night before turning out the lights and going to sleep. That someone had to be out there somewhere but, Lord knows, Linda hadn't been able to find her.

There was Karen, who Linda dated the year before. Karen was great except for the small problem she had with shoving cocaine up her nose on a regular basis. And then there was Julie, who Linda dated a few years earlier. Linda was totally in love with Julie. Only problem was Julie was not totally in love with Linda. Julie liked Linda and enjoyed being with her, but the chemistry just wasn't there for her. Even though Julie wasn't in love with Linda, Julie was in love with having a girlfriend. Linda sensed this all along, but it was only after six months that she brought herself to end it with Julie. It was the hardest thing she ever did. She had been deeply in love with Julie, but she had needed someone to return that love—she *deserved* someone to return that love.

Now, standing in a hazy lesbian bar, deflecting advances from a bizarre woman, a meaningful love life seemed more hopeless than ever. She didn't know where Gina had gone, or if she'd be back, so Linda decided she would grab a cab home. Gina was a big girl and could take care of herself. Something was vaguely familiar about the girl she saw Gina leave with anyway. Linda figured she must have been someone Gina knew, so she really wasn't worried.

Linda passed the strange woman who propositioned her on the way out of the bar.

"I hope you get some help," Linda said to the woman with a comforting smile as she walked out the door.

Maybe I should get some too, she thought, laughing slightly to herself as she hailed a cab to head home.

Cheap Wine, Lucy, and Sex

"I'm downstairs," Cheryl yelled into the intercom at the entrance of Peter's building.

"Okay, just a sec." Peter buzzed Cheryl into the building and hung up the phone. He had just put on a pair of loose exercise shorts. The ones that hung off his body but still highlighted the merchandise. After he buzzed Cheryl in, he shoved the Backstreet Boys video under the sofa. He'd been working out to it earlier that day, and, as thirty-year-old straight men were forbidden to enjoy the Backstreet Boys, he wanted it out of sight. He took off his shirt and threw it in the clothes basket. He knew he was looking pretty fine. Two hours at the gym every other day was really starting to have results. He glimpsed in the mirror and saw a very attractive tall man with dark brown hair and green eyes, features he inherited from his Italian mother. He flexed just a little, although lately he really didn't even need to flex. His chest was cut and his arms seemed to bulge just fine, even when he was relaxed. Recently, he'd taken to getting his chest waxed. Why build the buff body and hide it behind a hairy chest?

He never looked better in his life. There were days when

he'd spend several minutes looking at himself in the mirror. He didn't necessarily do it out of arrogance or narcissism. It was more to admire the way he was able to transform his body from the puny kid he once was. He didn't grow to six feet until he was seventeen and was small and scrawny most of his young adult life. He'd never forget high school—hiding behind the fat girl he sat behind in history class to avoid catching the gaze of Gus Rodman, the class bully. Every time she moved or adjusted positions, Peter would reposition himself and use her as a shield of sorts. If he could avoid Gus's gaze, maybe Gus wouldn't pay any attention to him.

He never did anything to Gus, but for some reason he singled Peter out and insisted on picking on him. Peter had suffered from severe asthma and allergies as a kid. He wasn't always able to participate in gym class and occasionally had wheezing attacks at school. Gus always called him Sickly Peter or sometimes just called him Afflicted. "Hey, *Afflicted*," he'd call to Peter, and then start making fake wheezing noises. "Call my mommy, I'm afflicted," he'd say. To this day the word "afflicted" sent chills down Peter's spine.

Looking in the mirror reminded Peter of how far he'd come over the past ten years. He'd learned to manage his allergies, and his asthma virtually disappeared over the years. The scrawny kid was history, and as far as Peter was concerned, he'd never resurface again.

As Peter quickly ran a comb through his short hair, Cheryl knocked on the door.

"I'm coming, I'm coming." Peter opened the door. "Hey, gorgeous. What brings you to these here parts?" Peter said with a fake cowboy accent.

"Well, don't we look comfortable. Always run around half naked when you're expecting company?" Cheryl replied in reference to his shirtless body.

"I can run around completely naked if you like."

"Maybe later. Got any beer?" Cheryl said, making her way into the living room. Peter watched her approach the sofa. At five feet five, she was quite a bit shorter than Peter, with light brown skin, and extremely short, curly black hair.

"No, but I have some wine. Interested?" Peter asked.

"Sure."

Peter went into the kitchen and got some wine out of the fridge. He ripped off the $5.99 label, unscrewed the cap, and took it to the sofa. Cheryl had found a rerun of *I Love Lucy* on cable and was laughing hysterically. "God, I can watch them over and over again and they still make me laugh. Isn't it weird how Ricky always calls Lucy a crazy redhead when her hair looks blond on TV? Guess red just doesn't show up on black and white, huh?"

Peter gave her the same look he always did when she said stuff like that. Cheryl took it to mean aren't you just a cutie pie. What the look really said was what a fucking box of rocks. Don't speak, honey, just sit there and look pretty.

It wasn't that Cheryl was stupid. She was actually quite intelligent and pretty successful, in her career anyway. She just had this habit of saying whatever came to her mind, regardless of how it sounded. Sometimes Peter found it charming, and sometimes it got on his nerves. He really was fond of Cheryl, and they had a good time together, but there wasn't any real chemistry between them, at least not beyond the strong sexual attraction. There was so much he liked about her—she was pretty, fun, and quite a chef. She was always taking some sort of cooking class or watching the Food Network to pick up new culinary skills. She whipped up some pretty impressive creations for Peter from time to time. It was a wonder she managed to stay so thin when she was such an excellent cook.

As Peter sat down next to Cheryl, he thought about how tired he was of their routine. They had to sit and watch television for a while, or sometimes a whole movie before the action got started. This way it didn't appear that they were just meeting for sex. He guessed it allowed her to save face.

Peter sat on the sofa next to Cheryl. He leaned back against the arm of the couch, and Cheryl laid her head on his chest. He was surprised when she softly kissed his chest and slid her cheek along the stubble coming from between his nipples, letting it lightly scratch her face. Peter was usually the one who made the first move. After all, she was supposedly over there only to talk.

"Aren't we forward this evening?" Peter said. She had caught him somewhat off guard.

"Sorry. I see you got your chest waxed again. You're turning into a regular muscle head."

"Yeah, I need to do it again. Get rid of this stubble."

"I kinda like it."

She began licking his chest with her tongue, running her tongue along his cut pecs and occasionally sucking on his nipples, trying to get them hard, so she could nibble on them. She knew this was his weakness and drove him crazy. It did, in fact, drive him crazy, but not the way Cheryl thought it did. He was usually wincing from the pain and wishing she would cut it out. But he didn't feel comfortable telling her this. She might think he wasn't man enough to take a little pain. Cheryl continued to follow the prickly hairs down to his navel and eventually slid her tongue under the elastic in his shorts, where the hair immediately thickened. With that, Peter quickly removed the shorts and lay back in position.

Obligations

It was after midnight, and having had quite a bit to drink at Penelope's wedding, Shirley was exhausted. After Gina dropped her off, she settled in front of the TV for the rest of the day and was just about to get in bed when her pager went off. She checked the number. Delighted to see it was from Collin (she hadn't heard from him in over a week), she picked up the phone to return his page.

When she first met him at the restaurant where she worked nearly a year earlier, she knew he was bad news. She spotted the wedding band right away but wondered why he was dining alone on a Friday night. A nice smile during his drink order, a little body contact while she was serving his food, some flirting during dessert, and, before she knew it, he was waiting for her when she finished her shift. Gina repeatedly asked Shirley to send him packing or, at a minimum, to not expect anything more than a fling, but Shirley ignored her. After all, she wasn't getting any younger. Fifty was only a few years away, and she didn't feel like she could be too choosy. As she always told Gina, "As your ass starts to sag, so do your standards." Collin would have to do for now.

"Damn," she said, remembering that her phone was disconnected. She wasn't going to be able to pay the bill until next week unless she asked Gina to lend her the money. Wondering if her old roommate's line might still be connected, she grabbed her phone from the socket in her room and took it across the hall into the recently vacated bedroom.

"Hey there, it's Shirley," she said, sitting down on the floor.

"Hello, gorgeous. Busy?"

"Never too busy for you."

"In the mood for a little company tonight?"

"You mean this morning. It's after midnight."

"I'd like to come over and see you," Collin said.

"I hope you want to do more than just see me."

"I won't argue with that."

"I'll see you in a half hour or so?"

"I'll be there."

Shirley hung up the phone and jumped in the shower. After drying her hair and putting on her makeup, she slipped into a silk robe (okay, polyester, but it was silk to Shirley). She was dabbing on a little perfume when Collin knocked on the door.

"Hello," Shirley said before pressing her body up against Collin and slapping a long slow kiss on him. She could feel him beginning to swell already.

"Baby, it's good to see you. Is your roommate home?" Collin said in between kisses.

"No, she moved out. She got all pissy about something. Who knows what. I was a little worried about you. I hadn't heard from you in a while."

"Sorry about that. You know . . . obligations," Collin replied, slipping his hand into Shirley's robe and caressing her breast. He released the sash on her robe and let it slip open. "I've missed these," he said, pinching her nipples. "And, oh, how I've missed this," he continued, lowering his hand.

Shirley unbuttoned his shirt and loosened his pants, letting them drop below his knees. Easing down his boxers, she let her robe fall off her shoulders and firmly grabbed his buttocks with her hands while she lowered herself to her knees.

* * *

Twenty minutes later, Collin was scuffling around Shirley's living room for his clothes. Shirley watched him get dressed from the sofa, wishing he would stay the night.

"Do you have to go so soon? You just got here."

"I'm sorry, honey. But you know . . ."

"I know, *obligations.*"

"You know I'd stay if I could. I really would."

"I know. I know. How'd you sneak away this time?"

"I had a friend of mine call the house. I told her the network was down at the office, and I had to go in and bring it back up. She was barely awake when I mentioned it, but I think she might be getting a little suspicious. We might have to cool it for a while. Actually . . . that's why I haven't called you recently," Collin said meekly.

"What do you mean, cool it?"

"Shirley, I think we have to take a break. That's really why I came over this evening. I wanted to tell you in person."

"What? Before or after you fucked me!"

"Shirley, I hadn't planned on that happening. I walked in the door, and you were all over me. What was I supposed to do?"

"Be honest with me. That's what you could've done."

"I'm being honest with you now."

"Well, let me get you a bozo button, you fucking bastard," Shirley said, raising her voice. "You know you'll just be back. You always come back. But, you know what, Collin? This is it. You can take your teeny little weenie and shove it somewhere else when that frigid wife of yours won't give it up."

"Fine, Shirley. If this is the way it has to be. I was hoping we could end this like grown-ups."

"Sorry to disappoint you. I'm not sure what makes you think you can do without me. What? Do you think Maggie's going to get that pole out of her ass all of a sudden?"

Collin remained silent in response to Shirley's comment.

"Wait a minute," Shirley continued. "This doesn't have anything to do with that wife of yours, does it? You've found someone else. Some other bitch to take that little toothpick of yours."

Again Collin remained silent (a sure sign of guilt) before responding. "It's over, Shirley. I'm sorry," he said calmly as he reached for the doorknob.

"Yeah, well, we'll see. The fat lady ain't sang yet," Shirley snapped as the door closed behind Collin.

Girls with Flair

————————————

"Can I get you a beer?" Annie asked Gina, pulling her keys from the lock as she closed the door behind them.

Gina knew she'd had way too much to drink and should probably say no. She could barely walk up the steps to Annie's apartment. She looked around the place in her drunken state. It was basically a dump. The one-room apartment was on the top floor of a converted row house—pretty much a bed, some other secondhand furnishings, and a little kitchenette in one corner. In the opposite corner from the kitchen was a large wraparound desk with vast amounts of computer equipment. Gina found it odd that Annie couldn't afford a decent roof over her head but managed to splurge on what looked like thousands of dollars worth of computer stuff.

"Sure, I'd love a beer."

Annie fetched a beer from the miniature fridge and started fumbling for some glasses.

"You have a cat," Gina said with a hint of disapproval in her tone as Annie's cat crawled out from under the bed. One of Gina's peeves was people with cats. It was always weird single people who had cats, or so Gina thought. Gina didn't understand the whole "cat thing." The idea of living with such a creature was absurd to her. Cats were obnoxious, self-centered, unfriendly, and, besides, who in their right mind would willingly change a litter box?

"That's Silky Sheen. She's my roommate."

Gina could barely contain herself. A cat for a roommate. That isn't pathetic at all. "I don't like cats," Gina said matter-of-factly.

"You'd like Silky. She's just like a dog."

This was another one of Gina's issues with cat people. They always said that she would like *their* cat because it was just like a dog. She wondered why, if these people wanted a cat that was just like a dog, they didn't just get a fucking dog in the first place.

"Is that so? This is a nice place you have here," Gina said as if she genuinely meant it.

"Thanks, me and Silky are pretty happy here."

It was almost sad to Gina that Annie talked about the distasteful cat like it was her roommate.

Annie added, "Money's been pretty tight since I started my own business a few months ago."

"Your own business?"

"I'm a bit of computer guru. I majored in psychology in college, but once I got into the workforce I just gravitated toward computers. I worked for a big insurance company for a few years, climbing the corporate ladder, but eventually decided to go into business for myself."

"Wow, that's pretty impressive."

"I sunk all my savings into getting it started. The biggest expense being that monstrosity over there," Annie said, pointing toward the computer before continuing to babble on about megahertz and gigabytes, leaving her guest confused, not to mention bored, by her computer jargon.

"So, what do you do with your business?"

"Well, like I said, I'm just getting started, but what I plan to do is help small businesses select the best computer hardware and software to meet their needs. Then provide support to them. I'm also a whiz on the Web, so I'm going to develop and manage Web pages for small businesses as well. It will be a long road to making some serious cash, but once I get going, I'm sure the money will follow." As Annie rambled on about her business aspirations, she realized Gina was still standing in the middle of the apartment not quite sure what to do with herself.

"I'd offer you a seat, but I don't really have any chairs," Annie said. "I usually just sit on the bed."

Gina sat down on the bed with her back against the headboard. After handing Gina her beer, Annie lay with her feet hanging off the side and her head in Gina's lap. While Gina was trying to get over the uncomfortable feeling of another woman lying on her private parts, she forced herself to begin massaging Annie's head and playing with her hair. Gina was amazed. Even Annie's hair had gone sour. It felt like straw. Poor Annie—cheerleader turned poverty-stricken lesbian living with a cat—and a computer geek on top of it.

Annie began to gently caress Gina's legs, enjoying their smoothness. Her caressing gradually got firmer as she made her way underneath Gina's skirt.

At this point Gina had had about all she could take. "It was awfully smoky at the Phase, Annie. What do you say we take showers and freshen up a little."

"Only if we take them together," Annie replied with a giggle.

"No, why don't you go first," Gina said with a friendly smile.

Annie headed to the bathroom, which, if the rest of the apartment was any indication, Gina imagined to be disgusting. Gina waited for the water to start running and promptly got off the bed and left the apartment, being careful not to make any noise. As soon as she was out of the apartment, she ran down the steps and out the front door. Much to her luck, she caught a cab right away.

She sat in the back of the cab feeling woozy and nauseated. She knew she would inevitably puke from all the liquor but wanted to do it in her own toilet, not in the backseat of a cab. She felt a little bad about being so cruel to Annie, but at least she didn't carry out her original plan. She pulled the notepad from her purse:

Sorry, I'm really looking for girls with flair!

She had planned to leave the note on the bed when she left Annie's but decided Annie's life was pathetic enough, and Gina just didn't have it in her to kick Annie when she was so far down. At least not beyond pretending to be lesbian and then running off into the night, leaving Annie hot, horny, alone, and feeling ridiculous. She felt a little guilty about the whole thing. After all, high school was a long time ago, but Gina couldn't help thinking of that awful moment when Annie tried to dissuade her from trying out for the cheerleading squad. Gina thought how she hated Annie, or at least how she used to hate her. Somewhere during the course of that evening the hate turned into pity. Maybe she'd call her in the morning and apologize. Then again, maybe not.

We Meet Again

"**S**o what was so traumatizing that you had to rush over here and talk to me about it?" Peter asked Cheryl even though he knew damn well what it was. Cheryl wanted to fuck him. That's what was so traumatizing. They both knew what the deal was, but Peter liked to put Cheryl on the spot every now and then just to get a reaction from her.

Cheryl lifted her head from Peter's chest. "I don't know. It was a hard day." That was the best she could come up with. As the words were coming out of her mouth, all she could think was, you prick—trying to embarrass me. She was feeling cheated anyway. She didn't even get close to an orgasm. Peter had been quick on the draw once again. It was always touch and go with him. Sometimes Peter was a great lover, and other times it was all over in a few minutes. What a selfish bastard, she thought. I sucked your cock for ten minutes and I don't even get an orgasm out of it. If she and Gina ever got on speaking terms again, she would love to compare notes with her about Peter's lovemaking abilities (or lack thereof).

Peter seemed to do better when he had a few drinks. He was much less inhibited and definitely lasted longer. One time she got him so drunk, he pretended to be her slave boy. She pictured Peter, completely naked, except for a bow tie and cowboy boots that she had made him wear—what a sight. She giggled a little to herself every time she thought about it. It made Peter really uncomfortable when she brought it up—if he even acknowledged that it happened.

Peter was about to get up, take a shower, and rinse his mouth out with Scope—as he did almost immediately after every sexual encounter—when someone started knocking at the door.

"Who could that be at this hour?" Peter said.

"If it's that Gina bitch, don't answer it."

Peter was about to yell "Who is it?" but decided to look through the peephole instead. Cheryl was right. It was Gina standing at the door.

"Peter, let me in. I know you're there. I saw your car outside."

Peter slipped on his robe and opened the door just enough to look out. "What are you doing here?"

"Peter, there's dog crap on my carpeting."

"I took him out and he wouldn't go. I *know* you're not over here in the middle of the night to bitch at me for walking your dog at midnight—going way beyond my neighborly duties."

"No, that's not why I'm here. I'm really here because my life just sucks."

"You're plastered, Gina. Aren't you?"

"Slightly."

"Well, go home and sleep it off. We'll talk in the morning."

"I can't come in? Is someone there? Not that whore Cheryl again?"

"Shhhh."

"It *is* her," Gina whispered, annoyed. "Has she grown a third tit or anything since your last fuck?" she added, raising her voice a little. In her drunken state she couldn't help hoping Cheryl would hear her. It was hard to believe that she and Cheryl were ever good friends. They'd roomed together in college for two years and were virtually inseparable the entire time. Their friendship continued only briefly after college, when Cheryl betrayed Gina, or at least in Gina's opinion that's what she did.

Before Peter could respond, a fully dressed Cheryl grabbed the door from him and pulled it all the way open.

"Peter, if you want to stand here all night and talk to what's-her-name," Cheryl said, gesturing toward Gina, "I'm leaving." Cheryl walked toward the elevators with neither Peter nor Gina trying to stop her. Cheryl had wanted to go anyway, and this was as good an excuse as any. She preferred to sleep in her own bed, and besides, the humidifier Peter ran every night was awfully loud and disturbed her sleep. Ever since he had two sinus infections a few winters ago, Peter was convinced he was especially prone to them and insisted on using a noisy humidifier every night to keep his nasal passages moist and ward off infections.

"God, Peter, what do you see in her anyway?"

"Good night, Gina. I'll talk to you in the morning." Peter closed the door to go take a shower and left Gina standing there.

Gina muttered something under her breath and headed down the hall to her apartment—another wasted Saturday night. If sitting through Penelope's wedding earlier that day wasn't bad enough, she had to walk in on Peter and Cheryl. Penelope had Donny, Peter had Cheryl, and Gina just felt very alone—very drunk and very alone. She passed the elevator just as it was opening.

"Mary, what are you doing here?"

Gina turned around to see the potbellied man who had paid for her drink earlier in the evening.

"I was just on my way home," Gina said, startled.

"Do you live here?"

"Just down the hall," Gina said, wanting to kick herself for telling the truth.

"That's amazing. A friend of mine lives down at the other end of the building. I don't usually use these elevators, but I couldn't find any parking near the other side. How long have you lived here, Mary?"

"Why do you keep calling me Mary?" Gina said before remembering she lied about her name earlier.

"Isn't that your name?"

"No, Gina. You must've misheard me." God, she hoped he'd buy it. After all, it was pretty loud at Rumors. She figured she could convince him that he misunderstood when she introduced herself as Mary, and hopefully he wouldn't ask about the White House.

"Well, Gina, can I walk you home?" Griffin asked.

"I guess so. Jerry, right?"

"Griffin."

"Oh, yeah," Gina said, taking a quick glimpse at his protruding belly, trying to decide if she could really ignore it.

God! Am I that desperate? she thought, heading toward her apartment. She wasn't sure if it was the liquor or the fatigue, but it was almost as if she were floating outside of her body and watching herself walk to her apartment with a fat, shapeless shlub.

What are you doing? she called to herself from above. No, no, no! But she wasn't able to stop herself. Somehow, tonight loneliness got the best of her and she needed a warm body, even if it was Griffin's. It was finally happening. She was settling for whatever she could get. Of course, she could get better, but in the wee hours of a Sunday morning, Griffin was there and available. He would have to do.

The thought of settling always scared Gina. She had seen so many of her friends do it—marry guys who were nice, and made a decent living, and might make good fathers— guys who they felt as passionate about as a doorknob. She didn't want that for herself, but that was an easy philosophy to have when she was twenty-two. It was getting harder to remain steadfast as the big three-zero approached. She was truly amazed on the rare occasions when she met couples that were truly in love—where both partners were really into each other. With most couples it was obvious that one person was totally in love while the other person was there just to avoid being alone.

There always seems to be a settler and a settlee. I don't care to be either one, Gina thought to herself as she put the key into the door of her apartment.

"Come on in," she said to Griffin as she struggled to push the door open.

The Personals

Cheryl closed the front door behind her and dragged into her living room. She was getting really tired of the whole scene with Peter, and having a run-in with Gina certainly didn't help matters. The whole mess had been going on for far too long. She was tired of being Peter's *friend*. She was so over hearing him say how much he cared about her and enjoyed her company—how he loved her but wasn't *in love* with her. She really didn't know if she was "in love" with him either. That's how she rationalized the whole ridiculous relationship. It was just as meaningless to her as it was to him, at least that's what she tried to tell herself. Neither one of them had a significant other, so their arrangement allowed them to have dates to weddings and Christmas parties, kept them from eating in restaurants alone, and certainly provided a sexual outlet for both of them. She knew the moment she or Peter hooked up with someone else, they would adjust their *friendship* to a purely platonic relationship. Cheryl just hoped she found someone before Peter did.

What the hell was Gina doing over at Peter's in the wee hours of the morning? She's worse than an ex-wife who won't let go of her former husband, Cheryl thought to herself as she kicked off her shoes and plopped down onto the sofa. The whole feud between her and Gina was so stupid,

but Cheryl had grown weary of trying to patch things up
with Gina and gave up trying a long time ago.

Cheryl missed having Gina as a friend. They were so
much alike—both attractive, young, smart women who just
couldn't seem to get their act together, especially when it
came to men. Cheryl used to think Gina would eventually
forgive her, and one day they would be friends again. But,
now that several years had gone by since they stopped
speaking to each other, Cheryl accepted the fact that her
friendship with Gina was history. And what made matters
even worse, Cheryl lost Linda's friendship as well. Cheryl
and Linda were never terribly close. In fact, Cheryl couldn't
think of when she and Linda ever really hung out by themselves, but they did spend a lot of time together because of
Gina. It was no real surprise that when Gina and Cheryl had
their rift, Linda dropped out of Cheryl's life as well. Gina
and Linda were close, worked together, and had a long history between them.

Thank God for *Nick at Nite,* she thought as she clicked on
a late night episode of *The Facts of Life* and riffled through a
couple of cooking magazines strewn on the coffee table.
After skimming through last month's edition of *Bon Appétit,*
she picked up a copy of the *Washington City Paper* that was
lying on the floor next to the sofa. Cheryl had never been
known for neatness. She wasn't a complete slob, but most of
the time her apartment was pretty much in a state of disarray,
and she constantly had trouble finding things. Her place wasn't
dirty or anything, just terribly disorganized.

As she started to flip through the paper, she remembered
how she used to comb through it every week to see where
the latest hot spots were—which bars were offering specials
or had themed evenings. In her early twenties it wasn't uncommon for her to hit the clubs three or four nights a week.
She remembered getting trashed at the Insect Club or Planet
Fred, two D.C. clubs that had long since closed. Before she
and Gina had their falling out, the two of them were almost
a staple at 15 Minutes. The doorman knew them on sight
and never made them pay the cover charge. He told them

they were both so young and beautiful that their presence alone would draw a crowd. They would spend the night drinking and dancing, rarely being troubled to actually pay for a drink. Cheryl remembered all the ridiculous one-liners she would get from guys at the bars—guys who eventually wanted to know if she wanted them to take her home. In her early days it didn't quite click with her why the guys rarely offered to take her to their own place, but she soon realized if the guys came home with her, they didn't have to worry about kicking her out as soon as the sex was over. They could just say they had to get home to let their dog out or something and be on their way. Besides, who wanted some one-night stand from a bar knowing where he lived?

Despite all the free drinks and offers to take them home, Cheryl and Gina usually ended up leaving the bars together. Not because they were morally above no-strings-attached sex. There were definitely times when Cheryl or Gina would leave a club in the company of a young man, but these instances were uncommon. It was just rare that either one of them found a guy who excited them enough to be bothered. Sometimes they were sluts, but at least they were picky sluts.

When she did actually have one-night stands, Cheryl remembered those awkward moments after the sex was over— how awful it was when she didn't get an invitation to stay the night and had to get out of bed and pick her clothes up off the floor. It was so humiliating, kneeling on the floor, trying to separate her clothes from the guy's she'd gone home with. She was never a smoker, but after a night at a bar her clothes would reek of cigarette smoke and pulling her shirt over her head would almost make her gag. Just thinking about it all gave Cheryl goose bumps.

Cheryl perused the ads in the *City Paper* for the newest dance clubs, most of which she hadn't been to. Now that she was pushing thirty, she started to feel a little out of place in many of the local clubs, particularly the ones that attracted the college crowd. Being surrounded by drunk eighteen-year-olds with fake IDs, who were about an hour away from puking their guts up in the bathroom was no longer Cheryl's idea of a good time.

A few weeks earlier, she went to Mister Days with a couple of the girls from work, when a young college guy approached her and tried to make conversation. Cheryl didn't have any interest in the kid, but it didn't hurt to be polite. After a few minutes they actually started to hit it off. He was a psychology major at American University, where Cheryl had graduated from, and they even had some of the same professors. The conversation went along smoothly until he inquired as to when she graduated. When she told him, his mouth dropped just a tad before he tried to recover by telling her how good she looked for twenty-nine. The young white boy then said he had heard that black people aged better than white people and she was surely proof of it. Annoyed and feeling about a hundred and ten, Cheryl joked that she used a lot of sunblock and tried to always get enough fiber. The young man politely laughed at her little joke and said it was nice to meet her before letting her know he was going to roam around a bit and maybe "they'd catch up later." He then extended his hand, offering a good-bye handshake. Feeling a tad humiliated, Cheryl shook his hand and forced a smile.

It all seemed so ridiculous. In the scheme of things, she was still very young. She wasn't even thirty yet, but she could remember back when she was twenty-one and thirty was just plain old. She also remembered being twenty-one and telling her friends to shoot her if she was still doing the bar scene when she was thirty. She had one more year to avoid a bullet.

Cheryl read an article or two in the *City Paper* and made her way toward the back. Eventually, she hit the classified section and flipped a few more pages until she reached the personal ads. She looked at the Matches section every couple of weeks and sometimes even circled a few ads she thought were interesting, but she was never able to make that final leap and actually place a call.

As she combed the ads, she laughed at herself. She hated how youth-obsessed people were and how a twenty-one-

year-old at Mister Days thought she was an old hag. But this
didn't stop her from immediately bypassing any ads from
guys who were over thirty-five. She skipped over the divorced ones, the ones with kids, the ones who said they were
hairy, and the ones who said they were stocky, which everyone knew was a marketer's term for big as a house.

Of course, she also passed on the ads that were specifi-
cally looking for white women. These ads annoyed her. It
was like she wasn't good enough for certain men because of
her skin color, but a part of her also felt sorry for men who
limited themselves to one race. There were so many people
out there, and it was just foolish not to give someone a
chance because they were African American or Asian or
Latino or whatever. Over the years Cheryl had dated men of
different races—a few black men, a Latino guy, and a man
of Native American descent. But mostly Cheryl seemed to
date white guys. In fact, most of the people in her life tended
to be white. White people were just what she was used to.
She grew up outside Portland, Maine, and was the only black
girl in her grade school and one of two in her high school. In
Maine she could go weeks without seeing a black person
other than her parents.

Now that she had been in D.C. for a few years, she had a
few black friends, but when she first moved to D.C. to go to
college, it was almost a culture shock. She had never seen so
many ethnic minorities in her life, and not just African
Americans. D.C. was the epitome of diversity. During the
brief walk from her dorm room to the Armand's Pizza on Wis-
consin Avenue she might see other black people, Cauca-
sians, some Latinos, an Asian or two, and sometimes women
in full Muslim attire. It took some getting used to, but
Cheryl eventually embraced the diversity of her new city.
This was one of the reasons she stayed in D.C. after she
graduated from college. She felt at home in a city with such
a varied population. Now, after ten years in a multicultural
city, when she went home to Maine it was almost like the
twilight zone—white people everywhere, no one speaking
foreign languages around her, and people who worked at

McDonald's and Ames actually spoke English as their first language.

By the time Cheryl reviewed the entire Men Seeking Women section, she only found two that were even remotely suitable. She circled them both with a red marker and set the paper aside. Maybe, just maybe, she would actually respond to one of them this time.

Immediate Regret

"Hey, pup. Aren't you cute?" Griffin said to Gomez as he walked into Gina's apartment. Gomez put on the usual show for Gina's guest. He yipped and barked and wagged his tail.

"Hush, Gomez. It's late. You're going to wake up the neighbors," Gina said, snapping her finger at the dog. Right then she had a terrible thought. She was talking to her dog the same way Annie talked to that feline beast of hers.

"Would you like a drink or something?"

"Sure," Griffin said. "Whatever you've got is fine."

Gina brought him a beer from the kitchen and got one for herself too. She was going to need even more intoxication if she was going to spend the night with Griffin. They sat on the sofa with Gomez and made small talk for a while. Griffin complimented Gina on her apartment and all the little knick-knacks she had displayed around the living room.

Gina had a one-bedroom apartment that was quite a bit larger than Peter's efficiency. The building was over fifty years old, but her unit had been remodeled a few years before so the appliances, carpeting, and such were fairly new. She furnished it with traditional pieces and solid colors. The overstuffed sofa was her favorite. It was light blue and almost swallowed her up when she lay on it. She and Peter lived on the seventh floor, but neither of them had views from their balconies. All they could see was the building across the alley.

Gina and Griffin sipped their beers and chatted for a while until Griffin got the nerve up to lean closer to Gina and kiss her. Gina immediately regretted ever letting him into her apartment. When she wrapped her arms around him, all she could focus on were the rolls of fat around his waist. His breath smelled like an ashtray, and he was a lousy kisser. He even kept his cap on the whole time they were on the sofa. It was so ridiculous to Gina. It was obvious that he was bald underneath, and he was silly to think he was hiding it with his stupid cap.

In spite of this, Gina continued to kiss him and agreed when Griffin suggested they move to the bedroom. She didn't quite know how to get rid of him without hurting his feelings. Why she cared about the feelings of a sleazy fat man she'd just met a few hours earlier was a whole different issue. Eventually, in her inebriated state, she decided it would be easier to just sleep with him and hope he would leave quickly afterward.

After all was said and done . . . mostly done . . . Gina lay in bed next to Griffin, feeling disgusted—absolutely disgusted. She usually felt a tinge of regret and a bit sleazy on the few occasions when she had brought guys home from the bars. But this time it was different. Generally, it was a nice-looking young man, about her age, lying next to her, and he was usually trying to figure out a good excuse for vacating the premises now that the sex was over. This time it was a short, fat, balding man who was probably old enough to be her father. She began to feel nauseated for the third or fourth time that evening and went into the bathroom. She'd had way too much to drink, and having sex with one of the seven dwarfs certainly didn't help her upset stomach. Feeling queasy, she sat on the floor, crossing her arms over the toilet seat. In a drunken haze she buried her head in her arms and began crying hysterically, all the while managing to keep it quiet, so Griffin wouldn't hear her. As she sobbed, she had an awful vision of herself still going to bars like Rumors twenty years from now.

As the crying quieted and the dizziness passed, Gina went to the sink and tried to gain her composure. She looked in the mirror and just wanted to cry again. Instead, she slipped on a robe, grabbed a towel, cleaned herself up, and went back into the bedroom. Griffin was asleep on the bed, and Gomez lay there wide awake, looking at her, his big brown eyes glistening in the darkness. She didn't even want to face the dog. She nudged Griffin awake and offered him the towel. He declined and started rubbing her leg.

"I think you should go. I'm really not feeling very well. Guess I had too much to drink," Gina said in a gentle voice, hiding her disgust at the fact that he wouldn't use the towel. He was gross enough without being wet and sticky on top of it.

"I really don't think I should be driving at this point. I had a little too much to drink myself," Griffin replied.

"Maybe you could stay with your friend down the hall." At that point, Gina didn't care if he ran his car into a telephone pole and decapitated himself. She just wanted him out of her apartment. Griffin ignored her suggestion and lay next to her with his eyes shut.

"Well, I hate to ask, but my mother's coming early tomorrow, and I don't think she would be pleased to find you here," Gina lied.

"Okay, I'll sleep for a few hours, then leave," Griffin replied, barely lifting his head from the pillow.

"Look! You have to go now. My friend, Peter, lives down the hall. Either get out, or I'll call him to get you out. I'm sorry to be such a bitch, but I really don't feel well. You need to go."

"Okay, okay," Griffin said, sitting up and fumbling for his clothes.

Gina looked the other way while he got dressed. She couldn't bear to see what she had gone to bed with—those rolls of fat and his ridiculous bikini undershorts. Griffin finished dressing, put his cap on, and Gina showed him to the door. He knew better than to try to kiss her good-bye or ask for her number.

Gina quickly closed the door behind him, thankful he was gone and hoping never to see him again. She locked the dead bolt and went back into the bathroom. She slipped off her robe and turned on the faucet in the tub, getting the water as hot as she thought she could stand it. After she stepped into the tub, she switched the shower on and let the hot water cascade over her. She soaped herself up from head to toe and scrubbed her body with a washcloth. She wanted every trace of Griffin off her. She soaped up and rinsed three times and washed her hair before finally getting out of the shower. As she toweled off and took a quick swig of mouthwash, she once again caught a glimpse of herself in the bathroom mirror and quickly turned away.

Once she was all dried off and had run a comb through her wet hair, she slipped on a cotton nightshirt and got back into bed. Damn! She could smell him on the sheets—kind of a musky cigarette smell. She immediately hopped off the bed and grabbed some clean sheets from the closet. She slumped the old linens into the corner of the bedroom and stretched the fresh sheets over the mattress. Once she had the clean sheets in place, she lay back down and the dog curled up next to her. The sun slowly started to rise as Gina tried to put the whole evening behind her and drift off to sleep.

Blue Sundays

Gina lay in bed, wishing Linda would stop calling. This was the fourth time since about eleven o'clock. After her first try she stopped leaving messages on the machine, but Gina knew it was her. She obviously was more than a little curious and wanted to know what had happened to Gina—why she had left the Phase without any notice. Linda must have been really intrigued and maybe a little worried. Gina never actually left her at a bar before—well, at least not without any explanation.

Gina groaned and reached over to get the phone. "Hello."

"So what happened to you?"

"What do you mean?" Gina replied, knowing exactly what she meant.

"What do I mean? I saw you take off from the Phase with that short girl with the bad perm. Are you like a fucking dyke now?" Linda said only half jokingly. "I saw that chick you left with, Gina, and believe me, you can do better."

"Very funny, Linda, and no, I regret to inform you, I'm not a lesbian. That was Annie from high school. Remember? I hadn't seen her since graduation, and we just went for coffee to catch up a little. It was too loud at the Phase. We could barely hear each other."

"Annie Harrison? Wow, how the mighty have fallen. She

looks like crap. Anyway, thanks for telling me you were leaving," Linda said, sounding a tad annoyed and wondering what on earth Gina and Annie had to catch up on. They had barely spoken to each other in high school.

"I'm sorry, Linda. I was a wee bit toasted at the time. I just didn't think about it. How was the rest of your night?" Gina asked, trying to change the subject.

"Nothing interesting happened. I left shortly after you and your new *girlfriend*."

"Ha-ha, very funny, Linda. Listen, that's my call waiting. Let me give you a ring later."

"Hello," Gina said after tapping over to the other call.

"Hey, sweetie. How are you?"

"Hi, Shirley. I'm really hung over and don't feel very well."

"Collin dumped me last night." Shirley responded as if she hadn't even heard Gina express her own discomfort.

"What do you mean, he dumped you? Don't you have to have a relationship in order to get dumped?"

"We had a relationship."

"Mother, he pages you a couple of times a week when his wife is asleep so he can come over and fuck you. That's hardly a relationship."

"It was more than that."

"Not to him, Shirley. I warned you over and over again."

"Thanks for the sympathy. I'm really upset. And do you know what the worst part is? He didn't even dump me to be faithful to his wife. He has another honey on the side, maybe two for all I know. Can you believe that?"

"Sure, I can believe it. What did you really expect from him, Shirley?"

"I don't know, but I'm upset, and I'm pissed—that's what I am."

"Look, Shirley, I'm really not feeling well. Do you want me to get him back for you?"

"How?"

"What's his home phone number?"

"Let me see. I have it, but I wasn't allowed to call him there. I could only page him or call him on his cell phone. Oh, here it is," Shirley said before reciting the phone number to Gina.

"Okay, I'll call you back later."

"What are you going to do?"

"I'll let you know, Shirley," Gina said before clicking the phone and dialing Collin's home phone number.

"Hello," Collin's wife said after picking up the phone.

"Hello, is Collin there?" Gina asked in the sexiest tone she could muster after just waking up.

"He's out for a couple of hours. May I ask who's calling?"

"This is Raquel," Gina lied before adding, "Oh, I'm sorry, is this the maid? He told me to hang up if the maid answered."

Gina hung up the phone, feeling that her work was done, and went to the kitchen to pop some aspirin and her antidepressant. She grabbed some orange juice and got back in bed to watch television. The night before was truly one of the most eventful nights she had had in a long time. She kept having visions of herself in the mirror, that lonely young woman standing there naked, with the bloodshot eyes from the crying and the drinking, and her hair completely frayed. But the worst, the absolute worst, was the look of sadness in her face. She felt like a character in a made-for-TV movie. One of those really cheesy ones where the nice girl becomes a slut and then has a revelation over the toilet and goes on to save poor children in India.

She tried to convince herself that she was being too hard on herself. Compared to other people she knew, she was almost saintly. Since college she'd probably only slept with a dozen guys, and she wouldn't go home with just anyone. She had to hit it off with them, and they had better damn well be attractive. In an age of AIDS and Lord knows what else, she wasn't about to take that kind of risk with any joe schmo who came along. But all of this changed after the "Griffin incident." What happened to her standards? Why had she sunk so low? She was only twenty-eight. She certainly wasn't looking old and haggard yet. She shouldn't have to settle for a guy like Griffin for at least another ten years. Maybe another fifteen if the Pond's Age-Defying Cream actually worked.

Passing on a
Milky Way

C heryl had just gotten back from Whatsa Bagel on 18th Street and was settling in for a relaxed Sunday afternoon. She was finishing her coffee and sitting next to the phone with the *Washington City Paper* in hand. She decided she was going to respond to the two ads she had circled the night before and was still trying to get up the nerve to actually pick up the phone. She hadn't really prepared anything to say. She didn't want her response to sound rehearsed. She wanted it to be relaxed and casual—even if she wasn't.

Eventually, she picked up the phone, dialed the 900 number, and responded to the appropriate prompts. When she entered the code for the first personal ad, she was immediately turned off by his recorded greeting:

"Hi. My name is Tyrol. I've been told that I'm very good-looking, but I don't get off on it or anything. I work out at Gold's four days a week and, if I do say so myself, I have a defined muscular build. I have short black hair, brown eyes, and skin the color of a Milky Way candy bar. I enjoy the finer things in life: wine, nice restaurants, fast cars, and beautiful

women. I own my home, drive a BMW 500 series, and work in high finance. I'm looking for an attractive woman with brains and beauty who doesn't mind taking care of her man. . . ."

As soon as Cheryl heard the part about "taking care of her man" she pressed the pound key to stop the message. She had heard enough. His tone was so pompous and patronizing, not to mention the "skin the color of a Milky Way candy bar" thing—how stupid was that? And although Cheryl had to admit that owning a home and driving a luxury car were certainly things she would like in a guy, she didn't think it was appropriate to put something like that in your initial greeting. Those were things you let your date subtly find out about, so it doesn't appear as if you're bragging.

Once she bypassed Tyrol, she skimmed the paper for the other ad that she had circled and punched in the appropriate code.

"Hi, thanks for answering my ad. My name is Hal, and I live just outside the city in Alexandria. I really hate talking on these things, so I'm going to keep it brief. Just to get the stats out of the way: I'm 32 years old, 5'10", 165 pounds, light brown hair, and have green eyes. I'm certainly not buff, but I know my way to the gym and I'm in reasonably good shape. I like doing virtually anything. I enjoy hiking in the summer, going to the beach, restaurants, movies, biking, reading, you name it. I guess I'm really looking to meet some new friends in the area and see what happens. So, if you would leave your name and number and tell me a little bit about yourself, I'll give you a call back and maybe we can meet for coffee or something. Thanks again for taking the time to answer the ad."

Cheryl really liked the sound of Hal's voice. He just sounded like a nice guy, not cocky or arrogant like Tyrol. He seemed friendly and maybe a bit humble. She pressed the key to leave a response.

"Hi, I'm Cheryl . . ."

She pressed the key to start again. "Hi, I'm Cheryl . . ."

Once again she pressed the key to start over. She couldn't think of anything to say.

"Okay, just relax, Cheryl," she told herself, hitting the key again.

"Hi, I'm Cheryl and thought I'd leave a quick response to your ad. I agree with you about talking on these recordings, so I will be brief as well. Let's see . . . I'm about five five, one hundred ten pounds, African American, short black hair, brown eyes . . . gosh, what else? I'd like to think I'm an attractive, fun person. I don't really have any specific hobbies, but I'm pretty much up for anything. I like doing things outside now that it's summer, hanging out with friends, and I enjoy cooking from time to time . . . things like that. Anyway, your ad seemed pretty nice, so I thought I'd go ahead and respond. Hope to hear from you."

Cheryl then left her telephone number and replayed the message to make sure it sounded okay. She wasn't overly thrilled with it but couldn't think of anything better to say. She held her finger over the appropriate key to send her message. She still wasn't one hundred percent sure this was something she wanted to do. She held her finger over the key a little longer before she took in a deep breath and gave it a quick punch. She still wasn't sure if the whole personal-ad thing was a good idea, but it was too late to change her mind now.

Name Tags

Linda was walking up Connecticut Avenue toward St. Margaret's Church for the evening service. St. Margaret's was an Episcopal church, but they let Dignity, a group for gay Catholics, hold a Catholic Mass there on Sunday evenings. Most of the time Linda didn't bother with it and went to the standard Catholic church closer to her apartment on Sunday mornings. Dignity's services tended to be long and, being in the evening, cut into her *Simpsons* watching time. It was just easier to go to a quickie forty-minute Mass in the morning and get it over with. Of course, she had issues with the Catholic church and its stance against homosexuals but, nonetheless, she always felt at home at church. She'd been Catholic all her life and even went through eleven years of Catholic school until her mother moved her and her sister to D.C. after the divorce. There Linda enrolled in Tenley High School, where she met Gina.

Linda had tried some other religions. She went to the Unitarian Universalist church a couple of years earlier but found their service to be more like a town meeting than a religious experience. She also visited the Metropolitan Community Church on Ridge Street, but when they wanted her to hug a complete stranger after receiving the Eucharist, she decided it was too touchy-feely for her. What was the big deal about being a gay Catholic anyway? It wasn't like every other Catholic didn't ignore the Pope's teachings—like half of the people that sat next to her at Mass weren't using birth control, having premarital sex, and even abortions. Please!

Linda was still a little annoyed with Gina for just disappearing from the Phase the night before—as annoyed with Gina as Linda could get. Long ago Linda decided to accept Gina for what she was—a mess. She knew that Gina cared for her, and that Gina would do anything for her. Gina took Linda under her wing in high school, helped her through her parents' divorce, and was right there through the rough times with Karen and Julie. Gina had even helped Linda move into her new apartment last summer, something Gina did for no one else. Linda remembered the time Peter asked Gina to help him move, and she told his "cheap ass" to hire movers.

Linda walked into the church and found a seat near the back. She didn't go to services there very often, so she didn't recognize anyone. Cursing herself for forgetting to set the VCR to tape her programs, Linda sat in the pew, reviewing the church bulletin, while she waited for the Mass to begin.

"May I?" a sharply dressed woman with a Dorothy Hamill haircut said to Linda, wanting to know if it was okay to sit next to her.

"Sure," Linda said, and scooted over just a tad.

"I haven't seen you around before. Are you new?"

"Sort of, I guess. I only come every once in a while."

"Well, it's great to have you," the woman, who was probably just a few years older than Linda, said with a smile. "I'm Amy."

"Linda. It's nice to meet you."

"You too. So, if I may ask, why do you only come every once in a while?"

"I usually go to another church in the mornings, but I was out late last night. I overslept and missed that service."

"I don't believe there is such a thing as oversleeping on a Sunday. That's what Sundays are for," Amy said with a quick laugh.

"Can't argue with that," Linda replied, not sure what the

woman's intentions were. Was she hitting on Linda? After all, there were plenty of empty pews in the church. Why had she chosen to sit down next to Linda? She had a look that Linda liked—a look that sort of said "I'm proud of being a lesbian, but I still want to look feminine."

"Certainly not. I hope you'll oversleep more often, so we get to see you here again."

Okay. She's flirting with me. Damn, I wish I had done my hair. "Maybe I'll do that," Linda said, smiling nervously, trying to sit up straight. It wasn't every day an attractive woman flirted with her. They chatted a bit more and started to get to know each other. Linda found Amy to be very interesting and well spoken. And, despite the fact that it was the beginning of the summer, Linda soon started thinking about what she always thought about when she began to hit it off with another woman—Christmas. She thought about Christmas and how this relationship might work out and how for the first time she wouldn't be alone for the holidays. She would have someone to put up a tree with and kiss at midnight on New Year's Eve. She knew it was silly, but she couldn't help it. The same way Pavlov's dogs started salivating when they heard a bell, Linda thought about Christmas the moment an inkling of a relationship seemed to be budding.

The girls talked some more before a rotund woman with graying hair plopped down into the pew.

"Amy, who are you harassing now?" the woman joked.

"This is Linda," Amy said to the woman before turning back to Linda. "And this is Harriet, my girlfriend."

Linda tried not to let her face drop. "Nice to meet you," Linda said, extending her hand and managing a smile.

"Yes, you too."

Why the hell did she sit down next to me and start talking to me as if she were interested, Linda thought to herself as the large woman fished a name tag out of her equally large purse.

"I brought your name tag, Amy."

"Oh, thanks," Amy said, pinning it onto her blouse. It said "Amy Garland, Greeter."

"You have to forgive Amy," Harriet said to Linda. "She has a habit of not wearing her Greeter name tag, and then people wonder why this brazen woman is approaching them and asking them all sorts of questions."

"Oh, no. I didn't think that at all. I just figured she was being friendly," Linda lied, offering a smile to Amy.

"Nope. Didn't think that at all," Linda repeated silently to herself as the music started, signaling the beginning of the Mass.

Another Short, Pudgy
Man for Gina

Gina hated Mondays. She was usually hung over from the weekend. Not necessarily from drinking too much—more from just napping here and there and staying up late. She found it impossible to go to sleep early on Sunday nights. Not getting up until noon on Sunday mornings may have had something to do with it, not to mention that *Entertainment Tonight* ran a special hour-long weekend edition around midnight.

The night before, she had stayed up even later than usual. She didn't leave the apartment the entire day or even get dressed. She watched reruns on channel five and napped off and on. It had definitely been a blue Sunday. She stayed up into the wee hours of the morning watching a tape of *The Sound of Music* her grandmother gave her for Christmas years ago. Now it was Monday morning, and she couldn't get the song "Climb Ev'ry Mountain" out of her head.

The day was getting off to a lousy start. Gina was down on her hands and knees in a skirt and heels trying to woo Gomez out from under the bed. She had forgotten to close the bedroom door before she took him out for his morning walk—big mistake. As soon as they got back inside, and she let him off the leash, he shot across the living room, into the bedroom, and under the bed. Once he was under the bed, he knew he was safe.

Gomez had a slight issue with doing his business on the floor when Gina wasn't home, so she had to keep him confined to the kitchen while she was at work. Gomez hated being restricted to the kitchen, and he knew hiding under the bed was his best bet for avoiding it.

"Gomez . . . here, boy. Look, I have your leash. Let's go for a walk," Gina called to the dog, waving his leash underneath the bed. He just looked at her like, Yeah, right. I'm really going to fall for that. Every time she'd try to reach him from one side, he'd run to the other. Gina would then hurry around to the other side just in time for Gomez to scurry back to the first side.

"Gomez, please!" Gina yelled, and grabbed the footboard of the bed. She pulled the entire bed a few feet away from the wall, exposing the little dog. He looked up at her and immediately scampered back underneath the bed to start the whole ritual again. Gina looked at her watch. She had to meet Dennis before work to get her hair done. Now that it was summer, Dennis spent most of his weekends at the beach in Rehoboth, Delaware. He didn't have any openings before he left for the weekend, but since they were friends, he agreed to meet Gina at seven A.M. to give her a quick touchup before the salon opened.

"Oh, forget it," she sighed while grabbing her purse and heading for the door.

Once Gina was gone and Gomez heard the front door shut behind her, he poked his head out from under the bed— ah, victory.

Gina pulled into the bank parking lot about nine-fifteen. She was one of those lucky people who actually drove against traffic to get to work from her apartment in the District to her job in the neighboring suburb of Arlington,

Virginia. One would think with this advantage she would usually be on time for work. She waited a minute or two before turning the ignition off and going into the bank. She wanted to catch the last bit of the story they were discussing on the radio. She was listening to some morning radio show, and the deejays were laughing it up. Some woman in nothing but bikini bottoms was washing the windshields of cars stuck in rush-hour traffic. They said the topless woman was causing traffic tie-ups from K Street to Constitution Avenue, and the cops had just arrested her. Gina laughed a little to herself. Some people will do anything for a buck, she thought as she cut off the engine, stepped out of the car, and headed toward the bank.

"Morning, Gina. You set such a great example for your staff, being so punctual and all," Linda said, noting Gina's tardiness with a friendly hint of sarcasm in her voice.

"Do you ever feel like you should have just stayed in bed?" Gina asked.

"Of course. Is today one of those days for you?" Linda responded before adding, "What happened to your hair?"

"Is there any coffee?" Gina asked, ignoring both of Linda's questions.

"No, I've only been here a few minutes myself."

"Why is Kelly working the drive-thru window?"

"Bob is late again, so I told her to go ahead and run the window until he gets here."

Gina sighed and went into the back to start the coffee-maker. She needed her morning cup of caffeine, especially since it was a Monday. Every Monday, Liz, the branch manager, didn't come in until noon, so Gina was in charge and, once again, she was late. With Liz out, Gina had to deal with all the tellers' little troubles and sign off on their large transactions, but the extra work was almost worth a morning without Liz. It wasn't anything personal, but she just creeped Gina out. Liz was a tall, stocky woman with broad shoulders and a deep voice. She tried desperately to look feminine but usually ended up looking ridiculous in floral print dresses with gaudy scarves tied around her neck.

Gina's early morning appointment with Dennis hadn't gone very well. She just wanted to get her roots covered and a trim; however, Dennis was in one of his manic phases and convinced her to go a few shades lighter. When all was said and done, Gina left the salon quite unhappy with the final product. Her hair had the yellowish hue of an overweight housewife who bought whatever brand of bleach was on sale at the drugstore. Dennis said she would have to wait at least a week before they could tone it down, to let her hair "rest."

She hated this stupid job. It had been six years since she started in the management training program at Premier Bank of Arlington, and she was still an *assistant* manager. She'd seen Linda go from teller to customer service representative to senior customer service representative while she stagnated. Fact was, Linda had saved Gina's butt on more than a few occasions. Linda started with the bank fresh out of high school and had been there for nearly ten years. She covered for Gina when she was late and helped her when customers asked her questions she didn't know how to answer. In fact, she was basically responsible for Gina even getting the job in the first place. When Gina graduated from American University, Linda referred her to a friend in human resources. Gina didn't understand why Linda wasn't bitter. The only reason Gina was in management over Linda was because she had a college degree and Linda didn't. Gina used to pester Linda about at least signing up for a few classes, but it just wasn't something that ever really interested Linda. Linda's parents would have helped out with the tuition, but they certainly couldn't afford to completely cover four years worth of higher education expenses. Linda would have needed to take out a plethora of student loans to get by. She spent a lot of time with Gina at American University and knew what went on at those supposed sanctuaries of higher learning—too much drinking, a lot of game show and soap opera watching, numerous naps, tons of sex, and every once in a while, someone might bother to go to class or study for an exam. Linda didn't care to get herself in debt up to her eyeballs to experience that. Besides, Linda was one of those people who could truly say money wasn't that important to her. She didn't drop a couple of hundred dollars at the salon every month or shop at fancy stores like Gina and Cheryl did. She simply wasn't a capitalist.

It always amazed Gina that Linda made significantly less money than she did yet Linda never seemed to be strapped for cash like Gina always was. Linda simply lived within her means and had more savings than most people her age who had much higher incomes.

Gina fumbled with a little packet of coffee and tried to get her morning cup of java going. As she thought about how she needed to manage her money better and be more like Linda, Bob came in the back to put his lunch in the fridge.

"Hey there," Gina said.

"Hi," Bob replied.

Gina figured she should probably ask him why he was late, but she really didn't care. He'd just lie anyway. He was probably late for the same reason she was—just didn't feel like getting out of bed. He was young and going to school. His bank teller job was just beer money to him anyway. If he got fired, he'd just go work at Kmart or some other service-oriented place that was desperate for help who spoke coherent English.

"Is the hair on purpose?" Bob asked, being a smart aleck.

Gina ignored his question. "Since you're running a little late, Kelly's running the drive-thru for you. Why don't you just set up in her station and wait on lobby customers today."

"I hate doing the lobby. I'll just switch with Kelly."

"I think you should do the lobby today to avoid confusion, Bob."

"It'll just take a second for us to switch."

Gina knew her lack of firmness was one of the major reasons she was still an assistant manager—aside from being late all the time, having virtually no motivation, and not asking for identification from a woman dressed like a nun, who ended up scamming the bank for over ten thousand dollars. She needed to be firm with Bob.

"Just do the lobby, Bob. End of discussion."

Bob looked at her with a disgruntled and somewhat con-fused expression. She'd always backed down before. Figur-ing she must have gotten laid over the weekend, he nodded his head and left the kitchen. Gina was as amazed as Bob. She only wished that Linda had been there to see her hold her ground and not let one of her employees walk all over her.

Standing over the coffeemaker, watching little droplets of coffee drip into the pot underneath, Gina wallowed through her typical Monday morning depression. She wasn't sure how much longer she was going to be able to do her job . . . how much longer she could honestly look customers in the eye and tell them that Premier Bank really wanted to help them reach their financial goals . . . how much longer she could watch lines of ten to fifteen people wait for one of two tellers to assist them.

A couple of weeks earlier, Premier had cut off all incom-ing phone calls into the branches. Customers were no longer able to reach their local branch directly. If they dialed their branch's number, they were routed to the 800 line, where they ended up in elevator-music limbo. Gina knew it was just another tactic to cut staff at the branches and save money. When irate customers complained to her about it, she had to tell them a bunch of crap about how a central ser-vice could serve them more efficiently. She wanted to tell them it was just another way to do her out of a job and pro-vide second-rate service to the customers. It was pathetic. She couldn't even discreetly suggest that the customer go bank somewhere else. All the other banks in town, which numbered in the single digits due to years of mergers and ac-quisitions, were owned by giant financial corporations and sucked just as much as Premier, if not more so.

As Gina started filling her cup with coffee, Kelly came running into the back room.

"Gina, we have a slight problem at the drive-thru."

"What is it?"

"Well, Bob and I were switching stations . . ."

"What do you mean, you were switching?"

"He said you wanted us to. Anyway, I was gathering my stuff, and this guy sent in a note demanding money. He says he has a knife," Kelly replied with a slight giggle.

"A knife? At the drive-thru? Is he joking?"

Gina left the kitchen, explained the situation to Linda, and told her to call the police as she hurried behind the teller line with Kelly. She glared at Bob and then leaned over the drive-thru counter just enough to peer outside. There was a short man with a stocking cap and sunglasses, sitting in his car, staring directly forward. She quickly drew her head back, starting to get a little nervous. Suddenly, the whole thing didn't seem so amusing anymore. The man was obviously crazy and might be dangerous. Kelly handed her the note the driver sent into the bank.

Send out 50,000 dollars in cash. I have knife!

"What a wacko," Kelly said, starting to get a little nervous herself.

Gina poked her head over the counter again and saw that the little man was gone. The car was empty.

"Shit, I'm going to lock the door," Gina said, running out into the lobby, but she was too late. The little man was already inside, standing about a foot from Linda, pointing some sort of kitchen knife at her.

"Who's in charge here?"

"I am," Gina called with her heart racing. This was the second time today she had surprised herself. She wasn't sure what possessed her to tell the wacko she was in charge. She hoped she hadn't just bought big trouble for herself. The little man turned around and glared at Gina. Gina tried to keep her composure as best she could. She was scared, and "Climb Ev'ry Mountain" began blaring in her head.

The robber stammered over to Gina, never losing eye contact. "Well, if it ain't Fried-Hair Barbie. I asked for fifty thousand dollars. This is a bank, isn't it? I don't want any trouble, blondie. Get me the cash, and I'll be on my way." The robber grabbed Gina's arm and raised his voice. "Move your bony ass and get me the cash."

Gina was virtually frozen. "Okay, please calm down. Let me get you your money." The robber pulled Gina's arm and led her behind the teller line. Between the smell of whiskey coming from her assailant and the blaring sound of Julie Andrews in her head, she thought she might faint. Gina opened one of the teller drawers and looked at the robber. He must have been at least sixty. He couldn't have been over five feet tall and, she wasn't sure, but he might have been wearing lipstick.

"Do you have a bag or anything to put the money in?" Gina asked the little man.

"Do you have a bag or anything to put the money in?" the robber mimicked Gina in a squeaky voice. "No, I don't have a bag, you whore. Why don't you take your bony ass and find me one!"

Gina was about to start looking for some sort of bag, when she saw two cops stroll into the bank as if it were Free Toaster Day. The robber saw the cops coming toward him but continued to stand next to Gina, pointing the knife at her.

"Had too much to drink again, Gladys?" the taller cop said casually.

"You guys stand back or there's no telling what I'll do."

"Settle down, Gladys," the smaller officer said, easily pulling the knife from the robber's hand.

"Don't worry," he said to Gina. "She's harmless."

She? It suddenly hit Gina, as she breathed a huge sigh of relief, that the nasty little man was, in fact, a nasty little woman. The police handcuffed Gladys, and the smaller cop led her out of the bank. The other officer looked at Gina and said, "I'll need statements from everyone. Are you in charge here?"

"No," Gina said, and pointed to Linda. "She is. Excuse me for a moment. I need to go to the rest room." As Gina left the teller line, she saw the cop approaching Linda. As soon as he had his back to her, Gina sneaked behind him and left the bank. She had to get out of there and didn't feel like co-ordinating some kind of robbery-debriefing ceremony. She didn't know the procedures, and she wasn't about to rummage through some policies and procedures manual to find all the goofy forms that needed to be filled out. Besides, she knew Linda would cover for her as usual.

Diving Right In

Cheryl had been up for only about an hour. Well, actually, she had been up briefly about two hours earlier to call in sick to work before she lay back down. She felt fine, but she hadn't called in sick for a few months, and she figured she deserved a day on the sofa, watching television. She was beating a couple eggs with a heavy-duty whisk her mother had bought her for her birthday and trying to remember everything she had learned about omelet making in one of the cooking classes she had taken. She remembered the instructor saying that it was important not to overbeat the eggs. The goal was to mix the yolk and the white so slightly that the final product would have striations of both. She dropped some butter in the skillet and poured in the eggs.

"Work it, work it," she said to herself as she swirled the pan and raised and lowered the skillet to control the heat. As the bottom of the omelet began to set, she lifted it up to allow some of the uncooked egg to run underneath. When the eggs were almost set, she turned off the heat and dropped in a few green peppers, tomatoes, and mushrooms.

"Okay, now for the hard part," she muttered as she brought the skillet over the edge of the plate and tipped and rolled the omelet out of the pan at the same time.

"Yes!" she said as the perfect omelet hit the plate. Cheryl

set two pieces of toast next to the omelet, pulled a cheese soufflé from the oven, and took the whole spread into the living room, where she set it on a TV tray in front of the sofa.

She went back into the kitchen and poured herself a glass of orange juice and grabbed some strawberry jam. As she walked back into the living room, she thought about how nice it would be to share her culinary creations with someone. When she lay her orange juice on the TV tray, she pictured a guy sitting in front of it, raving about what a great chef she was, and how lucky he was to have someone like her. As the vision passed, she clicked on the television to catch the last part of *The Today Show.* She didn't particularly care for Katie. But that Matt—he was hot!

As she sat down to eat her breakfast, she felt the same way she always did when she cooked herself an elaborate meal and then ate it in front of the television alone—pathetic. She only did it about once a week. Usually, she subsisted on Lean Cuisines, deli sandwiches, or restaurant meals with friends, but she really enjoyed cooking and wanted to keep up her culinary skills. She took classes every now and then through l'Académie de Cuisine in Bethesda and some of the adult education programs in the area. Sometimes she would invite friends over when she cooked, and every once in a while she would ask Bea, the middle-aged woman next door, if she would like to join her for dinner.

When she finally got settled in on the sofa and started to eat her breakfast, the phone rang. Cheryl hopped up and grabbed the phone.

"Hello."

"Is Cheryl there?"

"Speaking."

"Hi, this is Hal from the *City Paper.*"

Cheryl took a deep breath and tried to relax. "Hi, how are you?"

"Good, good. And yourself?"

"Just fine," Cheryl said.

"Did I catch you at a bad time?"

"No, not at all," Cheryl replied, staring at her breakfast, which was getting cold on the other side of the room.

"Great. Well, if you don't mind, I'd like to dive right in."

"Dive right in?" Cheryl asked.

"Yeah. I developed this questionnaire I'd like to go over with you. Do you mind?"

Questionnaire? "No, not at all," Cheryl said, not really sure if she minded or not. She would have preferred just having an informal conversation.

"Okay. Let's see. I think I have all your stats. You're five five, one hundred ten pounds, African American, short black hair, brown eyes. Correct?"

"Yep," Cheryl said, now knowing that she minded.

"You didn't say how old you were in your response."

"Twenty-nine."

"Great. Are you from the area?"

"No, I grew up in Maine, but went to college in D.C."

"Cool. You have a 202 area code, so I guess you live in the city?"

"You got it," Cheryl said, not sure if she would complete the rest of his dumb questionnaire before she just hung up on him. He sounded so pleasant and normal on his greeting.

"What do you do for a living?"

Cheryl didn't understand the logic of his questions at all. He went from where she grew up, to where she lived now, to what she did for a living. God, anyone with half a brain knew you were not supposed to ask someone what she did for a living when you first meet. It's one of those things everyone wants to know when meeting a potential love interest, but you're supposed to pretend it's not important.

What an idiot! Oh, well, she'd figured she'd get through his dumb questionnaire then just not return any of his calls if he ever phoned back. She was about to tell Hal about her job implementing new accounts for a health insurance company, when she had an idea.

"Well, I'm not working at the moment," Cheryl lied. "I'm out on disability."

"Disability?"

"Yeah. I'm having some mental health issues at the moment. My psychiatrist thought it would be good for me to get out and do things. That's why I answered the ad."

"Oh, well . . . good for you," Hal replied with some apprehension.

"Don't worry, as long as I take my antipsychotics I seem to do reasonably well. I haven't had an incident in several weeks," Cheryl said, not really sure what antipsychotics were.

"Oh . . ." Hal replied, not sure what to say and losing his interest in continuing with the questionnaire.

"I'm sorry. I probably divulged too much for a first phone call," Cheryl said innocently.

"No, no, not at all," Hal said before adding, "Oh, that's my call waiting. Can I take this call and try you back later?"

"Sure," Cheryl said. "I'll be home all day."

"Okay. Nice to talk to you."

Cheryl hung up the phone, slowly shook her head in frustration, and smirked slightly to herself. Only two ads in the whole paper even remotely interested her, and both turned out to be duds. Not to mention she had probably spent a nice chunk of change to respond to the ads. Maybe she could check the personals in the *Washingtonian* magazine or *The Washington Post*. She tried to think of a few other sources when she started to think about taking out her own ad. What did she really have to lose other than her pride?

As Cheryl finished her breakfast, she flipped through the *City Paper* and checked out the guidelines for placing an ad. It was only five dollars for fifty words, but Cheryl thought that some Web sites, like Digital City or Yahoo! let you take out electronic personal ads free.

Once she had cleaned up the kitchen and loaded the dishwasher, she stepped over to the computer and logged on to the Internet. After keying in the address for Digital City, she selected Washington, D.C. from the list of choice cities and made her way to the personals section. She took a look at some of the ads that were already posted to get an idea of what people were saying about themselves.

As she read the ads, she couldn't help but view most of

these people as desperate and pathetic. What was even worse, she was about to join them. After she reviewed a few dozen ads, Cheryl figured she was ready to create her own. She clicked on the Create Your Personal Ad icon and selected the Women Seeking Men category. She completed the fields asking for things such as age, occupation, ethnicity, hair color, and weight. That was the easy part. When she got to the field where she needed to write a personalized narrative describing herself in more detail, the exercise began to get a bit more difficult.

Cheryl played with her words for a few minutes. She wasn't sure how to present herself. It was hard to write about yourself and what you were looking for without appearing desperate. She may have been desperate, but she certainly didn't want to appear that way. In the end, she spent almost a half hour typing up the paragraph.

Hi guys! Thanks for taking a look at my ad. I'm really just looking to start some new friendships in the area that might lead to something more. I live in the city and enjoy cultural activities, fine restaurants, the theater, and an occasional night out at a trendy club for drinks and dancing. I enjoy the outdoors, movies, biking, and have become a rather talented amateur chef over the past few years. I'm 29, about 5'5", 110 pounds, African American, and have short black hair and brown eyes. I'm looking to meet nice, well-educated men to take advantage of all the nation's capital has to offer. Please be around my age, nonsmoking, and reasonably fit. Thanks again for reviewing my ad. Send me an e-mail, and maybe we can meet for coffee or something.

She liked the way Hal started his recording by thanking respondents for answering his ad, so Cheryl thought she'd do the same thing. Honestly, she wasn't looking for "friendships" at all but figured she didn't sound quite so needy by using that term. She wasn't sure what she meant by "cultural activities," but it sounded good. And she couldn't remember the last time she went biking. She really wasn't even sure where her bike was. She thought it might be in her basement storage unit, but she really didn't know . . . and so what if she was really 120 pounds? She could pass for 110.

Cheryl reviewed her ad one more time before saving it. Once she submitted the ad for publication on the Web, she actually felt pretty good about it. All she had to do was sit back, wait for the responses, and pick and choose whom, if anyone, she wanted to pursue. She didn't include a picture or her name, so she didn't have to worry about anyone she knew stumbling onto her ad and finding out that she had hit such hard times.

It might even be fun, and who knows, Cheryl thought, maybe I'll find the love of my life.

Mr. Right

"Take deep breaths ... relax ... deep breaths," Gina kept repeating to herself as she pulled into the lot at Rio Grande, a Mexican restaurant a couple of blocks down from the bank. She and Linda ate lunch there every couple of weeks. It was the closest place she knew of to get a drink so early in the day. She was still jittery over earlier events and was quite shaken from being held at knifepoint by a drunken old lady.

"Bitch, telling me I have fried hair. I hope they lock her ass up for good," Gina mumbled to herself. She contemplated switching hairdressers as she walked into Rio Grande, but she and Dennis had become pretty good friends over the years, and he usually did do a great job.

It was obvious that the restaurant had just opened. Gina went up to the bar, where another customer was waiting as well.

"Is anyone here?" Gina said to the man.

"I've only been standing here a few minutes, but there doesn't appear to be anyone around. I guess it's a little early for drinks, huh?"

"Well, I'm going to go look for someone," Gina said, turning around to find someone to get her a goddamn drink.

Gina returned with a disgruntled bartender behind her. "What may I get for you, ma'am?" the bartender asked Gina.

"The biggest, coldest margarita in the house, please."

"Make it two," replied the gentleman next to her at the bar. "Rough morning?" the dark-suited man asked Gina as the bartender began fetching their drinks.

"You don't know the half of it. I come into work after the weekend from hell, and some nutcase little man . . . I mean woman, comes into my bank with a knife, demanding money."

"Are you okay?"

"It turned out she was just some drunk. The cops came and hauled her out of there, but I'm still a little shaken up. I didn't even stay to coordinate a debriefing. I just took off," Gina said, embarrassed.

"The cops didn't make you give a statement or anything?"

"Well, I kind of didn't give them the chance. I sneaked out when they weren't looking. I was just so not in the mood . . . you know?"

The man next to her started laughing just a little. Apparently, he found her lack of responsibility quite amusing. Gina laughed with him, and for the first time since she walked in the door she realized how attractive he was. He looked a lot like Peter only with a darker complexion and sharper features. She wondered what he was doing at Rio Grande at ten-thirty in the morning.

"So what brings you to Rio Grande this time of day?" Gina asked.

"I'm meeting a client here for an early lunch. He's about as annoying as the lady who tried to rob your bank this morning. I thought I'd get a drink before he arrived to calm my nerves. He's a little easier to deal with after a couple of drinks."

"What kind of work do you do?" Gina asked, trying to sound like she was just making small talk and really didn't care what he did for a living.

"I manage porno stars. Well, they prefer the term adult film actors. Now, don't laugh. It's quite lucrative," the man replied. He started to break up with laughter after seeing Gina try to hide her reaction to his occupation. "I'm only kidding. Seriously, I'm a financial planner. This particular client I'm meeting today is a real pig. He makes quite a large sum of money and still prefers to meet here, so he can eat all the fajitas and refried beans he can stuff in himself. You know, I've been sitting here, babbling on, and I don't even know your name."

"Gina," she replied, a little distracted. He had just touched his forehead with his left hand, and she was trying to nonchalantly check it for a wedding band. To her relief, there wasn't one.

"I'm David. It's a pleasure to meet you."

"So, David, are you from the area?" Gina asked.

"No. I grew up in Connecticut and then went to college here. I graduated about five years ago and got a job locally."

"Where'd you go to school?"

"George Washington University."

"That's a great school. I went to American. What was your major?" Gina asked, realizing that she sounded as if she were at a college sorority mixer.

"Finance with a minor in economics," he replied.

"Interesting, I majored in—"

"There's my client," David said, interrupting Gina.

Gina turned her head and, to her horror, there was Griffin standing by the entryway. Once again he was wearing dress slacks and a tie, and that stupid cap that said "The Big G."

"I'll just call him over," David said, starting to lift his hand.

"No!" Gina replied abruptly. "You go and meet him. Maybe we can get together some other time. Let me give you my number." Gina reached into her purse for a pen, hoping David wouldn't notice her hands shaking. She quickly scrawled her name and number on a napkin and handed it to David, trying to appear calm. "I don't want to keep you from your client. You go, and I'll just finish my drink," Gina said, barely turning her head to speak to David. She didn't want Griffin to see her face.

"Okay, it was nice to meet you," David said with a smile, looking just a little confused.

"Call me, and we can hang out again soon."

David laid a ten-dollar bill on the bar and left the lounge area. Gina remained at the bar with her back to the doorway until she thought it might be safe to turn around.

"Damn," she muttered to herself as she gulped down the rest of her margarita. She walked out of the restaurant as quickly as possible, trying to keep anyone from seeing her face. She sat in her car and rolled her eyes and shook her head, not knowing whether to laugh or cry. She did neither.

"What were the chances?" she said once the car door was closed. "What were the chances of the fucking Pillsbury Dough Boy walking into the same restaurant where I'm actually getting along with a decent guy. Damn!" she yelled a little louder to herself while she started the car and drove out of the parking lot.

Busted

"Don't even speak to me—not a word, not one word!" Gina said to Shirley, who was sitting on the passenger side of the car. It had been a few hours since the attempted bank robbery.

"What's the big deal?"

"What's the big deal? You have no idea what kind of day I've had. Do you know this is the second encounter I've had with the police today? What were you thinking, Shirley?"

"I was thinking that I needed some money."

"Shirley, there are tons of ways to earn money."

"I know there are, and I found one of them."

"What do you mean, you found one of them? You ended up busted, Shirley. You're lucky you're not in jail right now."

"So my plan was flawed. Better luck next time."

"There'd better not be a next time. You pull a stunt like this again, and I won't come bail you out. I just don't understand, Shirley. What did you think was going to happen?"

"Get over it, sweetie. Would you? I saw something on TV about these women in New York who were making a fortune, so I thought I'd try it here. I figured if they were doing so well in bathing suits, I'd make a killing if I washed the car windows topless."

"And the small detail of going out in public topless being illegal wasn't an issue, I guess."

"I didn't expect such an uproar. I thought I'd squeegee a few windows, collect a few bucks, and be back home in an hour or so. Next thing I knew, men were hootin' and hollerin' at me to come wash their windshield and handing me masses of cash. I got twenty-dollar bills from some of them."

"And the women?" Gina asked.

"They were hootin' and hollerin', too, but to a different tune. Some old hen called me a Jezebel. Can you believe that? Who uses the word 'Jezebel' anymore?"

"And this didn't bother you?"

"Hell, no. They're just jealous."

"You think? They wished they were the ones Windexing cars half naked? I don't think so, Shirley."

"They might not have been wishing they were washing windows, but I bet they were wishing they had a rack like this," Shirley said, pulling her shoulders back and sticking out her chest.

Gina smirked just a little at her mother. It was futile. She had to remind herself that it was best to deal with Shirley the same way she dealt with Gomez. It was absolutely of no use reprimanding either one of them. They were both going to do what they wanted to do when they wanted to do it, and it was an exercise in frustration for Gina to try to keep either one of them out of trouble. This wasn't the worst stunt Shirley had pulled over the years. She had a long history of outrageous behavior. Gina sometimes dreamed of having a normal mother who wore dowdy clothes, made cookies, and went to PTA meetings.

It was probably about twenty years ago when Gina began to truly realize how different Shirley really was—Gina was eight or nine years old, and Shirley left her in the care of her grandmother to go to Los Angeles with a man—a man claiming to be a Hollywood agent, who had convinced Shirley that he would make her a big television star. He sold her a ridiculous line about how trouble was brewing on the set of *Laverne & Shirley* and the producers were looking to recast Cindy Williams. He said one of the producers sent him to the East Coast to scout possible replacements and joked that Shirley would be the new Shirley. He even promised Shirley her very own Boo Boo Kitty. Gina's grandmother begged Shirley not to go, but Shirley was head over heels in love with the man, and he charmed her into believing his story.

It wasn't long before Shirley was back in D.C. The scam artist had set his sights on Shirley when he saw her upscale home in Cleveland Park. It wasn't until they had gotten out west and Shirley was unable to "tide them over" until he got her some acting roles that he realized it was Shirley's *mother* who was wealthy. Once he found out Shirley didn't have any money in her own right, he sent her packing.

This began a pattern of Shirley moving in and out of her mother's house. She would stay for a while and then leave to live with some man. Then move back again when her relationship fell apart. It didn't seem like a big deal to Gina at the time. Shirley was always more like the fun aunt who came over to take her out for ice cream or sneak her into R-rated movies. Gina's grandmother certainly assumed the parental role and was ultimately responsible for raising Gina.

Now, in the car, dragging her mother home from the police department, Gina thought about how she would watch television as a kid and wonder why the woman she called "Mom" was so different from the mothers on TV. It wasn't like Gina was stupid or naive—she didn't really expect Shirley to be like Carol Brady or Marion Cunningham, but some resemblance would've been nice.

"Yes, Shirley. I'm sure all the ladies were jealous of your bare tits. Next time, would you let them be jealous with a bra and a top over them," Gina said in a resigned tone. It wasn't easy accepting Shirley for who she was, but somewhere along the line it was all Gina could do. She really did love her mother, and it was just too exhausting to try to do anything else.

"I'll try. Thanks for picking me up and taking me home, sweetie. I can always count on you."

I know, Gina thought. That's part of the problem.

"By the way," Shirley asked, looking at Gina. "What happened to your hair?"

Bedside Manners

It had been about a half hour since Peter finished filling out all the paperwork required of new patients when the nurse finally called him back to see the doctor. One time he actually typed up a generic form listing his name, address, health insurance, medical history, and all the other stuff doctors asked of new patients. He figured he could just copy and distribute it to each new doctor rather than spend twenty minutes filling out forms, but the first time he tried to use it, the receptionist looked at him like he was crazy. She had to data-enter all the information from their standard forms, which matched the screen on her computer and wasn't about to hunt all over his generic form to find the information she needed.

When he was finally called back to an examining room, the nurse did all the usual things. She took his blood pressure, temperature, and pulse rate, and told him the doctor would be with him shortly. Peter sat on the examining table, looking around at all the supplies and instruments on the cabinets, wondering what the purpose of some of them was. He hated meeting new doctors. He never knew what was in store. Some were friendly with a good bedside manner, while others were abrupt and rude and managed their patient load like an assembly line.

"Hi, I'm Dr. McKonkey. How are you doing today, Kenneth?" the doctor asked Peter as he glanced over his chart.

"I'm fine, thanks. Actually, it's Peter. Kenneth's my first name, but I go by Peter." Peter had yet to forgive his parents for naming him one thing and calling him another. Going by his middle name constantly wreaked havoc in his life.

"Well, Peter, what can I do for you today?"

"I've been working out a lot lately, and a few days ago I started getting this soreness in my chest while I was on the treadmill. I know it's ridiculous to think I might have a heart problem at my age, but, nonetheless, I thought I should check it out."

The balding doctor, who must have been well into his fifties, asked Peter a variety of questions about the pain and his family history. Then he listened to his heart with the stethoscope.

"You probably just strained a muscle or something even more benign, but I'll have Celia run an EKG to rule out any other problems." The doctor pressed a buzzer by the door, and within seconds an attractive nurse appeared at the doorway.

"Celia, we need to run an EKG on Mr. Virga," Dr. McKonkey said to the nurse. "I'll check back with you in a little while. Celia will take good care of you."

"You'll need to take off your shirt and lie down on the table."

Peter followed her instructions while admiring her backside as she began flicking switches on the EKG machine.

"We usually need to shave our male patients before we do this, but it looks like you've taken care of that for us," Celia said while she prepped his chest for the test.

This was one of the many times Peter felt his long hours at the gym were paying off. He knew his muscles must be turning her on. While she attached the wires to his body, he flexed his muscles as much as he could without it being obvious, hoping it would get her attention. Peter figured Celia was probably pushing forty. She had silky long, black hair

and an olive complexion. She was of some sort of Asian decent. Maybe Korean or Chinese. Peter wasn't sure.

While she continued to put little stickers on his chest,
Peter started having mild fantasies about Celia becoming
overwhelmed with passion and ripping the EKG pads from
his body. It was like some sort of low-budget porno movie.
Peter thought about what he'd call it—maybe "EKG-Spot"
or something like that. Peter smirked a little at the thought,
and before he knew it, the test was done.

"I'll give the reading to Dr. McKonkey," Celia said, leaving the room, closing the door, and, to Peter's dismay, not
seeming the slightest bit impressed with his muscles.

"Everything looks fine, Peter. If the pain comes back,
make another appointment and we will run a few more
tests," the doctor said, barely stepping into the exam room.

"Are you sure there's nothing else we should do?"

"Not at this point. It may have just been something you
ate, or a pulled muscle, or a number of things, but your EKG
was normal."

"Okay, thanks, Doctor," Peter said, relieved. He rushed to
put his shirt back on and left the examining room. He had to
hurry to an appointment with Dr. Ready, whom he was
going to see about some vague pain he'd been having in his
fingers. He thought it might be arthritis starting or something. He didn't want to tell Dr. McKonkey about the arthritis symptoms. Peter figured the doctor would think he was
just paranoid or something if he came for both chest pain
and discomfort in his hands. When he went to see Dr.
Powers last week because of headaches and a tiny numb spot
in his toe, he wasn't taken seriously at all.

The Life of
the Party

"Where are we supposed to park?" Gina asked as they turned into the housing development on a rainy Wednesday evening. Gina had convinced Peter to go to Penelope's party, and Linda had tagged along as well. Gina figured she wouldn't look too pathetic if Peter came to the party with her. Hopefully, everyone would assume they were together and, thank God, Dennis was finally able to fix her hair.

It had been a few weeks since Penelope's wedding and she and Donny had just bought a town house in a new development in the Maryland suburbs of D.C. When they finally found her house, they couldn't find any parking that didn't threaten to take their firstborn if they didn't have a parking permit for the development. Finally, they stumbled onto a visitors' lot with an open space, and Linda started to park the car.

"You can't park there, Linda," Peter called from the backseat while pointing out an old Cadillac next to the open parking space. "Next to that big clunker? You'll get your car nicked."

"Oh, please," Linda said, pulling the car into the spot. "I

refuse to spend my life worrying about a scratch on my car. I'm not going to be like those freaks who take up two spaces or park in the boonies so they don't scratch their precious car. It's pathetic."

"You mean like Peter does?" Gina joked as the three of them climbed out of the car and tried to huddle under one umbrella. The trio meandered toward the house with all the lights on and human shadows bobbing around behind the shades.

As they approached the party, they could hear the music coming from Penelope's house.

"Hi, guys, it's so good to see you," Donny said as he opened the door for them. He was short and skinny with red hair and freckles. He wasn't a bad-looking guy. He just sort of looked like a computer geek—one of those guys you might see in the parking garage of your office building and you just know they work in IS, even though you've never even seen them before.

"It's good to see you too. We had to park in Peru and walk quite a ways to get here," Gina replied with a smile, stepping through the doorway and closing the umbrella.

"The parking situation here kinda sucks," Donny said before calling to Penelope.

"Gina!" Penelope screamed, running up to Gina and hugging her. She was obviously drunk. "I never see you anymore. God. I haven't seen you since the wedding." She briefly acknowledged Peter and Linda and pulled Gina aside. She began chatting incessantly about her wedding, their new house, and her job as a manager at Bloomingdale's. Gina smiled and nodded as Penelope continued to babble. Gina wasn't really paying attention. She was amazed at the number of people in Penelope's house. She wondered when Penelope had met all these people—or were they all Donny's friends? When had Penelope become outgoing, and when had she become a manager at Bloomingdale's? The last time Gina saw her, she was still assaulting women with perfume as they walked through the cosmetics aisle. It had been a few

weeks since Gina met David at Rio Grande, and he still hadn't
called her. So listening to Penelope banter on and on about
Donny and her job wasn't exactly making her feel better.

"Gosh. Things are really going well for you," Gina said
with a phony smile.

"I'm a lucky girl."

Gina couldn't stand it anymore. "Where can a girl get a
drink around here?"

"Upstairs in the bathtub," Penelope replied.

"Great. Well, excuse me for a moment," Gina said, bound
for the stairway. She passed Peter and Linda on their way
down the stairs.

"I'm going to grab a beer, and I'll meet you guys downstairs," Gina said, feeling a little down about her life.
Penelope was such an introvert when they met in college.
Back then, Gina felt sorry for her and even made a point of
including Penelope when she made social plans. All of a
sudden it seemed like the tables had turned. Penelope was
the one with the husband, great job, and cutesy little house
in the 'burbs.

Gina stared at the selection of beers covered with ice in
the bathtub and decided on some foreign-looking beer she
had never heard of. As she reached for her beer, she noticed
the quaintness of the room. Penelope had decorated the
bathroom in lavender and, of course, the rug, towels, and
shower curtain were all perfectly coordinated. She even had
matching accessories—the soap dish, toothbrush holder, and
even the trash can exquisitely complemented the lavender
decor.

God, even her bathroom says I'm a happy-assed bitch,
Gina thought to herself. As she popped the cap off with a
bottle opener, the toilet paper roller caught her eye. After she
stood in the bathroom for a few seconds contemplating such
a silly idea, she peeked out the door and saw that no one was
on the steps. Then she took a breath and frantically began
pulling toilet paper off the roll and throwing it in the toilet.
She looked again to make sure no one was coming and
shoved even more paper in the toilet, all the while laughing

hysterically. She peeked out the door one more time, calmed herself down a little, and flushed the toilet. She then nonchalantly walked down the steps with her beer and joined Linda and Peter in the kitchen. They were leaning against the counter, chatting with an older black woman dressed in some sort of traditional African attire.

Gina was amused with herself as well as worried. God, she really had lost her mind. First she's sleeping with guys like Griffin, then she's overflowing toilets at parties. A few minutes later she saw some fat girl whisper something to Penelope, who immediately got a disturbed look on her face and ran upstairs. Slowly, more and more of the party guests wanted to see what the ruckus was about.

"What's going on?" Gina asked some stranger on the steps as if she had no idea what had happened.

"I think someone made the toilet overflow."

"You're kidding? God, that sucks," Gina said with a perfectly straight face, and headed back to the kitchen. Eventually the commotion on the stairs ended, and Penelope appeared in the kitchen.

"The toilet overflowed?" Peter asked Penelope.

"Yeah. Some fuckhead must have had an ass the size of Milwaukee. He threw a slew of paper in the can."

"That's awful, Penelope. You never know what drunk people will do," Gina said, relieved that Penelope had spoken of the culprit as a *he*. "I had a party a few years ago, and someone stole my shoes. Another time someone left a trail of chicken wings from my apartment to the elevator. You never know what will happen when you throw a party. People just have no respect."

Responses

Cheryl shook out her umbrella before she walked into her apartment. It had been a long day, and the rain wasn't helping matters. She hated the rain. The moment it so much as drizzled, people in D.C. somehow lost their ability to drive. Like Gina, she commuted from the city to her job in a neighboring suburb in Virginia. Driving *into* the city during evening rush hour certainly wasn't as bad as driving *out* of it, but it was still heavy. More and more corporations were moving their headquarters to the suburbs of Virginia and Maryland, so, during rush hour, people were snarling traffic in every direction. To avoid the whole mess, Cheryl stopped at the Starbucks in Seven Corners, had a few cups of over-priced coffee, and read the paper before heading home.

She closed the door behind her, flicked on the floor lamp in the living room, and walked into the bedroom. She unbuttoned her suit jacket and laid it on the bed. She was probably one of the last people on earth whose company made her wear business suits to work. Every day, when she went to lunch and saw everyone else in casual slacks and knit tops, she contemplated finding a new job simply so she wouldn't have to wear a suit every day. She had been with the same managed health care company for five years and recently got a nice promotion. She was now in charge of overseeing the implementation of new client accounts. It was her responsibility to make sure the appropriate phone lines were set up, brochures went out on time, staff were hired and trained to field calls from new members, etc.

The only advantage of a formal dress code at work was that changing into more comfortable clothes when she got home helped her let go of her work stress and feel more relaxed at home. She slipped off the rest of her suit, got rid of the heels and hose, and put on a T-shirt and shorts.

Much better, she thought as she pulled out the chair at her desk. She sat down and reached over to turn on the computer.

"God, this takes forever," she mumbled to herself as her computer logged on to the Internet. She'd bought the PC from her company a couple of years earlier, when they upgraded to new machines. In the fast-changing computer industry, her unit was probably considered an antique. It was slow and crashed now and then, but, for the most part, it met her needs.

Cheryl logged in to her e-mail account. She was hoping she might have several responses to her ad, but after she sorted through all the junk mail, it looked like she had gotten only three.

"How nice," she said sarcastically after she opened the first e-mail—a picture of a small erect penis. Under the picture was written "If you like what you see, let me know."

"Delete!" Cheryl said to herself as she clicked on the message and dragged it to the little trash can on the screen.

"Hmm . . ." Cheryl mumbled as she read the second response. At least it sounded normal. Cheryl actually liked the response, until she realized it was canned. It wasn't personalized to her at all.

This guy is probably mass-mailing this response all over the Internet, she thought as she finished reading the ad and clicked on the picture he had attached.

"Oh, my!" she said as the picture opened to reveal an extremely odd-looking elderly man. Cheryl also dragged this e-mail into the trash and clicked on the last one.

Hi! My name is Louis. I'm 30 years old and live in Falls Church, Virginia. I'm a restaurateur and enjoy my work, so we have a love for cooking in common. Like you, I'm mostly looking for new friends and then we can take it from there. I'm 5'10", 165, brn/brn, fit/lean, Caucasian, and nonsmoking. I love movies, eating out, hiking, the beach, and quiet evenings at home. Would love to hear from you.

Cheryl wasn't overly enthused by the response, but at least he seemed sane, and his stats were decent.

Well, beggars can't exactly be choosers, she thought to herself as she clicked on the reply icon. She sent him a quick note telling him a little more about herself. She then asked him to provide more detail about himself and possibly a picture if a digital one was available.

"Keep your fingers crossed that he isn't a freak," Cheryl mumbled to herself as she clicked on the mouse to send her e-mail.

Commiserating

Gina and Linda said good night to Peter as they entered Gina's apartment. Gina was somewhat depressed after seeing Penelope's little *Ozzie and Harriet* existence, so she invited Linda and Peter to come in for a nightcap. Peter declined, saying that he thought he might be catching a cold or something and wanted to get some rest. Once she and Linda got inside, Gina put an old Eagles CD on the stereo while Linda searched for a corkscrew in the kitchen. Gina felt terrible about the whole toilet incident at Penelope's. Why would she do that to a friend? She wasn't sure what came over her. Somehow she was just overcome with misery and jealousy and lost her head.

"Look in the first drawer next to the fridge," Gina called to Linda before plopping down on the sofa. Gomez jumped up next to her and starting digging into the sofa upholstery, as he was prone to do from time to time. Over the years, Gina had reprimanded him numerous times, but to no avail, and finally gave up.

"That's it, Gomez. Tear up the sofa, good boy," she muttered toward the dog with an utter lack of enthusiasm.

"You never keep stuff in the same place," Linda said, returning to the living room with an opened bottle of pink wine, two glasses, and a bag of Chips Ahoy.

"I know. I'm terrible. I just dump the silverware basket

from the dishwasher into whatever drawer has the most room. I organized the drawers once. I even bought one of those plastic tubs to separate the knives from the forks and stuff. That lasted about a week."

"I bet Penelope has everything perfectly organized in her kitchen. All those country geese made me want to puke," Linda snapped, sipping her wine and opening the bag of cookies.

"Bitch. I hate her. . . . Don't you ever tell anyone I said that," Gina said to Linda, feeling a bit guilty for talking about one of their friends like that. "I don't hate her. It's just not fair. She has everything I want," she added before turning her attention to Gomez, who had since hopped off the sofa and was on his hind legs, begging for cookies. "No, Gomez, you're not allowed to have cookies."

"God, we're pathetic, Gina. Sitting here at midnight on a Wednesday, drinking wine and trashing one of our friends."

"I know. I'm just so tired of everyone's life taking off but mine. Virtually everyone I went to high school or college with is married, and some already have kids. I hate all of them. Bitches," Gina hissed, raising her voice a little. She looked at the dog again, who was now slightly whimpering. "No! Gomez, cookies aren't good for little doggies."

"You! Well, at least there's hope for you. Even if I find Ms. Right, I'm legally barred from getting married. How do you think it makes me feel to see all of our friends settle down and start families? That's why I just couldn't bear going to Penelope's wedding."

"What? You weren't really sick? Why didn't you tell me?" Gina asked, sounding surprised.

"I was embarrassed . . . am embarrassed. I don't want to be known as some angry dyke who can't be happy for her friends," Linda said, staring at the floor.

"Well, I'm certainly no better. She asked me to be a frickin bridesmaid, and I snubbed her. I'm sure she knew I was lying about not being sure I could make it. I don't think she was mad though. I think she felt sorry for me. I hate that more than anything. Penelope Weils feeling sorry for me . . . Bitch," Gina said as she handed a cookie to the dog.

"Yeah, that's the worst."

"Well, I guess we're both pathetic, but it's not like we tried to hurt her or anything," Gina responded, dropping a few more cookies on the floor for Gomez to gobble up.

Linda sat quietly for a minute before responding. "Actually, I think I did mean to hurt her, a little anyway. I know I was never as close to her as you were, but it must be bothersome to get married with one of your good friends absent. Part of me wanted to upset her on her wedding day. I wanted to make her feel some of the pain I feel on a daily basis. Here she was, proclaiming her relationship with Donny in front of a few hundred people, and I can't even hold hands with a date in public without running the risk of being jeered or even physically attacked. It makes me so mad sometimes. Maybe I did want her to hurt. Everything else in her life was coming together so perfectly. She deserved to feel a little pain." Linda was starting to well up at this point and stopped talking to avoid a total breakdown. She didn't usually discuss things like this with Gina. How could she possibly understand?

Gina was seeing a part of Linda that only very rarely surfaced. Gina saw Linda's eyes beginning to water just a little and wasn't sure what to do. Linda always seemed so together. She was never in a bad mood and was always rather even-keeled and organized. She was Gina's "sensible lesbian friend." This was one of the few times since they met in high school that Gina had ever seen her like this. Linda rarely let down her guard in front of anyone. Linda was usually Gina's rock. Gina was the one whose life was always a mess. Even in high school Gina usually had her feathers ruffled over something, and Linda would be there to cheer her up and tell Gina how ridiculous she was being about not having a date to the latest dance or not getting invited to weekend parties. Linda never seemed to worry about having a date for the homecoming dance or not getting asked to the prom. It wasn't until after high school that Gina learned why.

Gina couldn't honestly say she was shocked by the news of Linda's homosexuality. She had suspected it for some time but figured Linda would tell her when she was ready. One night, about a year after they graduated high school, they had been drinking and were sitting on the floor in Gina's dorm room at American. At some point during the night, Gina, frustrated with her love life, joked that she may as well become a lesbian, and how much easier it would be if she were a lesbian. When Linda immediately fired off upward of ten reasons why it most certainly would not be easier, Gina started to get a clue. She remembered Linda telling her that if common estimates were right, lesbians were lucky to have five percent of the population from which to choose a life partner. She went on to explain that if only ten percent of the population was gay, and half of that population was men, that left lesbians with a meager five percent of the world to pick a mate. Linda assured Gina that she had much better odds with the forty-five percent of the general public that consisted of straight men.

Now, sitting next to Linda while the rain continued to pour outside, Gina didn't quite know what to say. She looked at Linda, who was about to cry while "Hotel California" played in the background.

She considered telling Linda that she was the one who purposely made the toilet overflow at Penelope's party. She thought it might make Linda feel better if Gina reminded her that she did pathetic things as well. Gina decided against it though. Bailing on a friend's wedding because you're gay was about a "4" on the pathetic scale, while stuffing toilet paper down the can at a party was a solid "10." No, Gina was keeping that little tidbit of information to herself.

"God, Linda. I didn't know you had it in you. So there is an evil bone or two in that body of yours. Thank God," Gina said with a little giggle, trying to break the tension.

Linda managed a slight laugh as she wiped her eyes.

"God, Gina, we need to get it together, girl, or Penelope isn't going to be the only one feeling sorry for us."

Change of Heart

Cheryl was at home, sitting at her desk and trying to balance her checkbook online. She was growing weary of all the numbers and decided she would give Peter a quick call. She hadn't talked to him since the night Gina barged in on them a couple of weeks earlier. Cheryl hadn't gotten any sex since that night and, with any luck, Peter might be equally horny and invite her over. She looked at the time displayed on her monitor. It was just after midnight. She knew it was a little late to be calling him, especially for a weeknight, but she figured she'd give it a shot anyway.

"Hello," Peter said after grabbing the phone with one hand and turning off the stove with the other. He had just been leaning over a pot of boiling water in the kitchen, trying to clear his sinuses.

"Hey. It's me," Cheryl said on the other end of the phone.

"Hi. What's up?"

"Nothing much. Just getting a little paperwork done. I thought I'd take a break and see how you're doing."

"Good. Well, actually, I think I'm getting a sinus infection, but otherwise I'm okay. I just got back from a party with Gina and Linda."

"Really? Whose party?" Cheryl asked.

"Penelope something or other. She's some girl Gina went to college with."

"Oh, yeah. Penelope. I remember her. Probably another person Gina has turned against me. I heard she got married a few weeks ago."

"Yeah, she and her husband have a nice house out in Maryland," Peter said.

Cheryl knew he was stalling for time to make up his mind about whether or not he should invite her over. She figured Peter wasn't sure if he was up for a visit from her or not. It was late, and he didn't sound as though he was feeling altogether well, although Peter generally didn't sound as though he was feeling altogether well.

"Just the three of you went?" Cheryl asked, trying to make conversation while she waited to see if he would ask her to come over. She didn't dare ask him. There was nothing worse than propositioning a man and having him turn you down.

Even if Cheryl called him for a date or an outing of some sort, she'd sometimes say she had plans with some friends (even though she had no such plans) and ask Peter if he wanted to come along. That way, if he said no, she didn't look like a total loser—she still had her friends to go out with, as far as Peter knew anyway. And if he agreed to join her and her friends, Cheryl told him that whatever friends she had mentioned had canceled on them.

"Yeah. We didn't stay that long. The toilet overflowed in one of the bathrooms, and it was all downhill from there."

"You're kidding?"

"Nope."

"God. Well, at least your evening sounds remotely interesting. Mine has been a total bore, but I don't quite feel like going to bed," Cheryl said, opening the door for him to ask her over.

"Really," Peter replied as a new e-mail notice appeared on Cheryl's screen. While Peter told her a little more about the party, Cheryl clicked on the newly arrived e-mail from Louis. After Cheryl read about how glad he was that she responded to his message, and that he would love to meet up with her sometime, she clicked on the photograph that he had attached.

"Wow!" Cheryl whispered to herself, forgetting about Peter on the other end of the phone.

"What?" Peter asked.

"Oh, nothing. I just found an error in my checking account," Cheryl lied as she inspected the photo of Louis. He had wavy brown hair and big brown eyes. He was wearing a tank top in the picture, which only highlighted his defined arms and cut chest.

"Well, when you're done with your checkbook, do you want to come over for a quick drink or something?"

"Ah . . ." Cheryl said, eyeing the picture. "You know what, Peter. I actually got tired all of a sudden. I'd better pass tonight."

"No problem," Peter said, more confused by her response than upset by the rejection.

"Why don't we talk later in the week."

"Sure," Peter said.

After they hung up, Cheryl read Louis's e-mail again and enjoyed the picture for a minute more. She was about to respond but figured she might seem too eager if she replied immediately. She decided she would wait until the next day to tell him she would absolutely like to meet up with him.

Reprimanded

"**G**ood morning, Linda. How are you?" Gina said as she walked into the bank at nine o'clock. She was hung over from Penelope's party, not to mention the bottle of wine she and Linda polished off afterward. She hated when people had parties on a weeknight. She didn't have the willpower to say no even though she knew it would make her worthless the next day.

"Okay, but you don't look too happy."

"I'm a little hung over, and there was some freak of nature jogging along the side of the road on my way here."

"Really?"

"It was some old man, and he had his shirt off. His breasts, which were bigger than mine, were flinging all over the place. I don't understand it, Linda. Why do most of us women manage to go our entire lives without taking our shirts off in public . . . except for Shirley, that is. But for some unknown reason, a sixty-year-old man with a beer belly the size of Mexico finds it necessary to jog along a major freeway half naked. He's liable to cause an accident."

"I guess he was hot."

"So what? That doesn't give him the right to gross people out," Gina continued, certainly not mentioning to Linda that the real reason the man had such an effect on her was because he reminded her of Griffin and that awful night with him. "If you're height-weight proportionate and go to the gym five days a week, fine, be naked for all I care. If not, keep your fucking clothes on," Gina responded before changing the subject. "Hey, I've been meaning to ask you, didn't your sister graduate from George Washington University?"

"Yeah, why?"

"Does she have an alumni directory?"

"I'm not sure. She didn't like it there very much."

"Can you ask her if I can borrow it if she has one? If she doesn't, would you do me a favor, and ask her to order one for me? I tried to get one myself, but they wouldn't send it to me. They'll only send it to former students like your sister. I guess they're afraid I'm going to try to hock Avon to all the graduates or something. I'll pay her for it."

"What do you want it for?"

"I just want to look up an old friend," Gina replied with a grin. "Here's the number to call and order a copy."

"Okay," Linda shrugged. "I'll do it after lunch."

"Thanks. Hey, do you think she would go downtown and pick it up? Or maybe she can have it FedExed?"

"I'll ask her. Are you going to tell me what it's for?" Linda asked.

"If things work out, I will definitely give you the scoop."

"Whatever, Gina."

Gina sat down at her desk and was starting to organize the files she left out from the day before, when she saw Jim Toosh walk into the bank. He was the regional manager and was responsible for Gina's branch as well as for four or five other offices in the area. He rarely came out to the branches, and when he did, it usually meant there was some sort of problem. Gina got completely out of sorts every time he showed up at the bank. She figured he was probably around forty. He was tall and thin and really didn't seem to have much of a sense of humor. She always wondered whether he owned anything other than a closet full of navy blue suits and black wingtips.

When they first met, Gina was amused by his last name, Toosh. From that day on it always reminded her of the word "douche." During Gina's first few months with the bank she and Linda decided to have a little fun at Mr. Toosh's expense. It was very late on a Friday or Saturday night. They had just returned from an evening of drinking and were polishing off a few more beers at Gina's apartment. At some point during their drunken conversation, Mr. Toosh's name came up, and they laughed about his long, bony arms and the awful way he slicked his hair back. Eventually, Gina got the idea to look him up in the local phone book and give him a ring. By this time it must have been three A.M.

"Hello," Mr. Toosh said, sounding as if Gina had woken him up.

"Hi. Is this Mr. Douche?" Gina asked, trying to disguise her voice even though he probably wouldn't have recognized it anyway.

"It's Toosh. Who is this?"

"Yes, what kind of douches do you sell, Mr. Douche? I would like to order a mountain-fresh-scented one. Oops, you'd better make it two. I'm having that not so fresh feeling," Gina replied, trying to hold back the laughter. As she waited for his response, she heard a click on the other end of the phone. It was Mr. Toosh hanging up. Gina put the phone back on the receiver, and she and Linda howled with drunken laughter. Seconds later Gina's phone rang.

"Hello," Gina said.

"Gina, this is Jim Toosh. You're quite the comedian, but would you please conduct your antics before midnight. I need my sleep," Mr. Toosh said as if he were talking to a five-year-old child.

Gina was so mortified, she couldn't speak. She just hung up the phone. In a split second it seemed as though her buzz was gone. Her heart was pounding, and she felt a wave of nausea. Linda figured out the circumstances just by looking at Gina.

"Oh, my God. He must have some kind of caller ID or

something. Shit! Shit! Shit!" Gina shouted at Linda in a panic.

Gina spent the rest of the night in a state of worry and disarray. Was she fired? Should she bother coming into work on Monday? What would she say to Mr. Toosh the next time she saw him if she wasn't fired?

As it turned out, Gina did go to work, and a few weeks later when she saw Mr. Toosh neither one mentioned the incident, but, since then, Gina was never quite herself in the company of Mr. Toosh.

Mr. Toosh, Gina, and Linda assembled around the small table in the back office. Liz Cox, the branch manager and Gina's boss, was also there. Mr. Toosh was his usual staid self. "How are you ladies doing?"

"Fine," they replied in unison.

"I wanted to get together to go over exactly what happened the day of the attempted robbery. I have to say that we have some concerns about your disappearance following the incident," Mr. Toosh said, looking at Gina.

She had wondered why no one had approached her regarding the incident, but it had been a few weeks, so she figured she was safe. After her margarita at Rio Grande she went home and called Linda. She told her to tell everyone that she needed the rest of the day off. Linda explained to Gina what happened after the robbery and how perturbed the cops were that she left without telling anyone. She also mentioned that Liz had finally arrived and was asking about Gina. After she got off the phone, Linda explained to everyone that Gina was traumatized from the incident and needed to go home. The police were supposed to call Gina later that day for a statement, but they never did.

Linda immediately came to Gina's defense. "I told both of you already that Gina needed to get out of here. She had just had some deranged lunatic shove a knife in her face." Linda spoke in a tone that only she could afford. She was probably one of the bank's best employees, not to mention one of the most underpaid.

"What exactly did you want to know, Mr. Toosh?" Gina said, interrupting Linda.

"Liz and I have been discussing your progress, and we both feel that your leaving the bank without any notice isn't something we can just let go."

Gina's blood pressure was beginning to rise. She could feel her pulse and was starting to get hot. She was especially embarrassed to have them speak to her in this fashion in front of Linda. She wasn't sure why it was necessary to include her.

"Mr. Toosh, she didn't leave without any notice. She told me she was leaving, and I said I'd handle things. Which I did, so I'm not sure I understand the problem," Linda said, looking at both Mr. Toosh and Liz.

"Linda, when I asked where Gina was the day of the robbery, you said you didn't know," Liz shot back at Linda.

"Well, I'm not sure what I said, but I do remember her telling me she was leaving," Linda lied.

"All right, Linda, it looks like it might be getting a little busy out there," Liz said, gesturing toward a customer waiting in the lobby. "You had better get back to work."

Linda walked out of the room, making it obvious that she wasn't happy about being dismissed.

"Despite what Linda said, Liz and I have some serious concerns about your progress with the bank. There are several areas where you need to improve if you want to excel with Premier. We like you, Gina, and want you to continue on with us, but for this to happen you are going to have to make a serious effort toward improving your performance."

"Well, what exactly are we talking about here?" Gina asked, feeling about two inches tall and wondering how a conversation about an attempted robbery had all of a sudden turned into her performance evaluation.

"We would like you to develop a plan—a written plan about how you are going to improve in the areas of organization, timeliness, sales, and overall progress toward a branch manager position," Liz said, looking at Gina. "You need to write down tangible goals and develop a time line for meeting these goals. Fact is, you can't make a career of being an assistant manager. It's supposed to be a springboard to bigger things, and you've been in this position too long."

"Can you tell me a little more about what you're looking for?" Gina said, trying to sound as if she gave a shit about their stupid plan.

Liz was about to elaborate, when Mr. Toosh interjected condescendingly, "I'm not sure how much clearer we can be, Gina. I think we're done here. We'll expect to see something on Monday. Have a good day, ladies," Mr. Toosh said as he got up from the table and left the room.

Gina sat there for a minute with Liz just staring blankly at her. Gina wanted to call her a bitch, get up from the table, pack up her desk, and leave. She knew she was being set up to be fired anyway. She got up from the table trying to make it look like she was about to cry, hoping this would make Liz feel sorry for her.

She left Liz's office and sat down at her desk. Luckily, Linda was helping a customer, so she wasn't attacking Gina for details just yet. She had no idea how she was going to come up with this ridiculous plan and wasn't sure if she would even bother. She was upset over the reprimand, but deep down she knew everything they said was true. She didn't like her job and barely made any effort beyond showing up and going through the motions. In fact, she really didn't want to excel at the bank. The idea was absurd. She had no desire to be anything like Liz or Mr. Toosh. They lived for the bank. It was their lives. To her, excelling at the bank might be more pathetic than failing.

In the midst of all this, Shirley showed up and wanted Gina to help her find some money she couldn't account for in her checking account. She stood over Gina's desk in a pair of cut-off jeans and a super-tight white T-shirt.

"Hi, sweetie. Can you give me a hand with this account? I'm off again."

Recognizing the voice, Gina responded without lifting her head. "Off again, huh? What is it this time?"

"I can't find thirty dollars."

"I'm sure it's just an ATM transaction you forgot to write down."

"Well, can we check in the computer? Then maybe I can take you to lunch?"

"Lunch? It's not even ten o'clock."

"A late breakfast, then."

"Not today, Shirley. It's just not a good time."

"You never have time for me, sweetie. Come on, I've got a coupon for the Olive Garden."

"I said no, Shirley," Gina replied in the same tone she often took with Shirley, as if she were speaking to a persistent teenager.

"How about you, Linda? Wanna go to lunch? My treat," Shirley asked, looking in Linda's direction.

Linda was about to say "sure," until she caught a glimpse of Gina's glare.

"I'm sorry, Shirley, but today just isn't good for me either."

"Well, maybe I can find some bum on the street and take him to lunch," Shirley snapped, starting to walk out the door.

"Won't be the first time," Gina said under her breath. "Just don't fuck him."

Gina watched Shirley sashay from the bank, wondering if there was any one woman on earth with a more chaotic life or screwed-up priorities than Shirley. Did anyone have the kind of relationship with their own mother that Gina did with Shirley? She loved Shirley dearly and looked out for her more than Shirley did for herself, but sometimes it seemed like such a waste of time and effort. Gina always felt like she was more of a mother to Shirley than Shirley ever was to her, and Gina acted the same way good parents always did—no matter how futile it seemed, she never gave up on Shirley. Gina knew—she just knew—that one day Shirley would make something of herself. Shirley had so much going for her. She was smart and attractive and so at ease with people. There were many times when Gina wanted to give up on Shirley—she wanted to ignore the phone when Shirley was calling to ask Gina to bail her out of whatever mess she had gotten herself into, she wanted to refuse to give Shirley money to make her car payments so that it wouldn't be repossessed, she wanted to stop hounding Shirley about her smoking, the list went on and on. . . . But Gina continued to help Shirley out, reprimand her, and offer advice even though she knew Shirley would usually just ignore it.

Sometimes Gina admired and was even jealous of Shirley's carefree attitude, but most of the time Gina feared, more than anything, ending up like her mother—middle-aged, alone, and trying desperately to look youthful.

The Stakeout

Damn, if only I had asked for his number, Gina thought to herself as she fumbled with the alumni directory from George Washington University she had asked Linda about the day before. Linda's sister actually did have a copy, so Linda brought it into work for Gina, still not knowing what the hell she wanted it for. Gina flipped to the section listing 1996 graduates. She remembered that David, the guy she met at Rio Grande, said he graduated about five years ago with a degree in finance. How many Davids could have graduated with that degree in '96? Of course, it could have been '95 or maybe '97. He did say he graduated *about* five years ago. She would have to check all three. Luckily, the directory was categorized according to majors. There were two Davids under the finance section for 1993, none in '94, and four in '95. Of all the Davids, only two still resided in the D.C. area, David Manion and David Capricio. She figured Capricio sounded Italian, and *her* David definitely looked Italian or maybe Latino or Middle Eastern.

Gina was about to mark and highlight the two names in the book, when she remembered that it was only on loan from Linda's sister. She copied down the names and their corresponding addresses and wondered if she might have time to check out at least one of the addresses during lunch;

however, she knew that she had better use her lunch break to start developing that plan Mr. Toosh and Liz were making her come up with. She only had a few days until it was due.

When lunchtime finally arrived, Gina tried to get started on her improvement plan. So far all she had was the title typed on her monitor. In exasperation she continued typing:

Career Improvement Plan

My plan to improve and excel with Premier Bank includes shoving a big ole board up my ass, so I can be just like Mr. Toosh. . . .

She began backspacing away her little joke before someone had the chance to see it. She decided she didn't have the mental capacity at that moment to develop the plan and figured she'd save it for the weekend. The pressure would be on by then, and she worked better under pressure.

"Linda, can you cover for me if I'm a little late getting back from lunch?"

"Why? What's up?"

"I have an errand I need to run."

"What's with the mystery lately, Gina?"

"Thanks, Linda. I'll be back as soon as I can," Gina said, ignoring Linda's question while she grabbed her purse and headed out the door.

She got into her car and looked at the addresses again. The Italian David lived close by in Arlington. The other David was out in Reston, about a half-hour drive from where Gina worked. She pulled out her local map and found David Capricio's residence. She could be there in about ten minutes. The route she chose took her in the back way to a new neighborhood of grand town homes. Land was so scarce in the inner suburbs of D.C. that you rarely saw detached houses being built. Instead, spacious brick town homes with luxurious amenities were sprouting up all over the place.

When she found David's house, she just casually drove by and saw a couple of BMWs parked in the driveway. She continued down the road for about a block and then turned around and stopped the car, taking it all in. She knew he must have some serious cash if he was living in such an up-scale neighborhood, and if the cars in the driveway belonged to him. She fought the urge to get out of the car and sneak around the house to peer in the windows. She would have to bring binoculars next time, and coming in the evening would definitely be a better idea. With the lights on inside the house, she would be able to see in, but he wouldn't be able to see out.

Gina looked at her watch and decided it was about time to return to the bank, when a trashy-looking woman with jet-black hair opened the door of the house. The woman walked down the front steps and got into one of the Beamers. Gina watched as she backed the car out of the driveway. She wasn't sure what to do. Gina wanted to follow her, but she needed to get back to work soon. She let the stranger drive off and then headed out of the neighborhood herself to get back to work. Gina wondered who the woman was. Maybe David was married. But he didn't have a wedding ring on the day she met him. He could just be living with someone. That woman, with her long, scraggly hair and black spandex, didn't look like his type. Maybe it wasn't even the right house. She'd have to check it out again and also stake out the house in Reston as soon as she had the chance.

When Gina walked back into the bank, Linda looked surprised to see her. "Wow. You're almost on time. Are you feeling okay?"

Gina smiled at her and pulled out her chair to sit down. Her "career improvement plan" was still up on the computer screen. She sighed and closed the document without saving it. All she had was the title anyway.

"I was looking through my mail a few minutes ago and guess what arrived?" asked Linda.

"I haven't the slightest idea."

"Just a little reminder about our class reunion next month."

"Shoot, I forgot all about it," Gina lied, not wanting to appear to be anticipating it too greatly. They sent out the reunion notice six months earlier, and Gina received the actual invitation a few weeks ago. She was more excited about it than she wanted Linda to know, and despite all the craziness lately, she had still been thinking about it quite a bit.

The Gina who was going to walk into the reception hall at the Omni Shoreham hotel for her ten-year reunion was a completely different Gina than the one who graduated from Tenley High School ten years ago. This Gina had it together. Well, as far as any of her old classmates would know, she had it together. There was no reason they had to know she was on the verge of getting fired, was fornicating with old fat guys, and spent her lunch breaks stalking strangers.

Since high school Gina had filled out nicely from the lanky teenager she used to be. Her hair was much longer, and the highlights Dennis added made it a more distinct luxurious shade of blond, and she was much better at applying makeup (thanks to Dennis as well). She hoped her nose job was subtle enough that no one would notice. Gina was glad she decided against the boob job. She didn't have much "up top," but people would definitely notice if she'd gone up a few cup sizes, and she didn't want any snickering behind her back. Besides, that would have only added to the outrageous Visa bill she was already paying every month. Thank God her grandmother barely charged her any rent for her apartment. Otherwise, between her own expenses and helping Shirley out from time to time, she wouldn't have any money at all.

Sitting down in her chair, Gina figured all she had to do was buy a killer dress to wear to the reunion and convince Peter to go as her date.

"Do you want to go shopping this weekend?" Gina asked Linda.

"Sure. What for?"

"What do you mean, what for? To find something to knock 'em dead with at the reunion. Something to make muffs like Annie Harrison envy us to hell," Gina replied as the name "Annie Harrison" registered in her mind. What was she going to do about Annie? She hadn't thought about the reunion when she scrambled out of Annie's apartment while she was in the shower. What would she say to her? Maybe Annie wouldn't be there. After all, she was looking pretty haggard. Gina decided to put it out of her mind. She did a stupid thing, and there wasn't much she could do about it. If Annie was there, she would just briefly acknowledge her and pretend nothing ever happened. Annie would only embarrass herself if she brought up the incident anyway, so a confrontation wasn't likely.

Malling

G ina and Linda were waiting on the platform for the sub-way train to come. They decided to take the Metro out to the Fashion Centre at Pentagon City, a semi-upscale mall in Virginia, not even a mile outside the District. The subway stopped right underneath it. Aside from the trendy shops in Georgetown, there really weren't too many places to do any major shopping in D.C.—at least not anymore. It was very upsetting to Gina and her grandmother when they closed Garfinkel's department store years ago. They had done most of their shopping there for years. A few years later the down-town Woodward and Lothrop flagship store was closed as well. Gina actually shed a tear or two when she read an arti-cle in *The Washington Post* about how employees with the most seniority each received a crystal from the chandelier that used to hang over the main level of the store. She hated that about D.C. She remembered visiting the major shopping districts of New York and San Francisco. It was kind of em-barrassing—in the nation's capital there was only one major department store left, and even many District residents didn't want to be bothered with it. It just made more sense to commute to the 'burbs, where parking was plentiful and there was a greater selection of stores.

"I'm not sure what kind of dress to get. I want it to be a

knockout, but I don't want any of those losers to think I went to too much trouble to look good for them."

"Gina, you look fine in a T-shirt and a pair of jeans. What are you so worried about?"

"I'm not worried about anything. I just want to look good. I want to look like a success. I hope all the muffs gained weight and look frumpy and fat. I'm going to make a point of standing next to the fattest one."

"Where did all this vengeance come from?" Linda said, laughing.

"I honestly don't know. I just want to feel superior to them. I spent my whole high school career feeling inferior and wanting to be like them. I guess I want to turn the tables a little," Gina said as she and Linda boarded the Metro.

Gina didn't care for riding the Metro. Every time she got on the subway she had flashbacks of riding to work with her mother during one of the phases when Shirley actually had some tinge of maternal instinct and wasn't punting Gina off to her grandmother. When she was just a child, Shirley would drag her to work because she couldn't (or wouldn't) pay a baby-sitter. They had to take the subway from Cleveland Park to the business district where Shirley worked at a convenience store. Gina would sit in the back of the shop and do her homework or watch television while her mother barely grunted at customers as she took their money and ineptly bagged their groceries.

When Gina and her mother would board the subway, there were never any seats left, and they would both have to stand all the way to their stop. One day they saw a pregnant woman get on the train with them, and a young man got up and offered his seat to her. Next thing Gina knew, every afternoon before they left for work, her mother was stuffing a throw pillow under her shirt before they left the apartment. Gina wasn't sure exactly how old she was at the time. But she was definitely old enough to be mortified by her mother's actions. Funny thing was that it worked only every once in a while. Much of the time no one offered their seat to the "pregnant" Shirley. Again Gina was old enough to know why. People were more apt to offer their seat to respectable-looking women who probably planned their pregnancy. They weren't as eager to help a saucy-looking twenty-something who probably got knocked up by some guy she hardly knew. That was just the look her mother had about her. Actually, it was kind of her whole persona. She radiated brash sexuality even though she came from an upper-middle-class family who lived in one of the most prestigious neighborhoods in the District. Luckily, Gina had to make this trek for only a few months before Shirley once again decided being a mother was more than she could handle and sent Gina back to live with her grandmother. This was shortly before Shirley quit her job at the convenience store and started her three-week stint as an Avon lady. Unfortunately, people were about as eager to buy cosmetics from her as they were to offer her a seat on the subway.

Gina and Linda got off the Metro and took the escalators up to the mall.

"Why don't we hit Nordstrom first?"

On their way, Linda spotted Peter in Brentano's. He was standing in front of one of the shelves and flipping through a large book.

"Look, there's Peter," she said, pointing toward the book-store.

"What's he doing here already? We're not supposed to meet him for a couple of hours."

"Well, let's go in and say hi."

They strolled into the store and snuck up behind Peter. Gina approached him first and gave his behind a little squeeze. Peter wasn't startled at all. He smiled and turned around. "What are you doing?" he said, suddenly looking surprised—as if he were expecting someone other than Gina to be standing there. "Gina, what are you doing here?"

"Scouring for nuts and berries," Gina replied sarcastically. "Shopping, you moron. What do you think we're doing?"

Peter seemed a little nervous as he put *Symptoms and*

Illness back on the shelf. His tongue wasn't feeling exactly right lately. It seemed rougher, or drier, or something to him lately, so he was trying to find some information about it in the medical section, when Gina and Linda arrived.

"What are you doing here so early? You hate shopping," Linda asked.

"I came with a friend. She wanted me to tag along to help her find a gift for her boss."

"You're still going to dinner with us, aren't you?" Gina inquired.

"Yep. I'll meet you at the restaurant at six."

"Okay, we'll see you later," Linda said, getting ready to continue on to Nordstrom.

"Wait a sec, Linda," Gina said before looking at Peter. "Who are you here with? Should we invite them to dinner?"

Before Peter had a chance to answer, Cheryl rounded the corner.

"I'd love to come to dinner," Cheryl said with a big smile. "How are you guys?" she asked Gina and Linda in an excited voice, as if they were good friends she hadn't seen in a long time.

"Pretty good," Linda replied while Gina just ignored her and rolled her eyes at Peter.

"We'll see *you* at six, Peter," Gina said to Peter as if Cheryl were invisible. She gestured to Linda, and they left the bookstore to continue their shopping.

Dalump

Cheryl was driving down Arlington Boulevard, headed toward Falls Church. She had just left the mall and was still upset about her run-in with Gina at the bookstore. Of course, she didn't dare let on that it bothered her. She didn't know how to react on the rare occasions that she crossed paths with Gina, so sometimes she put on a bright smile and talked to Gina as if they were still friends. She figured that being friendly would probably annoy Gina more than anything else. Cheryl didn't even let on to Peter that she was upset. She was afraid word would get back to Gina if she did. She just shrugged her shoulders as Gina and Linda left the store and tried to pretend that it didn't bother her.

God! Was what I did so horrible? I was drunk, for heaven's sake. It wasn't like I planned it. And it's been years. You would think Gina would have forgiven me by now, Cheryl thought to herself, truly sad that Gina was no longer a part of her life. Cheryl certainly had other friends to hang out with, and there was always Peter. But it was so rare that she met people on her own wavelength—someone with whom she could really connect the way she did with Gina. She had always assumed that the whole feud with Gina would eventually blow over, but it had been going on for so long, Cheryl was surprised either one of them even remembered what caused it.

Cheryl took in a deep breath and tried to erase the incident with Gina from her mind. She wanted to be relaxed when she met Louis. She drove into the Red Lobster in Falls Church with only a little apprehension. She knew she probably should have at least talked to him on the phone before agreeing to meet him, but he seemed so nice in their e-mail exchanges, and once she got his picture she was sold—the man was a looker. Besides, Cheryl figured that even if his personality was a dud, his hard body might be good for some no-nonsense sex. And, on top of that, it might be nice to flaunt a little eye candy in front of Peter.

When she got inside the restaurant, the fishy smell was a bit overwhelming. She found it odd that a restaurateur, as Louis had described himself, would want to meet in a chain restaurant famous only for its fried fish. She was about to sit down at one of the benches in the lobby, when she saw Louis approach from outside. She wasn't sure if the window was somehow distorting him, but something was odd about him—about the way he walked. It almost seemed as if one leg was significantly longer than the other. As she watched him walk through the threshold, *dalump . . . dalump . . . dalump*, she decided it was no big deal and she could just ignore it.

Yeah, she told herself. It's no big deal. So what if one leg is shorter than the other? He's still very cute. Maybe his "cuteness factor" has dropped five percent or so, but he really does look fine.

"Cheryl?" Louis asked, recognizing her from the picture she had e-mailed him.

"Yes. Hi. How are . . . ?" Cheryl tried to ask before Louis interrupted her.

"Good, good. Should we get a table? Why don't we get a table? I like booths. Hopefully, they will give us a booth. Booths are so much more cozy, don't you think? Better than those tables out in the open. I don't like being out in the open like that," Louis said very quickly and with purpose—like getting a booth at Red Lobster was his mission in life.

Cheryl followed him as they approached the hostess, *dalump . . . dalump . . . dalump*.

The hostess seated them and offered the menus, which Louis refused.

"I don't need a menu. I know exactly what I want. I'll have the Admiral's Feast with a baked potato with butter and sour cream, and a garden salad with ranch dressing, and a Coke . . . and lots of croutons on the salad please," Louis rattled off, his mouth going a mile a minute.

"I'm sorry, sir," the young woman replied. "I'm just the hostess. Your waiter will be right with you."

"Oh, okay," he replied as Cheryl offered a bit of a confused expression at his eagerness to place his order, when she hadn't even opened her menu. As Cheryl tried to give the menu a quick read, Louis lowered his voice.

"You know what?" he said with a grin.

"What?" Cheryl said, not sure she wanted to know.

"I knew that she was just the hostess, but sometimes I get them to take my order anyway and get my food really fast," Louis said like a mischievous child. "You know when you have to wait for a waitress it takes so much longer. And some waitresses are so slow. I hate when I get a slow waitress, especially if I need my drink refilled. Ya know?"

"You must really like the food here," Cheryl said, turned off by his loquacious manner and dropping his cuteness factor a few more percentage points.

"Oh, yeah, man. Have you had their cheddar bay biscuits? I just love their cheddar bay biscuits. And it's a great value. You get the biscuits for free, and a salad comes with your dinner for no extra charge, and they put salt on the skins of the baked potatoes. Yeah, this is my favorite restaurant . . . and free refills on the drinks too," Louis added as the waitress approached to take their order. Louis repeated his earlier order, and Cheryl asked for the Mainlander's Chicken Salad and a Diet Coke.

Okay, what kind of restaurateur held Red Lobster in such high esteem? Cheryl had to ask the question even though she feared the answer. He probably ran a Chuck E. Cheese or something.

"So, you said you're a restaurateur?"

"That's right. I like it okay, but getting up so early gets to be a drag, man."

"Early?"

"Yeah, you got to make the bagels early."

"Bagels?"

"Yeah. I make a mean cinnamon raisin. It's a pretty good job, and I get off at noon, in time for my second job."

Oh, it just keeps getting better. "Really? What do you do for your second job?"

"I . . . where are our biscuits? Excuse me, ma'am?" Louis asked a passing waitress who ignored him. "Miss?" he repeated. "Can you bring us some biscuits? And not just two or three, bring a whole mess of 'em, would ya?"

The waitress agreed, and Louis continued. "I'm sorry. I like to have a biscuit or two before the salad comes. Anyway, where was I? Oh, yeah, my other job. I'm a pharmacy technician."

A cashier at the CVS? "Really, that must be challenging." Cheryl replied for lack of anything else to say while Louis's cuteness factor continued to fall like the stock market on Black Monday. "Two jobs must keep you busy."

"Yeah, but I got them bills to pay. My parents keep telling me to get a job with benefits, but, you know, what do I really need health insurance for?"

In case you get sick, you moron. "I don't know," Cheryl said with a smile, resigning herself to just get through the date, hoping the food would arrive soon.

"I've actually been thinking about going to Japan and getting a job there."

"Oh? You speak Japanese?" Cheryl asked.

"Nah, but I hear Americans can go there and make lots of money."

"Really? Doing what?"

"I'm not sure. I haven't investigated it thoroughly yet. It's just something I heard. At least it would get my mother off my back. Last night me and Ma were watching *That 70's Show* . . . have you seen it? It's a riot . . . anyway, Ma keeps pestering me to look for another job, you know, just one job instead of two, but I like my jobs. Plus, I need jobs that are close to home, since my car got repossessed last year."

"Well, I'm sure your mother wants the best for you. Do you see her often?"

"Every day. I live in her basement. She doesn't even charge me any rent, and I have my own sofa and television and everything down there."

Cuteness factor just dropped off the chart. "Sounds like a great setup," Cheryl said, patronizing him.

"Yeah, it is. Sometimes it gets old 'cause Ma gets all caught up in my business and pesters me when I'm trying to play my computer games. But, for the most part, it works out okay for me and Juniper."

Oh, God! What the hell is a Juniper? "Juniper?"

"That's my cat. She's sixteen."

"Sixteen? That's old for a cat, isn't it?"

"Yeah, but she's in pretty good health. Although she had to have a kitty colonoscopy a few months ago. You know, she was having diarrhea all the time. It was gross. They took this camera and shoved it up her—"

"Oh, please! I don't want to hear the rest, we're about to eat," Cheryl said as politely as she possibly could.

"Yummy!" Louis said as the waitress slapped down a big plate of fried seafood in front of him.

The two of them ate their meals as Louis rambled on about his collection of Disney snow globes and the intricacies of bagel-making while Cheryl spent the bulk of her meal nodding and forcing herself to pretend she was remotely interested in anything he said. When the check arrived, Louis asked if she wanted to split it. Cheryl agreed, and the two of them got up from the table and headed toward the lobby, *dalump . . . dalump . . . dalump.*

Before they got to the door, Louis stopped. "So what do you think? Do you like me?" he asked Cheryl point-blank.

No. "Oh, I think you're lots of fun and very interesting," Cheryl lied before adding, "but, honestly, I'm not sensing any real chemistry."

Generally, Cheryl would just say yes and give the guy a wrong phone number or something, but she didn't want this guy thinking she was even remotely interested in him.

His faced dropped a bit. "That's okay. I wasn't sensing any either," he said, obviously disappointed.

"Well, maybe our paths will cross again," Cheryl said, praying that they never would. She extended her hand and Louis gave it a polite shake.

"Yeah, come by the CVS on Broad Street sometime. If you want, you can come to my register, and I'll forget to ring up some of your items. I do that for my friends," he said with the same grin he held when he shot his order at the hostess.

"Okay, maybe I'll do that," Cheryl lied again, and pushed the door open to head to her car.

Restaurateur! How did he even know how to spell restaurateur? Cheryl thought to herself as she put the key in the car door and watched Louis walk across the highway, *dalump . . . dalump . . . dalump.*

Cheryl got in the car and closed the door. The day was taking its toll. She had really had high hopes for Louis. He looked like such a cutie in his picture, and his e-mails were so nice. She even turned down Peter's invitation to come over the week before, thinking that maybe she would be able to get out of her dysfunctional relationship with him. She was already on edge from her encounter with Gina a couple of hours earlier, and the disastrous date with Louis was all she could take.

Thinking about the evening, she had such a strange feeling. One part of her wanted to laugh about her dinner with Louis, the first real-live moron she had ever met, and another part of her was so overwhelmed with sadness that she just wanted to cry. She looked in the rearview mirror at herself and let out a little smirk about how ridiculous the evening had been. Then she put her hand to her head and let the smirk fade into a steady stream of tears.

A Family That
Eats Together . . .

Shirley had gotten held up at work and was running late as usual. She was currently working as a waitress at the T.G.I. Friday's in D.C. She couldn't remember the name of the play, but some musical about a French guy who got caught stealing bread was playing at the Warner Theater nearby. The matinee let out just before she was due to get off, and a bunch of foo-foo suburbanites who were too cheap to pay for the evening show crowded into the restaurant. The manager asked Shirley to stick around and help with the crowd. She needed the tips, so she agreed to stay for a few hours, but she made sure the manager knew she was doing him a favor.

She had planned to take the subway to meet Gina and her friends for dinner but decided to drive since she was already late and had to swing by her apartment to pick up some Ziploc bags. She usually kept her eyes straight ahead when she was driving to avoid the nasty snarls she often got from people in passing cars. Her car emitted a foul-smelling white smoke when she accelerated, much to the disgust of the motorists behind her.

As she crossed the bridge into Virginia, she caught a

glimpse of a state cop in her rearview mirror. She decided to take the first available exit rather than risk getting stopped because of her expired tags—the ones she should have renewed six months earlier. She let the tags slide because she didn't have enough money set aside to pay for the new registration. Besides, if she did go to get the license plates renewed, she wasn't sure if the clerks at the Motor Vehicle Administration would want proof of insurance, which she hadn't set aside money for either. Next month she'd ask Gina or her mother to help her meet these expenses, but Gina had just helped her make this month's rent, and Gina's grandmother was already footing the bill for all of Shirley's medications—medications Shirley probably wouldn't even need if she would just quit smoking.

Shirley had very slight asthma as a child. It was so mild that it wasn't even diagnosed until she was an adult, and years of smoking had exacerbated it to a point where she would have frequent attacks. It had been so bad lately that Shirley had to keep switching medications to head off the attacks and keep her asthma at bay. Doctor after doctor told her she absolutely had to quit smoking. Sometimes Shirley would be honest and say she just couldn't. Other times, she'd just lie and say she had quit smoking or was going to right away. It was the way Shirley handled things—whatever way seemed easiest at the time, no matter what the long-term consequences were.

By the time Shirley got to the Kentucky Buffet and Salad Bar, Gina, Linda, and Peter were already seated and munching on some salads. Gina, as always, was trying not to watch Peter eat. She absolutely abhorred the way he ate. He insisted on eating only one item of food at a time. He had to finish all his mashed potatoes before he could eat his steak or scarf down an entire hamburger before he would even touch his french fries—and oh, God! The french fries! She couldn't stand the way he consumed french fries, the way he kept biting them continually as he propelled them into his mouth. It was like watching a tree go through a wood chipper. And the sound was worse, *CHOMP, CHOMP, CHOMP.* Gina had to listen to *CHOMP, CHOMP, CHOMP* for every single fry. Damn McDonald's and their stupid super sizes! If Peter hadn't been the one to break it off with Gina years ago, she may have had to dump him. How could she continue to date someone who drove her crazy at every meal?

Gina didn't particularly care for the Kentucky Buffet, one of those all-you-can-eat buffets filled with vats of lukewarm foods like mayonnaise salads, fish sticks, canned soup, and macaroni and cheese. It wasn't really the food that bothered her so much as the customers. Her stomach turned as grossly overweight people in polyester slacks and tight frocks slopped mounds of sloppy joe and fried fish on their plates—still chewing the food from their last round as they returned to the buffet to go at it again. It was like feeding time at the hog house. The only reason she agreed to come was that she felt a little guilty about snapping at her mother at the bank a few days earlier. Linda and Peter were happy to join in. They actually enjoyed Shirley's company. Truth was, Gina enjoyed her company too, when she could get over the fact that it was her own mother sitting with her friends, talking about the guy with the severely curved dick she went home with the night before, or the time she spent the better part of a Sunday sitting in a tub of vinegar because someone told her it would make her vagina tight again.

"Hi, gang," Shirley said with a smile before sliding into the booth next to Gina. "How are ya, sweetie? You seemed to be in a bit of a huff the last time I saw you."

"I'm okay. I had just had a rough day at work. They don't feel I'm performing up to speed, so now I have to come up with a written plan with goals for improving and things like that. It's due on Monday. Guess I'd better get started, huh?"

"Guess you'd better. If you lose your job, who's going to help me pay my bills?" Shirley said, only half joking. "So what's new in the world of young people? Young people with buff bodies, I might add," Shirley said, smiling and giving Peter a good once-over. Even on Shirley's worst days she was still sexy. A little cheap-looking, but always sexy. She even made Peter turn on the charm sometimes if she wasn't making him blush.

"Pretty good," Peter said. "Although my throat is a little scratchy today for some reason. Hope I'm not getting sick."

"We just did a little shopping," Gina added. "Our high school reunion is coming up, you know. Linda and I were trying to find something to wear."

"Did you find anything?"

"Just a cheap whore in the bookstore," Gina said, smirking at Peter.

"And who might that be?"

"Cheryl Sonntag, Gina's nemesis," Linda said, answering Shirley's question.

"I don't remember her."

"She's the girl I went to American University with. She was one of my roommates in college. She was around the house a lot the first summer after we graduated. I think you were living with Stan at the time, or maybe it was when you moved out for the umpteenth time to live with that guy whose mother was younger than you," Gina said, slightly slamming Shirley for her history of repeatedly moving in and out of the house she had occasionally shared with Gina and her mother, not to mention Shirley's taste for younger men.

"The black girl your grandmother didn't like you hanging around with?"

"Yes, Shirley, the black girl."

Gina's grandmother was a nice woman, but she did have one major flaw. She was a bit on the racist side. She didn't spend her evenings in white sheets burning crosses or anything, but she certainly didn't approve of Gina rooming with an African American. Gina's grandmother had old-fashioned ideas about how an upper-middle-class girl should behave, and it didn't include mixing with people of other races. But compared to Shirley's antics, Gina being friends with a minority seemed like small potatoes.

Growing up in such a strict household, Shirley learned to

abhor rules and discipline. As a child she felt like she wasn't allowed to have any fun. Her mother would tell her it wasn't proper to play in the dirt with the boys or run through the sprinkler on a hot summer day. She constantly pestered Shirley as a child to sit up straight, cross her legs, and conduct herself as a lady. She also forbade Shirley to wear pants outside the house, loaded her up with books on etiquette and proper presentation, and would not allow her to date until she was eighteen.

Looking back on her childhood, Shirley felt like she had been forced to stand on the sidelines, trying not to get dirty, while the other children played and were allowed to be kids. As she progressed into her teenage years and developed a mind of her own, she protested her mother's strict rules more and more, almost as often as she disregarded them—rolling her pants up under her skirt until she was on the school bus, passing on the etiquette books in favor of trashy novels and television, and sneaking around with boys long before her eighteenth birthday.

At first she violated her mother's rules only behind her back, but as Shirley got older, she became bolder and sometimes blatantly ignored her mother's wishes. If her mother wouldn't let her go to a school dance or get her hair permed, Shirley would do it anyway and be perfectly willing to face whatever punishment was doled out when her mother learned of her actions. It almost became a routine—Shirley would go to a party she wasn't supposed to or get home past her ridiculous ten o'clock curfew and then be grounded for a week. The following week she'd get caught with a cigarette or chatting on the phone after nine o'clock and be grounded for another week. The cycle continued for years until Shirley just plain wore her mother out. Gina didn't know if her grandmother's strict nature was really what made Shirley end up as such a wild woman though. Anyway, it couldn't have been totally to blame. Shirley's nature seemed so fully ingrained, it was probably just who she was.

Luckily for Gina, her grandmother mellowed with age

and had been thoroughly exhausted by Shirley. And, after witnessing Shirley's tremendous rebellion against her efforts, Gina's grandmother did her part in raising Gina with a more relaxed attitude—and, for the most part, she, not Shirley, raised Gina. Although her grandmother wasn't thrilled about Gina's friendship with Cheryl, she couldn't have been nicer to Cheryl when she came over to the house. She just occasionally raised her concerns to Gina and asked her not to spend so much time with that "nice colored girl."

It amused Gina that racism was usually handed down from one generation to the next, but not in her family. Her grandmother's feelings certainly didn't get passed on to Shirley, who Gina sometimes referred to as an equal opportunity slut. Shirley slept with guys of every race, color, and creed, although there was always the notion that she did it just to get under her mother's skin. Simply to amuse herself, Shirley would occasionally buy her mother ethnic gifts for her birthday and holidays. Last year she gave her a black animated Santa Claus figure. She was also sure to send her mother Hanukkah and Martin Luther King Day cards every year just to aggravate her.

"Oh, yes, Cheryl. I met her once or twice. Seemed nice enough to me," Shirley said.

"Yeah, well, she's *nice* all right," Gina added sarcastically.

"What? What did she do?"

"It's a long story. I can't believe you haven't heard it already."

"I've got all day, sweetie."

"Some other time, Shirley."

"Just tell her, Gina. What's the big deal?" Linda interjected.

"I think it can wait," Peter said, agreeing with Gina.

"Now you've really got me curious. Do share, Linda."

Realizing that Gina and Peter would be only slightly angry if she spilled the beans, Linda decided to go for it.

"Gee, I don't know where to begin. I guess it was the first Christmas after Gina and Cheryl graduated from American.

Gina, Cheryl, Peter, and I had just spent Christmas Day with Peter's parents out in the boonies, somewhere in Calvert County, Maryland. After dinner with Peter's parents we went to a local bar to have some drinks and shoot pool. Well, obviously, with it being Christmas Day, the bar was pretty empty. To liven things up, the bartenders started giving away free drinks and tequila shots. We certainly weren't going to give up free drinks."

"Certainly not," Shirley said as if it would be a tragedy to pass up free tequila.

"Needless to say, the four of us got schlossed. Oh, oh . . . I forgot one important detail. This was just a few weeks after Peter dumped Gina. Well, he did dump you, Gina," Linda said, looking at Gina, sort of apologizing for putting it so harshly.

"Whatever, Linda."

"Anyway, the four of us were three sheets to the wind by midnight. None of us were in any condition to drive, so I had the brilliant idea of catching a cab to Denny's. We were going to go there and have coffee and something to eat. After we sobered up we were going to grab a cab back to the car and drive back to Peter's house. So, anyway, we got into the cab. Peter sat up front, and us girls climbed into the back. I was sitting in between Gina and Cheryl, and not five minutes passed before I heard Gina make some quiet grunting noise like she was choking or something. Then I heard something splatter on her shirt like she had just spilled a drink. It was dark, and she was so quiet about it, I really wasn't sure what had happened. I was like 'Did you puke?' and she nodded her head. Then our lovely cabdriver asked if she threw up. He sounded rather annoyed. I told him that she did, but she mostly got it on herself and not on the cab. . . ."

Peter cut her off. "You would have been really proud, Shirley. She puked in a very ladylike manner. She was very quiet about it and just sat there with barf all over herself like nothing had happened."

"That's because I was hoping no one would notice, you jerk," Gina snapped at Peter.

"Why didn't you roll down the window and puke outside the cab?" Shirley asked Gina, trying not to laugh.

"Aaah, dah . . . I was drunk. I wasn't exactly thinking logically."

"When we finally got to Denny's, the cabdriver let us out. It was only after he took off that we realized it was closed for Christmas."

"Yeah," Peter said as Gina looked at him and Linda with a snarl. "It was freezing, and the place was closed, and we were too embarrassed to call the cab company again, so in our drunken stupor we started walking along the highway. I'm not sure if we knew where we were going. We just kept walking, in between laughing at Gina for blowing chunks in the cab. At some point Cheryl stumbled in a ditch and twisted her ankle."

"And she bitched about it the rest of the night and wanted Peter to carry her ass," Gina added.

"Well, this is where it gets interesting," Linda started again. "We finally got to some Super 8 Motel along the road and went in to get a room. Of course I ended up sharing a bed with Puke-Tisha, and Cheryl somehow finagled her way into sharing a bed with Peter. We were all so cold and tired that it didn't seem to matter anyway; however, shortly after the lights went off, strange noises started coming from Peter and Cheryl's side of the room."

"Strange noises, eh?" Shirley said, looking at Peter with a grin.

"Strange isn't exactly the right word. I guess the noises were more erotic. The kind of noises your parents make when you're a kid and they don't want you to hear them going at it. Come to think of it, it didn't even seem like they were really trying to be that quiet about it. Gina and I didn't know what to do. We just lay there like we didn't notice and—"

Gina didn't let her finish. "Basically, Cheryl fucked Peter's brains out right there in front of us like a paid whore."

"Wow, what a night," Shirley said. She was inclined to ask why Gina held a grudge against Cheryl for the evening's events, but not Peter. After all, his behavior was just as inappropriate and rude. But she knew better. Gina wasn't going to give up Peter's friendship for any reason. Cheryl was dispensable. Peter wasn't. Besides, he was a man. He was supposed to think with his dick.

"So you and Cheryl haven't spoken since?"

"She's tried to speak to me. I just ignore her. Who needs friends like that?" Gina said, stopping to think about Cheryl for a minute. Truth was, Gina was the one who needed friends like that. Of course, Linda was her best friend and probably always would be, but she and Linda didn't have the same roaring good time Gina had been known to have with Cheryl. Linda wasn't into gossiping and ragging on other people the same way Gina and Cheryl were. They had perfected it to an art form. They didn't mean any harm by it. It wasn't like Penelope could hear them trashing her new haircut or making fun of her taste in clothes. It was just something they did to entertain themselves. "If you're not going to talk bad about people, what are you supposed to do over lunch?" Gina would tell herself, trying to rationalize the gossip sessions she and Cheryl would have. In reality, Gina didn't actually hate Cheryl—at least not anymore. She was over the whole incident with Peter but was too proud to reconcile with Cheryl.

"Not me. That's for sure," Shirley said, getting up from the table to help herself to the buffet with the gang following.

They reached the food bar, and Gina and her friends meandered around, adding small samples of different items to their plates. Peter avoided anything that looked like it had dairy products in it. He'd recently come to the conclusion that he was lactose intolerant, and he'd forgotten to bring his dairy digestive supplement.

Compared to the others, Shirley was a woman on a mission. She quickly filled one plate with lumpy mashed potatoes and Jell-O salad. Then, while balancing that plate on her forearm, she filled another plate with turkey stuffing, and some sort of chicken with cream sauce all over it. She passed over the fried fish—it wouldn't keep well in the refrigerator. When she returned to the table, she just left the two full plates and immediately returned to the buffet to start again.

"Mother!" Gina said in a condescending tone as Shirley returned from her second trip. "Not again? I thought you gave this up?"

"Don't worry, sweetie. They don't care," Shirley said to Gina as she whipped out a gallon-size Ziploc bag and started spooning in the mashed potatoes. "What do they get paid? Five bucks an hour? Do you think they're going to confront me for five bucks an hour?"

"Mother, it has nothing to do with whether or not these people notice you shoving mounds of food into your purse. It's embarrassing. I should have known something was up when you came in with that duffel bag."

"I don't think it's embarrassing," Peter said.

"I don't either," Linda added smartly. "Want me to steal something for you, Shirley?"

"Well, as a matter of fact, can you grab some of the roast beef? Make sure you get the rare pieces. That way, when I heat it up, it will be medium, just like I like it. And if you can also get me some of—"

Gina cut her off. "No, she would not like you to steal something for her. For heaven's sake, are you that broke, Shirley? I'll go to the store with you and buy you a whole mess of TV dinners or something."

"I ain't eatin' that shit," Shirley replied, stuffing the last of the tuna casserole into another plastic bag as if what she was doing were completely appropriate.

"Gina," Shirley said, putting a couple of stuffed Ziplocs into the duffel bag. "I can eat for a week on this food, and it cost me only nine ninety-five."

"Nine ninety-five and your dignity, not to mention mine."

"Don't be such a whaaa baby. We don't all make big banker's salaries."

"I *hardly* make a big salary, and I'd be happy to help you out with groceries if you really need it. You work in a restaurant, for God's sake. Can't you eat there?"

"Just drop it, Gina. Would ya?" Shirley asked.

"Fine," Gina said, lifting her hands in exasperation, trying not to lose her temper with her mother. It wasn't like it did any good anyway.

"Here, sweetie, hold this. Will you?" Shirley said, handing a plastic bag to Gina. "I need to take my Zoloft while I'm eating. It upsets my stomach otherwise," she continued, looking through her purse for her antidepressants.

"Zoloft?" Gina said. "Yeah, that upset my stomach too. I take Paxil now," she continued before turning to Linda. "You take Paxil too, Linda. Right? Is it easier on your stomach?"

"No, I used to take that, but I switched to Prozac. Tammy, you know, from work, she takes Prozac and said it works well for her, so I had my doctor switch me."

"You guys got it all wrong," Peter said. "Effexor rocks. One of my docs . . . I mean, my doctor put me on that a few weeks ago. It's great."

"Well, the Paxil seems to be okay for me. For now anyway," Shirley said, downing her pill with some soda before starting her bag-filling process again. She didn't even try to be discreet about it. She just opened her bag, continued her conversation, and munched on the food as she spooned it into her bags.

"Shirley," Gina said, clearly frustrated. "Haven't you gotten enough? This is so embarrassing."

"Nobody cares," Peter said before Shirley could respond. "Do you think Shirley is the only one who does this?"

The thought had never really occurred to her, but as she looked around the large restaurant, Gina saw an awful lot of people with large bags of some sort next to them—duffel bags, beach bags, diaper bags. . . .

"Oh, my God, there's a whole colony of them," Gina said. "Why doesn't anyone do anything?"

"She already told you, Gina. If you worked here and got paid five bucks an hour, would you do anything?" Linda asked. "Hell no, you'd probably help them take their bags out the door and hope for a nice tip."

"How sad," Gina said with a look of confusion on her face. She suddenly felt a little better about the state of her affairs. So she screwed an old fat guy and didn't have a date to her high school reunion. At least she wasn't stealing coleslaw and hush puppies from the local greasy spoon.

Exasperated with the whole scene, Gina was about to get up and refill her soda, when she saw a familiar face at the food bar. It took her a second or two before she realized it was David. God, she couldn't believe it. Maybe her luck was changing. She wasn't going to have to use that dumb alumni directory to locate him after all. All she had to do was casually run into him, and he would remember how well they were hitting it off at Rio Grande and certainly ask for her phone number, which he must have lost. Yeah, Gina thought. He *must* have lost it.

After watching him add a few things to his plate and walk toward another corner of the restaurant, Gina excused herself, got up from the table, and followed him. She figured she'd just walk by his table and take it from there. As she turned the corner, she saw him sit down with his back toward her. She started to scurry toward his table, when the fat man seated across from David winked at her.

"Shit!" she thought, startled. She did a quick one eighty and started back to her table. David was, once again, wining and dining one of his best clients.

"Who was that?" David asked Griffin after noticing him winking at someone. He turned his head and got a quick look at a retreating female's back. There was something familiar about her, but he couldn't quite put his finger on it.

"She's actually one of the girls," Griffin responded.

"One of the girls?"

"Remember? I told you about the *girls*."

"Right. I forgot. God, she looked pretty good from behind. How'd you get her into bed?"

"You'd be surprised, David. It doesn't take much. You just get to them when they're vulnerable. Girls like her have a certain look about them. You know, lonely, a little sad. . . . You feed them a few drinks, and presto, before you know it, they've got your cock in their mouth."

"You're a piece of work, G-man. You know that?" David said, laughing.

"Do I ever."

"You really think we're going to make money with this scam?"

"Money?" Griffin replied. "Hell yes! Boatloads of money."

Super Cooper

It was almost time for bed, and after such a horrendous day, all Cheryl wanted to do was go to sleep. She had just finished canceling her personal ad on Digital City. Her date with Louis was enough to scare her away from any others. She was about to log off, when she figured she'd check her e-mail before she went to bed. She only had one new e-mail, which was another response to her ad. She had gotten about ten in total and Louis was the only one she had bothered to meet. The rest had either sent her canned responses or seemed like creeps.

She thought about just deleting the e-mail without even opening it. After all, she had no intention of meeting any more guys from the ad. She wasn't about to go through another date like the one with Louis. She decided that meeting people over the Internet wasn't for her. It was impossible to assess someone from an e-mail, even if it did include a picture. You still couldn't surmise the way they talked, their mannerisms, the whole way they carried themselves, or if they were blithering idiots who lived with a sixteen-year-old cat with diarrhea in their mother's basement.

Oh, what the hell, she thought, deciding to go ahead and read the e-mail. As she clicked it open and began to peruse the words, her eyes widened. But as she finished reading the ad, she let out a quick laugh—the kind of laugh that comes when you hit the punch line of a *Broom Hilda* or *Dilbert* comic strip.

Hi there! My name is Cooper. I read your ad and liked it very much. You have many of the qualities I look for in a woman. Hopefully, I will have some of the qualities you are looking for in a man. I'm looking for someone to be my soul mate and be with me all the time. Past girlfriends have called me high maintenance and needy, but I prefer to think that I just need a lot of attention. I'm looking for someone who will be honest with me. My last girlfriend lied to me, and I made her regret the day she was ever born (until the restraining order, that is). I hope you like cats, as I have seven, who sleep in bed with me every night. Don't worry about the smell, I have three litter boxes and change them frequently. I enjoy playing chess, bathing my cats, going to Star Trek conventions (Spock is my favorite!), and dressing my cats in cute little costumes so I can take their picture (I'm going to make a calendar). . . .

Scary enough?

Honestly, I'm just a nice, reasonably good-looking Christian black man looking for a nice, reasonably good-looking Christian black woman. I live in Alexandria and work for an Internet startup. I'm 31, 6'0", solid 190 pounds, have a shaved head and a great smile. I like biking, too, and have been known to be pretty good in the kitchen as well. I just moved here from Jacksonville a few months ago and don't know too many people in town. I would love to meet some new friends and take it from there. Feel free to give me a call sometime and maybe we can talk some more.

Cheryl liked the response. It was witty, and she actually dared to think that he might be normal. She had thought she was through with the online dating thing, but maybe it was fate that Cooper had sent this e-mail right before she canceled the ad. She looked at the clock. It was almost nine. It was still early enough for her to call him. She thought about it for another second, picked up the phone, and dialed the number he had included in the subject line of his e-mail.

"Cooper here," he said, answering the phone.

"Is Cooper there?" Cheryl asked nervously, only then realizing that he had already said his name.

"This is him."

"Hi. This is Cheryl. You answered my ad on Digital City."

"Yeah. Gosh, I just sent that e-mail a few minutes ago."

Shit! Cheryl thought. If she had given it more consideration, she would have waited at least a day to respond, so she didn't seem so eager.

"Really? I was just checking my e-mail now, and the phone was right here, so I figured what the hell."

"I'm glad you called, Cheryl."

She liked the way he said Cheryl. He had a deep, confident voice. "So, how are you?" she asked him.

"I'm well. And you?"

"Just fine. It's been a long day though."

"For you too?" he said with a bit of a laugh.

"Yeah," Cheryl replied, somehow feeling like he really empathized with her. "So tell me a little about yourself, Cooper."

"Sure," he said.

Cheryl liked the way he said "sure." So many guys would have said the typical "so what do you want to know?"

"Well, my first name is actually Everett. My last name is Cooper, but I've been called Cooper ever since I can remember. I moved here from Florida in March, so I've been in town only a few months. I got a job offer with an Internet company in Ashburn that was too good to turn down. I live in Alexandria, just outside of Old Town. I didn't know where to live when I moved up here, so I'm just renting a place until I get my bearings and figure out where I want to live permanently. I like doing all sorts of things and generally keep pretty busy," he said before hesitating for a moment and adding, "and, like I said, I'm a Christian, and religion is very important to me."

"Oh, me too," Cheryl lied. She wasn't really even sure she could attest to being Christian. She went to an African

Methodist service a couple of years ago; that must have counted for something.

"Really? Glad to hear that. You know, it's like being Christian is a bad thing these days."

"For some people maybe."

"Do you go to church?"

"Every now and then," Cheryl lied. Please don't ask me which one, Cheryl thought, trying to remember the names of some churches in the area.

"That's okay, religion isn't about going to church. It's about clean living and doing what's right."

"Absolutely," Cheryl agreed, finding his zest for religion a little odd but refreshing at the same time.

"I'm sorry. I didn't mean to go off on a tangent like that. Why don't you tell me something about you."

Cheryl went on to tell him about her job and her love for cooking. She mentioned that she grew up in Maine and moved to D.C. to go to college. They exchanged a few college stories and talked about the nuances of adjusting to life in an unfamiliar city. Before they knew it, they had been on the phone for over an hour, chatting and laughing and just enjoying some nice conversation. Cheryl assured him that D.C. had a lot to offer and asked him if he would like her to show him around the city sometime. He suggested that they meet for dinner but, after her Red Lobster experience, Cheryl figured a quick lunch might be a better idea.

"Why don't we meet for lunch one day this week?" Cheryl offered as an alternative to his dinner invitation.

"I'm off tomorrow. You work in Falls Church, right? Maybe I could meet you for lunch out there somewhere."

"Actually, I'm only working a half-day tomorrow. Why don't we meet somewhere in the city after I get home."

"Sure. Any suggestions?"

"Hmmm. Why don't we meet at the Italian Kitchen. It's just off Dupont Circle on Seventeenth Street. We can grab a quick lunch there."

"Okay? What time works for you?"

"Let's say two o'clock?"

"Great. I will see you at the Italian Kitchen at two o'clock."

As Cheryl hung up the phone, she read his e-mail again. It made her smile, but she wasn't about to allow herself to get her hopes up over this man. It just wasn't worth the letdown that was almost certainly in store for her.

He Works Hard
for the Money

"Hey, Peter, are you busy?"

"Actually, Doris, I am at the moment. I need to finish this report before lunch," Peter lied after Plant Lady called from the other side of the cube. He wasn't busy at all. In fact, lately, things had been rather slow. For the past few weeks Peter had been surfing the Web for large parts of the day just to pass time.

Peter had worked in the legal department of Saunders, Kraff, and Larson, a large accounting and consulting firm, for several years. He was a paralegal and mostly supported three lawyers by researching information and assisting on special projects from time to time. He also accessed the Internet and Lexis-Nexis from his desktop to research the multitude of requests that came his way.

"What report?" Plant Lady inquired further.

"Ah . . . you know, the . . . just something Mark asked me to work on."

"Can you just spare a second, Peter? I need you to hand me a plant while I stand on the desk."

For heaven's sake! It's already like the fucking Amazon rain forest over here. "I guess. Anything for you, Doris," Peter said, getting up from his chair.

He watched Plant Lady wobble up onto her desk and slip

a hook into the drop ceiling. Peter handed her the hanging spider plant and returned to his seat.

Peter had sat next to Doris for over a year. He and the rest of the office called her Plant Lady. One look at her desk, and there was no question why. She had at least ten plants in her cube and a few hanging from the drop ceiling. She was a very nice middle-aged woman, and Peter was fond of her. He thought her strong affection for plants was somewhat odd, but, aside from her constant inquiries about his lunch, she generally minded her own business.

Once he got settled in, he continued his *Yahoo!* search on zinc. He'd had a few hangnails lately, and he thought he'd read somewhere that brittle nails were a sign of a zinc deficiency. It often seemed that whatever syndrome, disease, or condition had been highlighted on the news the night before, Peter was either convinced he might have it, or wanted to make sure that he didn't. Some days he would spend hours on the Internet researching rare conditions that he thought he might be stricken with. He'd even taken to closing the blind of the window behind his desk so no one would see the reflection of his computer screen.

By the time he'd done enough research to rule out a zinc problem, it was afternoon. Shirley had offered him a Ziploc of mashed potatoes and another of carved roast beef from their foray to the buffet. After heating up the leftovers, Peter was sitting at his desk, getting ready to eat lunch, when Doris poked her head over the low cube wall.

"What's that?" she asked. "It smells really good."

"Just leftovers from the weekend," Peter said, wishing that just once he could eat his lunch without Doris inquiring as to what it was.

Peter was ready to dig in, when his phone rang.

"Peter, it's Mark, I need to see you in my office right away," Peter's boss asked with an uncomfortable tone in his voice. In all the years he had worked at the firm, Peter had never heard such an odd tone in Mark's voice. "I'll be right there, Mark," Peter replied before realizing that Mark had already hung up. He got up from his desk and maneuvered through the maze of cubicles that led to Mark's office. When he got to the doorway, Mark motioned for him to come in.

"Would you close the door behind you, Peter?"

Peter closed the door and sat down next to a perky young lady wearing a pink business suit and reeking of expensive perfume. Immediately after looking at her, Peter decided he didn't like her. Every hair was in place, and her makeup was perfect. She was sitting straight up in the chair, projecting confidence and authority, even though she was barely over five feet tall. She was just like those girls in high school who wouldn't give him the time of day.

Bitch, Peter thought to himself.

"Peter, this is Cameron Hartman. She's an operations analyst in information services downstairs."

"Nice to meet you, Cameron," Peter said, extending his hand and managing a slight smile.

"Yes, my pleasure," Cameron replied with an overly firm handshake.

Mark cleared his throat and looked at Peter. "Peter, Cameron called me this morning with some concerns."

"Concerns?" Peter asked.

"Yes, Peter," Cameron interrupted. "Part of my responsibility is to monitor and generate reports of staff member activity on the Internet."

Oh, shit, Peter thought while his heart started racing. He tried to look calm while Cameron continued.

"We're concerned about the substantial amount of time you've been spending on the Internet accessing sites that have nothing to do with our business. Honestly, it's hard for us to understand how you get any work done at all, considering the amount of time you spend hopping from one site to the next," Cameron added while handing him a report.

Peter eyed the document that listed the date and amount of time he spent at various Internet sites. Most of them had something to do with health or disease—migrainecontrol.com, multiplesclerosisforum.com, coloncancer.net.

Cameron rattled on, but Peter was so busy reviewing the report and trying to think of something to say that he didn't hear her. When she finally shut up, both she and Mark looked at Peter and waited for a response.

"Gosh, I'm not sure what to say. I guess I got caught up in the whole cyberspace thing and it got out of control. It won't happen again."

"Do you have anything else you want to say?" Cameron asked.

"I really don't know what else to say," Peter replied, shrugging his shoulders and trying to look apologetic.

"Thanks, Cameron," Mark said, signaling her to leave.

"Sure. Nice to meet you, Peter," she said as she got up to leave the room.

"You too," Peter replied. Maybe next time you can smash my balls with a sledgehammer.

"Peter, what were you thinking? Didn't you know you were being monitored?" Mark asked, sounding more like himself.

"Obviously, I didn't, Mark. I'm really sorry. How embarrassing this is."

"I haven't looked closely at the report, and actually I don't intend to. You've done good work around here. I can't imagine you've spent as much time screwing off on the Internet as Cameron implied. Let's forget this happened, Peter. And make sure it doesn't happen again."

"Thanks, Mark," Peter said, getting up to leave. He left Mark's office and went back to his cube. He didn't feel much like eating anymore. He was about to throw his lunch into the trash, when his phone rang again.

"Hello, this is Peter."

"Yes, Peter, it's Cameron Hartman. I just got back to my desk. I forgot to mention earlier that I need to get a copy of any written documentation about your inappropriate conduct on the Internet."

"Written documentation? From who?"

"From your supervisor, Mark Koffman."

"As far as I know, there wasn't any documentation," Peter replied, just slightly showing his annoyance with the pushy little woman.

"Well, it's company policy for anyone misusing the Internet to receive a written warning."

"Really? Mark and I discussed this, and he didn't feel it was necessary."

"Okay, I will talk to Mark directly."

"About what?"

"I just need to remind him about the policy and make sure a warning is placed in your file."

"If I may be so bold, Cameron, can't we forgive and forget? After all, if my supervisor is willing to let it go—"

"Peter," Cameron said condescendingly. "Wasting company time and money going to hundreds of Web sites for *afflicted* people is hardly something we can just let go."

"Afflicted people?" Peter said, seething. "Well, do what you have to do. I'd better go. Don't want to waste any *company time or money.*"

What a fucking bitch, Peter thought, hanging up the phone. It was almost as if she got some pleasure out of getting him into trouble. If Mark didn't write him up, what did she care? Something was seriously wrong with this chick. First she humiliates him in front of his boss, now she was going to see to it that he got a written warning in his personnel file, and, worst of all, she had called him afflicted. He was going to get back at her even if she was just doing her job. But how? He needed to come up with a creative plan for getting even. This called for some consulting services from an expert. He picked up the phone and dialed.

"Gina, hey, it's Peter."

Responsible Pet Owners

"Gosh, Peter, this is a bit of a tough one. I hope I'm not losing my touch."

"Come on, Gina, I'm counting on you. Cameron embarrassed me in front of my boss, she got me written up, and she's just plain mean. I've been here for over five years and never had a problem, and now all of a sudden I have a written warning in my file."

"Don't worry, Peter. We'll think of something to settle the score. I need to know a little about this girl. Tell me about her."

"I barely know her myself. I know you wouldn't like her. She's one of those I-have-it-all-together little bitches."

"Then I definitely wouldn't like her."

"And she's little and cute. She was probably a cheerleader in high school."

"Okay, okay. You didn't have to play the *cheerleader* card. Gosh, we could harass her by phone, but it's so hard to do nasty things with the phone these days, with caller ID and *69. If you want to get to her by phone, you'll have to do it with a pay phone."

"Gina, we're not in first grade. I'd like to do something a little grander than a couple of prank phone calls."

"That's not what I'm talking about, Peter. Phone calls would just be the beginning."

"The beginning of what?"

"The beginning of a steady stream of events. We could make her think she's crazy. Oh, the wheels are spinning now," Gina said, pausing for a moment when she saw Shirley walk into the bank with Gomez.

"Peter, I think I have a pretty good idea, but Shirley's here, so I have to go. We'll put our heads together later and flesh everything out. I'll stop by tonight," Gina said before hanging up the phone.

"Shirley, you know you can't bring him in here," Gina said, bending over to pet Gomez. "How's my baby? Have you been a good boy today?" she said to the pooch before looking up at Shirley. "We'd better get out of here. I'm in enough trouble around here without Liz getting on me for having the dog in the bank."

As Gina tried to usher Shirley and the dog out of the bank, Liz poked her head out of her office.

"Gina, you can't have that dog in here," Liz said sharply.

"What? This?" Shirley said, pointing to Gomez. "He's my Seeing Eye dog."

"Shirley!" Gina said, trying not to laugh before calling to Liz, who was not amused by Shirley's antics. "I know, Liz. I'm sorry. We're taking him outside right now."

Gina took the leash from Shirley's hand, and they went outside. Shirley generally worked nights at the restaurant, so she often stopped by Gina's apartment during the day to walk the dog. She loved to spend time with Gomez. He was always thrilled to see her and put on a big production every time Shirley came to visit. He barked and wagged his tail and ran around in circles at her feet to greet her.

The dog and Shirley had a special relationship. Gomez was the first living creature that she felt really gave her unconditional love. Gina and her mother certainly loved her, but they were always nagging about something—telling Shirley she should go back to school or get some vocational training. They always had some idea about how to reorganize Shirley's life and get her on track. Gomez never bugged her about anything. He just listened to her, gave her doggie kisses, and provided an often much-needed lift to her spirits. She hated giving him up only a few weeks after she adopted him.

About six years earlier, during a brief stint selling futons in Dupont Circle, one of Shirley's coworkers offered her the purebred mini dachshund pup, and she gladly accepted. Or, at least Shirley's friend told her that Gomez was a pure-bred mini dachshund. Gina found it somewhat suspicious that someone would *give* Shirley a purebred dog, not to mention that neither Gina nor anyone she knew had ever seen a dachshund with such a long, fluffy coat.

When she set out to name the puppy, Shirley was somehow under the impression that Gomez was a Chihuahua—maybe because he was so small. She had seen something on television a few months earlier that mentioned Chihuahuas were originally bred in Mexico. One of the deliverymen at the futon shop was named Gomez, and he was from Mexico also. Anyway, Shirley just liked the sound of "Gomez." She didn't get to say words with the letter "Z" in them very often, so Gomez was just a fun name to say. Gina didn't have the heart to tell her that Gomez was, in fact, a dachshund, a breed that originated in Germany. To this day, Gina wasn't sure if Shirley ever figured it out. It didn't really matter anyway. Gomez became the German dog with the Mexican name and, if anyone asked, Gina just told everyone her mother was a fan of the Addams family.

Shirley and Gomez became instant friends, and she took great care of him; however, it was just a few weeks after she took him in that one of the managers in her apartment building gave her forty-eight hours to get rid of the dog or be evicted. Gina's building allowed pets under thirty pounds, so she hesitantly agreed to take the pup until they could find him another home. Six years later Gina and Gomez were still together.

"Shirley, what's the matter with you? Are you trying to

get me fired? I'm on thin ice already without you being smart with my boss."

"I'm sorry, sweetie. I couldn't help myself."

"What are you doing here anyway?"

"You know Gomez, he loves to go for a ride in the car. I thought we'd drive out here, and I'd take him for a walk along the W&OD Trail. He needs some exercise. You keep him cooped up in that apartment too much. Want to come?"

"Sure. Let me tell someone I'm taking lunch. I'll be right back."

The girls and the pooch walked along the trail while Gomez ran ahead of them with his nose to the ground. It was a pleasant summer day, especially for D.C., where summers tended to be overcast, hot, and muggy. It was only about eighty degrees, and there was hardly a cloud in the sky. The trail was rather busy for a weekday during work hours. A fair number of people must have called in sick to enjoy the nice weather. Gina and Shirley kept to the right of the trail while an occasional biker or jogger whizzed by.

"So, whatever happened with that career improvement plan you were supposed to develop?" Shirley inquired.

"Linda and I worked on it last night. It's going to be a royal pain. I'm going to write a report to Liz twice a month to document my efforts toward improving my performance. I'm also going to start exactly recording my arrival and departure times to show that I'm putting in extra hours and arriving on time, and I promised to develop some programs to improve morale at the bank. It mainly consisted of things like that. Linda actually came up with most of the ideas."

"I'm sure you'll do fine. You've made it this far."

"I guess—" Gina didn't get a chance to finish. From what seemed like out of nowhere, she heard someone scream and, before she knew it, an overweight woman on Rollerblades came crashing into her—pushing Gina on the ground and tumbling on top of her. As soon as Gomez caught sight of this, he began frantically barking and running to Gina's aid.

As Shirley tried to help the ladies up, Gomez started growling at the fat woman and nipped her on the leg.

"Calm down, Gomez. It's okay, boy," Gina said, trying to calm the dog as she got up.

"Are you okay?" the lady asked Gina, pulling herself up.

"I'm fine. You?"

"Well, I was until your dog bit me," she said, pointing to what looked like a minor scratch on her shin. "He has his shots, doesn't he?"

"Yes," Shirley replied before Gina had a chance to respond.

"Why doesn't he have a rabies vaccine tag on his collar?"

"It's at home," Gina lied. In fact, Gomez hadn't been to the vet in a couple of years.

"I really need to see it, just to make sure. Do you live nearby?"

"No, I'm just on a break from work, but I can assure you he doesn't have rabies."

"Well, I need to know for sure. What's your vet's name? I'll call him directly," the woman persisted.

"Look, lady!" Shirley interjected abruptly. "Fact is, the dog hasn't had a rabies shot recently, so I guess you're out of luck."

"Then I'll have to call the animal shelter," the woman snapped while whipping her mobile phone out of her pocket. "They may have to quarantine him to make sure."

"No one's quarantining anyone," Shirley yelled, not knowing what the word "quarantine" meant. "If you hadn't plowed your fat ass into my daughter, the dog wouldn't have bit you in the first place."

"Hi. I need to report a dog-biting incident. I need the number for the animal shelter," the woman said into her phone, glaring at Shirley.

As the angry woman waited for a response on the other end of the phone, Shirley looked at Gina and gave her a long stare. She then picked up the dog, grabbed Gina's hand, and began running down the trail away from the fat lady. A few seconds later they turned around to see the woman fumbling on her Rollerblades, trying to catch up with them.

Just as she was saying "Get back here, God damn it!" she took another dive and fell on her face. As the woman struggled to get up, Shirley, still holding Gomez in her arms, stuck out her tongue and started shaking her hips at the lady in a nanny-nanny-boo-boo sort of fashion. She and Gina both started laughing and began running again. Eventually, the woman was out of sight, and they started back toward the bank.

"You are bad," Gina said to Shirley with a grateful smile as they approached the bank entrance.

"Thank God, huh. She's probably at the emergency room right now—getting some awful injections or something," Shirley replied with an evil laugh.

"You're terrible. I hope not," Gina said, laughing as well. "You're looking a little flushed. Are you okay?"

"I'm fine. The run was just a bit much for me," Shirley said, suddenly starting to breathe harder and heavier.

"Are you sure?"

"Actually no. I can't quite catch my breath," Shirley said, holding her chest and starting to wheeze.

"Come on," Gina said, pulling Shirley toward her car. "We're going to the hospital."

Jerks

Cheryl stood just inside the restaurant, waiting for Cooper to arrive. It was especially crowded, so she hoped they would still be able to recognize each other. Thinking that she should have asked him what he'd be wearing, she saw a sharply dressed black man with a shaved head walk through the door and give her a big smile.

She wondered what made him so sure she was his date, but then she realized she was the only black woman in the restaurant. He sauntered over to her, widened his smile, and extended his right arm. Cheryl smiled and shook his hand.

"Hi, I'm Cooper."

"Hi, nice to meet you. Cheryl."

"Let's get a table," he said, almost sounding authoritative.

"Sure," Cheryl said, pleased with the looks of her date and trying to read any early clues about what he thought of her. After the hostess showed them to a small table along the window, they gave their menus a quick read and set them down.

"Were you waiting long?" Cooper asked.

"No, no. I'd just got here."

"Great," Cooper said. "So, you live in the neighborhood?" he asked, trying to make conversation.

"Yeah, on P Street, near Seventeenth," Cheryl responded.

"Gosh, you're kind of stuck right in the middle of Queer World, aren't you?"

"Queer? Does anyone still use that word?"

"Sorry. You know . . . all the gays live around here, don't they?"

"Well, the neighborhood is pretty gay, I guess, but it doesn't make any difference to me. Why should I care?" Cheryl said, a little turned off by Cooper's apparent homophobia, not to mention his stupidity—who was dumb enough to use a word like "queer" at a trendy restaurant in the middle of Dupont Circle?

"I don't know, just seems a lot like Sodom and Gomorrah to me. As a Christian, I just can't condone that kind of behavior."

Oh, God, here we go with the Christianity thing again, Cheryl thought as she rolled her eyes at him.

Noticing her reaction, he softened his stance a little. "Well, like the Bible says, love the sinner, hate the sin. You know, it's the same with the Jews. I don't hate the Jews, I just hate the fact that they don't accept Jesus as the Son of God."

"Are you joking me?" Cheryl asked.

"Joking? No. Why?"

"Look, Cooper. Maybe this isn't such a good idea," Cheryl said, starting to get up from the table and swearing to herself that she would never place or respond to a personal ad ever again.

"Why? What's wrong?"

"I think we just have different philosophies of life."

"Oh, come on, give a guy a chance," he said, lifting his eyebrows. "I'm sorry. I really don't have anything against the Jews. I don't care about the gays either. I just wouldn't want to live in the middle of it. Suppose one of them tries to pick me up or something?"

"Well, one would guess you'd say no thank you, and that would be the end of it."

Cooper laughed to himself. "I guess you're right. Really, the queers don't bother me that much. It's not a big deal. Come on, sit back down. Let's have lunch. Give me a second chance."

Cheryl sighed and sat back down. "I think 'gay' or 'homosexual' is a better word to use than 'queer,'" Cheryl whispered, deciding that if she was going to stay, she may as well try to educate the buffoon a little. "You do realize half the people in this restaurant are probably gay?"

Cooper looked around. "Is this a gay restaurant?"

"No."

"Then what are all these gay people doing here?" Cooper asked, seeming almost alarmed.

"Eating lunch. Relax, would you?" Cheryl said with a slight smile. "All right, why don't we order?" she said as the waiter approached their table. She was somewhat amused with Cooper's obvious unease. She had concluded that he was a bit of a jerk, but then, there was something about jerks that was attractive to Cheryl. The nicer a guy was to her, the more boring she found him. A few years earlier she dated a man who treated her like a queen. He was head over heels in love with her and would have given her the world on a silver platter if she had asked for it. He would even do her grocery shopping and laundry for her sometimes. Only problem was he bored her to tears. He was a great personal assistant, but as a boyfriend, Cheryl wasn't interested. She needed someone to spar with every once in a while.

As the waiter took Cooper's order, Cheryl rubbed her eyes and thought about her dysfunctional taste in men. She knew she had an unhealthy attraction to gruff men who didn't treat her the way she deserved to be treated, but she couldn't seem to overcome it. In fact, if Peter ever decided to really commit to her, she'd probably lose interest.

Cheryl and Cooper actually ended up having a nice time through lunch. Cooper had an air of confidence about him that was attractive to Cheryl but bothered her at the same time. He had definite opinions about everything from politics and religion to where to get the best hamburger. It was nice to meet someone who was so decisive but a little un-nerving as well. There was a fine line between healthy confidence and annoying arrogance, and she wasn't sure which side Cooper fell on yet, but she was definitely attracted to him.

Latin Strangers

"Where is she?" Linda said to no one in particular. It had been almost three hours since Gina left for lunch. Linda was grumpy, not to mention hungry. She had just emerged from the women's bathroom. Lately someone hadn't been flushing the toilet after using it. It was maddening to Linda how disgusting some people could be. They did things in the bathroom at work that they wouldn't dream of doing in their own home, where they would actually have to clean it up.

The bank was short-staffed, and there was no way Linda could leave to get something to eat while Gina was still gone. She sneaked into the back to guzzle down some water before helping the next customer. About five of them were waiting for assistance, and she and Liz were the only ones on the floor. There were plenty of tellers behind the line, but they weren't trained to handle the sort of things Linda and Gina did. Liz had been with the same customer for more than a half hour. Linda figured that was the only reason she was ever promoted to branch manager—she was so slow and inept with the customers, the bigwigs wanted her in more of a managerial job. Guess they didn't realize she would be just as slow and inept in those duties.

Linda emerged from the back and greeted the next customer. She was faintly perspiring from the hectic day, which made her panty hose even more uncomfortable. Lately, she was growing more and more discontent with her job. She was a lesbian, for heaven's sake—what was she doing in a job where she had to wear hose every day?

"Hi, I'm Linda. What can I help you with?" she asked the exotic-looking young lady, extending her hand.

The petite stranger with an olive complexion and shiny black hair shook Linda's hand and smiled. "I need to open a checking account. I just moved here a few weeks ago."

"Sure, come over to my desk and have a seat."

As Linda pulled out her own chair to sit down, her customer slumped into her seat as if she'd been on her feet all day.

"What a day. I just got back from the Motor Vehicle Administration. It took almost two hours to get a driver's license. From here I have to go fight with U-Haul. They overcharged me for the truck I used to move here."

"Moving can be a real hassle. Where are you from?"

"Boston."

Feeling obligated to do so, Linda asked, "So what brings you to the D.C. area?" She didn't really care what brought her to town and, with a lobby full of customers, she didn't have time to chitchat.

"It's a long story."

"Oh." Linda paused. "So you're looking to open an account?" she added, hoping to move things along.

"Yeah, my girlfriend and I broke up a few months ago," the woman added, ignoring Linda's question. "She was the reason I moved to Boston in the first place. So after we went our separate ways, it was either go back home to my parents or accept a job in D.C. Obviously, I chose the latter."

Girlfriend? Did she say girlfriend? Linda thought to herself, suddenly forgetting about the other customers waiting.

"Girlfriend?" Linda asked, looking a little confused. This chick has straight written all over her face.

"Yeah. I'm getting too personal, aren't I? I just assumed you . . . well, what I meant to say was—"

"You assumed I was a lesbian," Linda said, finishing the young lady's response. "That's okay. I just give off lesbian vibes or something, even in heels and a skirt."

"Oh, you're not . . . ?"

"Yeah, I am."

"Oh, good. Some straight girls might have been offended."

"Some, I guess," Linda said, smiling. She didn't quite know what to say next. *So we're both dykes . . . want to see my L.L. Bean catalogue?* didn't quite fit the situation.

"You're busy. I'll stop blathering on. I really do need to get an account started."

"Sure. First thing I'll need is your name."

"Rosa," she replied. "Rosa Martinez."

"Is that Spanish? Where are you from?"

"I'm originally from New York. My parents are from Mexico, if that's what you meant."

"Cool. Do you speak Spanish?"

"No, not everyone with an 'ez' at the end of their name just crossed the border yesterday," Rosa responded sharply, as if this were a sensitive issue for her. "I'm sorry," she added. "It's just that I hear that all the time. I really don't speak much Spanish. My parents thought it was important for me to learn English, so that's all they spoke in the house. Forgive me?"

There was something about the way she said "forgive me?" that made it obvious to Linda that she was flirting with her.

"Of course. You're too cute not to forgive," Linda said, giving it right back to her.

Medication Money

"Ms. Perry," the young doctor at Arlington Hospital said to Shirley. "You need to carry your inhaler with you at all times. Why didn't you have it with you today?"

"I just didn't think about it, I guess."

"Ms. Perry, it's very important that you keep that inhaler with you. I'm going to write you a prescription for it just in case you can't find yours. I'll be right back," the doctor said, slipping behind the curtain that was pulled around the small area where Shirley was lying. She had a few monitors attached to her.

"You *are* getting your inhaler prescription filled, aren't you, Shirley?" Gina asked from the chair next to Shirley's stretcher.

"Yes, Gina, I got it filled. I get it filled every month."

"When I take you home, I want to see it."

"Gina, sweetie, I'm not in the business of displaying my medications to the world."

"Well, that may be, but Grandmother is also not in the business of giving you money for medicine and having you spend it on cigarettes or clothes and makeup."

"Okay, I didn't get it filled this month. I was running short on cash, so I had to use any extra money to pay bills."

"God damn it, Shirley! Medicine money from Grandmother is not *extra* money. Do you have any idea how much this emergency room visit is going to cost?"

"Don't worry about that, sweetie. Medicaid or someone will cover it. Really, Gina, what are they going to do if I don't pay? Take away my Mercedes and my estate in McLean? Oh, no!" Shirley added sarcastically. "It might affect my credit rating."

"I guess we're going to have to go back to the old system, where you give me your prescriptions and I fill them for you. You know I have nothing better to do with my time than babysit you."

"Can it, would ya? I didn't get one lousy prescription filled. I didn't run over a kitten with my car."

Gina sighed and shook her head. "I've got to call the bank and explain this whole mess you've gotten me into. I'll be right back."

"Please let Linda answer," Gina said to herself as she dialed the bank.

"Premier Bank of Arlington, Liz Cox speaking."

"Hi, Liz, it's Gina—"

"Gina, where are you? You've left Linda and me in quite a bind."

I'm fine. Thanks for asking, Gina thought to herself before responding. "I'm sorry, Liz. I went for a walk with my mother during lunch, and she had a severe asthma attack. I had to take her to the emergency room. I'm at Arlington Hospital right now."

"Oh, Gina, I'm sorry to hear that. Is she okay?"

Like you care, bitch! "She'll be fine. When we're done here, I'll have to take her home. I don't think I'll make it back today."

"Well, you take care of your mother, Gina, and we'll see you tomorrow," Liz responded in a concerned tone before adding, "And I'm sorry to ask, but please bring some sort of doctor's note or something just to verify your story."

"Okay, I'll ask for one."

"Thanks, Gina. Good luck."

"Hey, can you transfer me to Linda? I just want to let her know what happened."

"Sure," Liz agreed, and hit the transfer button.

"Premier Bank of Arl—"

"Linda, it's me."

"Where are you? Are you crazy? Liz is livid!"

"Screw her . . . that bitch. I'm at the hospital with Shirley, and do you know what that cow had the nerve to ask me?"

"Whoa . . . back up, girlfriend. What are you doing at the hospital? Is Shirley okay?"

"She is now. She had an asthma attack and didn't have her inhaler with her."

"But she's okay now?"

"She'll be fine . . . if I don't kill her. Anyway, I explained the situation to Liz, and she acted mildly concerned but then told me to bring a doctor's note to substantiate my story. Can you believe that?"

"That's ridiculous," Linda lied. In fact, considering Gina's track record at the bank, Linda didn't think it was unreasonable at all.

"Are things crazy busy?"

"They were insane for a few hours, but it's quiet now. Guess what? I have a date for Saturday night."

"Really?" Gina said, trying to sound enthused.

"Yes, with this woman who came to open an account today. She's very cute."

"Cool, you'll have to tell me all about it later. I'll give you a buzz tonight."

Gina hung up the phone, feeling a little unsettled. She always tried to be happy for Linda when she had a potential romance, but it made her feel somewhat apprehensive. The last time Linda had a steady girlfriend, she had very little time for Gina. Things got so bad, Gina joined a local church for its active young adults group just to try to make some new friends. She went on several outings with the group, going to local festivals and group dinners. She didn't find anyone in the group terribly interesting. In fact, between the girl who offered her some bizarre sugar substitute to put in her iced tea and the guy who thought it was oppressive to comb his hair, she found most of them downright weird.

During one of their dinner outings to a local Thai restaurant, one woman spent the better part of a half hour talking about milk. She explained that once milk is pasteurized and processed, if a baby calf were to drink it, he would die. Somewhere during this spiel, Gina sat there thinking, My God! This is what it's come to—spending a Friday night with a bunch of geeks, talking about milk. Shortly after this revelation, she excused herself from the table, said good night, and left the restaurant. She never saw anyone from the group again. Luckily, Linda and her girlfriend broke up a few weeks later, and things were back to normal.

Gina felt guilty about being apprehensive about Linda's date. Linda was her best friend and she really did want to see her happy. Linda in a relationship would have been much easier to swallow if Gina had a relationship of her own. She had seen a few guys here and there since the breakup with Peter, but nothing ever seemed to work out. She hadn't seriously dated anyone in years. She hadn't even met anyone who interested her in years, at least not anyone attainable. There was one guy she had really fallen for a while back. His name was Richard, a man she had met at a party at a friend's house in Rockville. She had scoped him out when he first walked in the door. He was cute but not overly cute, which was something Gina looked for in a guy. She certainly wanted to be with someone who was attractive, but not so attractive that she would feel inferior or unworthy. She had a mutual friend introduce her to Richard, and they ended up chatting for most of the evening.

They had a great first date when they went to dinner at the Carlyle Grand Café in Arlington. After dinner, at Gina's suggestion, they drove back into the city and walked around the Jefferson Memorial. Gina had never found a more romantic place than the Jefferson Memorial on a balmy night. They walked along the Tidal Basin and talked and laughed and got to know each other. When he dropped her off, he'd given her a long kiss good night and said he would call her.

Gina was so excited following her date. They had really hit it off and he obviously liked her. She jumped every time the phone rang for a week. When he didn't call, she was furious. It wouldn't have been so bad if they had had a lousy date, or he gave her a few clues that he wasn't interested. But every signal he sent, everything he said and did, led her to believe there was a mutual attraction. Of course, she thought about him possibly losing her phone number, but she was listed and they also had acquaintances in common. He could have tracked her down if he had wanted to. To this day, every time she heard Reba McEntire's "Why Haven't I Heard from You," she thought of Richard.

It wasn't until a few weeks later, when she ran into Richard, that she found out why he hadn't called. She saw him walking out of the Cheesecake Factory in Friendship Heights—he wasn't alone. He was holding hands with a woman who appeared to be a little older than him, maybe in her early thirties. She actually looked somewhat like Gina. She was tall and had a slender build and attractive blond hair. But she had something Gina didn't—boobs the size of honeydew melons.

Richard walked right by Gina and had the nerve to smile at her and say hello. Gina looked at him, took an obvious look at the woman's breasts, then lifted her eyes back to Richard as if to say "so that's what happened" or, more appropriately, "so *those* are what happened."

Something about the meeting actually made Gina feel better about Richard not pursuing her. At least it offered her some closure and explained a few things. She had thought about getting a boob job herself on numerous occasions and figured the woman on Richard's arm had done more than just think about it. Gina had even gone as far as making an appointment with a cosmetic surgeon. She figured if it was good enough for half the cast of *Beverly Hills 90210,* it was good enough for her. But she eventually canceled the appointment and decided to abandon the idea. The thought of having little bags of saline shoved in her chest was just more than she could stomach. She was going to have to land a man with the boobs the good Lord gave her.

Now, as she was walking down the hospital corridor back to Shirley's bed, she tried to forget about the Richards and the Peters of the world and force herself to be happy for Linda.

I'm glad she has a date, Gina tried to tell herself, and part of her was happy for Linda. It just made Gina a little anxious. Linda was pretty much the only single friend Gina had left. If Linda found a significant other, it would leave Gina all alone. Girlfriends had been in short supply lately—real ones anyway. Five years ago, Gina easily had five to ten girlfriends to hang out with or go shopping or on another outing of some kind. Most of these women were still friends in some way, but they were now toting a husband and some even had kids.

A few months earlier, Gina had called Rachel, a friend from college who had gotten married a year earlier but still went out with the girls from time to time. Gina was calling to see if Rachel wanted to go out dancing to Nation with Gina and a couple of others. Before Gina had a chance to ask her, Rachel mentioned that she was pregnant with her first child. After Rachel announced the news, Gina offered her congratulations and said she was just calling to say hello. Gina couldn't bear asking Rachel about going out to a bar. She felt pathetic. Here was her friend, getting ready to bring a new life into the world with her husband, while Gina was looking for someone to go to a bar with and get drunk. She couldn't stand the thought of Linda becoming a Rachel or a Penelope. Linda was all she had left. If Linda landed a relationship, Gina was truly on her own, and the thought terrified her.

No Big Deal

After a long lunch, Cooper offered to drive Cheryl home. Not wanting to be the eager beaver, she said it was only a few blocks and she could walk.

"Well, how about I walk you home, then?" Cooper asked.

"If you want," Cheryl said, trying to seem somewhat uninterested, when she had actually really enjoyed the afternoon with Cooper. They had some lively conversation over lunch and even debated over politics. Cheryl was a staunch Democrat while Cooper attested to being one of the few black Republicans. During their meal, they discussed everything from abortion to tax cuts to affirmative action. At first, Cheryl tried to avoid any controversial subjects, but their conversation seemed to naturally move toward contentious topics. She ended up enjoying these discussions with Cooper and getting his point of view. It sure beat sitting there with someone who agreed with everything she said.

She decided she liked that about Cooper—that he had strong opinions. She couldn't stand dating men who went along with all of her ideas just to avoid an argument. Cheryl liked to argue on occasion, and the heated discussion she and Cooper got into over lunch was actually kind of fun.

"You were just going to walk all this way by yourself?" Cooper asked as they approached Cheryl's building.

"Sure," Cheryl said.

"You don't walk around by yourself at night, do you?"

"Sometimes. There are always tons of people around, and streetlights are all over the place."

"Well, I don't think it's safe. But what can you expect in such an overwhelmingly Democratic city."

"Oh, please! Every city in the country has problems with crime. What does people voting Democratic have to do with anything?"

"Because Democrats are so wishy-washy and easy on crime."

"Just because we don't execute people for jaywalking doesn't mean we're easy on crime," Cheryl said with a smile, realizing Cooper was trying to start something with her again.

As they made their way to the lobby entrance of Cheryl's building, she thought about asking him up for a drink but decided against it. She actually kind of liked this guy and wanted to play a little hard to get.

"Thanks for walking me home," she said.

"No problem. Maybe I can call you sometime?"

"Sure," Cheryl said. "You have my phone number. Maybe we can do something later this week."

"Absolutely," he said before lightly touching her arm. "I had a good time."

Oh, kiss me already. "Me too."

"Take care," he said, and turned to leave.

"Sure. Bye," Cheryl replied, annoyed that he hadn't even tried to kiss her. Cheryl walked through the lobby to the elevators, and the flood of postdate thoughts began. She wondered if she had put her best foot forward. Maybe she shouldn't have been so opinionated during their discussion on politics. But, then again, maybe he liked that about her. She wished she had sat up straighter during lunch, and she hoped that she hadn't eaten too much. Should she have offered to pay the check when he pulled out his credit card? She didn't want him to think that she was cheap, but she didn't want him to think she was such a feminist that she wouldn't let a man buy her lunch. And why hadn't he kissed her at the end of their date? He seemed to really like her, and he wouldn't have offered to walk her home if he hadn't been interested. Would he have?

He said he was going to call. She wondered if he really would. She hated that about being a woman. Today's women could manage multimillion-dollar companies or even run for the presidency, but it was still taboo for her to be the first to call a guy after a date. She had to wait for him, if and when he chose to call.

She promised herself that she wouldn't think about it.

If he calls, he calls. If he doesn't, he doesn't. No big deal, she thought to herself as she walked into her apartment and went immediately over to the phone to make sure it was working.

The Ole MJ

By the time they released Shirley from the hospital, it was after nine P.M., so Gina took her straight home. She would have to take Shirley back to the bank in the morning and get her car.

"You want to stay the night, sweetie?" Shirley asked as they walked into her apartment with Gomez, who had been cooped up in the car the whole time Shirley was in the hospital. Considering her financial situation, Shirley's apartment was actually fairly decent. It had a spacious living room, a small kitchen, and two master bedrooms with private baths. It was old and creaky, and the furnishings left a lot to be desired, but, nonetheless, it was large and quite comfortable. The only way Shirley could afford it was to share the place with a series of different roommates. Most only lasted a few months. The last one left after only two weeks. Shirley lied to her initially and said she didn't smoke. When the new roomie came home to a living room full of cigarette fumes, she was furious and moved soon after.

Her current roommate was a guy of about twenty-five. Shirley knew very little about him. He worked as a bartender at Fridays for only three days before he was fired for leaving one night with a duffel bag full of vodka and tequila bottles.

But he was cute and young, and Shirley needed a roommate to help her make the rent.

"I don't know, maybe," Gina replied before crinkling her nose. "What's that pungent smell? Wait a minute . . . that's pot. Shirley, what's going on?"

"I don't know, Gina. You know I don't mess with drugs." Shirley messed with virtually everything else—men, booze, cigarettes—but she never did get into drugs.

"Sammy?" Shirley called toward the closed door of Sammy's bedroom. "Are you in there?"

"Hi, Shirley," he said, opening the door, which only spewed the smell of marijuana farther into the living room. He was a lanky young man with shoulder-length hair and was only wearing a pair of faded jeans.

"Sammy, honey. We had a deal—no drugs."

"What deal was that?"

"Oh, I don't know. It just sounded like the right thing to say," Shirley said with a giggle.

"Want a hit?" he said as he offered the smoldering joint to Shirley.

"No, she doesn't want a hit," Gina interjected. "And you need to pitch that thing and keep it out of this apartment."

"And who is this pretty young lady?" Sammy asked Shirley with a smile.

"This is my daughter, Gina. Sammy, you're going to have to keep that shit out of here. I don't want to go to jail because my roommate's a pothead," Shirley sighed at Sammy, more to appease Gina than anything else.

"It's gone," Sammy said, taking a final hit and walking into his bathroom. Shirley and Gina heard the toilet flush and then another voice from inside the bedroom.

"What the fuck are you doing, Sammy? There were a few more hits left on that."

"Who is that?" Gina asked Shirley as Sammy's bedroom door closed again.

"Some chick who's been staying here with him for the last couple of days. She's usually so doped up she's not very coherent. I don't know much about her."

"Doped up? Shirley, sometimes I wonder if you have any sense at all," Gina said, sitting down on the secondhand sofa and flicking the television on. She wasn't in the mood to lecture Shirley about her choice of roommates, so she let it go at that. As she and Shirley sat in front of the television, a young woman with a crew cut and wearing only a T-shirt emerged from the bedroom and went to the kitchen. Gina got up from the sofa and followed her.

"Hi, I'm Gina. And you are?"

"Sherri, last time I checked. You guys got any cookies or anything? You know how a little reefer can give you the munchies?" the girl asked with a dazed expression.

"Reefer?"

"You know, pot. Sammy couldn't score any hard stuff this week, so we're having to settle for the ole mj. What's good to eat in here?"

"I don't know. I don't live here, and I don't believe you do either. Where do you live?"

"Well, I was staying in Silver Spring for a few weeks. Now I'm just sort of hanging out here," the girl said before grabbing a bag of chips and returning to the bedroom.

Gina returned to the living room to find Shirley smoking a cigarette with Gomez curled up next to her.

"So, she's been *staying* in Silver Spring. She apparently doesn't *live* anywhere. Shirley, these people are bad news. You can't rent a room to a bunch of drug addicts. You may land your ass in jail."

"I know, sweetie. I'll kick 'em out soon," Shirley replied, paying more attention to the television than to Gina.

"Shirley!" Gina said in a strong whisper. "There's a drug dealer and his whore in the next room. What are you going to do about it? No . . . don't answer that. I'll tell you what you're going to do. You have till the weekend to ask them to leave, and if you don't, I'll call the police. I'm serious, Shirley."

"All right already! I'll talk to them tomorrow," Shirley replied, still distracted.

Before Gina could respond, there was a thunderous knock on the door.

"Who the fuck is it?" Shirley grumbled, not getting up or taking her eyes off the television.

"Where's Sammy?" a man shouted from behind the door.

Shirley got up and opened the door. There was a tall, sickly-looking man standing on the threshold in a pair of faded jeans and a tank top, which exposed the various scars on his arms.

"Sammy here? We had a deal. Where is he? He better not have dicked me, man!"

"Dicked you?" Shirley asked before yelling toward Sammy's room. "Sammy, you got company."

The man looked more closely inside and saw Gina and Gomez sitting on the sofa. Gina was facing the other way, and Gomez was ignoring the whole scene. He always barked at the pizza delivery man and bit nasty women on Rollerblades, but a derelict looking to score some drugs comes to the door, and he couldn't be bothered.

"Is this a private residence?" the man asked.

With that, Gina whizzed around. "Is this a private residence? No, it's the fucking Drug Depot, and we're a couple of crack whores! Yes, it's a *private* residence," Gina said to the man before getting up and heading for Sammy's bedroom.

She turned the knob. "Sammy, get out here. . . ."

As she opened the door and looked in, she realized the bedroom was empty and the window to the fire escape was open.

"Well, looks like he *dicked* ya after all," Shirley said with a gloating smile after peeking into the bedroom. "Maybe you can catch them if you hurry."

"Regardless of what you do, you come back here, and I'm calling the cops," Gina said to the man before pushing in front of Shirley and slamming the door in his face. She glanced out the peephole to see the man walking away from the apartment and down the hall.

"Shirley, what are we going to do? Sammy can't come back here. That guy could be dangerous, and you don't want to get caught in the cross fire."

"Oh, Gina, you're such a worrywart. He's harmless. Did you see him? Even I could kick his ass."

"Shirley, do you want to go to jail? If the cops come here and find a bunch of drugs, they'll haul you away with the rest of them."

Gina then grabbed the yellow pages and, after flipping for a few seconds, dialed the number for a twenty-four-hour locksmith. After she hung up, she pulled Shirley into Sammy's bedroom.

"Okay, grab anything that's his. We're putting it in the hallway."

"What? Are you crazy?"

"Me? You're renting a room to Cheech and Chong, and you're asking me if I'm crazy? Do you know what kind of things these people are capable of? The locksmith will be here any minute to change the lock, and you're not letting Sammy back in here. You'll stay at my place until he comes to pick up his stuff. Honestly, Shirley, would you for once just think before you act. You're going to end up getting yourself into some serious trouble."

The Wild Side

"A Sprite please," Peter said to the waiter.

"I'm sorry, we don't have Sprite. How about Mountain Dew?"

"No, Mountain Dew is loaded with caffeine. Do you have anything without caffeine?"

How the hell should I know, ya freak? "Afraid not."

"Just water, then," Peter said.

"Oh, go on, Peter. Live on the wild side and have a Coke," Cheryl said, smirking at Peter from across the table.

"No thanks. I've been on the wild side. It's overrated."

"Really? When did skipping your vitamins one day last month constitute the wild side?"

"Shut up."

"Testy, testy. Is Peter in a bad mood today?"

"I'm fine. Just tired."

"Me too. Mondays suck."

God, let's just get through dinner, Peter thought, bored with trying to make small talk with Cheryl. When she asked him to dinner earlier that day, he figured he had to eat anyway, and with any luck he might get laid out of the deal. Truth be known, Cheryl wasn't terribly into the evening with Peter either. Things seemed to be going pretty well with Cooper. She had been out with him again since their lunch, and they had had a really nice time, but she certainly wasn't ready to send Peter packing yet.

"I'm thinking of getting a perm in my hair. What do you think?" Cheryl asked.

Well, I was just lying awake last night, pondering that very thought. . . . "I don't know. Didn't perms sort of go out in the eighties sometime?"

"No, no. They're back in now. Two girls in my office just got perms."

"And they would be from Manassas or Woodbridge?" Peter joked, referring to the far outlying suburbs of D.C. where girls with big hair in TransAms were more commonplace. "I'm not sure what you would look like with your hair any curlier than it is already, but whatever."

"No, you nitwit. A relaxer to straighten my hair more. We call it a perm when we get our hair straightened. I'd be able to wear it much longer, but it would be a lot more work."

"Well, then, go for it. You can go to Dennis."

"That skinny gay white boy hairdresser of Gina's? I don't think so. Are you still going to him? Is he hot for your bod?"

"Yes, I still go to him to get my hair cut, and no, he's not hot for my bod. At least I don't think so. I'm sure he does okay without hitting on straight men."

"So how are Gina and Linda? Are you sure they both aren't lesbians? They spend a hell of a lot of time together."

"Well, when I used to sleep with Gina, she definitely wasn't a lesbian. I can't vouch for now, but I doubt it."

"Must we talk about you sleeping with *her.*"

"You brought it up."

"I did not."

"Whatever. Anyway, I guess they're okay. I haven't seen Linda in a while. She has a new chick though. I met her once. She's a hot Latin girl—looks like Salma Hayek. And Gina was over briefly last night. She wants me to go with her to her high school reunion."

"Are you going?"

"I said I would."

"So, she wants to pass you off as her date so she doesn't look like the dried-up old spinster that she is."

"I don't know, Cheryl. I'll just go and have a few beers and tag along. How bad could it be?"

"Well, I don't think you should go. Let her hire an escort if she wants a date so bad," Cheryl insisted, not at all happy with the idea of Peter escorting Gina anywhere. Gina was bound to look her best, and those kind of formal events always made people horny. Not that she had any right to care. She and Peter agreed that they were just friends—friends who had sex on a regular basis—but just friends nonetheless.

"I really don't mind. It might be kind of fun."

"Sometimes I wonder, Peter, if you want to spend so much time with her, why did you ever break up with her in the first place?"

"It's complicated, Cheryl."

"Complicated? How so?"

"I don't know. I really liked her. She was . . . is so much fun. She's pretty and smart and has a good sense of humor. And you don't fool me, Cheryl. I know you'd take her back as a friend any day."

"Hey, I'm not the one who severed our relationship. She did. But, okay, I do miss our friendship from time to time. But I still don't get it, Peter. If you liked her so much, then why? Why did you end it?"

"I guess . . . I guess I just couldn't deal with her drinking."

"Her drinking? Do you think she has a problem?"

"I don't know. I'm not saying she's an alcoholic or anything. Well, maybe that is what I'm saying. I don't know."

"I never really noticed. Although in college we sure did drink a lot. But so did everyone. It's just what we did."

"I know. It's not like she was a drunk or anything, or that she even got out of control that often. But every once in a while she'd get so drunk, it was like I didn't know who she was anymore. We'd go to a party, and she'd drink so much.

She didn't know when to quit. Then, other times, we'd go to dinner, and she'd have a glass of wine or a beer and that would be it. It didn't make any sense."

"I remember an occasion or two when she didn't have stopping sense. When she kept downing the beers one after the other and, come to think of it, she would freak me out a little sometimes too. But we've all had those moments. Peter, I remember last year, on the Fourth of July, you got so wasted you puked, and that still didn't stop you. You went to the bathroom and heaved and came back and grabbed another beer."

"I guess I shouldn't throw stones, huh. Maybe her drinking wasn't the reason. I don't know. I just couldn't be in a relationship with someone I worried was going to kill herself driving drunk or make a fool of herself at a party."

"Well, far be it from me to defend Gina, but I think you overreacted."

"Maybe. But one morning after Gina and I had stayed up late watching movies on HBO and drinking wine, I woke up, and she had wet the bed. That's when I knew I had to end it."

"She wet the bed?"

"We never talked about it, and I'm not sure if she even knows that I noticed. Anyway, what's done is done. Gina and I are over, as a couple anyway. It's much better for us to be friends. We get to enjoy each other but keep our distance at the same time."

Kind of like you and me, Cheryl thought to herself. "Well, you won't get any argument from me about that."

"Excuse me for a second," Peter said, getting up from the table to go to the bathroom. On the way, he stopped at the pay phone and dialed the number for Cameron Hartman, the analyst at work who snitched on him for misusing the Internet.

"Hello," Cameron said after picking up the phone.

Peter breathed heavily into the phone for a few seconds and hung up. It was about the sixth time he'd done it since she busted him for surfing the Web at work. It seemed kind of stupid to him, but Gina assured him it was only the beginning of Cameron's downfall.

Pizza Pizza

Griffin pulled his Mercedes into the parking lot in front of Myers' Books and Magazines. He climbed out of the car and sauntered into the store as if he owned the place, which he didn't, but hell, he might as well have. He spent more time there than anyone else. He couldn't even remember how long it had been since he started there.

"Hi, Brenda," he said to the small Asian woman behind the counter as he walked by and gave her ass a quick pinch.

"Hey, G-man," she responded with a smile.

Griffin walked past her and headed into the back. He went straight to his office and closed the door. As soon as the door shut behind him, he unbuttoned his shirt and threw it on the floor before reaching under his protruding belly and releasing the buckle on his pants. He kicked off his loafers, let them fling across the room, and slipped off his trousers. There was no need to remove his underwear—he wasn't wearing any. He left his clothes on the floor (knowing Brenda would pick them up later) and walked toward his desk.

Enjoying the comfort and freedom of full nudity, except for the socks he kept on to keep his feet warm, Griffin grabbed some hoagie rolls from his desk drawer, split them open, and started layering it on—salami, ham, bologna, sweet peppers, mayonnaise (lots of mayonnaise), and a few slices of American cheese. It was up to Brenda to keep his refrigerator filled constantly, and if Griffin was ever low on cold cuts, condiments, or his other favorite junk food, she would catch hell. He poured a stack of Doritos on the plate next to the sandwiches, popped the top on a can of sparkling fruit punch, and flicked on the television and VCR that sat on one side of his wraparound desk. He managed to do all of this without having to get up from his chair. He had the room configured so the TV, refrigerator, and stash of junk food were all within arm's length of the chair. He was about to dive into his sandwiches, when he decided he'd really rather have pizza—a nice deep-dish from Domino's with everything. After all, he was *The Big G.* If he wanted pizza, he should get pizza.

Griffin pressed the buzzer on his intercom. "Brenda, can you order me a pizza?"

"Sure, G-man. The usual?"

"Yeah, make it two."

"Okay, I'll bring them in when they get here."

Griffin was fumbling with some videotapes when the pizzas finally arrived. It only took thirty minutes, but it seemed like an eternity to Griffin. He hadn't had anything to eat since the two Egg McMuffins he downed about three hours earlier and was famished. When Brenda brought them in, with the smell of mozzarella and yeasty dough permeating the room, it was all Griffin could do not to pounce on them right away.

"Mmm, smells delicious!" Griffin said like a puppy waiting for his food dish to be filled.

"Sure does," Brenda said as she laid the pizzas on his desk and opened the lids. "You need anything, G-man?" she asked, looking at his naked body. "I stocked the fridge today. I put some Mounds and Snickers in the back behind the pudding."

"Nah, I'll be fine as soon as I get some of these pies in me," Griffin replied, gesturing toward the pizzas. "Help yourself if you want anything," Griffin added only because he knew she would refuse.

"Help myself to *anything?*" she said with a mischievous grin, eyeing the soft tool hanging limp between his legs.

"You little vixen," he said, starting to stiffen just a bit.

She walked behind his chair and put her arms around his neck. She made her way down his floppy chest, letting her hands glide over his nipples, down his hairy, bloated belly, before grasping his hardening penis. She stroked him with one hand and massaged his chest with the other as his tool continued to engorge with blood.

"Oh, yeah, that's it, baby," Griffin said as he took a big bite out of a slice of pizza. He chewed the cheese, and the pepperoni, and the anchovies while Brenda continued to stroke him. As he picked up a handful of Doritos from his sandwich plate and crumpled them on the pizza, Brenda moved around to the front of the chair and got down on her knees. She took him into her mouth while Griffin continued to feast. When tomato sauce dripped from the slice of pizza into Brenda's hair, she lifted her head.

"You think that will do it, G-man?" she said, rising to her feet, grabbing a napkin, and wiping her hair.

"You're the best. I got to take a quick look at one of these films, and I'll be right out."

"Okay, G-man. See you later," Brenda said, reaching for the doorknob. "But don't be too long. I don't want to have to come in here again," she joked as she walked out the door.

"Don't worry. I'll be out in a second," Griffin added before the door closed behind Brenda.

Unsolicited Advice

Peter and Gina swiped their cards under the little infrared light, and Gina signed Shirley in as a guest to the Fitness Results Health Club on Connecticut Avenue, just a few blocks from Gina's apartment. Peter had been pestering Gina to join his gym for some time and had already succeeded in recruiting Linda. As her class reunion approached, Gina figured it couldn't hurt to firm up a little, so she finally agreed to sign on as well. She also thought it would be good for Shirley to get some exercise. With her asthma and constant smoking, Shirley needed all the help she could get. Gina offered to take her as a guest, and if she decided to get serious about going to the gym on a regular basis, Gina agreed to pay for her membership.

Gina was already in her gym clothes, a T-shirt and shorts, so she waited outside the locker room while Shirley changed clothes. Gina was leaning against a railing when one of *them* walked by—one of those women who insisted on wearing makeup to the gym, had obviously just done her hair, and was wearing tight exercise pants and a half top. Gina hated those girls, and several of them had no business in their slinky outfits. They usually weren't exactly fat, but their stomachs were a bit flabby and certainly would have been better off covered with a sweatshirt than a skimpy outfit.

Whore, Gina thought, eyeing the slinky woman. She stood outside the locker room a while longer before Shirley finally emerged.

"What took so long?"

"I had to touch up my makeup and fix my hair. How do I look?" Shirley asked, twirling herself around in spandex and a crop top.

Gina and Shirley scanned the club for Peter. They spotted him on one of a row of about fifteen treadmills, trotting his tight little buns off, and proceeded in his direction. Peter offered to teach Gina and Shirley how to use some of the equipment in the gym and help them get a regular routine started. The last few weeks Gina basically just piddled around from one machine to the next, not really sure if she was doing enough reps, or using the right weight, or even using the machine correctly. Peter told them to warm up on the treadmill for about ten minutes, then he would take them through some of the circuit equipment. Gina got Shirley started on one of the treadmills and showed her how to increase the speed and the incline, although Shirley had no intention of doing either. Then Gina mounted one of the StairMasters. Someone at work had told her that the StairMaster was the best cardio machine for shaping the buttocks, so Gina preferred it to the treadmill.

As Gina exercised, she looked at everyone around her and thought about how laughable it all was—a room full of people bobbing up and down with sweat pouring from their skin, everyone in a desperate struggle to stay thin and youthful. She wasn't sure who looked more ridiculous—the women, with their boobs flinging all over the place and their ponytails shaking back and forth, or the men—strong, buff men, running and running but getting nowhere.

As the trio began to sweat on their respective machines, Shirley grew bored with the CNN coverage on the monitor displayed in the cardio room and decided to commit the most cardinal of health club sins. She wasn't sure how to turn off the treadmill, so she left it running while she hopped off and moved toward the television. Gina and Peter wondered why she was moving closer to the monitor. They knew it couldn't be that she was terribly interested in anything being broadcast on CNN. Shirley was hardly a connoisseur of the latest news stories.

Oblivious to the crowd, she reached up to change the channel. When she last saw the clock it was just after five P.M., which meant *Judge Judy* was on channel five. On her tiptoes, she flicked the channel to *Judge Judy* and returned to her treadmill. She couldn't imagine anyone was interested in CNN and didn't notice when the majority of the crowd scowled at her as she returned to her machine.

Peter and Gina exchanged looks, but neither was willing to give up their momentum to change the station back. As Shirley returned to her stride on the treadmill, an angry woman lifted herself off a stationary bike and stomped over to the television to return it to CNN. She then walked back to her bike, glaring at Shirley as if she had just killed her mother. Baffled by the woman's apparent interest in the news, Shirley took the hint and let it go.

Well, if she couldn't watch *Judge Judy* while she walked aimlessly on the treadmill, she figured she'd strike up a conversation with the woman next to her.

"So people really watch CNN?" she said to the stocky, middle-aged woman to her left.

"I guess," the lady replied, looking straight ahead.

"I prefer *Judge Judy* myself. Do you like her? Isn't she a riot?"

"Never seen her," the woman replied, being rather short with Shirley.

Sensing that the woman wasn't interested in conversation, Shirley shouted down a few treadmills to Peter. "Peter, I'm bored. Can't we do something else?"

Embarrassed, Peter pointed to his watch and mouthed the words "six more minutes."

When they finished on the cardiovascular equipment, Peter took the girls through ten different machines and helped them select the correct weights. He also started a workout card for each of them that listed the name of the machines and the appropriate weight, etc. He advised them to use the card each time they came to the gym to keep track of their progress. Gina was interested in what Peter had to say and tried to pay attention. Shirley was more concerned with checking out the other club members and making snide remarks about some of the women.

With their first real workout behind them, both women were exhausted but somehow felt energized at the same time. As Gina and Shirley retreated to the women's locker room, a stout young woman in tight exercise pants and a half top was putting her hair in a ponytail next to Shirley's locker. As the young woman zipped up her gym bag, Shirley leaned in close to her and whispered, "Can I give you a word of advice?"

"Excuse me?"

"Honey, your pubic mound is far too big for those spandex. I'd stick to shorts and a T-shirt until the pounds start to come off."

"I'll keep that in mind," the girl said, leaving the area with a perplexed look on her face, unsure if Shirley was genuinely trying to be helpful or just mean. Gina could never tell either, so she just pretended not to be with Shirley whenever her mother started spouting off unsolicited advice. A year or two earlier, when Gina introduced her to Tammy, one of the tellers at work, Shirley felt it necessary to provide her opinion on Tammy's slight facial hair problem, which she bleached. The overall effect was a rather thick white mustache above her lip. Shortly after their introduction, Shirley grabbed Tammy's shoulder and, with a look of concern, said, "I have three words for you, Tammy, sweetheart . . . laser hair removal."

Gina and Shirley decided to relax in the sauna before taking a shower and getting ready to go. Gina wrapped a towel around herself while Shirley proceeded to the sauna completely naked. She never was one to be uncomfortable with public nudity, as the poor souls stuck in traffic earlier that summer found out. Once they left the sauna and finished with their showers, Shirley went over to the mirror to comb her hair while Gina continued getting dressed. As Shirley approached the counter, she saw the woman who virtually ignored her on the treadmill. The mildly overweight woman was naked in front of the mirror, drying her hair with the communal hair dryer. Shirley stood nearby and toyed with her hair, waiting patiently for the woman to finish using the dryer. As Shirley parted her hair with the brush, she was disturbed to see the frumpy woman next to her move on from blow-drying her hair, now taking the hair dryer and waving it against her entire body with prolonged emphasis on her underarms. When the lady began whipping the dryer around her pubic region and on to her backside, Shirley had had enough.

"What the fuck are you doing?" Shirley huffed at the culprit. "Can you read? What does that sign say? It says *hair* dryer. Not *genitalia* dryer. How am I supposed to use it now that you've practically had it up your twat?"

The woman was aghast and speechless. She looked at Shirley and trembled a bit in fear of the angry naked woman standing in front of her. She managed a slight "I'm sorry" and scurried into one of the stalls before starting to cry. As she quietly wailed in the stall, Shirley finished combing her hair and walked back to the lockers, annoyed that she wasn't able to use the hair dryer, and not the least bit upset that she'd made a grown woman cry.

Collecting the last of their items, Gina and Shirley went back out to the gym to meet Peter, who was already waiting for them in the lobby. As they walked out, Gina noticed the flier taped to the glass door and mentioned it to Shirley.

"That's the self-defense seminar they're offering tomorrow night. Linda's been pestering me to go. Interested?"

"Will a big, hunky man be teaching it?"

"With any luck."

"Sure. What the hell. I'll go," Shirley replied as they began their brief walk back to the apartment building.

When they got back to Gina and Peter's building, the three of them walked toward the elevators, and Gina pressed the up button. When the door opened, there was a middle-aged black man in a suit and tie standing to one side. As they stepped behind him, Peter crinkled his nose and waved his hand in front of his face. The man had severely overdone it on the cologne, and the elevator reeked of Royal Copenhagen. Even Gina, who usually enjoyed the smell of most cologne, seemed bothered by the overwhelming smell. Shirley looked at Peter, who was trying to nonchalantly hold his breath, and then tapped the man on his shoulder.

"Excuse me, sir. I'm afraid you're wearing too much cologne. Peter, here," she said, gesturing toward Peter, "is allergic to cologne, and it really bothers him. I think he has a touch of asthma too. Don't you, Peter?"

Peter, feeling about five inches tall and not sure how to respond, shook his shoulders and offered an embarrassed smile. He felt humiliated and wished Shirley had just kept quiet.

"Ma'am, I'm afraid you're being quite rude."

"Me? You're the one stinkin' up the place. Why, you could cause Peter to have an allergy attack or something."

As the elevator doors opened, the man looked down at Shirley. "Look, you wretched little woman, I'm sorry your friend here is *afflicted*," he said, giving Peter a quick glare. "But I'll have you know I get compliments on my cologne all the time."

"Of course you do. If you came into a room wearing purple striped pants, you'd get compliments on them too—not because anyone likes them—just because they're so loud and obnoxious, people feel obligated to say something about them," Shirley said to the man as he stepped out of the elevator and the doors shut behind him.

"What an ass," Shirley said.

"He sure was, Shirley," Peter said, sounding a bit flustered by the man's remark as the three of them got off the elevator and headed down the hall.

Hijahh!

"**Y**um. I could put a little butter on him and eat him right up," Shirley said to the women checking out the handsome instructor of their self-defense class at Fitness Results. They sat on the floor of the aerobics room with about a dozen other women. The class was open to men as well, but apparently none felt the need to attend.

"Shirley, would you behave," Gina said, laughing.

"His sidekick isn't too bad either," Linda said, gesturing toward the young lady who was also going to lead the class.

"Okay, let's get started," the hunky male instructor said, trying to quiet the room. "My name is Will, and this is my co-instructor, Carla. We have a lot to accomplish in the next couple of hours. I'd like to start by asking a few of you what you hope to get out of the class. Any volunteers?"

"I was hoping to land me a man," Shirley joked to the group. "Where are you hiding all of them?"

The instructor smiled. "Unfortunately, we don't get a lot of men at these things. It's really a shame. Men are not immune to crime, but it's hard to get us over that macho attitude."

"I just want to feel more secure. I live in the city and want to feel safer when I go out at night," another woman in the crowd said to Will. She had just a tinge of annoyance in her voice—concerned that Shirley might not be taking the class seriously.

Carla stepped in. "Well, that's what we're here for. We are going to teach you how to avoid getting into any compromising situations in the first place, and if you still happen to become a victim of a crime, we want to teach proven techniques for protecting yourself and getting to safety. Have any of you ever been the victim of a crime?"

A few women raised their hands, but Shirley felt it necessary to share her story. "I was assaulted at the QuikMart on Twenty-second Street a few years ago."

"Really?"

"Yes. The security guard thought I was shoplifting. . . ."

That's because you *were* shoplifting, Gina thought to herself as Shirley continued.

"I was walking out of the market, and this big ole guard grabbed my arm and asked to check my pockets. Well, of course I refused, but he wouldn't take no for an answer and tried to pull my coat right off me. So I kicked him in the nuts as hard as I could and ran away."

"Well, that's not exactly the kind of example I was looking for, but kicking a male attacker in the groin can be a very effective self-defense method."

The instructors continued for almost an hour about various ways to avoid crime. They advised the women to walk in groups whenever possible and to always be aware of their surroundings. If they ever felt threatened by someone getting into their space, they should trust their instincts and yell "stop" at the assailant while putting their hands out in front of them.

Following the lecture, Will pulled out two large pads, and he and Carla gave a demonstration of what the women should do in the event of an attack. Will played the attacker, and Carla assumed the victim role. For the most part, the demonstration involved Carla thrusting her hand under Will's chin to distract him and then grabbing his shoulder and kneeing him in the groin. As she shoved her knee into the padding, Carla let out a loud "hijahh!" They ran through the demonstration again and then asked the ladies to divide into two groups and get into separate lines. Will led one line—the one Gina and Shirley made sure they were in—and Carla led the other. Each of the women would take her turn fending off one of the padded instructors. When it was Linda's turn, she gave a solid performance and seemed to impress everyone. Shirley did okay as well but was more concerned about getting close to Will than fending him off as an attacker.

Gina was one of the last to go. Feeling a little ridiculous, she made a weak attempt at going through the motions but couldn't bring herself to yell while she slightly kneed Will in the groin. He asked her to do it again and really yell this time. She tried it again, putting a little more strength into it, and letting out a weak noise, but still feeling too silly to really kick him hard or yell very loudly.

As the class wrapped up, Gina considered approaching Will and trying to get to know him better. After all, he appeared to be only a few years older than she was and wasn't wearing a wedding band. Only problem was, a few of her classmates beat her to it. She looked in his direction and saw two women hovering around him with goofy smiles on their faces. Deciding that she wasn't eager to join his fan club, she caught up with Linda and Shirley so they could walk home together.

As they crossed the street, Gina thought about the two women in the class that flocked toward the instructor after it was over. They were like piranhas moving in for the kill. The two looked so pathetic, standing next to him and smiling, trying to stick their boobs out and suck in their stomachs. What was even worse, the only reason it wasn't Gina standing there doing the same thing was that the two others beat her to it. Was it that bad all over? That attractive young women had to virtually tackle one another as soon as a decent eligible man was within range? The whole spectacle made her think of David. It had been about a month since she had met him at Rio Grande, and she had pretty much given up any hope of hearing from him. She knew it didn't serve any purpose to speculate why he had never called.

She had no way of knowing the real reason, but she couldn't get him off her mind. During their brief encounter something between them just sort of clicked. He seemed like a genuinely nice, normal guy. She felt so ridiculous the day she drove by what may have been his house on her lunch break. The more she thought about it, the more she knew it was in her best interest to just let it go and forget about him. Yes, that's what she needed to do—forget about him. If only she could do that.

Welcome to the
Hood

"Another Saturday Night and I Ain't Got Nobody" was blaring from the car stereo as Gina drove out to Arlington. She bought the cassette a few months earlier. She already had "All by Myself" and David Lee Roth's "I Ain't Got Nobody." They were all good tunes for Saturday nights spent by herself, languishing in loneliness. Generally, Gina would have spent the evening with Linda, but she was on a date with Rosa. Gina hadn't even met Rosa but already had a plethora of ideas about why she didn't like her.

At least it was summer. Not that being alone in the summer didn't suck, but it wasn't nearly as bad as being alone in the winter—the cold drives home from work, waiting for the car heater to warm up, knowing that she had only the dog to cuddle up with when she got home. Gina loved winter and the cold weather when she and Peter were dating. She loved coming in from the cold, heating up some hot chocolate or Irish coffee, and snuggling up with Peter to keep warm. Lately, winter nights were spent curled up under a blanket with the dog, reading *Cosmopolitan* or watching television. Yes, the summer was much easier to get through without a boyfriend.

She had taken a nap earlier that afternoon and was now

full of energy and raring to go. She didn't have anything else to do, so she loaded Gomez into the car and headed back to the town house in Arlington to try to catch a glimpse of David, the guy she'd met at Rio Grande weeks earlier. She couldn't explain it, but she had become infatuated with this guy she had spoken to only briefly and was determined to see him again. He just seemed like a decent guy. His only flaw seemed to be having Griffin as a client. She was considering actually getting out of the car this time, and she figured Gomez was the perfect diversion. She might even be able to get up close to the house and peer in through a window or two. No one was ever suspicious of anyone walking a dog. Any neighbors would just assume she lived down the street and was taking her dog for an evening stroll.

Gina had no clue what she would do if he did turn out to live there. Maybe she would follow him and engineer some sort of reunion—maybe she would *happen* to be at the grocery store at the same time he was, or the bank, or the dry cleaners. . . .

If he saw her again, he was bound to remember how well they had hit it off, not to mention her hair was back to normal. Gina decided that maybe he didn't lose her number. In fact, more and more she was convinced that the yellow locks she was sporting the day she met David were the major reason he hadn't called her.

She pulled into the exclusive community and drove up to the address she'd gotten from the GW alumni directory. She backed up and stopped the car a couple houses down from her stakeout point. After turning off the ignition, she muttered to the dog, "Okay, Gomez, I'm officially beyond pathetic now. My score has blown off the pathetic scale. If he'd wanted to see me again, he would have called."

Gina had been waiting only about ten minutes when the door to the town house opened.

"Oh my God," she whispered. "It's him." David was walking down the steps to his car.

"Gomez, it's him. Oh my God!"

She felt a wave of excitement and sank down in the car,

hoping he wouldn't notice her. Gomez must have felt the excitement as well. He stood up, resting his paws on the door
to see what all the fuss was about.

"Get down," Gina crooned to the dog as David drove
right by them, oblivious to the whole thing. Gina started the
car and caught up with David while keeping a safe distance
until they got to the first traffic light. She stopped about
twelve feet behind him. Then, deciding she would probably
draw more attention to herself that way, she pulled up closer.
Anyway, what were the chances of him recognizing her or
even looking back at her in the first place?

"This is so ridiculous, Gomez. Your owner is a freak. I've
finally lost my mind," Gina said to the dog.

Gomez had lost interest in the chase and was sound
asleep in the passenger seat. Gina continued to follow David,
and it became obvious that he was bound for D.C. When
they finally got into the city, Gina only faintly recognized the
neighborhood. It was somewhere in the dark recesses of
Southeast. The only time she'd been there was when her
hairdresser, Dennis, dragged her to some warehouse party.
The farther they drove, the more run-down houses and
boarded-up buildings Gina saw. She thought she might be in
Anacostia, the section of the city often referred to as the
"other side of the river." Gina had lived in D.C. her whole
life and had heard about Anacostia but had never been there.

David finally pulled his car into a small strip of dilapi-
dated shops and parked in front of one of the remaining open
businesses. The sign out front read "Myers' Books and
Magazines."

Why would anyone come into the hood to buy a book?
Gina wondered as she watched David walk into the store.

There were a few other cars in the parking lot and a fair
amount of traffic coming in and out of the store.

"What the hell, Gomez," Gina said with conviction, and
unbuckled her seat belt. Now was as good a time as any to
"accidentally" bump into him. Not that she had any idea
how she would explain what the hell she was doing in a
seedy-looking bookstore in Southeast D.C.

"Stay, Gomez," she called to the dog, and got out of the car.

When she opened the door to the bookstore, she stopped in utter amazement. The walls were covered from top to bottom with porn magazines, videos, dildos, vibrators, and every other sex toy imaginable. Gina gulped and took a deep breath. She didn't see David anywhere and really didn't want to run into him in the local Smut Hut. As she turned to go, a small Asian woman behind the counter called to her, "You the new actress?"

"Excuse me?" Gina said, wishing she'd just ignored her and walked out.

"Are you the new actress they're waiting for? The cameraman has been waiting for more than an hour."

"Actress? No, I'm not an actress."

"Aw, no use getting cold feet now, blondie. Come on into the studio in the back. David takes great care of all his girls."

"His girls? Does David work here?"

"Of course he works here. He manages all the actors. You shot porn before, sweetie? You seem like a newbee."

"Ah, there's a mistake. I have to go," Gina said, and turned to leave. Just as she was about to walk out, one of the videos on display caught her eye. On the cover was a naked young woman on her back, squeezing her silicone-enhanced breasts. She had her legs pressed against a fat man as he inserted his swollen organ into her with a look of ecstasy on his face. The fat man was naked as well—naked except for a ridiculous baseball cap with "The Big G" printed on the front of it.

Girls Night Out

"I've been working for the bank for almost ten years," Linda said to Rosa. They were seated at a corner table at the Mercury Grill just off trendy Dupont Circle. It was a quaint little restaurant in a converted row house—the perfect place for a romantic evening. This was their second date and they had talked on the phone a few times since they met, hitting it off better than Linda could've dreamed possible.

"Gosh, that's just unimaginable to me. I've had so many jobs since college. I just seem to get antsy and always need a change."

"Well, I guess that keeps things interesting."

"I suppose, but I'm thirty years old now. I think I'm ready for some stability."

"We should be perfect for each other, then. My friend Gina always tells me how stable I am."

"Gina?"

"She's a good friend of mine."

"Did you guys used to date?"

"Oh, no, nothing like that. She's straight as an arrow—your typical I've-got-to-find-a-man-before-I'm-thirty heterosexual woman. I love her dearly, but sometimes I wish she'd realize there's more to life than landing a man."

"How do you know her?" Rosa asked.

"Oh, God. I've known her for years. I met her when I transferred to Tenley High School. My parents had just gotten divorced, and my mother moved my sister and me down here from Pennsylvania. Gina was a godsend. I lived two houses down from her and she saw me walking to school and offered me a ride. We drove in together every morning after that and just hit it off. She introduced me to her friends and showed me around and really made me feel at home. I can't imagine what my last year of high school would have been like if it hadn't been for her."

"Do you have a crush on her?" Rosa asked mischievously.

"No, no, not at all. She's my best friend, and I'd never do anything to screw that up."

"Is she pretty?"

"She's actually quite beautiful, although she has yet to figure it out. She's very insecure."

"Well, enough about her. Let's talk about Linda. Tell me about Linda's world."

"Not much to tell, really."

"What do you like to do?"

"People always ask that, and I'm never sure how to answer. It's not like I lie around the house all day watching television, but I don't really have any specific hobbies. I like movies and wish I had more time to cook."

"Yes, I love to cook too. I worked in a restaurant for a few years in Boston, and I cooked for Renée all the time. I think she put on ten pounds after we moved in together."

"Renée? She's your ex, I take it?"

"I'm sorry. I shouldn't have brought her up."

"That's okay. She was obviously a big part of your life for some time. How long were you together?"

"Just over two years."

"Do you miss her?"

"Of course I miss her. But I know I did the right thing."

"The right thing?"

"It's complicated. Let's not talk about ex-girlfriends to-night. Let's talk about Linda and Rosa."

"Fine by me," Linda said, smiling, trying not to beam too brightly.

The Circus Comes
to Town

Cheryl was fidgeting in the uncomfortable plastic seat. Every time she tried to sit up straight, she would immediately begin to slide forward off the chair. She barely had any legroom at all. She didn't know how Cooper, who stood at just over six feet, looked so comfortable. She hated the stupid Cirque du Soleil. She had been once before a couple of years earlier and swore she'd never go back. But when Cooper called and invited her, she figured it was too early in the relationship to say she didn't want to go. He mentioned that he was taking some clients of his along as well. Apparently, they were interested in investing in the company he worked for. It made Cheryl feel good that he wanted to take her out with his clients and show her off.

The Cirque du Soleil, which was basically a glorified circus, usually came to the D.C. area in the fall, but it was just Cheryl's dumb luck that that year they arrived in McLean, Virginia, one of the ritzier suburbs of D.C., during the summer. She found it very amusing to look around her and see such a culturally diverse crowd attending the show—what with all the white people, and white people, and white people that were there. The circus set up camp in the parking area of the swankiest mall in the D.C. area. The Tysons Galleria boasted a Saks Fifth Avenue, Neiman Marcus, Hugo Boss, Versace Jeans Couture, Cartier—the list went on and on.

Over the years the circus had become the trendy thing for uppity white people to do. It became one of the "see and be seen" events of the season. It was almost laughable to Cheryl to watch people arrive. The same people who pulled up in Mercedes and Jaguars were about to hike across a mall parking lot, pee in Porta Pottis, and sit in a tent to watch little Asian girls contort their bodies in ways nature never intended.

Cooper and his business associates seemed to be enjoying themselves. In fact, most of the people around her appeared to be quite taken with the performances, but Cheryl wondered if they really were. Maybe it was like Shakespeare or the ballet—no one really liked it, but they were all afraid they'd be called boozy white trash if they actually said so.

"Oh, my God!" Cheryl said quietly, pinching her eyes shut as the tiny Asian girls onstage made a human pyramid with some of the top girls actually standing on the lower girls' heads—heads! Not shoulders. Heads! "They're going to break their necks doing that!"

"I know," Cooper said. "Isn't it cool."

"My God!"

"Aw, it's good for them. What doesn't kill you makes you stronger," Cooper joked.

"Yeah, but what if it does kill you?"

"One less person tying up traffic on the beltway. This area is so overpopulated as it is," Cooper joked again.

"Oh, it is not."

"Oh, it isn't? Have you been to the Home Depot on a Saturday?"

"You are terrible, especially for a *Christian*," Cheryl said, throwing his words back at him, laughing, and grabbing hold of his arm as the lights came up for the intermission.

Cooper held her hand as she carefully walked down the steps to the outside of the tent with Cooper's clients following. Negotiating the steep metal steps was a bit of a challenge. Cheryl hadn't been able to find her more conservative black pumps and ended up having to wear a pair of shiny black slingbacks with two-inch heels. One of these days she was going to dig out her apartment and get it organized so she could actually find things.

"So, what do you think? Are you enjoying it?" Cooper asked.

"It's definitely different," Cheryl said.

"Oh, it's spectacular!" Joanna, one of Cooper's guests, cooed with excitement. "Terry and I are going to run to the rest room. Meet you back here?"

"Sure," Cooper said as his guests scurried off to the bathrooms.

"This really isn't your thing, is it?" he said to Cheryl after his clients were out of earshot.

"Well . . . no . . . it's fine."

"Could you be any less enthusiastic?" Cooper said with a smile.

"I'm sorry. It really was a nice idea. I guess I'm just not really into watching people shove their feet behind their neck and spin around."

"It is a little freaky when you think about it. If it wasn't for Joanna and Terry, we could just bag the second half."

"That's okay. You've got your responsibilities."

"Thanks for being a trooper," Cooper said with a grin.

"No problem," Cheryl replied, smiling back at him.

When Joanna and Terry returned, the four of them headed back to their seats and Cheryl suffered through the rest of the show. When it was finally over, Cheryl walked quietly next to Cooper as he discussed business with Joanna and Terry. She was so impressed by his professionalism. He had a way of charming his guests without seeming phony. Watching him wheel and deal was a real turn-on for her. By the time they reached the car, it looked like Cooper had wrapped up the deal and Joanna and Terry would be making a substantial investment in his company.

After they said good night to Cooper's associates, Cooper

and Cheryl walked back to his car, where he unlocked Cheryl's door, opened it for her, and closed it behind her once she was safely inside.

"Thanks so much for coming tonight," Cooper said, climbing into the car.

"Sure. It turned out to be kind of fun actually."

"So what do you want to do now?" Cooper asked.

"I don't care. Maybe we can get a movie or something and go back to my place."

Mentioning the movie made her think of Peter. Suggesting they get a movie was Peter's and Cheryl's code for "why don't we meet for sex." Cheryl would usually run into the Blockbuster on 17th Street and just pick up something quickly on her way to Peter's apartment. She generally wasn't very picky about her selection. Lately, they had skipped the formality of actually watching the movie and just went straight for the action about a half hour into the show. As she thought about how ridiculous it all was, it hit her that she was always the one to travel. Why did she always have to pick up the movie and go to Peter's? He almost never came to her place. Reflecting on her screwed-up relationship with Peter made her all the more happy about whatever was burgeoning with Cooper.

Cheryl and Cooper headed back into the city and sat quietly for most of the ride. They had only been out a few times, but their relationship had reached a point where they were able to be silent around each other without it being completely awkward. They took Route 66 into D.C., crossed the Roosevelt Bridge, and headed toward Dupont Circle.

"Should we go to the Blockbuster on Seventeenth Street?"

"Sure," Cheryl said, wondering if asking him back to her place was such a good idea. The last time they went out, she had invited him up for coffee afterward. It took all the willpower she could muster, but Cheryl didn't even curl up next to him on the sofa while they drank their coffee and watched television. She really liked this guy and, as much as she wanted to, she was going to hold off on getting physical with him. When it did happen, she was going to make sure it meant something for both of them. She had to play it just right. He was one of a few persons she had met who truly seemed to be serious about religion, and there was no way he was going to respect a girl who jumped into bed with him.

After they stopped by the video store and picked up a couple of movies, they went over to Cheryl's apartment and settled in for the evening. Cooper put the tape in the VCR while Cheryl rummaged through the kitchen to find some munchies. She grabbed the last two beers she had in the refrigerator and a fresh bag of pretzels before going back into the living room.

"You want the Miller Lite or the Corona?" she asked Cooper.

"Corona's good," he said.

Cheryl set the beers down on the coffee table, ripped open the bag of pretzels, and sat down on the sofa next to Cooper, fighting the urge to lean in close to him.

Cheryl began to get restless halfway through the movie. How long could she watch Julia Roberts parade around in skimpy shirts and tight jeans, trying to save tainted-drinking-water victims. All she wanted to do was pounce on Cooper and devour him. But she had been down that road before. Her whole relationship with Peter started with a sexual encounter and look where that had gotten her. She was going to take things slow with Cooper—she was going to be wife material.

Poor guy, she thought to herself as she kept her distance on the sofa. He's probably wondering what the hell is going on. Cheryl also thought about how a part of him probably liked it. Men always wanted what they couldn't have, and Cheryl was going to make him want her really bad before she gave it up.

When the movie was finally over, Cooper yawned and got up from the sofa. "Guess I should get going. I've got church in the morning,"

"Okay," Cheryl said, getting up as well and walking over to the door with him.

"I had a good time tonight," she said.

"Yeah, me too," he replied with a grin, and put his hand on her upper arm. "I'll call you tomorrow," he added before leaning in and giving her a kiss.

Cheryl wrapped her arms around him and returned the kiss.

Stay, stay, stay, she thought to herself as he gently lifted his lips from hers.

"Good night," he said before giving her another quick peck on the lips and heading out the door.

God, this morality thing really sucks, Cheryl thought as she closed the door behind him. She didn't know how long she was going to be able to keep up the chastity charade. If she was going to continue being the girl next door with Cooper for any length of time, she was going to need some sort of sexual outlet. Feeling all hot and bothered, she picked up the phone and dialed.

"Hi, Peter. It's me," she said into the phone. "I just rented *Erin Brockovich*. Want to watch it with me?"

The Naked Truth

Gina gasped so loudly several customers turned to see what the unusual noise was.

"You okay, blondie?" the little woman called from behind the counter.

Gina didn't respond. She heard her, but her body was frozen. Her eyes were held tight on the videotape. The cover read "The Big G Strokes the Big G." She continued to stare at the tape in awe. She was speechless. When she finally managed to move her eyes away from the tape, they went straight for the one next to it, titled, "The Big G in the Big Apple," which was next to "The Bodacious Big G." There was a whole series of Big G movies, in which Griffin was the star.

Several seconds passed before Gina was able to put one foot in front of the other and trudge out the door. When she made it to the car, she climbed in and closed the door, only to immediately open it again and hop outside. She looked around her, still in somewhat of a daze, and then proceeded to vomit on the blacktop. She threw up her dinner in one quick heave, and the wave of nausea passed almost as quickly as it came. She pulled a few tissues from her purse, wiped her mouth, and threw them on the pavement before

climbing back in her seat and starting the car. Still completely dumbfounded and unfamiliar with the area of the city
she was in, she wasn't sure of the best way back home. In the
midst of seedy shops, boarded-up buildings, and run-down
homes, she could see the Capitol building in the distance.
She knew if she drove toward the Capitol, she would be able
to get home from there, so she made a left out of the parking
lot.

She had only traveled a couple of blocks when she noticed—where was Gomez? He wasn't in the passenger seat,
and his stubborn little butt wouldn't dream of going in the
backseat. As the revelation hit her, she began calling his
name and looking around the car while still trying to drive.

"Goddamn it, Gomez! Where are you?"

There was no way he could've gotten out of the car. Unless someone took him out. Oh, no! Had she forgotten to
lock the door when she went into the bookstore? Why would
anyone take her dog? What kind of sicko . . . ?

Gina began to panic.

"Gomez. Where are you?" she yelled, starting to cry.
"Oh, my God! What happened to the damn dog?"

She began to get hysterical and started bawling like a
baby. The remaining shred of sense she had left told her to
pull the car over until she calmed down. She was in such a
state, she wasn't aware of her surroundings. There she was—
a young woman in a Honda Civic, alone, late at night, in
what was basically a war zone. After a minute or two she
began to calm down somewhat, and her mind started functioning again. She decided to attack the problem at hand.

Who would take a little dog? Who do you call about a
missing dog? What can the police do? Put an APB out on a
dachshund?

Her complete lack of options made her want to cry again.
What could she do? Gomez could be anywhere in D.C. by
now. Then it hit her. It wasn't likely, but it was possible that
he got out of the car when she jumped out to throw up. She
probably hadn't shut the door. She said a little prayer that she

would get back to the bookstore, and Gomez would be meandering around the parking lot, waiting for her to pick him up. She merged back onto the road and tried to find somewhere to make a U-turn. As she looked for a crossing, she saw two scruffy-looking adolescent boys in super baggy jeans walking along the other side of the road. They could have only been seventeen or eighteen years old. Gina probably wouldn't have given them a second look except that it was a warm night, yet they were wearing jackets and had stocking caps on their heads, and, despite the fact that it was after ten P.M., one of them had sunglasses on. When she gave them a closer look, she noticed a furry little head sticking out of one of their jackets. She recognized that head. She had sneaked Gomez through the lobby of Shirley's building enough times to know exactly what he looked like with his head bobbing up and down, peering outside a jacket.

That was it. She had *had* it. Gina pulled the car onto the median strip and slammed on the brakes. In a fit of frustration and rage, she got out of the car and stomped across the road.

"Give me my dog!" she commanded in a more affirmative tone than she had probably ever used in her life.

"What dog? I ain't got no dog," one of the kids said as Gomez caught sight of Gina and began to squirm and try to get away.

"Give me my dog now, you little derelict, or I'm calling the police!"

"Hey, Simon," the one with sunglasses said to the other with a laugh. "Bitch gonna call the cops. Bitch think some cop gonna come and rescue her dog."

Gina was oblivious to any danger the situation posed and started to approach the two young men further. "I'm going to ask one more time . . ." she said.

"You gonna ask what one more time? If you can suck my big hard cock?" the stockier boy holding Gomez said to Gina. "Yeah, I think the bitch wants to suck my cock," he said again, and jerked Gina by the arm and pulled her closer to him. He held her firmly while Gomez continued to squirm. Gina was too angry and just plain fed up to be scared. With more strength than she knew she had, Gina pulled back her free arm and then, as hard as she could, bashed the young man underneath his chin with the palm of her hand, just like they had taught her in self-defense class. As his head flung back, he freed Gina's arm. She then braced herself by grabbing his shoulder with both hands, screamed at the top of her lungs "Hiiijahhhh" and kneed him in the groin with all her might—and after seeing Griffin on the cover of a porn video and having her dog stolen, boy, did she have some might. The delinquent let out a screech so high, he could have been the only hoodlum in the Vienna Boys Choir. He dropped Gomez and toppled over in pain. Upon seeing this, the other guy put his hands up and said, "I don't want no trouble, lady. He's the one that took your dog."

Gina ignored him and swiftly picked up Gomez and ran back to the car. She got inside and locked the door. Before she drove off, she turned her head and saw that the stockier kid had gotten on his feet and was shouting something at her. She wasn't about to stick around and find out what it was.

When she reached a safer part of town, she pulled over to catch her breath and take in the situation. She thought about Griffin on the cover of a multitude of porno videos, how David did, in fact, manage porn stars, and how she was almost raped and probably murdered. In some warped way the whole thing struck her as a wee bit comical. Maybe it was adrenaline or the shock to her system, but as she reviewed the evening, she began laughing. She looked at Gomez and said with a giggle, "I banged a porno actor." The giggle turned into a chuckle. "No, Gomez, he didn't make *a* porno movie. He's made *tons and tons* of porno movies." By this time she had erupted into hysterical laughter. She swung her head back and howled, "No, Gomez, I don't bang porno *actors*. I only bang porno *stars*. A girl's got to have standards."

When she calmed down, she once again pulled the car back onto the road and headed home.

"There's a few things I don't understand, Gomez. He's grossly overweight and not very attractive. How did he become such a big-time star of X-rated movies? And why the Big G? I've seen his G, and it's hardly big."

Salon Talk

"Nothing crazy today, Dennis. I just want you to blow-dry it out and make it look nice," Gina said to Dennis as she sat down in his chair. It had been a couple of weeks since she beat up the teenage boy to get Gomez back. She was dying to tell someone the whole sordid story but wouldn't dream of it. If she did, she would have to admit to the whole Griffin thing—and how would she explain following David to the porn shop?

"Not even a little trim?"

"No. The big reunion is tonight, and I don't want to risk any mishaps."

"Mishaps? Gina, I don't do mishaps."

"Shall I remind you of the yellow hair I ran around with for a week not too long ago?"

"Oh, that. Well, yellow's a good color for you. You should have thanked me."

"Sorry. Thanks for making me look like a military house-wife whose husband probably cheats on her."

"What time is Linda coming in? Does she still want me to do her hair and makeup?"

"She should be here any minute now."

"Just you and Linda going to the party tonight?"

"No, Linda is taking her new girlfriend, Rosa something-or-other, and Peter is going with me."

"When did Linda get a girlfriend?"

"She met her at the bank about a month ago, and they've been inseparable ever since."

"Do you like her?"

"She's fine, I guess."

"So, in other words, she's a bitch, and you hate her."

"Dennis! I do not. But must they do everything together? I don't think I've seen Linda independent of Rosa since they met."

"Someone's jealous," Dennis said in a catty tone.

"I'm not jealous. I'm happy Linda has someone. It just aggravates me that when people get involved in a relationship, they let it suck up their life."

"But it's nice she found someone. It's so hard, especially for us gay folks. We have such a smaller percentage of the population to choose from."

"Oh, boo-hoo," Gina joked. "It isn't any picnic for us straight girls either."

"Well, at least you can get married, adopt kids, join the military. . . ."

"Join the military? Since when did you want to join the military? I don't think I can picture you in fatigues, running around Kosovo."

"That's for sure. Do they have a Nordstrom in Kosovo? Because if not . . ."

"I don't think so, Dennis. You might have to actually wear synthetic fabrics."

"Heavens no!" Dennis replied, putting his hands over his face in mock horror.

Gina laughed. "Let's just agree that it's tough out there for both of us. What do you say if we're still alone in ten years we buy a house and grow old together? Just like Will and Grace."

"Only if I get to be Grace," Dennis joked. "Although I'd want bigger boobs than she has."

"God, even gay men are obsessed with big breasts. Maybe I should get that boob job after all," Gina sighed.

"Gina, I'm sure you'll find a great guy with your real boobs, and when you do—"

"When! More like *if.*"

"You and me both."

"What? Your love life is in the toilet as well?"

"Gina, I don't even try anymore. Although I did meet this guy the other night, but why would anything work out with him? Nothing ever does."

"Where'd you meet him?"

"JR's. He just walked up to me and introduced himself."

"So what happened?"

"We chatted for a little while and . . . well . . . eventually, I agreed to accompany him home."

"Slut," Gina said, laughing. "So, have you heard from him since?"

"Actually, he called the other day. We're supposed to go out next weekend."

"Well, good for you. I didn't think you went out that much anymore."

"I don't. It's just not worth it. I'm over the whole scene, for now anyway. The clubs don't even start hopping until midnight. First, I have to find a guy who doesn't make me want to puke. Then I have to strike up a conversation with him and pretend I give a shit about where he's from, what he does, his hobbies. . . . By the time we get back to my place and have to chat for a while again, it's almost morning when the sex finally gets started, and then I'm too tired to enjoy it."

"I hear you," Gina said, agreeing with Dennis. "And then you have the losers who want to stay the night."

"I know. I'm like 'Hello! You were okay to fuck, but get the hell out of my bed now that it's over.' "

"Or they want to go to breakfast the next morning," Gina added. "Like I want to eat breakfast with some stranger I met at a bar. It's a bunch of losers out there, Dennis. I've pretty much given up myself."

"Oh, please. You'll find someone."

"I don't know. No one interests me, and if by some remote chance I find someone who does, he isn't interested in me. It's not like I'm asking much. All I want is a fairly interesting, reasonably attractive guy. That's it. That's all I ask . . . well, I guess I'd also prefer he have a decent job and be taller than me and not smoke and be in decent shape and around my age . . . oh, and not have any cats. . . ."

Before Gina could finish her laundry list, the salon receptionist interrupted her. "Ms. Perry, there's a telephone call for you at the front desk."

"It's probably Linda running late," Gina replied, hopping up from the chair.

She reached for the phone. "This is Gina."

"Hey. It's me," Peter said in a hoarse voice on the other end. "Please don't hate me, but I'm sick. I've got the flu or something. I'm not going to be able to go to the reunion tonight."

God! You are such a hypochondriac! Who gets the flu in the middle of the summer? "Oh, no, Peter. Please say you're joking."

"I'm sorry, Gina. You know I'd go if I could."

Gina stood there in silence for a minute before responding. "All right," she said with resignation. "If you're sick, you're sick."

"I'm really sorry."

"Okay, Peter. Feel better," Gina replied, and hung up the phone. She knew better than to try to convince Peter to go out when he wasn't feeling well. With the wind completely out of her sails, she stumbled back to Dennis' chair.

"What's the matter?" Dennis asked. "Someone's not a happy camper."

"That was Peter. He's sick, so I get to go to my reunion alone—like a big, fat loser."

"Alone?"

"Yep. Damn! There must be someone to go with me," Gina said, sitting back down in the chair and catching

Dennis' reflection in the mirror. He was rather attractive with his blond hair and blue eyes and had a harder body than Peter's.

"Hey, Dennis? How about doing one of your best clients a favor?"

Ten Years Later

"This is weird. I actually feel a little nervous," Gina said to the gang as they pulled into the Omni Shoreham Hotel in D.C. Gina was in the front seat with Dennis. Linda and Rosa were in the back with their knees practically in their faces. They hardly had room to move in the backseat of Dennis' car, but they all agreed that his convertible Mustang was the best choice for transportation to the reunion. Gina and Linda both drove Honda Civics. Although not a bad vehicle, a Japanese economy car didn't exactly scream success.

"My stomach has a bit of a knot in it too," Linda replied, beginning to wonder if bringing her girlfriend to the reunion was such a great idea. When she made the decision, she was in one of her Melissa Etheridge moods with that I-don't-care-what-they-think! attitude. Now, when it was time to put up or shut up, she was having some regrets about not just coming alone and dodging boyfriend questions throughout the night.

Dennis handed the keys to the valet, and he and the girls got out of the car.

"You ready?" Gina smiled and turned to Linda. Linda just returned the smile, and they walked into the lobby. The official start time was about forty-five minutes earlier, but they didn't dare risk arriving early. How awful it might be to arrive before most of the guests got there. They might have ended up in the ballroom with two other early birds whose names they barely knew, and have to make forced conversation.

The girls waited while Dennis looked on the daily events schedule to see what ballroom the reunion was in. He asked a bellman where the Capitol Room was and led his three female companions to the lower level of the hotel. As they strode past the rest rooms, Gina suggested one last check to make sure everything looked perfect. Rosa declined and waited outside the powder room with Dennis. At Gina's suggestion, Dennis was wearing a standard charcoal-gray suit he usually reserved for funerals and Catholic weddings. He had a closet full of stylish double-breasted and three-button suits, not to mention a plethora of cashmere sport coats and linen slacks, but Gina didn't want him looking too stylish. She was trying to reduce the gay factor as much as possible.

In the bathroom, Gina lightly brushed her hair with her fingers while Linda just stood and watched her. Gina was pleased with her overall look. Dennis had done a great job with her hair and even applied her makeup for her. She knew all the women would be in black, especially the ones who'd ballooned since high school, so she chose a simple red dress she picked up at Neiman Marcus in Chevy Chase—a store she hadn't been into in years. She couldn't afford the prices there. But she and Linda didn't have any luck the day they went shopping at Pentagon City, so Gina decided to go even more upscale. Besides, it was for something special.

She spotted the dress almost as soon as she walked in the store. The dress itself was not overly formal, but the black belt with sequins on just the buckle gave it a flair of elegance and style. She saw the price when she first pulled it off the rack but chose to ignore it and try it on anyway. When she went in the dressing room and slipped it on, one look in the mirror and she knew she had to have it. It fit her perfectly and fell just above her knees, allowing her to show a little leg without looking like an Ally McBeal wanna be. The red was a great contrast to her blond hair and gave her face a bit of a rosy shade. A few minutes later she opened up a Neiman Marcus account and charged the nine-hundred-dollar dress.

Looking in the mirror in the hotel rest room, Gina knew it was worth every penny, even if she was going to have to live in the dark and eat cat food for a few months to pay for it. Besides, she put on extra deodorant and was wearing a slip just in case she decided to pull a Shirley and return the dress the next day. A few years earlier, Shirley got her hands on one of those little machines that click out plastic threads and hold the price tags onto garments. She could easily put the tags back on the dress for Gina. Although it meant Gina would have to swallow her pride and ask for help with something she constantly reprimanded Shirley for doing.

Linda was looking pretty good herself. Gina had convinced Linda to let Dennis do her up as well. A few weeks earlier, Gina persuaded her to buy a snazzy black pantsuit with gold buttons from Bloomingdale's. The price of Linda's outfit didn't compare to Gina's purchase, but it was still quite a stretch for Linda to spend as much as she had on one outfit.

"Okay, let's do it," Gina called to Dennis and Rosa as she and Linda emerged from the bathroom. They continued down the hall and approached the reception table where two perky young ladies were sitting.

"Gina Perry and Linda Collins!" the young lady to the left announced with a toothy smile. "How are you?" she added as she fumbled through the name tags strewn all over the table. "One for you, Gina, and here's yours, Linda."

"Oh, no! They have our senior pictures on them," Gina groaned, somewhat concerned about pinning the name tag to her nine-hundred-dollar dress. "Nice to see you again," Gina said to the women behind the table, although she had no idea who either of them were. Linda nodded in agreement with Gina, and they proceeded into the ballroom with Dennis and Rosa following.

"Oh, God . . . there's Kathy Wolwine," Gina whispered to Linda.

"Gina!" Kathy screamed, and trotted toward her. She gave Gina a big hug and then smiled at Linda and hugged her too. "Girlfriend, you got it goin' on! Look at you . . . like a super-model," she crooned to Gina, and then with somewhat less enthusiasm turned back to Linda. "And, Linda, you haven't aged a bit. You look great."

"You're not doing so bad yourself. How are you?"

"Oh, you know. I'm performing anywhere I can."

There was one in every class—the girl who thought she could sing and dance and act and look pretty—the girl who was going to become a star—the girl who usually ended up in a mouse suit at Busch Gardens. In Gina's class, that girl was Kathy Wolwine. She was in every school play and de-manded that she have solo performances when the school choir sang at various events. Unfortunately for her (and for those who had to listen to her), she had a high-pitched, nasal voice and an uncanny ability to make the latest pop tunes sound like opera—bad opera.

"Really. We're all still waiting to see your name in lights," Gina said with a smile.

"You never know. I'm doing community theater and just signed with a modeling agency."

"That's great."

"It's called Spectra Models. They're in Baltimore," Kathy replied with a proud smile. "Oh, look. I need to go say hi to Laura. Let's chat some more later."

After Kathy was out of earshot, Linda quietly said to Gina, "A model—with those hips? What does she model? Muumuus?"

"Oh, please, I've heard of Spectra Models. They're one of those agencies that send fat ladies to the mall to scout so-called *potential* models. They give you their business card and tell you that you have a great look and could have a bright future as a model. Then, when you go to meet with the agency, you learn that you have to pay *them* for some ridicu-lous training that supposedly prepares you for a modeling career. I think it's around a thousand bucks to learn how to walk down a runway. Shame she got suckered into it."

"How do you know so much about it?"

"I don't know. I saw a report on the news or something," Gina said, starting to blush.

As the evening progressed, Gina and Linda perused the room and caught up with old classmates while Dennis and Rosa sat at a table and discussed all the things a gay man and a lesbian have in common. Twenty seconds later they began to get antsy and wished their respective dates would return.

Eventually, the girls returned to the table. Gina sat next to Dennis and Linda next to Rosa. Gina was soon busy pointing out various class members she suspected were gay to see what Dennis thought of them. She was always amazed at his ability to sniff out other homosexuals before he even spoke to them. They might see a guy who looked perfectly heterosexual to Gina, and Dennis would confidently assess that he was gay—and he was always right. Gina tried to get Dennis to let her in on the clues, but he claimed there were no definite clues. It was just a feeling . . . a radar. Gina wasn't sure if he was telling the truth or not. For all she knew, there could've been some universal identifying gay symbol or gesture homosexuals were forbidden to share with straight folks.

As they conversed about various classmates, Jenny Parks showed up at their table.

"Dennis! What are you doing here?"

"Hi, Jenny. I'm here with a friend," Dennis replied, gesturing toward Gina.

"Gina Perry! How are you? How do you know Dennis?"

"We've been friends for a while."

"Really, well, I've been one of Dennis's clients for years. He's the best colorist in town."

Oh, shit, Gina thought. If Jenny's mouth was anywhere near as big as it was in high school, it would be mere minutes before the entire room knew Gina was at her high school reunion with her gay hairdresser.

"You didn't say anything about a reunion this morning when I was doing your hair," Dennis said to Jenny.

"Yes, I did. I must have mentioned it a hundred times."

God, I've got to actually start listening to these broads, Dennis thought.

"A hundred times, Dennis," Gina said. "She must have mentioned it a *hundred* times, and you didn't *tell* me. You little *devil* you," Gina continued, starting to feel flushed. She could see Jenny plotting behind her phony smile—plotting to matter-of-factly tell Gina's entire senior class that she couldn't get a date to the party. She must have been aching to get away from the table and start spreading the news.

"Well, it's so nice to see you guys. What a hoot to run into my hairdresser at my reunion. Listen, I've got to mosey, but let's catch up later."

"Sure," Gina replied, and turned to Dennis. "Great, just great! Now she knows I'm here with a gay guy."

"Watch it, Gina, or you'll be here with *no* guy."

"I'm sorry, Dennis. I know you're doing me a favor, but I just had a plan for how this evening would go, and this wasn't part of it."

"Why do you even care what these people think? You never see any of them."

"You know what, Dennis? I really don't know," Gina replied.

"Think about it, Gina. Everyone here is so caught up in themselves, they're all worrying about how *they're* being perceived. Believe me, no one in here is concerned in the slightest with you. And if they look outside their self-obsessed little worlds for a moment or two to pay you any attention, they'd see a stunning young woman with beautiful blond hair . . . thanks to me, of course, and killer legs that rival Tina Turner's," Dennis said before coyly adding, "and they most certainly would wish their date was half as handsome as yours."

Gina let herself smile just slightly. "You're sweet, Dennis."

"Gina, you're a beautiful girl with everything going for you. If only you weren't so thickheaded and could see that."

Gina thought about what Dennis said for a moment—about her being a beautiful girl and having killer legs. Part of her did believe she was beautiful, but part of her also believed she just plain wasn't. Tonight, the "wasn't" part of her was winning out.

I only wish you were right, Gina thought to herself, looking at Dennis. God, how I wish you were right.

Afflicted

"God, would you hurry up, I'm starving," Cheryl said to Peter as he finished putting his shoes on. Cooper was out of town on business and Cheryl hadn't seen Peter in a couple of weeks. She didn't have anything else to do, so she called Peter to see if he wanted to grab dinner with her.

"You know, Gina would absolutely kill me if she knew I was going out tonight."

"What's the big deal?"

"I was supposed to go with her to her reunion tonight, but I just felt sick this morning. I was really feeling bad when I called her to cancel."

"So now you're feeling better, and you're going to grab a bite to eat. Besides, who's going to tell her?" Cheryl said as they walked out of the apartment.

Cheryl needed to swing by her office in Falls Church, so they headed out to Virginia and planned on grabbing a quick dinner there. After Cheryl retrieved the file she needed, they drove around Falls Church, trying to find somewhere to eat.

"There's a Ruby Tuesday's. They have a good salad bar," Cheryl said.

"Salad bar? Cheryl, you know I don't like salad bars. All those people and their germs, cavorting over communal food dishes. I don't think so. I'm still having flashbacks to that awful buffet we went to with Shirley last month."

"How about that place?" Cheryl said, pointing toward a small, nondescript restaurant in a little strip mall along the highway. "Look, the sign says they've been in business for thirty years. It must be good."

"All right, we can give it a shot."

They pulled into the parking lot, hopped out of the car, and headed toward the restaurant. When they were through the doorway, a heavyset woman gave them a curious look.

"May I help you?" she asked the couple as if they were lost or in the wrong place.

"Hi. Two for nonsmoking please."

The woman raised her eyebrows, grabbed a couple of menus, and gestured for Peter and Cheryl to follow her.

As they strode past the tables, Cheryl couldn't help but feel that people, all of whom were white, were staring at her. Her radar was beeping, signaling that she was in unfriendly territory. As a black woman, she developed a sort of sixth sense about when she was in racist company. Sometimes it was off, but usually it was pretty accurate.

The hostess sat them at a small table in the back, laid the menus in front of them, and left without saying a word.

"For heaven's sake," Peter said to Cheryl as they took their seats.

"What?" Cheryl asked.

Peter pointed his eyes toward the wall behind Cheryl. She turned around to see a gigantic confederate flag virtually covering the entire wall.

"Let's go, Cheryl. I doubt we're welcome here," Peter said, getting up to leave.

"Sit your ass down. We're not going anywhere. That's exactly what they want us to do."

"I didn't know places like this still existed, at least not around here."

"Naive little white boy," Cheryl said, opening her menu.

"Everyone is looking at us, Cheryl. Are you sure you want to stay?"

"Just ignore them, Peter, ya big baby. It's a free country. We can eat wherever we want," Cheryl replied, trying to put up a brave front. She was actually quite nervous herself. She looked at the wall next to them and viewed the plethora of framed photographs. Apparently, they were taken at special events at the restaurant and were mostly of customers—not a single person of color in the bunch. A mature waitress came and took their drink order and was actually quite friendly. As the couple continued to review the menu, a large man with a heavy beard and tight flannel shirt strode past their table on the way to the rest room. As he walked by, he mumbled under his breath, "Someone's here who's not supposed to be."

"I'm sorry, did you say something?" Cheryl said loudly, although she heard him clearly the first time.

"Cheryl, what are you doing?" Peter asked.

"The gentleman said something as he walked by. I just wanted to be sure I heard him correctly."

"I said," the bearded man continued, turning around, "that someone is here who's not supposed to be."

"And who might that be?" Cheryl asked while Peter gave her a look that pleaded for her to just let the whole thing go.

"Look, lady, it's nothing personal, but is it really too much to ask to have one place—one damn place, where we can be with our own kind?"

"If you want to be with your own kind, wouldn't you be more comfortable in a zoo?"

"Miss, I'm afraid you're going to have to leave," the hostess said sharply to Cheryl before the man could reply.

"Me?"

"Yes, you. Now, get on out of here before it gets ugly. You have no business here in the first place."

"Come on, Cheryl. Let's go," Peter said as the whole restaurant watched. Peter tugged on Cheryl's arm, coercing her to follow him. Steaming, Cheryl started to walk out with Peter.

As they passed the last few tables, the man called to Peter.

"Yeah, take your colored girlfriend out of here. Dating a colored girl—you must be *afflicted* or something."

Peter probably would have ignored him and kept walking if it weren't for the racist man's fatal choice of words. Every other word the man had spoken became a blur, and the word "afflicted" stung Peter's ears. All of a sudden he was thirteen again, and Gus was making bogus wheezing noises and laughing at him.

From what seemed like out of nowhere, Peter swung around and lunged straight for the bearded man. Something inside Peter had just snapped, and he rammed into the stout man, throwing him against the wall. Peter had caught him totally off guard, and the bigot was pinned against the wall as Peter repeatedly wailed on him. Peter hit him in the face, in the chest, the shoulder—anywhere his spiraling arms could make contact.

"Get him off of me," the man shouted to the crowd. "Get him off of me!"

He tried to push Peter off and get in a few punches of his own, but it was pointless. Peter was in his own world and struck the man with such force and speed that his opponent didn't stand a chance. When two of the customers were able to pull Peter off the bloody and swollen man, Peter finally regained his senses and realized what he had done. The two men pulled him by both arms through the restaurant and out the door with Cheryl following. They dropped him outside without a word.

"Come on," Cheryl said. "Let's go before they call the police."

As they got into the vehicle, Cheryl asked with a comforting smile, "What the hell happened, Peter?"

"I don't know. He just pissed me off, I guess," Peter said, still a little dazed.

"When you started hitting him, my first instinct was to yell 'Stop,' " Cheryl said. "But then I realized you were kicking his ass, so I just enjoyed it. It was such a spectacle, Peter. I wouldn't believe it if I hadn't seen it myself."

"I did kick his ass, didn't I?" Peter said, feeling his eyes start to water. He felt like a huge chip had been lifted off his shoulder. He felt lighter, freer—he felt proud of himself. Sitting in the car with Cheryl at the wheel, he smiled, and he laughed, but mostly he wept. He wept like a baby and didn't even care that Cheryl saw him.

"Are you okay?" she asked.

"I'm fine. Actually, I'm pretty damn fine," Peter responded, trying to wipe the tears from his eyes. "He looked pretty bad, didn't he?"

"I think they might have to take him to the hospital."

"I guess you might say he's *afflicted?*" Peter said.

"I guess," Cheryl said. "I guess you would."

A Ride Home

"I need another drink. You guys want anything from the bar?" Gina asked the gang, figuring the evening was a wash. She'd have another drink or two and then just go home and try to forget about it.

"Nothing for me," Dennis said. Linda and Rosa declined the offer as well.

Gina got up from the table and made her way through a maze of familiar faces. Several guests smiled at her and almost attempted to engage her in conversation, but she just ignored them. The night was now a disaster. She was probably the laughingstock of the party. The only thing worse than coming to your reunion without a date was coming with a pretend date and getting busted. She was lost in thought when she ran into Karl Mullins.

"Oh, excuse me . . . ?"

"I'm sorry. I wasn't paying attention to where I was going," Gina said to Karl.

"Don't be sorry. I'm going to be honest with you. I can't quite remember your name, and I can't imagine how I could forget someone as radiant as you," Karl said, tilting Gina's name tag up. "Gina Perry. Oh, yes. Now I remember. Thank God for name tags, huh?"

"Well, with any luck, I've improved with age. Honestly,

you look familiar to me also, but I can't quite place the name," Gina lied. She knew damn well who he was. She had only yearned for him for most of her high school career. He played varsity football and was salutatorian of their graduating class. He had a solid build, light brown hair, big brown eyes, and was just over six feet tall.

"Karl . . . Karl Mullins."

"That's right. Karl."

"Were you going to the bar?"

"Yes, I was. You?" Gina asked.

"I am now."

Gina smiled as Karl followed her to the bar. As they stood in line, they continued to catch up.

"So what have you been up to?" Gina asked.

"I live in D.C. . . . Georgetown . . . just bought a house on P Street. I'm a lawyer with a firm downtown. They work me to death, but I enjoy it for the most part. How about you? What have you been doing for the last ten years?"

"Gosh. Where to begin? I went to college at American University. I live over near Dupont Circle."

"What kind of work do you do?"

"I'm in management with Premier Bank of Arlington."

"A banker, eh? That's cool. So, did you come with anyone?"

"Yes, I'm here with a friend. You?"

"No, I came solo. I just finished law school last year and I've only been back in town about six months. It's hard to meet people in this city."

Tell me about it! "Oh, not at all. I'd be glad to introduce you around."

"I'd like that."

When they finally got their drinks from the bartender, Karl asked, "Are you much of a dancer?"

"I guess. I dance some."

"Well?" Karl asked, pointing toward the dance floor.

"Lead the way."

Eighties music seemed to be the theme of the evening and Debbie Gibson's "Shake Your Love" was blaring from the speakers. They laid their drinks on one of the speakers and hit the dance floor, with Gina trying not to stare at Karl. He was so good-looking, and he could actually dance. Good-looking and rhythm—how often did that happen? They stayed on the dance floor through Def Leppard's "Pour Some Sugar on Me" and Janet Jackson's "Nasty." Eventually, the music slowed as the deejay played the New Kids on the Block's "I'll Be Loving You Forever." There was an awkward silence when the song came on until Karl raised his shoulders, smiled, and gave her a look that said "interested?" She was definitely willing and met him in the middle, putting her arms around his neck.

They swayed to the music as the dance floor got more and more crowded. All the guys who wouldn't dream of dancing to an upbeat song were usually willing to suffer through a slow tune with their significant others. As space tightened, it gave Gina and Karl an excuse to move closer together. By this time, Gina's mouth was dry, and her heart was slightly palpitating. Karl felt warm and strong and just plain good. When the song ended, they slowly pulled apart and exchanged smiles. At this point Linda, waving her hands from the table, caught Gina's attention. She had forgotten all about Linda and the rest of the group.

"You remember Linda . . . Linda Collins? We came together," Gina said, walking toward the table and gesturing at Karl to follow.

"Hey, Linda. Remember Karl?"

"Yes. Hi, Karl," Linda replied, offering Karl a distracted smile. She then looked back at Gina. "Gina, Rosa's really sick."

"What's wrong with her?"

"She just got nauseous all of a sudden. Dennis is with her now. They're outside. We've got to take her home."

"Take her home?"

"Well, we can't have her spend the evening outside puking in the courtyard. Why don't Dennis and I take her home, and we'll come back and get you. I know this night means a lot to you."

"No, not at all," Gina said, embarrassed by Linda's comment. "It's not a big deal."

"If you want to stay, Gina. I can take you home," Karl interjected.

Yes! Yes! Yes! "Oh, I don't want to trouble you."

"Believe me. It's no trouble."

"Are you sure?"

"It's settled, Linda. I'll take Gina home."

"Okay. Have fun, kiddies." Linda smiled and winked at Gina before walking out into the hallway.

Opening the Candy Store

"That's Gomez, my dog. He's a little monster," Gina said in reference to the barking coming from the other side of her apartment door. Before Gina got her key in the door, Gomez would somehow always know she was home and immediately start barking in anticipation of being let out of the kitchen.

"A dog? What kind?" Karl asked, following Gina into the apartment.

"He's a miniature dachshund. He's perpetually in trouble. Couldn't behave himself to save his life."

"He's so cute," Karl said, watching Gomez run in circles around his feet.

"Thanks. Listen, why don't you have a seat and make yourself at home while I run him outside for a walk," Gina suggested to Karl while she attached the leash to Gomez's collar. She wasn't thrilled with the idea of leaving him alone in her apartment, but he was a former classmate, and scooping poop wasn't exactly the way she wanted Karl to see her at that moment.

When Gina got back inside with the dog, Karl was sitting on the sofa with the television on.

"Can I get you something to drink?" she asked, passing him on her way to the kitchen.

"No thanks. I'm fine."

"Okay," Gina replied, filling a glass with water for herself and replenishing Gomez's water dish. She had been rather parched the entire evening, and sipping the cold water provided some relief. The night had gone splendidly. So she was at her reunion with her gay hairdresser, and everyone probably knew it. Everyone also watched her hit it off with Karl Mullins and leave the party with him.

How about them apples, Gina thought to herself before returning to the living room.

She sat down next to him on the sofa but kept a slight buffer zone between the two of them. She wasn't sure how to handle the situation. She wanted to sleep with him but knew it was probably in her best interest not to. Guys always had more respect for girls who waited awhile before "opening the candy store." She looked down at the floor and saw that Karl had taken his shoes off—a sure sign he was getting comfortable.

"He's so funny," Karl said, gesturing toward Gomez, who was now lying on the chair opposite them. "I think he's lost interest in me."

"He does that. When guests first walk in the door he's all over them, but the novelty wears off really fast, and then he basically ignores you."

"Well, as long as his owner hasn't lost interest in me," Karl said, moving in closer and pecking Gina on the lips. Gina just smiled and gazed at him. He kissed her again and moved his body closer to her. He wrapped his arms around her waist and pressed his chest against her.

Gina melted and took a deep breath as he kissed her neck. Any thoughts of being a good girl that evening were history. Well, Gina thought. Guess the candy store's open for business.

Karl continued to passionately tongue her neck as he reached for the zipper to her dress. Gina held tightly on to his back as he slowly maneuvered the zipper down. With her dress now loose on her shoulders, she flipped up from underneath him and sat on his lap to more easily unbutton his shirt. As she loosened the buttons, an exquisitely cut chest and solid abs emerged from the fabric. Gina massaged his chest firmly with her hands until Karl decided to help her get out of the dress. She stood up and let the dress flow to the floor as Karl watched her. He pulled her toward him and shifted Gina onto her back. He tossed his shirt off and then reached up under her slip and delicately pulled her stockings down to her feet and off onto the floor. As he started to lie back on top of her, Gina unbuckled his belt and loosened his pants. Karl then finished the job himself and pulled his pants off and laid them over the sofa arm. He lifted Gina's slip up above her breasts and pressed his nearly naked body against her. He firmly grabbed her buttocks and teased her mouth with his tongue. Gina was enmeshed in pure pleasure until she reached her hand down into his boxers and felt a small, flaccid penis.

This was totally new to her. At this stage of the game, all the guys she'd ever been with were hard as a rock. She couldn't recall ever feeling a limp dick *before* sex. She played around with his soft member for a few minutes to no avail, somewhat baffled by the circumstances. Finally, Karl broke away from her and with a look of frustration said, "I don't know what's the matter. This has never happened before."

"It's okay. It happens to guys all the time," Gina lied. It wasn't okay, and she had never known it to happen before.

"Well, this is a first for me. But it has nothing to do with you."

Me? Who said anything about it having to do with me? "You just need to relax," Gina said, pulling her slip back down and feeling a little ridiculous.

"I guess you're right, and I know something else that might help. Please don't take this the wrong way. But did you have onions for dinner or something?"

"What? No. Why?"

"I'm sorry. God . . . there's no polite way to say this . . . but your breath is just sort of foul. I think that's why I'm not performing up to speed."

"Oh, my God!" Gina said, putting her hand to her mouth as she scurried toward the bathroom. She frantically brushed her teeth and rinsed with some mouthwash before returning to the living room.

"God, that is so embarrassing. All this time I had bad breath. I could just die."

"No, really, it wasn't that bad. I'm just supersensitive to smells. It's more me than you. Anyway, where were we?" Karl asked before leaning in closer to her and giving her a kiss. He then pulled away and said, "You know what, Gina? I just don't think this is going to work."

"Oh?"

"It's just not happening for me. You're very nice and . . . oh, nothing."

"No . . . what? What is it?"

"I don't know. I usually do okay with women with small breasts, but . . . oh, I don't know. I think I just need to go," Karl said, grabbing his pants and beginning to get dressed. "I'm really sorry."

Gina was mortified, and she wasn't about to beg him to stay. "Small breasts? Funny thing for a guy with a small dick to say."

"Oh, *that* was necessary. I'm outta here," Karl snapped, pulling his shirt off the floor and heading for the door without bothering to put it on.

"Don't let the door hit ya in—" Gina couldn't finish before the door shut behind Karl. She sat there, staring at the door, upset and confused. She was totally stunned, and all of a sudden her mind flashed to that fateful night with Griffin. She thought about how she had felt that night and how disgusted she was with Griffin and with herself. She had just wanted to kick him out before the sex was even over. God! Was that how Karl felt about her? Did he take her home and suddenly decide he was too repulsed to have sex with her?

Was she that horrible that a guy had to run out on her right in the middle of a heated encounter? Dennis had just told her how beautiful she was a few hours earlier. How was she supposed to believe that? She felt like Mia Farrow in *Rosemary's Baby*. Of all the billions of people on the planet, why had the devil picked her to torture?

As Gina sat upstairs, hopelessly trying to understand what had just happened, Karl slipped his shirt on in the elevator and walked out of the lobby. As soon as he was outside the building, a beat-up Ford Escort drove up next to him, and the driver rolled the window down.

"Get in. How did it go?" called a short lesbian with a bad perm from inside the car.

"Exactly according to plan," Karl responded.

"Move over, Silky," Annie continued, picking up the cat and putting her in the backseat to make room for Karl.

The Truth Comes
Out

_D_ennis had dropped Linda and Rosa off a few hours earlier. The couple were lying on the sofa, watching
Saturday Night Live. Rosa was feeling much better.

"Thanks for including me tonight. It meant a lot to me,"
Rosa said.

"I'm glad you went. I had a good time," Linda said, glad
to be home. She really had had no burning desire to go to the
reunion in the first place, but she knew she'd catch hell from
Gina if she didn't go. Linda was generally content to stay at
home and watch television or curl up with a good book.

This is where she was happiest—lying on the sofa with
Rosa, totally relaxed. It was nice to leave events like her reunion with someone—to have someone to talk about the
event with on the way home, and someone to snuggle up
with after it was all over. She and Gina used to talk about
how you could always tell who was single at social events.
The single people were always the last to leave. The married
couples might show up and make an appearance, but they
would only stay briefly because they had someone to go
home with. Half the time the janitor had to sweep the single
people out with the trash to get them to go home.

Watching television with Rosa, Linda thought about how

lucky she was. She didn't have to stay late at parties anymore to avoid going home to an empty apartment. Things really seemed to be clicking with Rosa, and Linda was starting to think they might really have a future together.

"I don't think Gina likes me very much," Rosa said.

"Don't be silly. She's just lonely and worries that I won't have time for her. She'd never admit it though."

"She must really hate me for prompting you to leave the party early."

"Actually, I don't think so. You probably scored some points. It gave her the opportunity to get a ride home with Karl Mullins."

"Do you think there was something going on there?"

"I'm sure if Gina had anything to say about it, there was. I'll call her in the morning and get the dirt. Maybe we can meet her for brunch if you're feeling up to it."

"I'm sure I'll be fine."

"Have you been to the doctor? You've been under the weather for a while now."

"Yes, I've been to the doctor. I go once a month. That's what we pregnant women do."

"Excuse me?"

"I'm sorry to blurt it out like that, but I've been trying to figure out a way to tell you for a while."

"How long have you known?"

"I found out just before I moved here."

"Well . . . care to splain, Lucy?"

"God, where to begin? You know Renée and I were together for quite some time before we broke up."

"Well, unless Renée sprouted testicles, you're losing me here."

"Last year we came to a decision together. We decided we wanted to start a family. Well, with nature's limitations, we certainly couldn't do it on our own, so we started to investigate the whole sperm bank thing. We decided that I would carry the baby. Needless to say, I went to the sperm bank numerous times but never got pregnant."

"Well, you obviously got pregnant at some point."

"Yes, I did. When it finally took, and I got the results, I was so excited I ran home in the middle of the day to tell Renée. That's when I met Bianca. She was the cleaning lady I had hired a few months earlier. Even though I hired her and wrote the checks, I'd never met her. Renée was always there to let her in. Anyway, I walked in the door, eager to tell Renée the news, and found her in her Victoria's Secret best. I saw Bianca's cleaning basket on the floor and asked Renée what was going on. She said she forgot the cleaning lady was coming and hadn't bothered to get dressed. 'So, you changed from your nightshirt to a skimpy teddy instead?' I asked. I heard some clunking in the bathroom and went to open the door. Bianca was scrubbing the bathtub. She was completely nude.''

"Nude?"

" 'Ah . . . may I help you,' I asked her, and she said, 'No, thank you, ma'am,' and continued cleaning the tub as if the whole scene were perfectly normal. She tried to tell me that she didn't want to get her clothes wet while she cleaned the tub, so she just took them off. She had a harder time explaining why she had taken them off in the living room and scattered them all over the place."

"Oh, my God."

"Yes, the whole thing was so ridiculous. I told Renée she had a few days to find another place to live, and I went and stayed with my parents for a while. When I got back, she was gone, and I haven't seen or heard from her since."

"Don't you think you should tell her about the baby?"

"Hell no! She sealed her fate the moment she banged the cleaning lady. She has no claim to this baby. I'm sorry I didn't tell you sooner, Linda. It just isn't a comfortable thing to talk about."

"Well, I'm glad you did."

"So, what do you think?"

"Gosh, I don't know what to say. It's quite a surprise."

"Do you still want to see me?"

"Of course I still want to see you," Linda said, not really knowing if she did or not.

"Oh, thank God. I really like you, Linda, and don't want to lose you."

"You won't. Unless, of course, you hire me a sexy lesbian cleaning lady," Linda joked, trying to sound like she wasn't bothered by Rosa's news. Couldn't Rosa have prepared her a little? She just blurted out the news of her pregnancy like she was announcing the weather forecast.

I should have known it was too good to be true, Linda thought about her relationship with Rosa. Something had to come along and complicate it. What was she going to do with a pregnant girlfriend? If she had known Rosa was pregnant from the beginning, she never would have agreed to go out with her. After all the craziness with Karen and Julie, she didn't need to take on something like this. But it was too late now. She couldn't just walk away.

Another Morning After

Gina was still in bed. She was awake but had no intention of getting up anytime in the near future—if ever. The evening before—an evening she had anticipated for months—was a complete nightmare. Her whole class probably knew she couldn't get a real date to the reunion. She thought the evening was salvaged when things began to click with Karl Mullins, but that whole scene ended up rivaling the *Hindenburg* disaster. Her phone had been ringing since ten A.M. It was probably Linda, but Gina did not know for sure. After the phone rang for the fourth time that morning, Gina made a mental note to herself to get caller ID, and picked up the receiver.

"Hello."

"So, is he still there?" cackled Dennis from the other end of the line.

"Who? What are you talking about?"

"Linda said some hot guy who used to play football at your school agreed to take you home."

"Oh, Karl. Why would he still be here? Last night was the first time I'd seen him in ten years," Gina said as if the idea of her letting a guy she'd just met stay over was ridiculous.

"Karl? Not Karl Mullins? The guy I saw you dancing

with before Rosa got sick? I had no idea that was who Linda was talking about."

"Yeah, he said he'd take me home while you played nurse-maid to Rosa."

"Well, I guess he's not there, huh? Not much chance of getting lucky with him."

"What do you mean?" Gina asked.

"What do I mean about what?"

"For heaven's sake, Dennis. Why isn't there much chance of getting lucky with him?"

"Ah . . . perhaps because he's queer as a three-dollar bill."

"What?"

"Don't tell me you didn't know? You danced with him, Gina. He's good-looking, buff, and has rhythm. How could you not know?"

"You know for sure he's gay?"

"Unless straight guys started rowing on my *gay* rowing team, yes, I know for sure he's gay."

"Thank God!" Gina sighed with relief.

"What?"

"Nothing. Why didn't you tell me he was gay?"

"I didn't get a chance. Besides, I thought you knew. Gina, you know more gay people than I do. I figured he was just one more of your many homosexual friends."

"So, I'm the ultimate fag hag eh?"

"Fag hag, maybe. The *ultimate* fag hag, certainly not. You'd have to gain at least a hundred pounds and wear black everywhere to qualify for that title. I've been rowing with Karl for more than a year now. I didn't realize he went to the same high school as you—until last night anyway."

"You seem to know a lot of people who went to my school—Karl, Jennie Parks."

"Actually, I must know another one. At least I think she and Karl went to the same school. I've heard them reminiscing about it here and there. I didn't see her at the party last night though."

"Who?"

"I forget her name. She's the coxswain for our rowing team."

"What the hell is a coxswain?"

"She basically sits at the front of the boat and shouts orders at us to keep us rowing in unison. It's a great job for a pushy lesbian. I'm surprised she and Karl didn't go to the reunion together. They're very tight. God, what is her name? Annie something-or-other, I think."

"Oh, my God! Not Annie Harrison?"

"Yes, that's it. Annie Harrison. She and Karl are really good friends. They drive down to the river together every morning."

"You are fucking kidding me?"

"What?"

"Nothing. Listen, Dennis, I've got to go. Let me give you a buzz later," Gina said, hanging up the phone and shaking her head. She wanted to be angry with Annie—the little bitch had engineered the whole embarrassing evening with Karl—but Gina just sat in bed next to the phone and couldn't help smiling. First of all, she was relieved that Annie had put Karl up to humiliating her the night before. At least she really didn't have bad breath, and he had no intention of sleeping with her from the very beginning. But beyond that, Gina was impressed with Annie's ingenuity.

Gina called information and asked for Annie's number.

"Hello."

"Annie?"

"Yes, who is this?"

"Gina Perry. How are you?"

"I'm fine," Annie said after hesitating for a moment.

"Yes, I bet you are."

"Is there something I can do for you, Gina?"

"Beyond last night? No, I don't think so."

"Last night? What are you talking about?"

"Don't worry, Annie. I'm not mad. I had it coming."

"Worry. Why should I worry?"

"Okay, Annie, let's cut the crap. You got me back, and I must say you're a real pro. I could learn a lot from you."

Annie laughed. "Yeah, I am pretty good, aren't I?"

"Yes, you definitely have an evil mind. Are you an Aquarian by chance?"

"As a matter of fact, I am. How did you find out I was behind the whole thing?"

"Let's just say Karl and I have a friend in common."

"Well, women are always hitting on Karl, and I figured you'd fall victim to his charms like every other girl. Besides, I had backup plans if that one failed."

"Like I said, I deserved it. It was a pretty awful thing I did to you. If it makes any difference, I was unbelievably drunk, and I'm really sorry."

"Apology accepted. But why? Are you some kind of homophobe? Do you regularly hang out at gay clubs and lure away poor, unsuspecting women just to dick them over?"

"Homophobe? Hardly. Like I said, Annie, I was really drunk and, I'll be honest here, I was unbelievably jealous of you in high school. I don't know what I was thinking. I thought it would make me feel better about my high school experience if I did something mean to you. It was really stupid, and I was wrong."

"Yes, you were, but what's done is done. High school seems a world away now. Funny how things turn out."

"Yes, they never work out as you'd expect them to."

"Or would like them to."

"Right again," Gina said, realizing how easily she was chatting with Annie.

"Well, I appreciate the apology, Gina, and let's just call it even. Maybe our paths will cross again sometime."

"Maybe," Gina replied, realizing the conversation was wrapping up. "Annie, would you like to go to lunch or something sometime?"

"Sure. You have my number. And, Gina, just in case this is some warped plan to get back at me for the Karl incident—don't even think about it."

"Annie, I'm not stupid. I wouldn't mess with the master," Gina said. And she really meant it.

Strictly Business

Peter had gotten into work early that morning. He needed to be there before anyone else to take care of the stinky flowers that Plant Lady in the cube next to him insisted on displaying on her desk. Peter wasn't thrilled to sit next to a jungle of potted plants, but he was never really bothered by it until Plant Lady brought in some scented geraniums a few days earlier. Peter was very sensitive to smells, and the geraniums had a pungently sweet aroma. Many in the office enjoyed the scent and asked Plant Lady what smelled so wonderful; however, Peter was convinced such a strong odor was making his nose run and might eventually lead to one of his dreaded sinus infections.

He considered asking Plant Lady to take the geraniums home after explaining his allergies to her but figured she might take offense to such a request and decided to take care of it on the sly. He pulled a small container of bleach out of his briefcase and stepped into Plant Lady's cube. He felt a little sleazy doing it, but nonetheless, he proceeded to pour a few ounces into a cup so he could more easily drain it into the pot. The bleach had a strong smell of its own, and, after catching a whiff of it, Peter wished he had used some other mechanism. Maybe saltwater or weed killer would have been a better choice. Oh, well, at least it would be done.

Peter felt a tinge of remorse as he lifted the cup, but he decided this way was best. The plant would drop dead in a few days. Plant Lady would have to get rid of it. The stench would be gone, and no one would be the wiser. He tipped the cup over the pot, and just as the bleach was about to flow, he tilted it back the other way.

Damn, he thought to himself. He just couldn't do it. He could freak out in the middle of a crowded restaurant and beat up a bigot, but he couldn't kill a stupid plant. If Plant Lady was a normal person, it probably wouldn't have been a problem. But her plants were her babies, and he didn't have it in him to kill her pride and joy.

After the whole plant fiasco, it was time for Peter's vitamins, so he went to the kitchen to get some water. On the way, he stopped by his mailbox and removed a letter marked "Confidential: To Be Opened by Addressee Only." The envelope piqued his curiosity, and he opened it immediately. It was a letter from the director of Human Resources. As he scanned the letter, his face began to flush. He recently applied for a promotion to the position of departmental supervisor. He'd been with the company for years and was virtually functioning as a supervisor anyway. He trained all the newly hired staff and monitored their work. He also handled all the major research projects. It was his job for the taking. It would have meant a nice raise and, more important, an end to cubedum—he would finally have an office.

The letter informed him that due to the recent written warning placed in his personnel file regarding abuse of his Internet privileges, he was not eligible for the promotion. He also would be unable to apply for any promotions or position changes for one year from the date of the warning.

Peter was livid.

That bitch! That fucking bitch! That fucking Cameron Hartman! With Gina's help, Peter had put a few benign things in place to aggravate Cameron for having him written up, but now he was beyond mad. He was ready to bring out the big guns and really get back at her. It was just a matter of figuring out how.

* * *

As Peter tried to sort things out, Cameron Hartman arrived at her cube a few floors below. She was usually in early but was delayed by three different moving companies coming to her front door, wanting to load up her furniture and take it to her new house in Indiana. Cameron had no intention of moving and had never been to Indiana. She thought they might have had her confused with one of the neighbors, but all the orders had her full name and correct address. Someone was obviously playing a joke on her. Between the movers and the person who had repeatedly been calling her house and breathing into the phone, she was beginning to get a little paranoid. Just as she was sitting down to her desk the phone rang.

"This is Cameron."

"Ms. Hartman?"

"Yes."

"This is Sylvia at Dr. Remly's office. We're just wondering why you didn't arrive for your appointment yesterday."

"I didn't have an appointment yesterday. I don't even know who Dr. Remly is."

"Well, I have your name and number right here. You had an appointment yesterday at four o'clock."

"I most certainly did not. I think someone is playing a little joke."

"Well, we don't find it very amusing."

"Sorry," Cameron said, and hung up the phone before it rang again.

"This is Cameron."

"Hi, Ms. Hartman. This is George at Travel America. I've booked your reservations at the Stone Gate Nudist Resort. Would you like to book the airline tickets now?"

"Who is this?"

"George at Travel America."

"George, I'm afraid I don't need any reservations," Cameron said before hanging up the phone.

Her phone rang again, but she didn't dare answer it. Instead, she went to her mailbox just to get away from the phone. Aside from a couple of memos and fliers, there was a plain manila envelope. She opened it up to find a recent copy of *Give It to Me Baby*. She pulled out the magazine and looked at the cover in astonishment. Who was sending pornography to her at work? She didn't know what to do with it. With her heart pounding, she shoved it back in the envelope and raced to the kitchen to throw it away. She certainly didn't want it in *her* trash can. She dumped the magazine in the kitchen trash and threw a few paper towels over it; however, realizing that someone was seriously harassing her, she thought it prudent to keep the magazine. She might even want to have it checked for fingerprints or something, not that she had the slightest clue how to go about such a thing. She was starting to get scared.

Cameron pulled the envelope from the trash and went back to her desk. After sliding it into her briefcase, she saw that her voice-mail light was on and proceeded to check her messages. It took her a few minutes to get through messages from doctors wanting to confirm appointments and a Realtor wanting to know when he should meet her to look at various houses. Once she settled into work, she would then spend the better part of the day fielding such calls, including a caterer wanting to know if she still wanted chicken Kiev to be served at her wedding (she wasn't even engaged), and a psychic healer wondering if she still needed help with vaginal dryness.

The One

"Hello," Cheryl said, picking up the phone while still searching through a drawer in her living room. She couldn't find the gold hoop earrings she wanted to wear that night.

"Hey. It's Cooper."

"Hey there," Cheryl said, perking up a little. It had been a tedious day at work, and she was looking forward to her evening with Cooper. He had been out of town on business the past couple of weeks, and Cheryl had seen him only once since their night at the circus.

"Would you mind doing me a big favor tonight?"

"No, not at all. What?"

"My boss just asked me if I could take a couple of clients out to dinner tonight. They're in from New York for the evening and apparently they're very interested in buying into the company. Do you mind if they join us? We can go somewhere really nice, and my company will pick up the tab."

"Sure. I don't mind," Cheryl lied. Virtually every outing they went on, Cooper dragged along some sort of business associate. She admired him for being so committed to his career, but he needed to make some individual time for her. Besides, she figured tonight it was about time to let him take things a little bit farther—maybe some above-the-waist action.

Hanging out with his colleagues was always so boring. Cheryl had to think about everything she said and make sure it couldn't possibly be construed as offensive. She chose her words carefully during these outings. She didn't want Cooper to think she wasn't cultured enough to hold her own during a business dinner. At least she must have been doing pretty well at schmoozing in the big leagues. Why else would he keep inviting her along to these events?

"Thanks, you're a doll. I promise—next time it will be just you and me."

"I'm going to hold you to that," Cheryl said in a friendly tone.

Cheryl was walking up P Street toward Gabriel, a nuevo Latino restaurant in the Radisson-Barceló Hotel. Cooper was supposed to pick her up, but he was running late and asked her to meet him and his companions at the restaurant, which was several blocks from her apartment and not an easy walk in her favorite blue dress and high-heeled black slingbacks. She never did find her pumps with the lower heels. As she approached the hotel, she figured she had to choose between buying a new pair and cleaning out her closet to try to find the old pair.

Guess I'm going shoe-shopping tomorrow, she thought to herself as she walked into the restaurant, where the others were already seated. When Cooper saw her walk in, he stood up and waved her over.

"Hi, honey," he said to Cheryl, and gave her a quick kiss on the lips.

Honey? Cheryl thought. They had been on a few dates, but they certainly weren't at the "honey" stage. "Hi."

"Cheryl, this is John Carpenter and Will Frankel. They're in town from New York," Cooper said.

"Nice to meet you," Cheryl said, shaking their hands as they rose from the table.

Cooper pulled out Cheryl's chair, and the three gentlemen remained standing until she sat down.

"What did I tell you?" Cooper asked his guests. "Isn't my girl beautiful?" Cooper added, gesturing toward Cheryl.

Your girl? What's going on? We've barely been on five dates, Cheryl thought as she smiled in response to the compliment. "You're sweet," she said while John and Will nodded their heads in agreement with Cooper.

Once Cheryl got situated at the table, the four of them perused their menus and ordered a variety of tapas. They had some light conversation over dinner, and throughout the meal Cooper talked about himself and Cheryl as if they had been dating forever. He told his associates about how much Cheryl enjoyed socializing with his business partners and what a great girlfriend she was.

Cheryl played along. Maybe Cooper really was starting to have strong feelings for her. Maybe her good-little-girl routine was actually paying off. After giving it some thought, Cheryl decided she wasn't going to give Cooper any above-the-waist action after all. She knew she was right—men always wanted what they couldn't have, and they fell in love with the girls who didn't give it up too easily. He certainly wouldn't be taking some one-night stand to dinner with important clients. He was taking her. For once she was making the right decisions, and a relationship was coming her way.

Oh, thank God, she thought to herself as they wrapped up dinner. I play my cards right, and this guy might just be the one.

Plotting Revenge

"You can't apply for anything for a year? You're kidding?" Gina asked Peter as he sat down on her sofa.

"That's right. Thanks to that little Cameron bitch, I'm stuck in my position for another year. That promotion was mine for the taking. It would have meant more money and an office. God, this really sucks."

"Well, I have an idea to really get that Cameron chick, but I'm not sure it will work. We'll need the help of someone I'm not sure will be willing to help me out."

"Who?"

"This girl I went to high school with. Her name is Annie Harrison, and apparently she has turned into a regular computer geek."

"So how does she fit into the whole thing?"

"I need someone who's computer savvy."

"Why?"

"Let me talk to her first, Peter, and then I'll share my idea with you. It may not even be feasible. Hand me that notepad, would you? It has her phone number on it."

Gina grabbed the pad from Peter and went into the bedroom to call Annie. As she picked up the phone, she heard knocking on the apartment door.

"Peter, get that, will you? It's Shirley. She took Gomez for a walk for me."

"Hey, gorgeous," Peter said to Shirley as she walked in the door with Gomez and another dog, a little cocker spaniel or something.

"Hi, Peter. Where's Gina?"

"She's in the bedroom, making a phone call. Who's Gomez's little friend? Did you get a dog?"

"No, this is Rascal. He belongs to Mr. Borkourski, upstairs. He saw me walking Gomez the other day and offered to pay me to walk his dog. I figured, what the hell, I'm never one to turn down an easy buck."

"Really? That's great."

"So, how are you, Peter?"

"I've been better, having some work troubles."

"You and me both. I waited on this fat lady at the restaurant, and she got all huffy—complained to my manager that I gave her the check without asking her if she wanted dessert."

"She ratted on you to the manager just for that?"

"Well, not just that. She was really bitchy when I gave her the check, so I told her that her big ole caboose didn't need dessert. I guess that's what really set her off. Like it's my fault she's a pig."

"Hey," Gina said to Shirley, emerging from the bedroom. She then looked at Peter. "Well, Annie agreed to help us out. But you'll have to get a picture of Cameron."

"How am I supposed to do that?"

"She must have one on her desk—of her and her boyfriend, or with her dog or something. Just steal it and bring it back."

"I don't know, Gina. I'm already in trouble at work."

"Don't be such a pussy, Peter. Just do it," Shirley joked even though she had no idea what they were talking about. "So what's all this about anyway?"

"It's a long story, Shirley. I'll explain it over dinner," Gina said before turning to Peter. "So, Peter, want to come to dinner with us?"

"No thanks. I'm not the best company tonight."

"Are you sure?"

"You guys go ahead. Maybe I'll just stay here with the dog and watch TV."

"Sure, you can take him for another walk if you want," Gina said as she and Shirley went out of the apartment and closed the door behind them.

"What about Linda? Is she coming?" Shirley asked Gina as they headed down the hall.

"No. She said she was going to some appointment with Rosa. Actually, I haven't seen too much of her lately, since she started dating Rosa."

"Rosa? Is she still doing that lesbian thing?" Shirley joked.

"It's not a *thing,* Shirley."

"I know. I was just joking. But it must get awfully boring. Don't you think? My God. There's only so much you can do with a pair of high heels and a couple of boobs."

Lady with a
Baby

"You really didn't have to come," Rosa said. She and Linda were sitting in the waiting area of Rosa's doctor's office. Rosa had the last appointment of the day, and they were the only two left in the room.

"I know," Linda said. She really wasn't sure whether she wanted to be there or not. She had known Rosa for only a month or so. It seemed odd to be tagging along to obstetrician appointments. After all, it wasn't *their* baby. It was Rosa's baby.

Linda convinced herself that she was just there to offer some support. What's wrong with accompanying a friend to a doctor's appointment? She'd do it for Gina or any other friend. It didn't mean she was expecting to be co-parent of the baby or anything.

Linda tried to look at Rosa's stomach without being too obvious. Rosa was only a few months along, but her belly was already starting to protrude. If Rosa hadn't been so petite, it probably wouldn't have been noticeable at all.

Rosa caught her looking at her abdomen. "Guess I couldn't have kept it from you much longer, huh?"

Linda smiled. "You may have been able to disguise it a

little longer. You certainly couldn't have done any worse than the *Frasier* people did with that Daphne woman."

"Maybe you just would have thought I was getting fat. Which would you have preferred? A fat girlfriend or a pregnant one?" Rosa asked, obviously trying to get a read on how Linda really felt about the whole thing.

Linda smiled and ignored the question. She didn't want to say that she really didn't want either one.

"I know this is unexpected and probably much more than you bargained for," Rosa said. "If I had known things with Renée were going to go so sour, I would never have gone through with it. But I'm carrying a child now, who I love with all my heart. I know we haven't known each other very long, but I hope you will give us a chance."

Linda looked at Rosa. Damn it, she thought. Why did you have to be pregnant? "Rosa, I have to admit, this is a lot to take in. Being honest, I'm not sure how I feel about the whole thing, but you're not going to get rid of me that easily. Let's just take it one day at a time and see how it goes," Linda said just as the doctor called them back to the examining room.

Rosa introduced Linda to her doctor, and they were shown to a large examining room. The doctor asked Rosa to get changed, said he would be back in a few minutes, and closed the door behind him. As they waited for the doctor to come back, Linda looked around her—at the sterility of the environment, at the box of latex gloves on the counter, at Rosa, sitting on the examining table in a paper gown. If someone had told her a few months earlier that she would be accompanying her girlfriend to her first ultrasound, Linda would have told them they were crazy.

The doctor knocked at the door.

"Come in," Rosa said.

"Are you ready?" the doctor said as he started to maneuver the ultrasound equipment.

"You bet. Much longer and I might burst," Rosa said. She

had had to drink some sort of glucose solution and keep a full bladder for the test.

The doctor shifted Rosa's gown and squeezed some rather cold gel onto Rosa's slightly protruding belly. He pressed a few buttons on the machine and started rolling what looked like a telephone receiver over Rosa's abdomen.

"Oh, my God!" Rosa exclaimed. "There it is."

Linda thought she saw the baby on the monitor as well. It was wavy and blurry, but she could see a tiny little baby. Her mouth dropped, then curved in a little smile. She stared at the monitor, trying to get a clearer view of the baby, and then looked at Rosa, whose eyes were starting to water. There was no turning back now. Like it or not, Linda was going to be part of this pregnancy.

It's a Small
World After All

After dropping off Mr. Borkourski's dog, Gina and Shirley began their walk to dinner. That was one of the best parts of living in the Dupont Circle area in the summer. There was a plethora of restaurants with outdoor seating. Gina and Shirley tried to take full advantage of the season and ate out a lot during the summer. Linda and Peter weren't big on eating outside. Linda didn't like the heat, and Peter, for reasons no one understood, somehow found eating outside unsanitary. But Gina and Shirley loved to sit outside and have a pitcher of beer or margaritas. Sometimes they barely talked. They just enjoyed their food and people-watched. Some of the restaurants even let Gomez sit on the patio with them.

When they finally reached their destination, Trio's on 17th Street, they nabbed a table on the patio and didn't bother looking at the menu. Trio's was basically a pizza place/diner—nothing fancy, but it had outdoor seating. It was also fairly cheap, and since Gina usually picked up the check when she and Shirley went to dinner, Gina tried to choose reasonably priced restaurants for their outings. They ordered a pizza and a couple of beers and watched the crowd stroll by.

The stretch of 17th Street where they were having dinner was one of the major hubs of restaurants and bars in D.C., and Trio's had prime seating along the busy sidewalk to accommodate the sport of people-watching.

"So, how are things on the roommate front?" Gina inquired.

"Well, since you made me kick Sammy out, I haven't had any luck finding a new one."

"Why don't you run an ad in the *City Paper?* I think it's pretty cheap."

"No, I don't think so. I have another idea."

"Oh?"

"A friend of mine at work mentioned this foster child program to me."

"What?"

"Yeah. She said if you take in a foster child, you get six hundred dollars a month. Man, what I could do with that."

"Oh, Shirley, please tell me you're joking."

"No. How hard can it be? I have the extra room. The kid can sleep in there. And think about it. I get six hundred dollars a month. How much can a kid eat? I figure I spend a couple hundred on food and clothes and stuff for the kid, and then I can do whatever I want with the rest. You think they'd let me have two or three? How many do you think I can fit in that room?"

"Shirley, you can't take a kid in for the money. That's not what it's about."

"Oh, please, Gina. I'd be nice to the kid."

"Shirley, your life is very erratic and unpredictable. You can't take on a child."

"Well, we'll see."

"Oh, Lord, I hope not," Gina said, letting it go at that. She would have tried harder to talk Shirley out of it if she thought there was a chance in hell of Shirley actually getting approved to take in a foster child. Although, with the current state of the District's government, anything was possible.

"So what is this plan you and Peter were talking about when I came in earlier?" Shirley asked, changing the subject.

"This colleague at his job reported him for surfing the Web too much. Her name was Cameron or something like that."

"What's wrong with surfing the Web?"

"I'm not sure what the whole story was, but he was visiting sites he shouldn't have on company time."

"Like porn sites?"

"Actually, he didn't say. Anyway, the whole ruckus caused him to lose a promotion he was in line for, so he really has it in for this woman."

"So, how do you fit into all of this?"

"I ran into an old high school classmate a while back. Her name's Annie Harrison, and she's really into computers and graphics and such, so I had this idea . . ."

Before Gina could finish, she caught sight of a short, fat man walking along 17th Street, headed straight for them.

Gina gasped and cleared her throat. "I'm going to run to the bathroom. I'll be right back," Gina said, abruptly getting up from the table.

"Okay."

As Gina lunged for the doorway, she heard Shirley's voice behind her, talking to the rotund little man.

"Griffin? Is that you? God! It's been forever," Shirley called over the patio railing.

"Shirley Perry. Aren't you looking fine."

"You know it."

Gina's heart pounded wildly as she stood just barely inside the doorway and continued to listen to their conversation. How on earth did Shirley know Griffin?

"How are you?" he asked Shirley.

"I'm hanging in there. You? Still in the business?"

"Oh, yes. You know, you do something for so long, you get pigeonholed into it."

"Not me. I don't get pigeonholed into anything."

"Well, glad to hear it, Shirley. Listen, it was great to see you again. I'm actually in a bit of a hurry. Got to run."

"Okay. Nice to see you. Keep that chin up."

As Griffin continued down the sidewalk, Gina came back to the table.

"Who was that you were talking to?" Gina asked, feeling flushed.

"Just some guy I used to work with."

"Work with?" Gina said sharply, praying to God that Shirley wouldn't tell her that she used to act in porn movies and slept with Griffin. She certainly wouldn't put it past Shirley.

"I worked at this sleazy bookstore years ago, and he worked there too."

"Doing what?"

"Me? I worked the counter and waited on customers. Griffin, well, he was an actor of sorts."

"An actor?" Gina asked, relieved that Shirley had only worked the counter.

"He shot porn movies actually. They had a studio in the back of the store."

"Are you kidding?"

"No. He used to be really popular in the porn world. He might still be for all I know."

"Why? I caught a glimpse of him. He's not very attractive."

"That's why he's perfect. They make porno movies to please men, not women, Gina. Guys love it when they turn on a porno flick and there's some nasty fat guy getting it on with a hot chick. I guess they figure if someone like Griffin can get the girls, then there's hope for them."

"Interesting, I don't remember you working at a sleazy bookstore?"

"It was years ago, and I didn't stay very long. After I had been there for a while, they wanted me to start getting Griffin *ready* for his performances, if you know what I mean. You know, make sure everything was *up* and running. I passed on that little duty. Right before I left they got this woman—Brenda I think her name was—to man the counter and be Griffin's fluffer or poofer or whatever they call it."

"Is there anything you haven't done, Shirley?"

"If there is, I'm working on it."

"So what do people in the porn industry tell others they do for a living?"

"I don't know. Most of them were pretty open about it— even proud. Although I remember Griffin used to tell his mother he worked for the Public Broadcasting System."

"PBS?"

"He said he produced documentaries, which wasn't actually a lie, I guess."

"He sounds like quite a character. Well, at least you didn't sleep with him. You didn't. Did you?" Gina inquired, hoping to sound like she was just asking a casual question.

"Sleep with him? Gina, you saw him. He's sweet, but come on. Who'd be pathetic enough to sleep with his fat ass?"

"I don't know, Shirley," Gina said, slightly shaking her head at the whole situation. Not only did she, in a drunken stupor, screw a porn star, but he ended up being an acquaintance of her mother's. Oh, well, what was done was done, and Gina just needed to move on. She was just thankful that Griffin had used a condom when she slept with him.

Oh, my God! He did use a condom—didn't he? Gina thought. She was so drunk that night, and had tried so hard to put the experience out of her mind, she honestly couldn't remember.

Trying to Look
Busy

It was nearly noon, and Gina was dead tired and trying to stay focused on her work. She hadn't slept well at all the night before. She kept up a decent front through dinner with Shirley, but when she got home she began a full-fledged panic session. She sat on the sofa with Gomez curled up next to her, trying to replay that awful night with Griffin. She went over the evening step by step in her head—meeting Griffin at the bar, running into him again in the hallway, sitting with him on the sofa, moving into the bedroom. . . . As she reviewed the night, she could feel the emotions from that evening creeping up on her—the disgust she felt with Griffin on top of her, just wanting him off her and out of her apartment but not having the guts to say so until it was too late. She shuddered as she remembered crying in the bathroom—how she looked in the bathroom mirror with tears streaming down her face. If her life had ever hit rock bottom, that night was it.

As she sat at her desk, trying to look busy, she again traced the evening with Griffin but, as hard as she tried to remember, she just couldn't recall if he had used a condom. The thought petrified her. He was an X-rated movie star, for heaven's sake. Lord knows what kind of diseases he might be carrying.

She wasn't sure why she hadn't questioned it before, but she never really worried about things like sexually transmitted diseases in the past. She had always been careful, and subconsciously she must have just assumed they had used protection. Up until the Griffin incident, she could honestly say she had always been careful. Even after she and Peter had been dating for quite a while they still used protection, actually more at Peter's insistence than hers. Peter always *always always* used condoms.

Gina found it impossible to concentrate on work. She knew she needed to see a doctor and have some tests run just to make sure she was okay. At least she knew she wasn't pregnant.

It was so frustrating for her. The night with Griffin was a couple of months earlier, and she was drunker that night than she'd been in years. Damn! Why couldn't she remember?

She couldn't believe it. How did it happen? She took it seriously when they lectured about reproductive health in high school and college. She read the articles in women's magazines and was constantly passing them on to Shirley. She even regularly bought Shirley condoms and insisted that she use them. If she was worried about anyone getting a sexually transmitted disease, it was Shirley, not herself.

Gina kept rearranging papers and clicking on her mouse in an effort to look busy while she had only one thing on her mind. She thought about going in the bathroom and sitting in one of the stalls to think. But the last time she went in there, someone hadn't flushed the toilet after using it, and Gina didn't feel like running into that again.

Oh, just what I need, Gina thought to herself as she watched Tammy come through the bank entrance with a stroller. Tammy had been out on maternity leave for several weeks and was due to start back in another day or two. As Tammy wheeled her infant through the lobby, Gina's first instinct was to flee to the back room. She hated when new mothers brought their stupid babies into work to show them off. Gina was about to get up from her desk, when Tammy called to her.

"Gina. Hey. Come see my little angel."

Gina forced a smile and walked over toward Tammy and the baby.

"What do you think, Gina?" Tammy asked, eyeing her baby, who looked like a wrinkled alien with a big head.

Hmmm . . . add horns and a tail and you've got Satan. "Oh, he's so precious."

"She's a girl," Tammy said.

"Oh, I'm sorry. *She's* adorable. You're so lucky," Gina said before adding, "Listen, I've got to make a phone call. I'm glad you stopped by. It was nice to meet the little one," Gina fibbed. She had bigger things on her mind than a new-born with drool hanging off his chin—her chin.

The only way to get any peace of mind was to go to the doctor, but this wasn't exactly the kind of thing she wanted to see her regular physician about. Gina knew the clinic where Linda volunteered had health programs for women. She could have easily asked Linda for the phone number, but that might lead to questions, so she got out the yellow pages, found the number for the Women's Reproductive Health Center, and copied it onto a slip of paper. Liz was out to lunch, so Gina went into her office to make the call. As she reached for the phone, she felt very alone and desperate. She never had a clear picture of what her life would be like by the time she was nearly thirty years old, but whatever picture she did have, it certainly didn't involve calling a public health clinic to get tested for a host of sexually transmitted diseases.

Rock Bottom

Time after time, Gina thought she must've hit rock bottom—joining a church singles group, overflowing a toilet at a party, sleeping with a porn star—but this had to be it—this had to be rock bottom. She was about to walk into the Women's Reproductive Health Center in Fairfax. Of course, there were clinics in D.C., but Gina figured a place in the suburbs might be cleaner and attract a more upscale clientele—a more upscale clientele of women getting testing for venereal diseases or waiting to have abortions, that is.

"May I help you?" the receptionist at the front desk asked her as Gina closed the door behind her.

"I have a six o'clock appointment. Gina Perry."

"Sure. Let me give you a few forms to fill out," the woman said, handing Gina a clipboard and a pen. "Fill these out—front and back, and bring them back when you're done."

"Thanks," Gina said, taking a seat and starting to complete the paperwork. Just as she was finishing it up, a middle-aged woman with a deep voice called her back to be examined.

"I'm Ellen," the woman said. "How are you?"

"Good. Thanks," Gina lied.

After Ellen gestured for Gina to follow her, they made their way down the hall and entered a small examining room.

The woman looked over Gina's forms before asking, "You have some concerns about sexually transmitted diseases?"

"Um . . . yes . . . some," Gina said nervously, embarrassed even to be talking about it.

"It's okay, Gina. We see this all the time here. Try to relax," Ellen said, noticing Gina's obvious unease. "Are you having any symptoms you're concerned about?"

"No, not at the moment, but I thought I'd better get checked out just to be sure."

"Is there a particular incident that you're concerned about?"

"Yes."

"You've had unprotected sex with someone?"

"Um . . . yes," Gina said, hating herself—hating herself for having to say yes to such a question. Her real answer should have been "I can't remember," but Gina figured it was easier to just say yes.

"Well, we'll check you out for everything. We can do most of the tests today, but if you like, you can come back for the HIV test and do that anonymously. We do anonymous HIV testing twice a month."

"HIV?" Gina said, startled. "The guy . . . the guy I'm concerned about wasn't gay."

"Well, that's good to know," Ellen said. "But AIDS isn't just a gay disease. We should still run the test, particularly if you're not sure of his history."

His history? Gina thought. His history includes sex with hundreds of women . . . all caught on film. "I don't think he was into drugs either. Do you really think I need the HIV test?" Gina said, hoping Ellen would say no.

"There's no reason to be alarmed, Gina. But just to be safe, yes, I definitely think you should have the test. We're doing testing on Wednesday. Why don't we draw some blood and run a few other tests today, and you can come back next week for the HIV test."

"Okay," Gina said, suddenly becoming overwhelmed with fear. HIV had crossed her mind, but it seemed so impossible until the nurse actually said it out loud. HIV couldn't happen to her. She was a straight white girl. It was unthinkable.

But what if it's not unthinkable? Gina thought to herself as she only faintly heard Ellen tell her to get undressed and slip into one of the gowns behind the door.

"I'll be back in a few minutes," Ellen said, and closed the door behind her.

As the door shut, Gina felt an impending sense of doom come over her. She was scared, and not the kind of scared she got from watching *Scream* or *The X-Files*. This was a different kind of frightened. It was the way she had felt when she was a little girl and had gotten separated from Shirley at King's Dominion and thought she would never find her again.

Now, sitting on an examining table, she felt like that scared little girl all over again. Then, just like she did when she was a six-year-old child lost at an amusement park, she started to cry. What had made her be so stupid as to sleep with Griffin? What was she doing in a women's clinic? How was all of this happening to her? She was a nice girl . . . wasn't she? Things like this were not supposed to happen to nice girls.

"Gina, you've got to hold it together," she said to herself, wiping her eyes and getting up from the table. Things are going to be okay, she tried to tell herself as she grabbed the gown from behind the door. If only she believed they actually would.

Up to No Good

P eter was working on a report for his boss. It wasn't due for a few weeks, but he had to stay at work late anyway, so he figured he might as well get a head start. It was after eight-thirty, and most of the staff had gone home, but Peter set nine o'clock as the time to head downstairs and see if he could snatch a picture of Cameron from her desk. He had run into her in the elevator a few days earlier. She actually smiled at him and asked how he was doing. Peter couldn't believe her audacity. He said he was fine and politely smiled back at her. He didn't want to give her any indication that he was the one behind the movers, and the phone calls, and fourteen "for sale" signs he and Shirley put in front of her house (once Shirley found out about the whole deal with Cameron, she was eager to offer her ideas and assistance).

When it finally hit nine o'clock, Peter shut his computer down, went to the kitchen to down his evening vitamins, and walked downstairs to the seventh floor. He stuck his head out of the elevator to make sure no one was around and stepped out into the hallway. As he walked toward Cameron's cube, he wished he had asked Gina to get the picture. They couldn't fire her. Wishing he thought of asking her earlier, he stepped into Cameron's area and hit the jackpot. She had several photographs thumbtacked to the cube wall and a couple in frames on her desk. There were so many pictures, Peter surmised that he could probably take one of them off the wall and it would be days before Cameron even noticed. Then he remembered that it was Cameron Hartman he was thinking about, and her obsessively organized ass probably took inventory of them every day.

He disregarded the ones in frames on her desk and started reviewing the ones up on the wall. There were at least a dozen. Most of them were of her and what appeared to be her friends from college. In several of the pictures the women were wearing sweatshirts with Greek letters on them.

Gee, who would've guessed the little princess was in a sorority, Peter thought as he pulled down a picture of Cameron with one of her friends. The picture was a pretty close shot, so the image of Cameron was quite large and vivid. He figured that particular picture would give Annie the most to work with. As he replaced the thumbtack, he heard someone clearing her throat behind him. It was Plant Lady.

"Plan . . . Doris," Peter said, startled but trying to act relaxed and casual. "What's up?"

"You, stealing pictures apparently."

"What? Stealing? Don't be silly," Peter replied, trying to think quickly on his feet. "I'm just borrowing one. Cameron and I are good friends, and I need a picture to make her a birthday present."

"A birthday present for Cameron? You and Cameron aren't friends. Cameron doesn't have any friends here."

"Of course she does."

"Peter, what are you up to? A birthday present? Is that the best you could come up with? No one likes the perky little bitch, so don't try to convince me that you do."

Peter had never heard Doris use the word "bitch" or anything half as harsh. "Honestly, Doris . . ."

"Whatever, Peter. I'll just have to ask Cameron about your *friendship* with her myself."

"No. No. This is supposed to be a surprise," Peter pleaded, starting to sound desperate.

"So I guess you're going to surprise her with this sudden friendship," Doris said, laughing at Peter. "Peter, I was only hoping to get in on the action with you."

"What action? Why?"

"A few months ago she reported me for spending a few minutes online in my horticulture chat room. Okay, it was more like hours, but one of my peace lilies was dying, and I needed advice."

"So she got you too?"

"She's in the doghouse with most of us around here. I'm not sure how she shows her face every day. I've worked for this company for eight and a half years and never had any problems, and now, thanks to her, my record is jaded. Mark said he didn't even want to write me up, but Cameron wouldn't hear of it."

Figuring that making Plant Lady an accomplice might be the best way to keep her quiet, Peter told her about Gina's idea. She was amused and offered Peter a picture she had of Cameron from an office luncheon, so he wouldn't have to worry about returning the one he took from Cameron's cube. After Plant Lady retrieved the picture from her desk, she wished Peter luck, and they walked out of the building together.

Testing Day

———————————

Gina was a basket of nerves as she swung open the door to the Women's Reproductive Health Center. There was a receptionist standing in the lobby who immediately asked if she was there for testing. Gina nodded, and she directed her into the next room. Gina was about ten minutes early, but the room was already more than half full. She was a little taken aback by being sent into a room full of people. The nurse she had seen earlier said that the HIV testing would be anonymous. She assumed she'd meet one-on-one with a counselor or something, get her blood drawn, and that would be the end of it. Getting tested with thirty or forty other people hardly met her criteria for anonymous.

Gina sat in the very back of the room and took in the scene. As her eyes roamed the room, for a split second she thought she might be in the wrong place. She hadn't expected to see such a variety of women. The crowd ranged from professional women in business suits to college kids in fraternity sweatshirts. Somehow the diversity in the room was comforting to Gina. It made her feel less alone.

Gina continued to eye the new arrivals, wondering what their stories were. How did they all end up there? They all knew how not to get HIV, and everyone seemed to be reasonably intelligent. One would think that once people knew how to avoid a devastating disease like AIDS, no one would get it anymore. Yeah, right—the way people knew how to avoid getting pregnant, yet countless unwanted pregnancies happened every day.

Gina grabbed the form that had been lying in her chair when she walked in and gave it a quick read. It was an anonymous questionnaire asking for things like sex, age, race, etc. Then it got into more detailed questions about her sexual history and practices. It was odd to see her sexual history on paper, right in front of her in black and white. She was curious to see what the others put on the form and how her history compared with theirs.

As Gina completed the form, the room continued to fill up, and one of the few remaining seats open was next to her. Just as she was finishing up the form, a young black woman hurriedly slid into the seat next to her. Gina lifted her head from the paperwork to check out the latest arrival.

"Gina . . . hi," the young woman said nervously to Gina.

"Cheryl . . . hey," Gina replied, uttering the first words she had spoken to Cheryl in years.

"How are you?" Cheryl asked Gina, wondering if she should be saying anything at all.

"I'm okay, I guess. I'll be better once I'm done with this," Gina replied. She wasn't sure what was making her be civil to Cheryl. If she had run into her anywhere else, she would have just ignored her, but somehow it was nice to be able to commiserate with someone.

"Have you been through this before?" Cheryl asked.

"No. It's a first for me. You?"

"I got tested at my doctor's office a couple of years ago. This is the first time I've been here."

While Cheryl and Gina were talking, a young woman stepped to the front of the room and introduced herself and a few other clinic volunteers as testing counselors. She welcomed the group and explained the testing procedure. First the participants would listen to a lecture and slide show about HIV, and then they would start the actual testing. Gina was surprised by the graphic sexual references made during the presentation. If the language used in the presentation surprised her, the props were downright astonishing. The young woman leading the presentation slipped condoms onto dildos and even had a plastic vagina to demonstrate safe sex practices.

Gina had geared herself up to be stuck with a needle for a blood test; however, during the presentation the counselor mentioned that they would be tested orally. When the presentation was finished, the volunteers began handing out little plastic packets to everyone in the room. Gina and Cheryl examined them and waited eagerly to rip them open. The counselor told them to go ahead and open the packets and remove the cotton swab. She then instructed them to put the swabs in their mouth, between the lower cheek and gum line. They had to keep the swab in for a minute or two. Everyone in the room looked a little ridiculous. It looked like a room full of overgrown children awkwardly sucking on lollipops. Gina and Cheryl looked at each other with little swabs of cotton sticking out of their mouths. Unable to say anything, they just slightly smiled at each other, further breaking the tension between them.

When the test was done, they removed the swab and placed them in individual plastic containers. They labeled the containers with their respective code numbers and then waited for their rows to be called to the adjoining room, where they dropped off the specimens and were told the results would be back in two days. At that time they could come back and use their code numbers to get their results.

Gina and Cheryl walked out of the clinic together. When they got outside, it was still daylight.

"Do you want to get a cup of coffee or something?" Cheryl asked meekly.

"No," Gina said. "But I'd love to get a drink of the alcoholic variety."

"That does sound like a better idea than coffee. What's around here?"

"I have no idea. I don't get out to Fairfax very often."

"Why don't we head back downtown? Maybe the Big Hunt or the Front Page?"

"The Big Hunt sounds good. Why don't I meet you there," Cheryl replied as they walked toward the parking lot.

Post-testing Drinks

"Oh, this is good," Gina said, taking a long sip of her draft, a Kilian's Irish Red. She and Cheryl were sitting in a booth at the Big Hunt, a bar on Connecticut Avenue with a huge selection of beers.

"Yeah, I really needed it. I hate doing this testing thing. I was a nervous wreck a few years ago until I got the results back."

"I've been a real bitch for a few days now. I can't concentrate on anything at work. Yesterday I just called in sick and lay in bed all day."

"Are you really that worried about the test results?"

"Aren't you?"

"A little, but I don't think the chances are that high that it will come back positive."

Didn't have sex with a porn star, huh? "Yeah, me either, but it still grates on my nerves," Gina lied. She was worried sick that the test might come back positive. "If I may ask, I guess there have been others?"

"Others?" Cheryl asked.

"Someone other than Peter. I can't imagine you're concerned about catching something from him."

"From Peter? Always-wear-a-condom Peter? Jump-out-of-bed-immediately-after-sex-and-take-a-shower Peter? Rinse-his-mouth-out-with-Scope-every-five-minutes Peter? No, Peter is the least of my worries."

Gina laughed. "God, he still does that. Don't you hate that?"

"It used to bother me, but I just chalk it up to one of his quirks—one of his many quirks. How about the stupid humidifier he runs all damn night?"

"Oh, God, I'd forgotten about that. I used to sneak out of bed in the middle of the night and turn it off. I'd try to wake up before him and turn it back on, but sometimes I didn't, and I'd catch hell the next day. How does he sleep with that thing humming all night long? The more I think about it, he is very odd, isn't he? I was over there the other day, and he was sprinkling some kind of anti-allergy powder all over the carpet to kill dust mites or something."

"He's also doing some bizarre broccoli diet where you boil the broccoli and drink the juice. It's disgusting."

Gina laughed again. She had almost forgotten about why she and Cheryl were once such good friends. They both enjoyed trashing people, and they were both so good at it. Whoever was out of earshot was fair game. In college they would stay up into the wee hours of the morning, Gina on the top bunk and Cheryl on the lower bed, discussing the girl down the hall with the bad haircut or how the girl with the big ass in their stats class had no business wearing that tight miniskirt. They were always up to no good.

They constantly terrorized their suite mates, Chiller and Lisa. Their dorm room at American University was actually part of a suite, which meant their room was connected to an adjoining room by a shared bathroom. Chiller spent a lot of time at her boyfriend's house, so she wasn't around that much, but Lisa always seemed to be in the dorm with her loudmouthed boyfriend, Troy. The walls between the two rooms were fairly thin, and Gina and Cheryl were treated to a regular sexual sound-fest a few nights a week. They didn't hear much from Lisa, but Troy was quite a talker—a loud talker. For kicks Gina and Cheryl would listen to them, and when Troy started with his "oh baby, oh baby, ride the pole, ride the pole," Gina and Cheryl would call Lisa's room, and the phone would start ringing, interrupting their love session at the most inopportune time. Juvenile? Yes. But it was good for a laugh or two.

For a brief period, Cheryl adopted a cat and kept it in their dorm room for a few days, unbeknownst to Lisa or Chiller (or Troy, for that matter). Growing ever tired of Troy and his clamorous sex talk, one night during one of his and Lisa's escapades, Cheryl slipped into the bathroom with the cat and quietly jarred the door to Lisa's room open. She left the cat in the bathroom and closed the door leading to her and Gina's room. She and Gina lay in their beds and waited patiently. As usual, Troy started moaning and groaning and saying "oh baby, oh baby, ride the AAAAAHHHH- HHH!!!!!! What is it? What is it? Is it a rat?"

Now, several years later, Gina and Cheryl were speaking civilly for the first time in quite a while. Cheryl had approached Gina numerous times over the years. She apologized incessantly for the incident with Peter, but Gina wouldn't accept her apology and continued to ignore her until Cheryl finally gave up. Gina wasn't exactly sure why she was finally thawing out. Maybe the sting of Cheryl's actions was finally subsiding or maybe it was just nice to commiserate with someone going through the HIV testing process—even if that someone was Cheryl. Or it could have had more to do with Linda spending every waking moment with Rosa and having less and less time for Gina.

"So, if I may ask, why are you getting tested?" Gina asked Cheryl.

"I made a mistake—a stupid mistake," Cheryl said, wanting to leave it at that. She really didn't care to tell Gina about the night she hooked up with someone from a bar a couple of months earlier, long before she met Cooper. She hadn't even mentioned Cooper to Gina. Actually, she hadn't really mentioned Cooper to anyone. Things were going so well with him, she didn't want to jinx it.

"A mistake?" Gina asked.

Oh, what the hell, Cheryl thought. I may as well tell her.

"I was at a bar with some of the girls from work. It was a Friday night, and it had been a long week. I guess I had more to drink than I should have. Oh, Lord, this is so embarrassing. I met this guy. He wasn't much to look at, and he was older than me, but he was so nice and attentive."

"Really."

"He kept feeding me drinks," Cheryl continued. "And before I knew it we were back at my place, and one thing led to another and . . . now I'm getting tested. I can't believe I was so stupid. Every time I think about it, I get nauseous. I keep seeing his fat moon-pie face and this stupid cap he was wearing when we met. I think it said 'The Big C' or 'The Big G' or something."

Family Planning

"What do you think of this?" Linda said, holding up a pink baby sleeper. She and Rosa were in the infant department at Lord & Taylor in Tysons Corner.

"Suppose it's a boy? We can't put him in pink."

Linda noted how Rosa said *"We* can't put him in pink." More and more Rosa seemed to be indicating that she wanted to raise her baby in partnership with Linda. Almost as if Linda would be co-mom. Linda wasn't sure how she felt about the situation. Everything was happening so fast. She had only known Rosa for a short time but had never had such intense feelings for anyone in her life. Even though she was falling hard for Rosa, she had mixed emotions about the baby and what her ultimate role would be.

"Why not? He or she isn't even born yet, and you're gender-stereotyping already," Linda said.

"I am not. It's not a gender thing. It's a tradition thing. Little girls wear pink and little boys wear blue."

"So if you're not going to find out the sex before the baby's born, how do we know what to buy?"

"I guess we buy lots of yellows and greens."

"Blah. I don't know why you just don't let the doctor tell you whether it's a boy or a girl."

"Again, Linda, it's a tradition thing."

"Rosa, there isn't anything traditional about this baby. It was conceived in a doctor's office and is going to be raised by a lesbian."

Rosa remained silent following Linda's comment, as if it had upset her.

"I'm sorry," Linda said. "I was only joking."

"I know. I know. It's just that sometimes I wonder if I'm doing the right thing."

"What do you mean?"

"You know, having this baby by myself. He needs his father."

"Father? You don't even know who the father is."

Rosa hesitated for a moment. "Yeah, I know, but it just— Do you think I'm doing a terrible thing? Bringing a baby into the world without a father?"

"Please, all that baby needs is your unconditional love. You can find a father figure for him if it's a boy—or if it's a girl, for that matter."

"You think?"

"Of course, maybe Peter would be up for the role."

"Maybe," Rosa replied with a little giggle. "Gosh, I'm just scared. This is so new to me. Some days I just can't believe it. There's a little baby growing inside me, and in a few months I'm going to be a mother. Me—Rosa Martinez—a mother."

"You'll be a wonderful mother."

"Thanks, Linda. Really, thank you for everything. If I hadn't met you, I can't imagine what things would be like."

"Well, I can say the same."

"I've been sort of wondering about something, Linda. I'm going to need to start birthing classes eventually, and I need a partner. I guess I was wondering . . ."

"I'd be happy to be your partner."

"Thanks. That takes a big load off my mind—one less worry for me."

"You've got to stop worrying. Everything will be fine."

"I know, but there's so much to deal with, and I just can't get past the baby not having a father."

"Why are you so worried? Plenty of kids grow up fine without a father. Look at Gina. She didn't have a father, and she's a normal, well-adjusted gal."

"I guess you're right, Linda. I guess you're right."

Screwed by the
Same Man

"**O**h my God!"

"What?" Cheryl asked Gina, somewhat taken aback by Gina's reaction to her news.

"Oh my God!" Gina said again.

"What? What?"

"It said 'The Big G' didn't it? The cap—it said 'The Big G'?"

"Come to think of it, I guess it did. Yeah, now I remember. His name was Griffin . . . Griffin Cirelli."

"I don't fucking believe it."

"Gina, if you don't tell me what's going on . . ."

"Okay. Okay. It's just hard to get the words out," Gina said. "Okay, here I go. . . . I slept with him too," Gina continued, wincing at the mere thought of it.

"You slept with Griffin? The Big G?"

"Oh, yeah. He landed me the same way," Gina said, conveniently leaving out the fact she ran into him in the hallway of her building and invited him into her apartment.

"Is this some kind of sick joke or something?" Cheryl asked suspiciously.

"Oh, God, how I wish it was," Gina reassured her. "You don't know how much I wish it was."

"This is unbelievable, Gina. He was fat and old and bald. What the hell happened?"

"I don't know, Cheryl, but that's not the end of it."

"What do you mean?"

"Brace yourself. How do I tell you this?"

"Spill it, Gina. You're scaring me."

"Griffin. The Big G. He's a porn star."

"What? Oh, now I know this is a joke. How did you know about me and Griffin, and how did you know I was going to get tested today?" Cheryl accused, starting to get angry.

"You don't believe me? Want proof? Let's go for a ride, Cheryl," Gina said, dropping a ten on the table and getting up to leave.

"Where, Gina? I don't like this."

"Come on," Gina said, walking toward the car in front of Cheryl. "I only hope I can find the place."

It didn't take the girls long to travel across town to Myers' Books and Magazines. Rush hour had just passed and traffic was pretty light. Gina made a couple of wrong turns but eventually recognized the neighborhood and was able to find the store.

"What the hell are we doing here? This neighborhood looks scary," Cheryl said.

"I want to take you in the bookstore and show you something."

"Gina, now is hardly the time to look for the latest bestseller."

"Just come with me," Gina said, getting out of the car. Cheryl followed once again, and as they came through the front door, Cheryl was visibly disturbed.

"What kind of place is this, Gina?"

"What's it look like? It's Fucking Pervert Central Station."

"I want to go, Gina. Now!"

"Look," Gina said, pointing toward a group of videos on display. Cheryl turned her head and observed The Big G collection. She was speechless.

While Gina was feeling a certain degree of comfort knowing that someone else was going through the same horrific moment she did when she saw the videos, a small woman called to the girls from behind the counter. She was the same woman who was there during Gina's last visit.

"You girls like The Big G?" she asked.

The girls ignored her, so she called again. "If you like The Big G, I have his Web site address."

"Excuse me?" Gina said.

"He has a great Web site."

"Really?" Cheryl asked, finally able to speak again.

"It shows clips from his movies and tells you about his upcoming films. And get this. Soon we're going to be launching The Big G Cam."

"The Big G Cam?" Gina asked.

"This is such a hoot. You know the baseball cap he wears in all his movies?"

"Do we ever," Gina replied regretfully.

"Well, it actually has this tiny hidden camera in it. For the past six months or so, he's been seducing these pathetic women and getting it all on film."

"What!" Gina shrieked.

"Oh, yeah. He finds these poor bitches at bars and goes back to their place. Then before the performance gets started, he takes off the hat and strategically places it where it can record all the action. We're going to load all the recordings online and charge money for people to view them. Isn't that hysterical?" the woman said to the two girls, who had suddenly become severely flushed and dumbfounded.

"What the fuck are we going to fucking do?" Gina said to Cheryl as they drove away from the bookstore. "Any day now we could be all over the Internet in all our glory."

"I can't believe this. This is insane. He can't do this. It's not legal. It can't be."

"You're right, Cheryl. It has to be illegal."

"Then we'll go to the police."

"And say what? Oops, Officer, I banged an old fat guy. Please lock him up."

"Let me ask you something, Gina. Why did you get tested for HIV? You can't remember if Griffin used a condom. Can you?"

"How did you know?"

"Because I can't remember either. The whole night is a daze. I think he drugged us, Gina."

"You think? I guess it's possible. I had a couple of drinks with him. He could have slipped something into one of them. I don't remember much about my encounter with him, but I wasn't ever unconscious or anything."

"I've seen pieces on the news about that date rape drug, Rohypnol. Maybe he drugged us with Rohypnol. If that's the case, we can press charges," Cheryl said.

"I don't think it was that date rape drug. I've seen information about it on the news too. I think it basically renders its victims unconscious. I wish I could say I was unconscious, but I wasn't. I just don't remember the night very well."

"Okay, so maybe it wasn't Rohypnol, but it could have been something else."

"Sure it could have. Anything's possible. Anyway, at this point it doesn't really matter how it happened. We need to figure out what we're going to do about it."

"I guess you're right."

"Grab the phone from the glove compartment, would you?" Gina asked Cheryl, who reached for the mobile phone and handed it to Gina. Gina dialed information and asked to be connected to Myers' Books and Magazines.

"Bookstore," the woman at Myers' said.

"Hi, I'm trying to reach Griffin . . . ?"

"Cirelli," Cheryl said.

"Griffin Cirelli. Is he there?"

"No, he's not here right now, but I expect him any moment. They're filming tonight. May I take a message?"

"Any moment? No. No message," Gina said, hanging up the phone and switching lanes so she could turn around. "Well, Griffin is apparently on his way to the bookstore as we speak. I say we just confront him and tell him we'll go to the police if he doesn't give us the films."

"God, we have to see him again. I'm not sure I can bear it."

When the girls reached the store, they went back to the woman behind the counter and asked for Griffin.

"He's busy right now. If you want to leave something, an article of clothing perhaps, I'll have him autograph it, and you can come back and pick it up."

"Autograph? We don't want his autograph," Gina said, trouncing behind the counter toward the back room with Cheryl following.

"You can't go back there," the woman called behind them, but it was too late. Gina and Cheryl were already in the back of the store, which was more than four times the size of the front area. What appeared to be two stages or television sets took up the bulk of the space, and professional lighting and camera equipment was strewn about. A short, skinny man was directing a young woman in the bedroom set. She had long, black hair and was wearing a tiny silk bathrobe. Gina recognized her as the woman who was walking out of David's house the day she was on her stakeout. When she saw Gina and Cheryl walk into the back, she got distracted, prompting the director to speak to the two girls.

"May I help you, ladies?"

"We're here to see Griffin," Cheryl said.

"He's not available. He'll be having a publicity event later this month, if you'd like to come back."

"No, we wouldn't like to come back. We'd like to see him now," Gina said firmly.

"What part of my words did you not understand? I said he is unavailable."

"I don't care . . ." Gina started to say, when Cheryl nudged her on the arm and pointed toward a door to the left of the set. It had a small star and the words "The Big G" painted on it.

Gina and Cheryl started toward the door.

"Where do you think you're going?" the man asked.

Ignoring him, Gina banged on the dressing room door. "Griffin, open up."

"Who is it?" Griffin called from behind the door.

Without answering, Gina opened the door and saw Griffin sitting, stark naked, at his desk, which was loaded with food.

"I'm in the middle of my dinner, ladies. What do you want?"

"We know all about your little scheme, Griffin."

"Who are you?"

"Don't pretend you don't recognize us."

"You look vaguely familiar, but I can't place the name. What? Did I fuck you? 'Cause I fuck a lot of women. You can't expect me to remember every pathetic bitch I prod, now, can you?" Griffin said, dropping every pretense of the shy, middle-aged man the girls had met at Rumors.

"Asshole!" Cheryl said.

"Don't waste your breath, Cheryl," Gina said. "Now, listen, Mr. Big G. We know all about your sad little baseball cap with the hidden camera. We want any films of us, and we want them right now. We don't care about the other women, but give us our films or we'll go to the police."

"The police?" Griffin said, laughing. "You chicky babes are stupider than you look. Go ahead—call the police. What do you think will happen besides this whole story reaching the media and your faces being plastered all over the news? Please, go to the police. At worst I get a slap on the wrist and tons of publicity for my movies and my Web site."

Gina and Cheryl stared at him briefly in silence.

"You're going to give us those films. You may not know it yet, but we will get them back. Let's go, Cheryl, before he stands up and we have to look at that tiny little dick of his," Gina said to Cheryl before turning her glare back to Griffin. "Big G. What does that stand for, Griffin? Do you have a very big goat?"

Griffin laughed. "I love a feisty little filly. Keep talking, and I won't need to stand up for you to see my—"

"Bastard!" Gina said, interrupting Griffin before following Cheryl out the door.

Pretty Girl

Gina, Peter, Linda, and Annie were at Pizzeria Paradiso, enjoying some of the best pizza in D.C. They had just come from Peter's office. Gina and Linda had waited in the car while Peter and Annie went up to Cameron's cube to work their magic. Annie had tried to write out detailed instructions for Peter that told him exactly what he needed to do, but as she went over them with him, she could see his utter confusion at the daunting task. Annie worked with computers all day, every day, so it wasn't uncommon for her to discuss technical jargon with the less computer savvy and often get impatient with their lack of understanding. Such was the case with Peter. Rather than field his questions for an hour and help him through the job over the phone, she decided just to come along and do it herself. The least Peter figured he could do was take her out for a bite to eat.

"God, Annie, you're amazing. I can't believe you did it so quickly," Gina said from across the table. She tried to add to the conversation every once in a while, but she was hardly in the mood to be out on the town. Her test results were due back the next day, and she was a nervous wreck. If that weren't bad enough, her drunken image was about to be plastered all over cyberspace, having sex with an old fart.

The only good thing about the whole mess was that it

helped Gina put a few things into perspective. She may have been single with no immediate hope for a meaningful relationship and stuck in a dead-end job, but recent events prompted a few revelations. For one, she had her health, something she rarely thought about until there was a possibility that it might be taken away. If her results came back negative, she swore she would never take it for granted again. She had really great friends who would do almost anything for her. Gina realized that even Shirley, with all her faults, was a blessing in her life. Under a cloud of HIV and unwanted Internet exhibitionism, she realized the silliness of being jealous of her friends and generally miserable over the state of her life. Once it was over (and oh, how she hoped it would be over), she vowed to live her life differently.

"Please, it was nothing. Actually, it's more fun than I've had in a while. Little did I know, I'm in the wrong business. I shouldn't be helping businesses with software issues. I should just start helping people screw over their colleagues."

Peter laughed. "Not a bad idea really. I'm sure your services would be in great demand."

"How did you learn so much about computers?" Linda asked Annie.

"I don't know. It just sort of happened. I was temping as a secretary in the IS department of an insurance company downtown, and I guess I really started to get into it. I wasn't that busy, so I offered to help one of the programmers. He showed me some of the basics. I was eventually hired as an analyst and then took a few courses at George Mason. I kept taking classes and continued to learn on the job, and a few years later I was the vice president of Systems and Programming."

"That's fantastic. I'm terrible with computers."

"I'm sure you're not. Everyone is so afraid of technical jobs. People think you have to be some kind of computer geek or math genius to work in technology, but it's really no different than banking or any other field. You just get the training and keep learning as you go."

"I'd be afraid I'd screw up."

"Of course you'd screw up. I screw up all the time, but you learn from your mistakes, and you make less and less of them. You should think about it. You're a bright girl, Linda. I'm sure you could learn to do anything you wanted. Not to mention technology jobs are booming, and employers are paying steep price tags for qualified candidates."

"Really?"

"I do some consulting for my old company, and they pay me two hundred dollars an hour. Who knows, get some training, Linda, and maybe you can be my first employee."

"Careful what you offer. I might just take you up on that."

"That's fine with me. I'd love to have such a pretty girl work for me."

Oh, that was subtle, Gina thought, observing the two girls.

Linda almost started looking around to see who the "pretty girl" was, when she realized that it was her. Lord, when it rained it poured—first Rosa, and now Annie. Linda smiled at Annie, acknowledging the compliment and sizing her up.

She is sort of cute, although a little pudgy, and she'd have to do something with that hair, Linda thought to herself, although not really interested in bantering with Annie. She was so happy to be with Rosa, someone she actually found terribly interesting and sexy. It was so nice to be hit on by Annie and be able to essentially say "Thanks, but I'm taken."

Caught in a Lie

Thank God, it's almost lunchtime, Cheryl thought to herself. She'd been in the same meeting for over three hours. Ever since she was promoted to implementation manager she had to go to so many meetings. When she was promoted to oversee the implementation of new client accounts, it was going to be her responsibility to make sure everything got up and running smoothly. Only problem was her company hadn't landed any new clients in months. This left Cheryl without an exact job to do, so she was constantly pulled into various projects. Today she was supposed to have reviewed a one-hundred-page quality improvement plan that everyone was discussing in the meeting.

"I think it was a bit too long, especially the account management section. We should probably tighten up the claims section as well," Cheryl lied. She hadn't read either section, but she had overheard another manager saying almost the same thing in the hallway before the meeting. There was no way Cheryl could concentrate on some convoluted document about quality improvement initiatives the company was never going to spend the money to implement anyway. Her HIV test results were due back today, and she had been such a nervous wreck all week, she had barely gotten any work done at all.

"Well, it's almost time to break for lunch," Cheryl's boss, Sandra, said. "Why don't we wrap things up. Let's do a quick round-table. Why don't you guys update me on your projects, and then we'll call it quits until two o'clock."

Sandra looked at Veronica on Cheryl's left and gestured for her to begin.

"Well, I'm working on the new account management manual that I told you about last week. I've pared it down to four hundred and twenty pages and should have a draft for you to review next week. I've also been meeting with Janice in the Claims Department about developing some standard letters to send to clients. ... ."

Cheryl just looked at Veronica as she continued to drivel on about all her various projects. Veronica was a major workaholic and was always juggling several different projects at once. As Veronica continued talking, Cheryl desperately tried to come up with something she could say she had been working on. She had been so preoccupied with her HIV test, and the whole mess with Griffin, she really hadn't accomplished anything all week.

"Thanks, Veronica," Sandra said as Veronica finished up. Then she looked at Cheryl.

Shit! Cheryl thought. If Cheryl had known Sandra was going to ask them for progress updates, she never would have sat next to Veronica. She certainly didn't want to have to follow her. Cheryl had been working on a project to revise one of the company databases with a guy in Information Services the week before. Maybe she could just say she was still working on that.

"Gosh. I've been real busy this week. I've been working with Ron Lopez in IS on revising the client database and—"

Cheryl didn't finish before Veronica cut her off, "Ron Lopez? He's been on vacation all week."

Fuck! Cheryl thought.

"Yeah, I think he's in Bermuda or the Bahamas or something," another meeting attendee interjected.

Fuck! Cheryl thought again, starting to feel flushed. "Oh, that's right. Not Ron . . . I meant . . . ah . . . I don't remember the name of the guy, but I've been working on that data-base."

"I thought that was finished," Veronica added. "I saw Ron last week, and he said you guys had finished that."

Bitch! "Yeah, well, there were a few finishing touches that need to be done, and then it will be wrapped up."

"Okay, thanks, Cheryl," Sandra said with a questionable look.

As the rest of the meeting attendees detailed what they had been working on all week, Cheryl sat in her chair, want-ing to dissolve into thin air. Everyone knew she was lying about the database, and she was totally embarrassed. This was all she needed on top of everything else.

What was she going to do if her test came back positive? What would Cooper think? That would sure blow her good-little-girl facade. Initially, she really hadn't been that wor-ried about the test. It had just been a little precautionary thing she was doing until Gina told her about Griffin and his porn star status. Damn Gina!

As the meeting wrapped up, she thought about how she had to get through the next few hours, and then she would meet up with Gina and go get the results.

Blast from the Past

Gina was feeling very anxious. After work Gina could go to the clinic and find out if her life had changed forever. She was so worried about the test that The Big G Cam was only a secondary concern for her. She just wanted to get through the testing procedure. Then she would take care of Griffin and his stupid Web site.

She had just finished helping a customer with a credit line and was trying to clean out some files she'd been ignoring for a few days. Liz was holed up in her office, and Linda was in the rest room, getting ready for her lunch date with Rosa. Gina was the only one working the lobby, when an elderly woman approached her desk.

"Excuse me, dear. The young man behind the counter told me I have to pay a dollar for a deposit ticket. I'm sure he must be misinformed. What is that about?"

It's about one more way for the bank to dick you over. "Actually, ma'am, he's right. The bank charges a fee for counter deposit slips."

"For heaven's sake—that's insane."

Yep. "Actually, the bank does it to encourage customers

to use their pre-encoded slips. It helps to avoid errors," Gina said, offering the standard bank spiel.

"Well, charge me for a deposit ticket, and I will close my account right now."

"It's okay, ma'am. It really is the bank's policy, but here're a couple of slips on the house," Gina said just to avoid any further confrontation with the woman.

"God, I hate this place. You know, this was a decent place to bank about three name changes ago. Charging for a slip of paper—insane!"

"I'm sorry, ma'am. I understand your frustration, but it's really beyond my control," Gina responded in complete agreement as the woman walked away.

As Gina watched the woman head back toward the teller line with her deposit tickets, Linda came from the rest room with a disgusted look on her face.

"Hey, what's wrong?" Gina asked.

"Have you noticed anything strange in the ladies' room lately?"

"Strange? You mean the person who is doing their business and not flushing the toilet? Yes. I've run into it a few times."

"It's disgusting. I think we should talk to Liz about it."

"And say what? Someone's pooping in the toilet and not flushing?"

"Why not?" Linda asked.

"I don't know. It's not exactly pleasant conversation. Anyway, she already hates me. I'm not going to talk about poop with her. Besides, I think it's her."

"What do you mean?"

"I mean I think she's the one doing it."

"Oh my God! Why?"

"Well, remember last Saturday? The only women here were you, Kelly, Liz, and me. Well, *it* happened last Saturday. I know it's not me or you and, God, look at Kelly," Gina said, pointing her eyes behind the teller line at Kelly. "She's barely five feet tall and maybe a hundred pounds. There's no way she's putting out stuff that big," Gina said with a disgusted giggle.

"Why would Liz do that?" Linda asked.

"Maybe she's angry about something or because she's . . . oh, I don't know . . . a FREAK!"

Linda and Gina laughed together. It was one of the few times over the past couple of days that Gina's mind actually strayed from the HIV test.

As the girls tried to get back to work, a small man with blond hair came into the bank and approached Linda.

"I'm trying to find Rosa Martinez. I went by her office, and they said she was meeting a friend here."

"Well, I'm the one she's meeting. She's not here yet. Can I help you with anything?"

"No, I'll just wait for her here, if that's okay," the man said.

"Sure. By the way, I'm Linda. May I ask your name?"

"Sure. I'm René, Rosa's husband."

As Linda stood flabbergasted, the elderly woman who questioned Gina earlier passed by.

"Charging for a slip of paper . . . insane!" she mumbled on her way out the door.

Husband

"Excuse me?" Linda said.

"I said I'm René, Rosa's husband."

"Husband? Really? That's funny. She never mentioned a husband."

"No? René? She never mentioned me?"

"Oh, she mentioned a Renée, just not a *husband* named René."

"Well, we've been separated for a few months."

"Still, she should've mentioned you. She's going to have some serious explaining to do when she gets here."

Gina watched the scene unfold in front of her desk but remained silent. She knew how awful the news must have been for Linda, but she couldn't help feeling a tinge of relief that maybe Linda's relationship with Rosa was headed for disaster and Gina would have her best friend back.

"Explaining?" René asked.

"I can't even begin to tell you. Did you guys have a cleaning lady named Bianca?"

"Oh, God, did she tell you about Bianca?"

"She mentioned her."

"It was one time. I can't believe she told you about her," René said, sounding very defensive. "Bianca seduced me. She basically forced herself on me."

"Okay, okay. You don't have to explain yourself to me. It's none of my business," Linda lied. It most certainly was her business. She was about to inquire further, when Rosa appeared at the door. She smiled at Linda as she walked into the bank. Then she caught sight of René and immediately halted. She looked at René with a startled, angry glare and then back at Linda.

"Linda, I'm sorry. What did he tell you?"

"Not much, just that he's your husband, significant other, spouse, life partner. . . ."

"You fucking asshole!" Rosa yelled at René. "What are you doing here?"

"I had to find you, Rosa. Don't be mad. I only came because I care."

"Really? How much were you caring about me when you were rolling around the living room floor with the maid?"

"It was a mistake, Rosa—a really big mistake. I don't know why it happened. It was just that one time. I swear. God . . . I don't know!"

"It was just the one time? Well then, I guess I was irrational. You should leave your husband only if he screws the maid twice? Is that it? Is that what you're trying to say?"

"No. Goddamn it, Rosa! I'm not trying to explain anything. I'm just asking that you forgive me, or at least consider forgiving me. I love you, Rosa. I was so stupid. Please! You have to—" René didn't finish his sentence. He had finally noticed the obvious.

"Rosa?" he asked. "Are you pregnant? Is it mine? It's got to be mine. Oh, Rosa," he said, suddenly smiling and walking closer to Rosa. "We're going to have a baby?"

"We aren't going to have anything. *I* am going to have a baby."

"Come on, Rosa, this is a sign. We are meant to be together. We need to raise this baby together. You *have* to give me another chance."

"I can't talk about this now," Rosa said between tears. "You hurt me, René. You ripped my heart out. Do you have any idea what it was like for me to walk in on the two of you? How do I know it was just one time? How do I know it won't happen again?"

Linda and Gina, not to mention the rest of the bank, had been watching the spectacle unfold. Completely dumbfounded, Linda observed the two of them as lie after lie unraveled before her eyes. There was no lesbian lover, no sperm bank, hell, Rosa wasn't even a lesbian. Linda was especially disturbed when Rosa began asking questions—questions like "How do I know it was just one time?" or "How do I know it won't happen again?" Words like that meant she was starting to cave. She was starting to consider taking him back. She wasn't telling him to go away and never return. She was asking him to explain himself and assure her that he wouldn't hurt her again.

"It won't happen again, honey. I promise. I could never bear to lose you again," René said, lightly stroking Rosa's arm. "Rosa, please, let's try. Please, for the baby—*our* baby."

"I can't. I can't get hurt like that again," Rosa said, sobbing.

"I promise, Rosa. I will never, with God as my witness, hurt you again."

Rosa looked up at him and stared into his eyes. She just looked at him for a long pause before turning in closer and nuzzling her head into his chest. He hugged her tightly as she continued to cry.

"It's okay. It's okay," René said, trying to calm her. "What do you say we get out of here and talk for a while?"

René grabbed her hand and started to lead her out of the bank.

"Wait a minute, René," Rosa said, wiping the tears from her face before turning to Linda. "Linda, I just don't know what to say. I'm so sorry."

"There's a lot of sorrys floating around here today, aren't there? A lot of sorry people."

"I'll call you, Linda, once I get my head together."

"Don't bother."

Rosa just looked at her for a minute longer, lowered her eyes, and turned to leave.

"Rosa?" Linda called behind her. "If you love him and you really think he loves you . . . well . . . just let me know that the baby was born and that it's okay."

Again Rosa just looked at her, nodded her head, and gave her a weak smile before pushing open the door and letting it shut behind her.

Fill 'Er Up

Cameron was dragging a little these days. She had been with the company for almost a year, and this was the first time she had ever been late for work. It was nearly noon by the time she got in. She was so tense lately, she wasn't sleeping well. She was still getting hang-up calls at home every now and then—sometimes well into the wee hours of the morning. She tried to remember to turn the ringer off before going to bed, but sometimes it slipped her mind. Thank God the weird phone calls at work had stopped. There hadn't been any since the man who wanted her to spank him repeatedly with a Ping-Pong paddle. Maybe the whole thing was finally winding down.

The past few days she just had a sense that no one in the office particularly cared for her. She always figured people would understand that she was just doing her job when she produced her monthly reports about Internet and e-mail misconduct. After all, they were all adults. There was no reason to take it personally. Cameron prided herself on being efficient and doing her job with a certain degree of perfection. She wasn't about to let a bunch of losers who insisted on sending around e-mail jokes about bearded midgets get her down. As she stepped off the elevator, she threw her shoulders back and lifted her head, trying to put herself in a better mood.

Project confidence, Cameron. You're a winner in a world of losers, she thought to herself as she approached her desk. She flipped on her computer and sat down. After logging on to the network, Cameron waited for her e-mail to open and started reviewing her messages. There was an urgent request from her boss to compile her monthly reports and get them to him as soon as possible. Cameron immediately began riffling through her desk drawers to find the necessary documents.

When she found the last report, she swung around in her chair, and her computer monitor came into view. As she caught sight of her screen saver, her jaw dropped as she gasped for air. Staring directly at her was a picture of "Virtual Cameron," completely naked aside from a pair of stilettos and a gasoline hose—or, more accurately, a picture of Cameron's head superimposed onto someone else's body that was completely naked aside from a pair of stilettos and a gasoline hose. Shocked, Cameron hastily pecked at the keyboard to make the screen saver go away. Her first keystroke sent the figure into a fit of erotic masturbation. Virtual Cameron began gyrating—masturbating herself with one hand and swinging the hose with the other. Panicked, Cameron hit the keyboard again, only to add sound to the monstrosity on her screen. The sound system was set at full volume. (Annie had recorded the voice in a deep, throaty tone, but one of the settings must have gone astray, because the voice coming from the computer was more that of a vinyl record being played at high speed.) The voice of an excited chipmunk shouting "Fill me up! Fill me up!" blared from the speakers, sending sound waves into the office corridors and prompting staff to approach Cameron's desk to see where the noise was coming from. In a complete frenzy, Cameron hit the escape button on her keyboard. Thank God—that finally made it go away. Virtual Cameron disappeared and was replaced by a notice that popped up on her screen. It said "Thank you. Message sent to all company users."

Peter finally had justice. The annoying woman who had cost him a promotion and embarrassed him in front of his boss—the woman who made a career out of policing employee use of the Internet—had just sent Virtual Cameron to come alive on the computer screen of every employee at Saunders, Kraff, and Larson.

Must Think of Linda

"**O**h my God, Linda. Are you okay?" Gina said, realizing what a stupid thing that was to ask.

"I'm fine," Linda responded, staring down at her desk.

"I'm so sorry," Gina said, ashamed for feeling even remotely glad to see Linda and Rosa part company. Yes, Gina was jealous of Rosa and all the time Rosa and Linda had been spending together, but over the past month or so, Linda had an aura of contentment and confidence about her that Gina had never seen before. Gina was glad to see her doing so well and knew that she, probably more than anyone Gina knew, deserved to be happy. Linda was always even tempered and rarely moody, but she never really seemed genuinely happy until she met Rosa. Lately, it hadn't been uncommon for Gina to see her singing at her desk, and, once in a while, she caught her smiling like a Cheshire cat for no apparent reason.

"Why don't we go for a walk or something? It's not that busy, maybe we can sneak out for a minute or two."

"Thanks, Gina, but I'm fine, really. Easy come, easy go," Linda said, lifting her head and awkwardly shuffling through a few papers on her desk. "Why don't you go on to lunch, and I'll man the fort for a little while."

"Linda, you're not okay. You can't be. I wish I knew what to say."

"God, Gina! I'm fine. Would you drop it, please?" Linda said.

"I can't believe you asked her to call you when the baby was born. The little bitch rips your heart out and stomps on it, and that's all you have to say to her. Hey, if you won't give her a piece of your mind, then maybe I will."

"Gina! Everything is not a crisis. We don't all handle things the way you do. The whole fucking world doesn't revolve around Gina Perry and what she thinks of people," Linda said with a shortness in her tone that Gina had never heard before.

"I'm sorry, Linda. I'll shut up," Gina replied with a terribly hurt expression on her face. Linda had never spoken to her like that before, and it took Gina by complete surprise. She was used to being snapped at by Liz, and Mr. Toosh, and even Peter on occasion, but never by Linda. With the added stress of her impending HIV testing results, it was too much. Gina's eyes began to water, and she turned her face away from Linda.

"No, Gina, I'm sorry. You were just trying to help. I'm upset, and I'm taking it out on you."

"That's okay. You're right. I do tend to be a bit self-involved at times."

"You and the rest of the world. But I love you anyway."

"All right, Linda, please stop trying to make *me* feel better. I should be there for you," Gina said, wondering how she'd managed to do that. Linda was the one who just got dumped and humiliated in front of everyone at the bank, and somehow Gina ended up crying with Linda apologizing to *her* and trying to make *her* feel better.

God! Maybe I do think the world revolves around me. Oh, no! There I go. Linda's had her heart broken, and I'm worried about the world revolving around *me*. How can I do that? Stop. Must think of Linda. Must think of Linda. "Are you sure you don't want to talk about it? I wish there was something I could do."

"You and me both," Linda said before catching a glimpse of Rosa walking back through the bank entrance.

Linda stared icily at Rosa as she approached her desk, and Gina gave her the most evil look she could muster.

"Linda, can I talk to you for a minute?" Rosa asked meekly. "Please, let me try to explain."

"I really don't want to hear it, Rosa," Linda said. "I think my ears have heard all they can stand for one day."

"Linda, I—"

"What part of I REALLY DON'T WANT TO HEAR IT did you not understand?" Linda said, interrupting Rosa.

"Can I just have a chance to—"

"Please get out," Linda said, her cheeks swelling and tears beginning to form.

"I never wanted to hurt you, Linda. I promise—"

"You promise? You PROMISE? Who are you to promise anything? Please, Rosa, just get out," Linda said before raising her voice and saying it again. "Get out!" Linda called, trying to keep back the tears.

Rosa looked at her, clamped her eyes shut for a moment, and turned to go.

As Gina watched, she had a fleeting desire to attack Rosa the same way she had the kid who stole Gomez a couple of weeks earlier. She had never seen Linda in such obvious pain. Gina looked at Linda as Rosa walked out the door and walked over to give Linda a hug. She reached her arms out to Linda, who looked at her and backed away just a bit.

"Gina," Linda said with watering eyes. "I'm fine. Please, I'm fine," she said again, and walked away from Gina toward the bathroom. Gina hated that about falling in love. It made you so vulnerable and let someone else hold such power over you. The day before, Linda was all smiles and humming pop tunes at her desk, and next thing you know, she's crying in the bathroom. It was all so ridiculous to Gina—love, relationships, all of it. It was pointless. Nothing ever seemed to work out.

Gina watched Linda go, deciding to let her have her space for a while. She went back to her desk and watched the bathroom door close behind Linda.

God, I really don't act like the world revolves around me, do I? she thought again as she sat down at her desk.

And the Results
Are In

The whole spectacle between Linda and Rosa at the bank was terribly bothersome to Gina. She spent the rest of the workday walking on eggshells around Linda, who emerged from the bathroom determined to go on as if nothing happened. It drove Gina crazy that Linda didn't show more emotion. Gina tried a few more times to get her to talk about the whole mess, but Linda wouldn't hear of it. She kept insisting she was fine. If one good thing came of the whole situation, at least it took Gina's mind off her impending test results and made the day go by faster.

Gina and Cheryl drove out to the clinic together. They had chatted on the phone both nights since the testing day, and Gina was actually pleased to have Cheryl back in her life. Deep in conversation, they were almost able to forget about the test on the way over. They spent the better part of the drive discussing Peter's annoying habits and his hypochondria. His birthday was also coming up and, despite their latest drama, they knew they had to think of something to do for him.

The girls entered the clinic and checked in with the receptionist, who directed them to a waiting area down the hall. They signed in with their identifying code numbers and were told to have a seat until their numbers were called.

"Nervous?" Cheryl asked.

"Nervous. More like on the verge of a breakdown. I hate this waiting."

"Try to relax. Really, what are the chances of the test coming back positive?"

"Well, if we hadn't slept with a porn star who's slept with hundreds of women, they would probably be pretty slim."

"Even so, we only did it one time. Keep that in mind."

"It only takes one time."

"Okay, okay. I can see it's pointless to try to reassure you."

"I'm sorry, Cheryl. I know this is just as difficult for you as it is for me. I'm so thankful you've been around to lean on the past couple of days."

"No problem. I'm thankful you're speaking to me. I wasn't sure we'd ever be friends again."

"Honestly, I didn't plan on it. You just made me so angry that being nasty to you just sort of became a habit. Every time I thought about returning one of your phone calls, I forced myself to remember that night in the motel. You have to admit it, Cheryl. What you did was mean."

"You're right. I was wrong. I tried to convince myself that what I did was okay. After all, you and Peter were no longer together. He was fair game. But I knew you still had a thing for him, and I shouldn't have done that to a friend. But I wish you would've cut me a little slack. I was unbelievably drunk, and we ended up in the same bed together. It wasn't like I planned it."

"Maybe you didn't plan that night, but you kept seeing him from then on."

"What was I supposed to do? You ignored me. You basically forced Linda to stop seeing me. Peter was all I had left. This whole thing is so ridiculous, especially considering Peter and I have absolutely no future together."

"Why do you say that?"

"You know why, Gina. I know Peter enjoys my company and has genuine affection for me, but he would never seriously consider a long-term committed relationship with a black woman. Now, don't get me wrong. It's not that I think Peter is racist, but his parents would forbid it. Besides, I know Peter isn't ready to deal with all the other baggage that comes with an interracial relationship, and frankly, I'm not sure if I want to deal with it either," Cheryl replied. More and more she was realizing how unhealthy her relationship with Peter was. Regardless of what happened with Cooper, Cheryl was starting to believe that it was probably time to stop having sex with Peter.

Cheryl considered telling Gina about the night Peter lost it in the restaurant, but she wasn't sure Peter would want her to. Cheryl liked to think that Peter had been defending her when he attacked the racist bastard, but she sensed it went deeper than that. Whenever Cheryl brought it up, Peter quickly changed the subject, as if he didn't want to talk about it. Cheryl figured she'd let Peter tell Gina about it if he ever wanted to.

"Here we are, into the twenty-first century," Cheryl continued, "and we still get stares and an occasional snarl when we're together in public. And this is D.C. I shudder to think what it might be like in more rural areas or the South, where people aren't so politically correct. Good heavens . . ."

"Gosh. I never really thought about it. I don't think it was ever meant to be between Peter and me either. I know everyone says this when they've been dumped, but, honestly, if he hadn't broken up with me, I think I would have eventually ended the relationship myself."

"Really? I had no idea. Why?"

"I just couldn't take his drinking anymore. Cheryl, he used to drink so much."

"Peter?"

"Yes, you must have noticed it. Every time we got together, he'd have a beer in his hand. He drank every night of the week. It's so odd considering he's such a health nut in every other area of his life."

"Now that you mention it, I guess he does drink a lot. But so what? So do a lot of people."

"I know, and maybe I'm overreacting. Lord knows, I like a beer every now and then myself. It just worried me."

"I don't think there's any need to worry, Gina."

"Probably not, he just scared me sometimes when he got really drunk. It was almost as if I didn't know him anymore. That stuff's okay when you're in college, but when you're pushing thirty, it's time to grow up."

"Come on, Gina. He *scared* you?"

"Sometimes he really did. I think the last straw was actually right before he broke it off with me. I've never told this to anyone before, but one night we had stayed up late, watching movies on HBO, and had a bottle of wine or two. The next morning I woke up, and Peter had wet the bed. Can you believe that? It was disgusting. We never talked about it, and I'm not even sure he knows that I know, but that morning I really started to think that I had to end it. Oh, I don't know, I guess—"

"031272," called a woman from the hallway, interrupting Gina.

"Oh, God, that's my number," Gina said, standing up, her heart beginning to palpitate. "Wish me luck."

"Hi. I'm Carol. How are you?" the woman said to Gina. Scared shitless. "Fine, thanks."

The woman led Gina to a small room with two chairs and gestured for her to have a seat. Gina sat down and waited for what seemed like an eternity while Carol sorted through her papers. She asked Gina to verify her number again to make sure she had the correct results. Gina confirmed the number anxiously, wishing she'd get on with it.

"Your results were negative. There was no evidence of HIV."

"Oh, thank God!" Gina said, letting out a deep breath. "You're sure?"

"Yes, ma'am. The results are negative. Do you have any questions?"

"No. Thank you."

The woman then offered some brief information about the clinic and explained how to contact a counselor if she had questions later, and Gina left the room. As she closed the door behind her, Cheryl emerged from another room across the hall. Gina gave her the okay sign with her hands. Cheryl smiled and returned the gesture. They gave each other a quick hug and headed down the hallway.

"Thank God this is over!" Cheryl said as they walked out.

"Over? Cheryl, honey, it's hardly over."

"Yeah, I know we need to be tested again in a few months, but the counselor said the possibility of those results coming back positive is about as likely as us getting struck by lightning."

"No, I wasn't talking about that. I'm talking about Griffin, The Big G. He put us through hell. We've got to get back any films he has of us and make him shut down that Web site."

"How do you suppose we do that?"

"I'm not sure, Cheryl, but I'll think of something. I always do."

The Mad Pooper

Gina smiled at the last customer and held the door for him as he walked out of the bank. Her smile was genuine. She had a perpetual smile all day, thanks to her negative test results. She still had to figure out a way to keep her naked body off Griffin's Web site, but the test results were such a relief that for a brief time she was able to put it aside. She also needed to keep her own spirits up for Linda, who was a complete wreck, even if she wouldn't admit it, following the whole disaster with Rosa and René.

Gina locked the door behind the gentleman and walked back to her desk. She wanted to finish up some paperwork so she could leave right after the meeting. Once a week, Liz held a staff meeting after the bank closed. Liz usually attempted to turn them into her own version of a high school pep rally as she tried to get the staff riled up about cross-selling checking accounts and credit cards. Every once in a while she'd come up with some scheme to try to improve sales at the bank. Last week's offer of two free movie tickets to the teller with the most referral points was greeted with such overwhelming indifference, Liz withdrew the offer in a huff and adjourned the meeting. Gina was not looking forward to the coming meeting, but she was in such a good mood, she didn't let it bother her. As the staff assembled in the middle of the lobby, dragging chairs behind them, Gina's phone rang.

"Premier Bank of Arlington, Gina Perry speaking."

"Hey, sweetie, what's up?"

"Hi, Shirley, I'm just about to go into a meeting. Can I call you back?"

"Sure, but I just wanted to ask you a quick question," Shirley replied, figuring that asking Gina while she was in a hurry might be a good idea. "Sweetie, can I borrow fifty bucks?"

"You mean can you *have* fifty bucks that you never plan to return? What for?"

"I've got to pay this . . . this stupid . . . traffic ticket."

"No, Shirley, I've told you over and over again to stop speeding."

"I wasn't speeding. I was at the gas station, minding my own business, when I got the ticket."

"Somehow I doubt that, Shirley."

"I was at a gas station in Arlington, and I needed to vacuum the car. I figured I might as well do it while I was in the 'burbs. The dog was in the car with me—you know how Gomez likes to ride in the car. Anyway, I was afraid if I left him in the car while I was vacuuming, he might jump out and get hit or something."

"What does this have to do with anything?" Gina asked impatiently.

"Well, like I said, I was afraid he might jump out, so I put him in the trunk for a few minutes."

"What? Shirley, you put the dog in the trunk?"

"It was just for a few minutes. He didn't mind. He was just napping anyway. Well, someone must have seen me do it and called the police. Next thing I know, I'm getting lectured about pet care from some little Nazi in a police uniform. I think he was all of twenty-two or something. Can you believe that? Someone calling the cops on me. They probably trip over homeless people on the way to their Mercedes, but one little dog in the trunk, and they have to call the cops."

"Well, good. He should have given you a ticket. You ever

stick my dog in the trunk again, and I'll stick you in the trunk."

"I'm telling you, Gina, he didn't mind. It was quite a sight. The cop was trying to be all serious and uppity, and the whole time Gomez was barking at him and panting—"

"Gina?" Liz's unnerved voice came from the lobby. "We can have the meeting in the parking lot if we're disturbing your phone call."

"Shirley, I have to go. I'll call you later."

"Okay, but can I borrow the money? Hello? Gina?"

Gina hung up the phone, pulled her chair around to the front of her desk, and joined the meeting.

"Let's get started," Liz said to the bored group. "First thing on the agenda is our new sales incentive program. I've asked Gina to tell you about it."

Part of Gina's career improvement plan was to further develop her leadership skills, so Liz thought Gina would like to start running some of the staff meetings. Liz had met with Gina earlier that day and discussed her idea for an employee-of-the-month program. Gina thought the concept was as stupid as the free movie ticket idea. She gently tried to dissuade Liz, and recommended offering time off to employees who met their sales goals. She knew that just like her, most of the bank's employees would do almost anything if it would get them a day or two of paid time off. As usual, Liz ignored Gina's suggestion and stood firm about her employee-of-the-month program. If that wasn't bad enough, she asked Gina to present the idea to the group.

"Liz asked me to speak to everyone about *her* idea to incentivize all of us to improve our sales performance," Gina said to the crowd. *"She* thought it would be a good idea to identify an employee of the month based on who best meets or exceeds his or her sales goals."

Gina felt like a complete idiot handing out a stack of convoluted forms that explained the scoring system and the criteria for being named employee of the month.

"So what does the employee of the month get?" Bob, one of the tellers, asked.

Trying to muster up something that resembled enthusiasm, Gina said, "Your name engraved on the employee of the month plaque and your picture posted on the bulletin board." I know, whoopty fucking doo!

"That's it?"

"Yes, I'm afraid so."

Once again Liz's idea was met with unilateral apathy.

"It's a chance for you guys to get some recognition for your hard work. Being employee of the month will make you a Premier celebrity of sorts. I'll make sure Mr. Toosh knows who each employee of the month is," Liz added, trying to raise some excitement for the idea but succeeding only in getting a few polite nods. Discouraged with the group's reaction, Liz decided to move on to other business. She discussed some upcoming changes in the bank's fees and some other policy revisions, then opened up the floor for questions.

"Does anyone have any other issues they would like to bring up?" Liz asked the group.

"Yeah," Tammy, who was never one to mince words, added, "Someone's dropping turds in the toilet and not flushing."

"What? Dropping turds?" Liz responded.

"You know, taking a dump and then leaving it in the can without flushing."

"She's right," Linda added. "I've seen it a few times, and it's pretty nasty. The other day they did it right *on* the toilet seat."

As the other women in the room nodded in agreement, Liz dropped her mouth as if the news were a total shock, which just confirmed Gina's suspicion that she was the culprit. How was it possible that every other female in the bank had come upon the Mad Pooper's (as Linda and Gina had started calling her) little gifts but Liz?

"That's terrible," Liz responded, starting to turn a bright shade of red. "I'm not sure what to do about this."

"Why would someone do that?" Bob asked no one in particular.

"My cat does that when she gets mad," Tammy said. "Whenever we leave her for long periods of time, she shits all over the place—on the sofa, the bedspread. . . ."

"Enough, Tammy," Liz snapped. "I will put up a sign in the bathroom reminding people to flush. Sometimes individuals from other cultures aren't aware of proper bathroom etiquette," Liz said, condescendingly smiling at Jabeen, who was from Iraq.

How dare you! Gina thought, sending an angry glare at Liz before adding, "Oh, I don't think that's the case. I've seen it happen on several occasions when no one from *another culture* was here."

Something about the way she had smiled at Jabeen unleashed a new disdain for Liz and made Gina terribly angry.

"In fact, Linda and I were comparing notes, and the only consistency we could come up with was that *you* always seem to be here when it happens," Gina said to Liz.

A tense silence fell over the room. Gina had just shot a bullet, and everyone waited to see what Liz would do—dodge it, suffer a minor injury, or drop dead. Liz responded to Gina's jab by sitting in her chair stone-faced. She couldn't respond. She didn't have any words. She sat in silence, and Gina almost felt sorry for her but couldn't because Liz had been perfectly comfortable trying to put the blame on Jabeen.

Oh, God. I've just pissed off a woman who regularly defecates on toilet seats. What else is she capable of? "Well, what's it really matter who's doing it as long as it stops. I think the meeting's over, guys," Gina said to the group, gesturing for them to move on before turning to Liz. "Liz, I'm sorry. I didn't mean to imply anything. Are you okay?"

Trying to hide her humiliation, Liz responded, "Of course I'm okay. Now, I'd better go put up that sign. We have to try something to make this person, whoever it is, stop this."

Now Gina really did feel sorry for her. What fantasyland was she living in? Everyone knew she was the Mad Pooper, and there she was, trying to save face anyway. Gina was really starting to question Liz's sanity.

"God! Is this what seventeen years at Premier does to a

person?" Gina said to Linda as they watched Liz walk back into her office.

"She's trippin', Gina. I'm worried about her."

"I'm sorry I embarrassed her, but she was trying to pin it on Jabeen."

"I know. That was dirty."

"Well, if she didn't hate me before, I'm sure she hates me now."

"What do you think?" Liz interrupted the girls, holding up a sign that read "Please flush the toilet after use." She was smiling as if nothing had happened.

"It looks fine," Linda responded.

"Great," Gina added.

The girls watched her march into the ladies' room with her sign.

"Gina," Linda said. "I don't think you need to worry. I don't think she even remembers what you said. I think she deleted it from her hard drive, if you know what I mean."

"I hope so," Gina replied, pausing for a moment. "You know what, Linda? We need to get the fuck out of here."

"Okay, I'm right behind you."

"No. I mean permanently. This place sucks the life out of people. Look at Liz and Mr. Toosh. They're deranged."

"Gina, I'm sure they were deranged before they ever started working here."

"Linda, I've got to find another job. How do you stand it here?"

"It doesn't bother me that much. In fact, some days I like it here. I like the customers for the most part, and I like helping them work the system so Premier doesn't get the best of them. Besides, I'm good at it."

"Yes, you are, but I'm certainly not."

No, you're not. "Sure you are. You just don't have any motivation. You know, Annie was rambling on about her business the other night. If you want out of here so bad, why don't you call her?"

"I think she was just hitting on you, Linda."

"Maybe so. Who could blame her?" Linda joked, and actually cracked a smile, one of few since René had shown up at the bank. "But I'm sure she can offer some advice and maybe even a job."

"You know, Linda. I might just do that. This place makes me nuts. I mean, my God, Liz is acting like an angry animal. Gomez does that every once in a while. He gets mad when I leave him alone too much or try to feed him cheap dog food, and then he pees in the apartment."

Gina forgot to mention that Gomez also got annoyed when she had guests over and didn't pay enough attention to him. Like that night a few years earlier when she and Peter stayed up late, watching movies on HBO and drinking wine. They hardly paid any attention to him at all. Gomez got so mad, he peed right on the bed while Gina and Peter were sleeping.

The Birthday Boy

Gina, Linda, and Dennis added their names to the waiting list at Lauriol Plaza, a popular Mexican restaurant with some of the best margaritas in town. The hostess gave them a beeper and they waited in the bar area. It had been over a week since Linda found out about Rosa's husband. She had been keeping to herself the past few days, but Gina wouldn't hear of her missing Peter's birthday party. The three of them had spent most of the day in the middle of Dupont Circle, catching rays, and they had all picked up slight tans. Once again, Gina swore it was her last summer in the sun. Next summer she'd stay under an umbrella. She saw what years of heavy tanning had done to Shirley's skin, and Gina was determined to age more gracefully than her mother.

"Any prospects?" Gina asked Dennis, eyeing the crowd, looking for someone to fix him up with.

"Gina, we just got here. I haven't even gotten a drink. What do you guys want from the bar?"

Gina and Linda both asked for margaritas, and Dennis headed off toward the bar. They were still waiting for Cheryl and Peter, and Shirley was also due to show up later. She had started walking a few more dogs in Gina's building and needed to get them squared away before coming to the restaurant. It was Peter's birthday, so the gang was celebrating with dinner at Lauriol Plaza and maybe some dancing later at Rumors or Polly Esthers. They were all trying to put on a happy face for his sake but, truth be known, the assembling group was rather gloomy. Linda was still down in the dumps over the whole Rosa fiasco, and Gina and Cheryl were totally distracted with trying to keep their naked bodies off the Internet. But they agreed to try to relax and have some fun for one evening.

The girls leaned against the wall and looked around. Gina felt a sense of relief being in a bar and just hanging out with her friends rather than man hunting. As she thought about it, going out to bars seemed more like work than anything else. She couldn't quite place the exact time that it happened—when going out to clubs turned from seeking a fun evening of drinking and dancing with her friends to the task of trying to find a decent guy. And the older she got, the more urgent the task seemed to be. She read somewhere that if she wasn't married by the time she was thirty, she had a better chance of getting hit by a bus than landing a husband. Or was it thirty-five? God! She hoped it was thirty-five.

"So Cheryl is coming and you don't mind," Linda asked, intrigued by Gina's sudden reconciliation with Cheryl.

"No, we had a chat the other day. We've decided to put the past behind us."

"Really? What happened?" Linda questioned again, still having trouble believing Gina and Cheryl were going to sit down to dinner together.

"Nothing," Gina lied. She wasn't ready to tell Linda about the whole mess with Griffin, and she wasn't sure she ever would be. "I guess I'm just getting soft in my old age."

"Whatever," Linda said, not really buying Gina's story but willing to let it go for then.

When there was a quick lull in their conversation, a young man leaned toward Gina and Linda in the crowded bar area and spoke to Gina. "What's a nice girl like you doing in a place like this?" an unbelievably gorgeous, and obviously gay, young man joked to Gina.

"Because the margaritas rock," Gina said.

"They do, don't they," the young man with killer blue eyes and dark brown hair replied. "The pretty boys are just an added bonus."

"For you, maybe."

As they continued talking, Dennis came back from the bar with three margaritas in his hands. He offered two to Gina and Linda.

"Thanks. Dennis this is . . . well, actually, I don't know who this is."

"Christopher."

"Chris, this is Dennis, and Linda, and I'm Gina."

"Christopher," he said, correcting Gina. "It's a pleasure to meet you guys. What brings you out tonight?"

"It's our friend's birthday. He's not here yet. We're taking him to dinner here and then out for some more fun," Linda said to the young man.

"Sounds like a fun evening."

"I hope so," Gina said. "And what about you? What's your deal, *Christopher?*"

"My boyfriend and I are just waiting for a table."

"So where is this boyfriend?" Gina asked, curious to see what his boyfriend looked like.

"He's right over there," Christopher said before calling to his significant other. "Hey, Karl," he yelled across the bar. Karl didn't hear him, so he yelled again. "Karl . . . Karl Mullins, you twit!" he yelled again, waving for him to come over and meet Gina and her friends.

"What's up?" Karl said to Christopher before catching a glimpse of Gina.

"I just wanted you to meet these guys."

"Oh, we've met," Gina said with a bit of a glare.

"Yes, we have. How are you, Gina?"

"Oh, since I cut out onions for dinner, I'm doing pretty well," Gina responded somewhat awkwardly. She felt herself tensing up and just wanted to get away from Karl and Christopher. Even if the whole thing was a joke, she still felt embarrassed. She had her hands down his boxer shorts, for heaven's sake.

"I'm so sorry, Gina. Annie put me up to the whole thing, but I guess you know that already," Karl responded, equally uneasy. It was bad enough when he ran into guys he'd had a one-night stand with, but this was beyond uncomfortable.

"I guess I do," Gina said, trying to think of something to say to ease the obvious tension.

"Don't worry about it, Karl," she added, trying to sound relaxed. "I deserved it."

"Deserved what?" Linda asked.

"Nothing," Gina said.

"Nothing? It doesn't sound like nothing," Dennis added.

"Nothing is another word for none of your business," Gina responded, giving Karl a look that forbade him to share any details. Luckily, Peter and Cheryl sauntered through the door before Dennis and Linda could continue the interrogation.

"There they are," Gina said. "Well, it was nice to meet you, Christopher. Wish I could say the same for you, Karl," Gina joked, trying to offer a slight smile to show there were no hard feelings.

When their beeper finally went off, the gang approached the hostess and was seated at a big round booth upstairs. Just as they were sitting down, Shirley arrived and took a seat next to the birthday boy. They enjoyed a huge platter of fajitas and shared a variety of desserts that the waiter brought out with candles for the happy birthday singalong. They finished two pitchers of margaritas by the time they got around to opening Peter's gifts.

"Thank you, Shirley," Peter said after opening his birthday present from her. It was a black tank top with a white stripe.

"Sure, hon, I thought you'd like it. It'll show off your muscles."

Hmm, where'd she steal that from? Gina thought, looking at Shirley.

"Did you buy it small enough, Shirley?" Linda asked. "You know Peter only shops in the boys' department these days. It's the only place he can find shirts tight enough."

"Open mine! Open mine!" Cheryl said like an anxious child. She picked up a small box from the floor and handed it to Peter. "Hope you like it."

Peter ripped off the wrapping and opened the box.

"It's a picture," Peter said before flipping over the frame.

"No, no," Cheryl said. "It's a poem. I wrote it myself."

Peter examined the framed poem, pretending to read it, and tried to muster a smile.

What the fuck am I supposed to do with this? Next! "Thanks, Cheryl, that is so cool." He attempted to admire it for a few more seconds, then set it aside.

What a dumb girlie thing to do. What guy wants a poem? Gina thought as she handed him her gift. It was a casual Timberland watch she picked up at the Fashion Centre at Pentagon City. He had been complaining that his watchband broke a few days earlier. Peter opened the package and seemed genuinely pleased with the contents. In fact, he put it on right away.

"Do you like it?"

"It's exactly what I need. Thank you, Gina."

"You're quite welcome," Gina said, pleased with herself. He obviously was much more enamored with the watch than with Cheryl's stupid poem. She and Cheryl may have been friends again, but where Peter was concerned, there would always be issues.

"I know it's Peter's birthday, but, Shirley, I have a gift for you as well," Gina said, handing Shirley a small box.

"For li'l ole me?" Shirley said, accepting the box and ripping it open. It was a box of business cards that said "Shirley's Dog-walking and Pet Care Services." It had Shirley's name, address, and phone number, and a small cartoon of a dachshund, a poodle, and a German shepherd.

"What's this about?"

"Shirley, you've practically started your own business. How many dogs are you walking now? Four? Five? You might as well make it official."

"Yeah, I guess I have," Shirley said with a proud smile. "Thank you, sweetie. This means a lot to me."

"Okay, back to the birthday boy," Linda said, and handed him her gift. As Peter started to unwrap his present, Gina peered over his shoulder and saw a petite woman lingering on the steps near the bar area. Gina gave the young lady a nod and then whispered to Linda.

"Linda, there's someone at the bar who would like to have a word with you."

Linda looked over toward the bar. "What is *she* doing here?"

"Give her a chance, Linda. At least listen to what she has to say."

"Did you tell her to come here?"

"No, I didn't tell her to come here, but I did mention that you would be here tonight."

"You've been in touch with her?"

"She's called a couple of times just to see how you're doing."

"Gina, I really have nothing to say to her, and what's with you? You were never a huge fan of hers."

"Linda, I don't like *anyone* who takes your time away from me, but I'll get over it. I've never seen you as happy as when you were with her. I want you to have that. How often does someone come along who makes your knees wobbly, Linda? Believe me, I know. Go on."

Linda excused herself from the table and walked out to the bar toward Rosa.

"Hi, Linda, thanks for seeing me."

"I'm not sure what to say, Rosa. Why are you here?"

"I need to apologize."

"You did that already."

"I know. Linda, I can't undo what I did. I lied to you, and I hurt you very badly. I don't blame you for hating me, but I have to try . . . I have to try. . . ."

"Try what?" Linda asked.

"I shouldn't have let you go. And for René of all people—what an idiot."

"He did seem like kind of an idiot," Linda said with a slight laugh, softening her stance just a bit.

"I meant me. But you're right. He is an idiot. He's back in Boston. It's over between us."

"Rosa, I can forgive you, but, honestly, I don't see us getting back together."

"That's fine, Linda. I just want you in my life in some form. If it can only be as a friend, then I will accept that for now. Shoot, I don't even deserve that. I was really stupid. René hurt me so much, and then I go and do the same thing to you."

"That you did," Linda said, not afraid to further lay the guilt on Rosa.

"I don't know what happened. The best way to get back at him was to have an affair of my own, and when I met you at the bank, I figured if I did it with another woman, that would be the ultimate revenge. I didn't plan on falling in love with you, Linda. God, I'm so sorry."

"It's going to take a little more than an apology, Rosa. I can't believe that everything I thought we had was a farce."

"In the beginning maybe it was, but only in the beginning. I never would've told you about the pregnancy if I wasn't planning long-term with you. For God's sake, I asked you to be my birthing coach. Do you think I would've done that if I didn't want to be with you?"

"I don't know what to believe, Rosa. You don't exactly have the best track record."

"No, I don't. I'm just asking for a chance."

"I have to think about it," Linda fibbed. She knew she would take Rosa back. She knew the moment she saw her in the bar and her stomach got that familiar knot. Rosa was all she had thought about for the entire week. Linda was so hurt and angry with Rosa for lying to her. She had tried to convince herself that Rosa had lied to her because she cared about her and didn't want to upset her. Rosa had no way of knowing René was going to show up at the bank and blow the lid off everything she had told Linda. But when was Rosa going to tell her? Had she planned on ever telling her?

Ever since the confrontation at the bank, Linda had wanted to call Rosa and give her a chance to explain. Rosa had become a part of her life and so had Rosa's unborn baby. Linda wanted there to be a good explanation, but how could there be one? Rosa had purposefully lied to her for months, but Linda had wanted to forgive her from the beginning. That's what you did for people you loved—you tried to believe the best about them and give them the benefit of the doubt.

"Listen, it's Peter's birthday, and I have to get back to my friends. I need time to think things over. Maybe you can give me a call, and we can talk about this some more."

"I'll do that," Rosa said.

Linda walked back to the table, wanting to let a huge smile burst on her face, but she remained calm and unaffected. She didn't want her feelings to show to Rosa. She wasn't sure how much pleading she was going to make Rosa do before taking her back.

Wench

While Linda was conversing with Rosa at the bar, Peter started to stack his gifts in a little pile, while the rest of the table finished their coffee.

"It was nice to see you again, Cheryl," Shirley said. "I think it's been years. You look great. I love that dress."

"Thanks," Cheryl said. "I had to put it on at the last minute. I have this great navy-blue dress that I love. I was going to wear that tonight, but I think I forgot it at the dry cleaners or something. I couldn't find it."

"Well, if your place is as messy as it used to be, it's probably buried under some papers or something," Gina joked.

Cheryl smiled. "Yeah, one of these days I'm going to get organized. I have to, or I'm going to end up running around naked."

"Maybe Dennis can give you some lessons, his place is the neatest I've ever seen."

"That's 'cause I'm never home," Dennis said.

"Really?" Shirley asked. "So, what have you been up to, Dennis?" she continued as the group watched Peter neurotically try to pile his gifts on top of each other according to size.

"Nothing . . . nothing interesting anyway. During the week,

all I do is work, go to the gym, watch a little television, and then go to bed."

"What about weekends? I thought you'd be at the beach?"

"I'm not going to the beach every weekend anymore. It just got to be too much. I need a few weekends in town to get things done . . . you know . . . my laundry, grocery shopping. . . . I think this is going to be my last year participating in a house for the whole summer. Guess I'm just getting old."

"God, if you're old, what does that make me?" Shirley asked.

Dennis laughed at Shirley's comment. "I don't know. I'm just a little tired of the whole beach scene—the themed parties, and the drinking, and the attitude. It's fun when you're twenty-two, but I guess I'm growing out of it."

"Well, good," Gina chimed in. "It will be fun to have you in town on the weekends next summer. Besides, how are you supposed to land a man in town if you're at the beach every weekend?"

"Oh, please, it's not like half the guys at the beach aren't from D.C. And it's not like I'm having any luck lately anyway. Remember that guy I told you about a few weeks ago? The hot black man I met at JR's?" Dennis asked Gina.

"Yeah, but when you said you met him at JR's, I assumed he was white," Gina said. JR's wasn't exactly known for the ethnic diversity of its clientele.

"What a loser he turned out to be," Dennis said.

"What happened?"

"We went out a couple of times, and things seemed to be going well until, get this, he tells me about his *girlfriend*."

"Girlfriend? What kind of gay man has a girlfriend?" Shirley asked.

"It's so pathetic, Shirley. He told me he works for this Internet company. He's mostly in charge of securing interest from outside investors, so he has to do a lot of wining and dining."

"What does that have to do with anything?" Gina asked.

"He said some of his investors are from the Midwest and

pretty traditional, so he has to put on the ole straight act. Apparently, he's conned this poor girl into going on his outings with him and has led her to believe he's interested in more than just a companion for his business functions."

"Doesn't the poor bitch get a little suspicious when he doesn't try to get in her panties?" Shirley asked.

"You know, it's the strangest thing. He said she hasn't really even tried to get physical with him—a few kisses here and there, and that's been it. He said he hasn't had to dodge her advances at all."

"Well, it's bound to come up sometime," Gina said.

"He apparently has it covered," Dennis replied. "He told this girl he's all Christian and shit, so he figures he can tell her he's waiting until he gets married. He even told her he's a Republican. Can you imagine? A black gay Republican? The whole thing is so ridiculous. I didn't want any part of it, so I told him to hit the road."

"God, you kind of feel sorry for whatever poor wench is caught up in that mess," Cheryl, who had been quiet up to then, added from the other side of the table.

"Yeah, sounds pretty sad," Gina said. "With my luck, I'm surprised it's not me. What's his name, anyway?"

"Cooper. Everett Cooper, actually, but he goes by his last name."

"What?" Cheryl shrieked.

Dennis just looked at her, not sure what she was asking about or why she seemed so startled.

"What did you say his name was again?" she asked, trying to appear calm.

"Cooper."

Oh, God! It can't be the same Cooper. "Really?" Cheryl asked, trying to sound casual. "What's he look like?"

"He a pretty good-looking black man. He's tall, with a shaved head, nice build . . . shame he's such a loser."

"Oh," Cheryl added, still trying not to sound bothered. "Hey, I've got to run to the bathroom. I never remember where they are. Can you show me, Dennis?"

"They're just down the steps over by the bar."

"Oh, just show me, would you? I hate wandering around aimlessly."

"Okay," Dennis said, getting up from the table, a little confused by Cheryl's need for an escort to the bathroom.

As they walked down the steps to the lower level of the restaurant, Dennis heard Cheryl let out a loud "Fuck!"

"What?"

"That fucking bastard!"

"What are you talking about?" Dennis asked.

Cheryl looked at Dennis. "I'm the pathetic wench."

"The pathetic wench?" Dennis questioned before realizing what Cheryl was referring to. "Not Cooper's pathetic wench?"

"That's me. I'm the wenchiest wench of all."

"Oh, my God! He's been taking you around with his clients?"

"God, I should have known. We had only been out a few times, and he was referring to me as his *girl* in front of his business associates."

"Well, he is nice-looking. I can see why you fell for him," Dennis said, trying to offer some condolence.

"He isn't going to be so nice-looking by the time I'm through with him. As soon as I get home, I'm going to call him . . . no! I'm going to go see him and tell him off in person. Do you know where he lives?"

"You don't?"

"No. He always came to my place."

"Cheryl, I don't think it's a good idea to go over there now. Let yourself cool down a little."

"Dennis, tell me where he lives."

"Cheryl, what are you going to accomplish—"

"Dennis," Cheryl said, interrupting him. "Tell me where he lives. I'll just find out some other way if you don't."

"I'm not really sure I could tell you where he lives. I'd probably have to show you. I've only been there once."

"Oh, God! You've slept with him? I don't even know where he lives, and you've slept with him! Take me to see him, Dennis. Now!"

"What do you expect me to tell everyone at the table?" Dennis questioned.

"Tell them I don't feel well and you're going to take me home."

"Cheryl, let's just stay here for—"

"Tell them NOW!" Cheryl said, raising her voice.

"Okay, okay," Dennis said, and went off to deliver the news.

Hot Stuff

——————

"This is so ridiculous. I should have known it would never work out. He's cute and interesting and employed. Of course it couldn't work out. What was I thinking?" Cheryl said to Dennis as they drove toward Cooper's apartment.

"My God! He told me all about how he was a Christian. He even pretended to be uncomfortable around gay people," Cheryl added before thinking for a moment. "Maybe he isn't gay, Dennis. Maybe *you* were the one he was lying to," Cheryl said, not believing her words herself. But maybe there was some sort of explanation.

"Lying to me about what?"

"About being gay and using me to go along to work functions with him."

"I don't know, Cheryl. He seemed pretty gay the night he had his mouth wrapped around my—"

"Dennis!"

"Well, he did."

"Then maybe he's bisexual," Cheryl pondered, grasping at straws at this point, trying to come up with anything that might explain what Cooper said to Dennis. "I can't believe this," Cheryl said as they hopped out of Dennis' car and headed up the steps to Cooper's apartment.

"I don't know. When you think about it, it's actually kind of funny," Dennis replied before getting a look at Cheryl's glare. "Okay, not so funny."

As they climbed the steps, they heard music coming from Cooper's apartment. He had Donna Summer's "Hot Stuff" blaring from the stereo.

"He plays Donna Summer? And you didn't know he's gay?" Dennis said to Cheryl as he knocked on the door.

"I never heard him play Donna Summer. And he's bi! Not gay!"

Dennis knocked again. "The boy's gay as a twenty-four-hour gym."

"He is not," Cheryl said again, trying to convince herself as much as Dennis. Logically, she knew Dennis was right, but she had to hold on to something.

"Have you seen his CD collection?" Dennis asked.

"What does that have to do with anything?"

"I've seen it—Cher, Madonna, Barbra, Bette, Patti . . . shall I go on?"

"Well, unless you saw some Ricky Martin in there, I'm not convinced."

"Cooper," Cheryl called as she knocked again. "Oh, for heaven's sake, he can't hear us with the music up so loud."

"Yep, gay boys can't listen to Donna Summer at half mast. We've got to crank her up."

"I'm telling you, Dennis, he's bi."

"Gay!"

"Bi."

"Gay."

"Bi!" Cheryl repeated, finally having enough of the waiting and turning the knob to open the door.

"Oh, my God!" Cheryl and Dennis said in unison as the door flung open to Cooper decked out in a blond wig, Cheryl's favorite navy-blue dress, black pumps, and her gold hoop earrings. He was gyrating around the living room, lip-syncing to Donna Summer.

"Oh, my God!" Cheryl said again. "My clothes! You're wearing my clothes! You stole my clothes!"

"Cheryl? Dennis? What are you doing here? Haven't you ever heard of knocking?" a clearly flustered Cooper asked.

"We did knock, *Donna*. We knocked numerous times. Maybe you should lock your door before you parade around in women's clothes . . . my clothes." Cheryl put her hand to her head and sighed.

Cooper tried to think of something to say . . . anything to say, but there wasn't any excuse in the book that he could make up to explain his attire, so he just stood quietly, looking at Dennis and Cheryl.

The three of them languished in the awkward moment— each of them totally silent while Donna Summer blared in the background, until Dennis just couldn't hold it back any longer. He held his stomach with one arm, pointed at Cooper with the other, and burst out laughing.

"This is funny to you?" Cheryl said crossly to Dennis.

"I'm sorry," Dennis said, trying to keep his composure. "But look at him."

Cheryl looked at Cooper, a stocky black man in a blond wig, full makeup, and *her* clothes.

"I don't find it funny at all," she said, starting to laugh just a little. "But he does look ridiculous," she added, letting the giggles come out a bit more and eventually starting to really crack up.

"What were you thinking?" Dennis said to Cooper. "That dress is all wrong for you. And who styled that wig? Atrocious!"

"You know, you're right," Cheryl said, trying to control her laughter and giving Cooper a good once-over herself. "He isn't exactly petite," she continued, eyeing Cooper, who was about to burst out of Cheryl's dress. Somehow he'd managed to get it over his hips, but the dress was way too small for it to actually go over his shoulders for the zipper to meet properly in the back. "He should really be in black. Black is slimming, you know," Cheryl added as she and Dennis looked Cooper up and down, talking about him as if he weren't in the room.

"Black is not slimming. That is such a myth," Dennis said.

"Oh, it is too," Cheryl insisted.

"Oh, please. All these people, big as hippos, thinking they look like Jennifer Aniston because they're in black. There's only one thing that's slimming, Cheryl. It's called losing some damn weight."

"Whatever, Dennis. But he should at least be in something with more of a waistline, don't you think? And what made him think he could carry off that blond wig?" Cheryl said as she and Dennis starting circling Cooper to get a view of him from all sides.

"Look how he's stretching out those shoes. How did he get those canoes of his into your little black pumps?" Dennis asked.

"Could you two just get out?" Cooper scowled to the laughing duo.

"He'll have to get some bigger shoes. And what about that snazzy black dress I've seen you in—you know, the stretchy fabric one. That might suit him," Dennis said, ignoring Cooper's request.

"You know. You're right . . . probably look better on him than me."

"Cooper, you should really let us fix you up," Dennis said to a clearly frustrated Cooper. "We could take you from trailer park tacky to Park Avenue style in no time."

"Thanks, but no thanks," Cooper said. He was trying to look stern, but in a blond wig, high heels, and an unflattering dress, he couldn't quite pull it off. He awkwardly wobbled toward the door in Cheryl's heels, held it open, and gestured for them to leave.

"Guess, he doesn't want our help, Dennis," Cheryl said.

"Oh, well," Dennis replied as they walked out the door, giggling, with Cooper shutting it behind them.

Dennis and Cheryl laughed some more before they started into their own version of "Hot Stuff." They sang Donna Summer and did a little dance as they walked back to the car.

After they had gotten in the car and settled down, Dennis looked over at Cheryl, sitting next to him.

"I'm sorry things didn't work out," he said softly.

"Oh, I've been dicked over by better guys than him. I'll be okay. Besides, I can't date someone who looks better in my clothes than I do." And Cheryl meant what she said. She *had* been dicked over by better guys than Cooper, and she *would* be okay. Dealing with the whole Internet mess with Griffin and going through the HIV testing process had been a nightmare, but it did teach Cheryl how strong she could be when she needed to. It also helped her see her life more clearly. There would be other Coopers to date (hopefully, Coopers who didn't steal her clothes), and, until then, she had her friends. Gina was back in her life, which meant Linda was back in her life as well. So what if Cooper was a lying thief. She had her friends, and they would help her get through anything.

Talk Show

Gina heard a slight ruckus from the crowd as she stood backstage, waiting for Star Jones to announce her. She was surprised by the way the set looked close up. Somehow it seemed bigger than on television. She clenched her fists as Star began the introduction.

"Ladies and gentlemen, we have a super special guest with us today on *The View.* You've all seen the story in the news lately—how a pudgy, balding man managed to seduce a slew of young, attractive women and get it all on film—film many of you naughty boys may have seen on the Internet already. Well, one of those young ladies is speaking out. Come on out, Gina. Gina Perry, ladies and gentlemen."

As the crowd offered polite applause, Gina tried to confidently saunter onto the stage. Star gave her a big hug, like they were best friends, when, in fact, they were meeting for the first time. Gina then shook hands with Lisa, Joy, and Meredith (Barbara was off that day) and took a seat between the four co-hosts.

"Hello, Gina. How are you today?"

"A little nervous. It's so exciting to be here," Gina offered, hoping a little humility might win over the crowd.

"So you've had quite a summer. Haven't you?"

"Oh, Star, you can only imagine."

"Well, let's start from the beginning. How did you meet this Big G character?"

"I was at a bar with a friend, and when I ordered a drink, he stepped in and paid for it."

"Is that when you think he drugged you?" Joy asked, joining the conversation

"I'm certain of it. I don't go home with guys from bars," Gina lied. "I never would have done it if I weren't under the influence of some mind-altering drug."

"And we know of at least one other victim who suspects she was drugged. But, Gina, what do you say to those other women he filmed who said that they weren't drugged, and you're probably lying about it?" Joy continued

"I say they're sluts," Gina replied. Her remark was followed by a mixture of laughter, clapping, and a hiss or two from the audience. "Honestly, Joy, do I look like a girl who would go home with a guy like that?"

Joy lifted her eyebrows instead of answering Gina's question, before asking, "So how did you find out that Griffin . . . Griffin was his name, right? The Big G?"

"Yes, Griffin Cirelli."

"How did you find out about his Web site? And worse yet, that you were a part of it?"

"A friend of mine happened to mention the Web site in general terms, so I checked it out."

"What did you do when you found out?" asked Meredith, who was seated a couple of chairs down from Gina.

"What did I do? I freaked. I cried. I was so upset. I felt so helpless." Again Gina tried to win the crowd over with emotion.

"So if you could say anything to Griffin now, what would it be?" Lisa, who had been quiet until then, asked.

Burn in hell, you fucking tiny-dicked bastard! "I would say that I feel sorry for him, and I wish that he hadn't been so evil as to take advantage of fellow human beings. . . ."

Before Gina could finish pontificating, a large woman rose from the audience.

"Slut! Slut! Slut!" she shouted from the crowd.

Shocked, Gina peered out into the audience. She recognized the woman. It was the fat lady on Rollerblades Gomez had bitten a couple of months back.

"You lying whore," she shouted. "You slept with him willingly, and you wanted to get it all on film so you could play Little Ms. Victim and get all this press and attention," the woman said to Gina before addressing the general audience. "I know for a fact, she and The Big G are in cahoots together. They want to make Gina Perry the biggest star in the adult film world. What better way to do it than make a media circus out of some whore who pretends to have been drugged and seduced? She's evil, I tell you. Gina Perry is pure evil. Look what her dog did to my leg," the woman yelled before standing up with the help of a cane and showing the crowd a huge gaping wound in her leg. "She's a conniving bitch, I tell you. Die, you conniving bitch! Die! Slut! Bitch! Whore! Die, you slut! Bitch! Whore!" the woman said, trying to get the crowd riled up. "Die, you slut! Bitch! Whore!" the woman said again.

A few audience members joined in. "Die, you slut! Bitch! Whore!" A few more. "Die, you slut! Bitch! Whore!" The entire audience began shouting at Gina and stamping their feet. "Die, you slut! Bitch! Whore! Die, you slut! Bitch! Whore!"

Completely taken aback, Gina yelled back at them, "I'm not a slut. I'm not! I'm not a bitch. I'm not a whore." She was terrified. "Star, help me," Gina said. "Please! Call security or something."

Star looked at her in silence as she and her three co-hosts moved in a little closer to Gina's face. "Die, you slut! Bitch! Whore!" they said in sync with the audience. . . .

Beep Beep Beep Beep Beep—Gina reached over and slammed the alarm clock with her hand. She was still hearing "Die, you slut! Bitch! Whore!" as she woke up in a cold sweat. What was she going to do? The nasty little man was even invading her sleep. She had to rid herself of him once and for all. She had to.

She riffled through the nightstand for Annie's phone number. She had come up with the idea a few days earlier but was hesitant to ask for Annie's help again.

"Hello, Annie?"

"Gina? It's seven o'clock in the morning," Annie said, sounding dazed and tired.

"I'm sorry. Did I wake you?"

"As a matter of fact . . . Why are you calling so early?"

"I hate to do this, Annie, but can I ask for your help one last time?"

"Maybe. What is it?"

"I've heard you can use the Internet to find people, where they live, their phone number, stuff like that. I was wondering if you could help me locate someone."

"That's easy enough. Who do you want to find?"

"It's such a long story, Annie. Can I meet you later today? We can talk about it then," Gina said, trying to buy some time. She'd have to make up a good story to tell Annie. She wasn't about to tell her the truth.

Feeling Like an
Absolute Heel

"Have a seat and the doctor will be right with you," the receptionist told Peter after handing him some forms to complete. He didn't really think it was multiple sclerosis or a brain tumor, but he woke up a few days earlier with some numbness in his arm and just wanted to get it checked out. Never mind that his affected arm had been lying up above his body all night under the weight of his head. Peter was also considering talking to the doctor about his hair. Lately, it wasn't behaving the way he thought it should. He was afraid it might be thinning. His father had a full head of hair, and both his grandfathers died with all their hair intact, but Peter wasn't taking any chances. He wanted to get a prescription for Propecia or Rogaine to stop his hair from thinning, if, in fact, it was thinning. He had no intention of ever going bald.

As Peter scanned the waiting room for a seat, he noticed a familiar face. He tried to avoid eye contact so he wouldn't have to acknowledge her, but it was too late. She had already seen him.

"Hi," Cameron said to Peter, offering an awkward smile. She had probably wanted to avoid a conversation as much as he did.

Peter returned the greeting and gave Cameron a quick once-over. It was the first time Peter had seen her in several weeks. He heard through the rumor mill that she had taken some time off after the screen-saver incident. Cameron's demeanor had changed since the last time he saw her. Peter couldn't quite put his finger on it, but something was different. Her shoulders weren't back as far, or her head wasn't as high. Even the smile she gave him was missing the energy that annoyed Peter so much.

Peter felt obligated to sit next to her and lowered himself into an empty chair.

"How have you been?"

"I'm hanging in there," Cameron said in a resigned tone. "It's been a tough couple of weeks."

"I can imagine. I'm so sorry. I heard what happened. It's unbelievable."

Cameron tried to smile at Peter in response to his sympathy but, instead, began to well up. "I don't understand why someone would do that to me," she said, trying to keep herself from crying. "How am I going to face anyone in the office?"

Peter looked at Cameron, and his heart dropped to the floor. He felt a sudden deep sense of regret for his actions. Feeling like an absolute heel, he lifted his hand and lightly touched her upper arm. Cameron looked down to the floor as tears started to drip from her eyes.

"Sometimes I feel like I'm losing my mind. I've been getting these hang-up calls at all hours of the night. I'm afraid to fall asleep because I don't know what terrible thing awaits me the next day. I get all these phone calls from strange people—doctors I've never heard of, psychic healers, movers. Someone is just torturing me. I can't stand it anymore. That's why I'm here, Peter. I need some help—some sedatives or something."

"It will be all right. People have already forgotten about the whole thing."

"Yeah, right," Cameron said sarcastically, wiping the tears from her eyes. As she tried to compose herself in the chair, the receptionist called her name and said the doctor was ready to see her.

"Cameron," Peter called as she got up from the chair. "Wait." He wanted to tell her it was him. That he was behind all the terrible things that had been happening to her. And, more important, that it was over. Strange things wouldn't be happening to her anymore, and she could get on with her life. Yep, that's what he *wanted* to tell her.

"Cameron, I don't know who would do such terrible things to you," Peter lied. "But I do know one thing."

Cameron looked down at him. "What?"

"I know that you're stronger than this. Not that I know you very well at all. But I've seen you around. I've seen you in action. Where is that feisty young lady that got me in trouble for surfing the Net? You're bigger than this freak, Cameron. If you let him . . . or her know that they're getting to you, it will just entice them to keep it up."

"You're probably right."

"Come on, let's see a Cameron smile."

Cameron offered a reserved, almost shy smile, something Peter never would've guessed she was capable of.

"Well, that will have to do for now."

Cameron's smile brightened a little more. "Thank you, Peter. You're very sweet."

"Think you might have time for lunch after your appointment?"

"Sure. I guess so."

"All right, wait for me when you're done. Will you?"

"Okay. I could really use a friend today."

"Then it's a date," Peter said with a grin as he watched her walk back to the doctor's office.

Six Hundred a Month

Shirley was just putting the finishing touches on her apartment. It was cleaner than it had been in years. She actually dusted with Pledge instead of just a damp cloth and borrowed a neighbor's vacuum to clean the rug. The bed was made for the first time in months, and all the ashtrays in the house were empty and sparkling. Shirley was fluffing the lone pillow on the sofa, when there was a knock on the front door.

"Hello," Shirley said to the mature, silver-haired woman at the door.

"Hi, I'm Dorothy from the agency."

"Nice to meet you. Shirley Perry," Shirley said, introducing herself as she gestured for the social worker to come inside. "Please sit down."

"I'd love to, but how about I take a quick look at the apartment first. It's important that I evaluate the apartment if you want to take in a foster child."

"Sure. Well, this is the living room. I like to read the classics in here. That's my reading light over there," Shirley lied as she led Dorothy toward the vacant bedroom and opened the door. "This is where my foster child would stay. It's a great room . . . lots of light."

"There's no furniture in here."

"Yes. I'm getting some," Shirley lied again.

"Really. When?"

"Ah . . . I thought the kid and me could pick it out together."

"And what is *the kid* supposed to sleep on until you get this furniture?"

The floor? "He can have my bed. I'll sleep on the sofa."

"That will never do. You'll have to get some furniture."

Well, give me my money, bitch, and I'll get some. "Sure, I can do that. No problem."

"Do you smoke?" Dorothy asked. "It smells faintly of cigarettes in here."

"No, no, that's from my old roommate, ah . . . ah . . . Chester. He was a smoker. Nice old man, smoking was his only vice. I took him in after his wife passed away. He lived with me for years until he finally passed on," Shirley said, impressed with herself for being able to make up a story so quickly.

"Really. What happened to his furniture?"

"Ah . . . well . . . you know . . . you know, his greedy kids . . . yeah, his greedy kids didn't want to be bothered with him when he was alive, but the moment he died, they descended on this place like it was a yard sale. They took everything."

"What a shame," Dorothy said. "How about your room?"

"My room?"

"Yes, I'd like to see it."

"Okay," Shirley said, leading the way. She opened the door to her bedroom, and Dorothy followed behind her. Dorothy took a long look around before holding her gaze on the ceiling.

"Mirrors?" she asked Shirley.

"Oh, those. This is so funny," Shirley said, stalling for time. "I . . . I . . . I do yoga at night. I do it on the bed and use the mirrors to make sure I'm doing it right."

"Really," Dorothy said in a questionable tone. "I practice yoga as well. Do you prefer Kundalini or Integral?"

"Ah, I like that condelingi kind myself."

"The ashtray by the bed? Is that yours?"

"Oh, no, no. That's Chester's. It's the only thing I have left of his, so I keep it by the bed."

Following the bedroom tour, Shirley ushered Dorothy into the kitchen. After Dorothy perused the refrigerator filled with little more than beer, cold cuts, and a couple of sodas, Shirley realized it was probably over but agreed to sit in the living room with the social worker and fill out some paperwork. As they talked intermittently while Shirley completed the forms, someone knocked on the door.

"Who is it?" Shirley asked.

"It's me, Shirley," the voice called from the other side of the door.

Shirley recognized the voice immediately. But it couldn't be him. She hadn't heard a word from him in months.

"Excuse me," she said to Dorothy and opened the door.

"Collin," she said.

"Hi, honey. Can we talk?"

"I have nothing to say to you."

"Shirley, please, may I come in?" Collin asked, stepping into the living room without letting Shirley answer. "I'm sorry. I never should've let you go. Screw my wife. I don't care about her. I just want to be with you," Collin said in a full voice, not noticing Dorothy on the sofa until it was too late.

"This is obviously a private moment," Dorothy said, gathering her paperwork. "I'll come back later."

"Great, Collin, just chase my guest away, not to mention six hundred bucks a month," Shirley said to Collin after Dorothy walked out the door.

"I don't care about your guest. I just care about you. What do you say, Shirley? Can we try again?"

"Hmmm . . . let me think . . . ah . . . FUCK NO, YOU FUCKING BASTARD! Does that answer your question?"

"Shirley, just hear me out."

"I don't have time for this, Collin. I'm a career girl now."

"A career girl?"

"Yes, I have my own business," she said, pulling out a business card and handing it to Collin. She grabbed a couple of leashes from the hook next to the door and stepped into the hallway with Collin following. "I've got dogs to walk."

"That's great, Shirley, having your own business and all."

"Yeah, it is," Shirley said, shutting the door to her apartment and heading toward the stairwell, leaving Collin behind.

"Shirley?" Collin called behind her.

She didn't answer.

Settling the Score

"So your flight went well, Sophia?" Cheryl asked the elderly woman. She and Gina just picked Sophia up from the airport, and they were seated at a table at the Palm, a pricey steak house where beautiful people dined and power deals were brokered over large cuts of beef and jumbo lobsters. Gina and Cheryl had spared no expense. They flew Sophia in from Cleveland first class, put her up at the luxurious Hotel Washington, and were currently treating her to dinner at one of the more upscale restaurants in D.C. What did they care. After all, they had no intention of paying for any of it.

"Oh, yes, dear. It was quite comfortable. I don't get to fly very often," she replied with just a hint of an Italian accent.

"I'm so glad we were able to bring you here, so you could be involved in the festivities," Gina said. "It's so exciting."

"Yes, it is. I'm very happy to be here. When you reach my age, you don't know how many more visits to the nation's capital there will be."

"Oh, please," Cheryl said. "You look healthy as a horse."

"I guess I can't complain," Sophia said before a waiter briefly interrupted their conversation.

"Are you ladies ready to order?"

"We're waiting for one more person," Gina said.

"Okay, take your time. I'll check back in a few minutes."

"Thank you. Actually, I think I might go check the lobby and see if he's here," Gina said, about to excuse herself from the table when she saw Griffin walk into the dining room. It wasn't easy getting Griffin to agree to meet them. Gina first told him she had a business proposal for him, without offering any details. She figured curiosity would be enough to lure him to the restaurant, but he sharply rebuffed her invitation and reiterated that she wasn't getting the films. After his refusal, she decided to sweeten the bait and contact him again. She explained that if she couldn't get the films back, and if she and Cheryl were going to be the porn world's latest darlings with or without their consent, then they might as well consider making a career of it. She expressed an interest in possibly shooting a real live adult film with him. She pictured him drooling as she proposed her and Cheryl's lesbian sex scene. The mere thought of even being near Griffin again made her crazy, but she was determined to get him to the restaurant.

Gina, who was facing the entrance, waved Griffin over to the table where Cheryl and Sophia had their backs to the door. Griffin glided over to the table and offered Gina a big smile—a smile that quickly turned into a perplexed look of surprise.

"Griffin! It's so good to see you," Sophia said, standing up to hug him.

"Mom! What are you doing here?" Griffin responded.

"These lovely girls flew me in from Cleveland to surprise you, dear," Sophia said to Griffin.

"Oh, they did, did they? How did they find you?"

"The Internet is full of information, Griffin. You of all people should know that," Gina replied. "We called your mother a few days ago and told her all about your budding career."

"My career?" Griffin said, seeming slightly panicked.

"Yes, we told her all about it, Griffin," Cheryl said. "We wanted to bring her to town to celebrate your latest production."

"My latest production?" Griffin asked, clearly agitated. "You know, The Big G Cam you're planning to launch."

"What's The Big G Cam?" Sophia asked.

"Should I tell her, Griffin? Should I tell her the short story about how The Big G Cam has to do with your job at PBS, or should I tell her the longer, *more interesting* version?" Gina threatened.

"Is everything okay, Griffin?" Sophia asked. "I'm sorry. Maybe I shouldn't have surprised you. I should have called."

"He's fine, Sophia. He's just nervous about the new Web site he's planning to launch. You know, he plans to show clips from all his recent PBS documentaries. Don't you, Griffin?"

"I guess," Griffin said, confused about how to respond.

"In fact, Sophia," Gina said, "we have some of his latest *documentaries* on video in the car. What do you say we go back to your room and pop a few of them in the VCR after dinner?"

"That would be lovely, dear. I never get to see my son's work."

"Mom, I'm sure you're tired. We could do that some other time."

"I guess we could," Gina said. "Actually, Cheryl and I would like to have two of your films back to do some final editing before they go on the Web."

"Editing?" Griffin said.

"Yes. Well, who knows. We may take a look at them and decide they have no business in cyberspace and just *destroy* them."

"You girls are film editors?" Sophia asked.

"Yes, we work very closely with Griffin," Cheryl said to Sophia before arching toward Griffin. "What do you say, Griffin? Do we get the films?"

"Yeah, Griffin," Gina added. "Do we get the films?"

"Griffin, give the nice girls the films already."

Looking baffled and defeated, Griffin relented. "Okay, girls, I'll give you the films."

"Then it's settled. Cheryl and I will meet you at *PBS headquarters* tonight after dinner."

"Does it have to be tonight?" Griffin asked.

"Now, Griffin, we don't want you to have any time to make extra copies."

"Fine. Tonight it is."

"So when do I get to see my son's documentaries?"

"Sophia, I think you'll have to ask Griffin about that one. Why don't we let you guys have a quiet dinner. Cheryl and I aren't very hungry anyway."

"Yes, that would be nice," Griffin said, irritated.

"Good. We'll meet you in a couple of hours, Griffin," Cheryl said.

"It was so nice to meet you ladies. Thanks so much for the plane tickets and the limo and that beautiful hotel suite."

"Don't thank us. Griffin can expense it all and charge it to PBS. Right, Griffin?"

Griffin sighed. "Right. Good night, ladies."

"Night," Cheryl replied. "It was lovely to meet you, Sophia."

"Yes, it was," Gina said before standing up and flicking off Griffin's cap with her finger, exposing his bald head. She set his hat down on the table before adding, "And, Griffin, mere words can't describe my feelings."

"The feeling is definitely mutual."

"Good-bye, Griffin," Gina said with a superior grin—the grin of a chicken that just outsmarted a fox—a nasty, fat, obnoxious fox. Gina and Cheryl walked out of the restaurant with gloating smiles. The pompous little man had finally gotten his due, and they no longer had to worry about showing up on the Internet in all their glory. It was over. The whole saga was finally over!

Griffin and Sophia watched the girls leave the restaurant as the waiter approached the table.

"Shall I wait for the young ladies to return?" the waiter asked.

"No, they're not coming back," Sophia said. "How about a nice bottle of your finest champagne for me and my son."

"Do you believe those two?" Griffin asked his mother.

"Yeah, that's too funny. You know, they flew me in first class. It was fantastic. PBS—that's hysterical."

"Mmm, I'm gonna get me some of that," Griffin said as a platter of the Palm's famous cottage fries went by. "And one of those," he added, eyeing a three-pound lobster being carried to a neighboring table.

"Are you celebrating a special event this evening?" the waiter asked, returning to the table and popping the cork on a bottle of champagne.

"Most definitely," Sophia said without elaborating.

As the waiter walked off, Sophia whispered to Griffin. "Honey, you may as well give the films back to those two broads. They're hardly worth the trouble. Neither one had very big titties, and we got plenty others to load up on the Web."

Epilogue

Gina followed Cheryl down the center aisle of St. Margaret's Church. As the maid of honor, she had the pleasure of pushing the stroller with little Grace in it. She had been born just a few weeks prior to the wedding. When Gina and Cheryl reached the front and assumed their positions, Dennis did some final primping on Linda and Rosa in the back of the church.

The wedding march sprang from the organ, and Linda began to walk down the aisle with both her parents. She was wearing a beautiful ivory gown with long sleeves and lace around the shoulders. Rosa followed in an equally stunning lavender dress with her father in tow. Linda had gotten more involved with Dignity, her group for gay Catholics, over the past year and, aside from the fact that there was no groom, she insisted on having a traditional wedding.

Gina watched the couple present themselves before the minister. Her eyes wandered around as she took in the beauty of the evening. It was Valentine's Day weekend, and the church was decorated with red roses and soft white candles. There was snow on the ground outside from a brief dusting the night before. It was a crisp winter evening, but the church was warm, and the lit candles shined a glow on the two brides about to commit to a lifelong relationship. Gina couldn't help but be touched.

She was in an extremely good mood. Earlier in the day, there was a clip on the news about an illegal porno ring being raided in her building. Not only were the culprits filming in the back of a D.C. bookstore, they also leased an apartment in Gina's building. It was only a brief spot on the news, but the anchorman mentioned words like "criminal behavior," "jail time," and even "illicit drugs and prostitution." It was one of Gina's happier moments in life when she saw the police drag a fat little man out of her building in handcuffs. And what a relief it was to hear that in an effort to avoid being arrested, Griffin had destroyed all the films taken with The Big G Cam.

From the steps in the sanctuary, Gina could see everyone in the church. She smiled at Annie, who was sitting with one of Linda's friends who Gina had introduced her to. In addition to her job at the bank, Gina was doing some part-time work for Annie while she took some computer classes. It wasn't the ideal situation, but until Annie landed a few more contracts and was able to hire her full-time, Gina had to stay at the bank. Luckily, Premier had a tuition reimbursement program and was bankrolling Gina's ticket out of there.

Gina looked at Peter sitting next to Cameron and then exchanged glances with Cheryl. Cheryl was particularly hurt by Peter's sudden relationship with his nemesis, but she had little right to voice any complaints. She agreed from the get-go that she and Peter would just be friends, and deep down she knew it was best to let him go and get on with her life. It had been a rough year, but she wouldn't have traded the experience for anything. The whole ordeal brought her friends back in her life and offered some closure to her pointless relationship with Peter. She learned how strong she could be and that good friends and a sense of humor could get you through almost anything.

Looking at Peter, Gina thought about how she and Cheryl had come to loathe Cameron, the perky little bitch who stole Peter's heart. They also held the information that could destroy Peter and Cameron's relationship in a nanosecond. One mention of Peter's involvement in the Virtual Cameron occurrence, and he could kiss Cameron good-bye. But for all his faults, the girls cared deeply for Peter and wanted to see him happy.

Shirley was in the pew next to Peter, clutching her gift to Linda. It was a hand-painted tea set from Ireland that Shirley actually bought with her own money, something she recently had more of. Her pet-sitting business was taking off, and soon she would be able to quit her waitress job at Friday's and take care of animals full-time. Her two jobs kept her so busy, she had to turn down the foster child the agency wanted to send her. No one knew what happened. Did the agency get Shirley's paperwork mixed up with someone else's, or did they figure she needed a foster child to take care of her?

Penelope was a few aisles over with Donny. Gina wasn't even feeling jealous of her today, even though Penelope driveled on and on before the ceremony about her job and how she was remodeling her kitchen. She even bragged about how they had just hired a cleaning lady—some woman named Bianca who just moved to D.C. from Boston, and how, since he mostly worked at home, Donny was always there to let her in and keep an eye on her.

After giving the church one final sweep, Gina again focused on the happy couple at the altar. For the first time, she was happy as a bridesmaid, and she actually liked the evergreen velvet dress, which Linda let her pick out herself. She wanted for herself what Linda and Rosa had found, but she truly was happy for both of them, especially for Linda. And Gina was glad that she had played a role in bringing them back together. She'd learned a lot over the past year, and having so many awful things happen to her gave her a new appreciation for the little things in life. She realized how stupid it was to be at war with Cheryl for so long when they were so good for each other. She also realized that life had to be about more than just finding a man. The more she thought about it, the more she realized how full her life was without one. It wasn't like she was going to stop trying to land a man with every feminine bone in her body, but, until then, life was going to be okay—life for Gina Perry was going to be okay.

Feeling only genuine happiness and joy for Linda, Gina could hardly believe it herself. There was no envy, no fear of losing a friend, no hopes for disaster. That's how she knew Linda was a true friend. That's how she knew she herself was a true friend.

Following the initial blessing, Linda and Rosa took their seats behind the altar, and Gina and the others stepped down from the sanctuary into a pew. The priest stepped to the pulpit and began the Mass. He was a tad long-winded, offering all sorts of advice, thoughts, and feelings on marriage. He rambled for quite some time about fidelity, trust, "until death do us part," blah, blah, blah. By the time they got to the first reading, Gina was uncomfortable in the hard church pew. Damn Catholics, she thought. Their weddings are just too fucking long.

Please turn the page for an exciting sneak peek of

MURDER WITH FRIED CHICKEN AND WAFFLES

the first book in Patrick Sanchez's

Mahalia Watkins Soul Food Mystery series

coming from Kensington Publishing in March 2015!

Welcome to Mahalia's Sweet Tea!

When I launched Mahalia's Sweet Tea I dreamed it would be a success, but I had no idea it would become *THE* restaurant of choice for delicious soul food. When I came up with the idea to open my own establishment, which that would allow me to prepare and serve my favorite foods, I couldn't have predicted that "my baby" (which is how I often refer to Sweet Tea) would make the Top 100 restaurant lists of local magazines and newspapers, or that people traveling from as far away as California and Texas would make a point of stopping by for a glass of iced tea and a taste of my collard greens topped with homemade hot sauce.

Many of the mouth-watering items you see on the menu are based on my grandmother's recipes . . . if you can call my grandmother's way of adding "a dash of this" and "a sprinkling of that" a recipe. I prepare many of the dishes the same why I did thirty years ago when I learned how to cook by helping Grandmommy make Sunday dinner for crowds of up to thirty people every week. Entrées like my fried chicken and waffles and my cream of turkey over thick cut Texas toast are made just as they were when I was child. The complementary sour cream cornbread we bring to your table— that's Grandmommy's recipe through and through. And, although I've updated a few recipes to make them a bit more contemporary and add a little flair (e.g., Grandmommy didn't include roasted red peppers in her macaroni and cheese), I mostly like to keep things simple here at Sweet Tea. You won't find any cilantro or curry in my kitchen, and a few menu items, like my creamy mashed potatoes for instance, are simply seasoned with only salt and pepper.

We make virtually everything here at Sweet Tea—from my chicken and dumplings to my fried catfish to my salad dressings and even my croutons—from scratch. About the only thing not made in-house is that bottle of ketchup you see on the table (and don't think I haven't considered making that as well).

I could go on for days about my food, but let me take a moment to talk about something even more important than that: YOU.

You, the customer, are what makes Sweet Tea great, and no matter how many best-restaurant lists it graces or how long a wait we have for a table on a Saturday night, my staff and I strive to treat each and every one of you as if our very existence depends on you thoroughly enjoying your guest experience with us. Why? Because it does!

We make every effort to ensure we provide the best food and the best service at reasonable prices. If you ever find we are doing otherwise, I hope you'll let me know. I'm usually on the premises and easy to spot, running around keeping this wheel of a restaurant in motion.

Sincerely,

Mahalia Watkins

Proprietor

Chapter 1

I still remember the first time I tasted my grandmother's cornbread. I was maybe four or five. It was some time in the seventies. If I close my eyes, I can still see the heavy cast-iron skillet being set on her wobbly table with a couple of pot rags underneath to keep from burning the laminate.

"Now, don't you touch that pan, ya hear. It'll burn the skin right off your fingers, Halia," she said as she sliced into the piping-hot bread . . . all golden and steaming and smelling of sweetness. I watched her lift the first slice onto a plate and wished it was for me, but the first slice always went to Granddaddy.

"When you work the night shift at the factory to pay the bills around here, you'll get the first slice," Grandmommy said to me as I watched the slice of cornbread pass on by me and land in front of my grandfather. I guess I really didn't mind though. I loved Granddaddy. I didn't see him too often. He worked nights and slept during the day, but he always had a kind word for me, and, according to Grandmommy, "he was one of the good ones." She'd say it all the time: "I've got myself a good man. He's one of the *good ones*."

When I did get my slice I wasted no time in cutting off a big piece with my fork and plunging it in my mouth. It had a taste that danced on my tongue . . . a sweet yet salty flavor with a texture somewhere between bread and cake. Unlike a lot of cornbread, there was no need to spread any butter on my grandmother's recipe. It was so sweet and moist that more butter would have been overkill. She made it with corn meal, flour, sugar, an entire stick of butter and a full cup of sour cream. She'd add a can of cream corn and a can of regular corn, and then mix it all up before pouring it into a cast iron skillet to bake to a golden brown in her prize possession, her 1964 Lady Kenmore oven.

From then on, whenever I ate that decadent cornbread, I thought that it should be served in restaurants. And now, more than thirty years after I first tried it, I serve it to all my customers—small two-top tables get a small pan, four-tops get a medium pan, and six-tops get a large pan. Eight-tops? Those get two medium pans. And don't ask me about ten-tops. If customers come in here with more than eight in their party, I tell them I can only accommodate them at two tables. As my cousin, Wavonne, who has a way of telling it like it is, says, "Ain't nothin' worse than a large party. They'll run us ragged with special requests and complaints 'til our tongues be hangin' out our mouths and then leave a five-percent tip."

The first pan of Grandmommy's cornbread is on the house, but we do charge for additional pans. I love and appreciate my customers, but we do get the occasional low-class fools in here who would have no problem filling up on my free cornbread and ordering virtually nothing else. I'm a cook (I've never felt comfortable with the term *chef* considering I don't have so much as a day of professional culinary training), and I love to see people enjoy my food, but I'm also a businesswoman, and a sister has to make some money.

When I opened Mahalia's Sweet Tea four years ago, I thought long and hard about whether or not my grandmother's cornbread was going to be free or available on the menu for a charge. I didn't like the idea of my customers filling up on heavy cornbread and later skipping appetizers or desserts . . . and affecting my bottom line. But I think restaurant patrons really like the idea of getting something free with a meal, so I decided to work it into my prices and make it complementary, one of the many times I've followed the advice of Wavonne. "You know, Halia," she said to me when she was helping me launch the restaurant, which mostly amounted to her doing her nails or reading the latest issue of *Us Weekly* while I did all the work, "what would Red Lobster be without those free salty biscuits with the all the cheese up in 'em? Hell, I wouldn't even go to the Olive Garden if I didn't get that big ol' free basket o' bread sticks . . . even if those greedy buggers do charge you for somethin' to dip 'em in."

I thought about what Wavonne said. I certainly wanted my restaurant held in higher regard than Red Lobster and Olive Garden (not that I don't like to help myself to one of those "salty biscuits with the cheese all up in 'em" every now and then myself), but she did have a point. Wavonne is not a girl of academic intelligence—I swear the only reason she graduated high school was because the teachers couldn't bear another year of her mouthing off. She's more concerned with Beyoncé's latest video than who was confirmed onto the Supreme Court, and, if she didn't work for me (and I use the term "work" loosely), I'm not sure she'd be able to hold a job at all. But the thing about Wavonne is that she has a sense about what makes people tick . . . what makes them behave the way they do. She warned me that the customers who kept their Bluetooth ear pieces on during dinner were most likely to be the ones to run my staff to death with complaints about everything from the location of their table to the prices on the menu . . . and then tip worse than a certain former Washington D.C. mayor. She gave me some good advice about going with black linen napkins instead of white: "The white napkins'll get lint all over those tight black hoochie dresses your customers gonna be wearin'." And I even followed her advice about the dinner lighting in the restaurant. "Halia, you gotta lower the lights in here. A sista wants to look good for her man over dinner and ain't all the Oil of Olay in the world gonna make some of the heifers who be comin' in here look presentable in this light."

So the cornbread, thanks to Wavonne and her vast insight, comes with my meals along with a small . . . *tiny* really, house salad. I'm looking at that very cornbread right now as I take it to table fourteen while thinking about my grandmother, Mrs. Mahalia Howell. Everyone assumes my restaurant is named for myself, but it's really in honor of Grandmommy after which I *and* my restaurant were named. Grandmommy's name on the marquee is much deserved—almost half the items on the menu are based on her recipes.

"Girl, he makes my wig go crooked!" Wavonne says as I head back toward the kitchen after making a cornbread delivery. I turn to see who her gaze is on and find Marcus Rand coming through the door of my restaurant. I suppose I should say *our* restaurant—Marcus is practically a co-owner. I didn't want his help or his money, but I got in a little over my head when I opened the place and turned to him as a last resort. I don't like Marcus nor do I trust him . . . and I'm quite certain that the money he invested in Mahalia's Sweet Tea isn't exactly clean. Not that I think Marcus is involved in anything illegal. Unethical? Yes. But *illegal*? Marcus is too smart for that.

I think he makes some of his money as a financial planner although financial *salesperson* is probably a more accurate description of what he does for a living, considering the mutual funds and other products he sells pay steep, some might say predatory, commissions. He's also involved in some of those Ponzi-type schemes where you recruit members to sell all sorts of nonsense and everyone pretends that members, or "associates" as Marcus calls them, make lots of money selling quality items when the real money is made by finding other suckers to join the scheme as your underlings so you can take a percentage of their sales (think Amway, Avon, Mary Kay). Marcus is as smooth as butter and uses his charisma to recruit associates, most of them women, all over town. Despite his success in this area I don't think you net a mansion on five acres in Upper Marlboro or a BMW 5-series by recruiting members for pyramid schemes. I'm not sure where his big bucks come from, but some of the people he brings in here for business meetings over my fried chicken and waffles look like they're into things far more serious than Tupperware or scented candles.

I met Marcus more than ten years ago when I was a line cook and occasional server at a restaurant a few miles outside D.C. in Virginia. Marcus was in his early thirties at the time and looked about the same as he does now. He has a shaved head, big brown eyes, and a smile for days. He's charismatic and charming and confident. What he isn't, though, is tall. I'd go almost as far as to call him petite. He tops out at about five-foot-six with a good heel on his shoes, but he does keep his body firm and likes to wear tight shirts that show no hint of fat around his abs and highlight sculpted biceps so fine you just want to squeeze them. His skin is a rich dark color and, to this day, his complexion reminds me of those Palmer hollow milk chocolate bunnies they sell at the drug store before Easter, which is quite fitting—much like those hollow bunnies, while pretty to look at, Marcus is made with cheap ingredients that leave a foul taste in your mouth, as I'd learn shortly after I met him so many years ago.

"Hi sugar, how's it going today?" Marcus, decked out in one of his Hugo Boss suits with coordinating French-cuffed shirt and silk tie, says to Wavonne as he reaches for her hand, giving it a quick kiss.

Wavonne smiles. "I'm just fine," she says, titling her head and doing that thing she does with her eyes whenever an attractive man is around. "Don't you smell nice."

"Thank you, sugar," Marcus says. "It's my new custom scent. I had it made just for me."

Wavonne inhales deeply. "It smells good. Sort of like spiced rum." She takes another deep breath. "And maybe some dark chocolate."

Marcus, like so many brothers, wears too much cologne. I don't care if it smells like spiced rum, or dark chocolate . . . or Taye Diggs for that matter. I'm just not a fan of cologne and perfume. It gives me a headache and irritates my sinuses. Marcus's cologne is so strong, and he wears it so heavily, that it often lingers in the restaurant for hours after he's left. Sometimes, just from me standing near him, the scent gets in my clothes and doesn't come out until I wash them. I ask my staff to refrain from wearing cologne or perfume, even though Wavonne defies me here and there and sprays herself with all sorts of stinky nonsense. When customers come into Sweet Tea, I want them to smell my food, not Mary J. Blige's latest overpriced fragrance.

"And you, Mahalia?" he says to me, stopping himself in mid-reach. Not only does he know better than to call me sugar, he also knows I'll refuse to offer my hand for him to kiss. I ain't buying what he's selling, and he's knows it.

"Busy. What do you want, Marcus?" I ask, knowing that the only reason Marcus would come by in the middle of the day is because he wants something.

"Can't I just stop by to say hi to my two favorite ladies?"

"Sure you can. It's just that you never do."

"Well I *did* come just to say hi, but I also want to talk to you about reserving a table tonight. I've got three associates to entertain this evening and Régine and Jacqueline will be joining as well."

"You could have called, Marcus. You know I'll have the big table by the window all ready for you."

"Great. I'm sure you'll be serving plenty of fried chicken and waffles, but one of my guests is a vegetarian. Any chance you'll be making that famous sweet corn casserole of yours?"

"No," I say flatly.

"Are you sure? I mentioned it to Lindsey, my guest who's a vegetarian, and she was very exited about it."

"Tell her to hold on to that excitement for a few more days. It will be a special on Tuesday night." I often reserve some of my best specials for Tuesday and Wednesday nights (we're closed on Monday) when people tend to eat out less and need a little more motivation to come in here and spend their money.

"Can you move it up on the schedule? For me? Please." Being the snake charmer that he is, Marcus says this like he's asking. But, we both know it's more of demand than a request. If I refuse, he'll slyly remind me of the money he loaned me to get this place off the ground . . . how he helped me when I needed it, and now it's my turn.

"Marcus, that dish takes a lot of time. And I can't just make it for your guests. If other customers see it coming out of the kitchen, they'll want it too."

"Great. Cha-ching Cha-ching. You'll rack up some serious sales."

"I don't have enough fresh corn in the kitchen today, and I can't get it wholesale at this late hour. You get me the corn, and I'll do the best I can."

"Where should I get it from?"

"The Safeway for all I care. Wendy at Shadow's Catering always has a lot of fresh produce on hand, and she owes me a favor. Maybe you can work out a deal with her." I'm willing to cave to Marcus to an extent, but I'll be damned if I going to run around buying fresh corn on the cob at the last minute while I'm trying to run a restaurant. I'm sure he'll just push the job off on his sister Jacqueline anyway.

"Okay. I'll get Jacqueline on it. Thanks Halia. You're the best."

"Yeah yeah. . . ."

"If I can't get fresh corn, will frozen do?"

"You *did not* just ask me that? The only frozen thing I serve in this restaurant, Marcus, is ice."

He smiles. "My bad . . . my bad. That's why everything is so good."

And he's right. The best food starts with the best ingredients. Everything we serve at Sweet Tea is made from scratch. All of our meats and vegetables are fresh, many from local farms. We even cut and broil our own house-made sourdough croutons because no package variety comes close to my recipe. We make all our salad dressing in-house because the bottled brands just don't have the creamy thickness I want, and we chop lettuce daily for all our salads—taste the lettuce that comes precut in a plastic bag, and you'll know why. And, of course, all of the tea at Sweet Tea is fresh brewed on the premises. Every day we offer unsweetened, sweetened, and a special flavored tea. Today's special tea is honey clove.

As Marcus leaves I think of all the reorganizing I'll have to do to get a special on the menu that I hadn't planned for.

"I'm going to need your help husking corn." I say to Wavonne, who's watching Marcus's ass (and it is a fine one) while he walks out the door.

"I just got a manicure, Halia. I can't be huskin' no corn."

"Would you prefer bathroom cleaning duty?"

Wavonne groans. "Let me know when Marcus gets back with it."

"Oh, don't worry. I will."